I stopped dead in my tracks.

Ten feet away stood the most beautiful man I'd ever seen in my life. More beautiful than my new neighbor, Mr. Fine-ass. I felt light-headed and realized I'd ceased to breathe. Sandy blond hair, full lips, eyelashes that belonged on a girl, and a build like a brick shithouse. He didn't fit in here. His jeans and dark gray T-shirt covered by a rockin' black leather bomber were hotter than hot. He was holding a folder and kept glancing at it. No ring on his left hand. Aces! He looked about thirty-five or so. Absolutely perfect. With my luck he was probably gay.

What the hell was wrong with me? I wasn't here to pick up guys. I was here trying not to get arrested. My brain knew that, but all my girlie parts were screaming something else entirely. There was no security guard in sight . . . maybe, just maybe . . . No, absolutely not. I couldn't take the chance of going back to jail. It wasn't a parking violation; it was a restraining order, for shit's sake. But if I didn't show myself, there was no way my future husband would notice me. I was covered up like a fashion-impaired nun. Maybe I could remove the disguise just for a minute . . . make eye contact, ask him to marry me, and then finish what I came here for. No, wait, maybe I'd deliver the package first and then tackle him to the ground and have my way with him . . . No, wait, what if he left while I was delivering the goods? And what if I got arrested before he noticed I was alive? Jesus Christ, I needed to get laid. This was the second stranger I'd considered marrying in two days and I'd only seen the other one's butt.

How Hard Can It Be?

ROBYN PETERMAN

KENSINGTON
Kensington Publishing Corp.
www.kensingtonbooks.com

KENSINGTON BOOKS are published by

Kensington Publishing Corp.
119 West 40th Street
New York, NY 10018

All Kensington titles, imprints, and distributed lines are available at special quantity discounts for bulk purchases for sales promotions, premiums, fund-raising, educational, or institutional use.

Special book excerpts or customized printings can also be created to fit specific needs. For details, write or phone the office of the Kensington special sales manager: Kensington Publishing Corp., 119 West 40th Street, New York, NY 10018, attn: Special Sales Department; phone: 1-800-221-2647.

KENSINGTON and the k logo are Reg. U.S. Pat. & TM Off.

First Electronic Edition: January 2013

ISBN-13: 978-1-60183-062-3
ISBN-10: 1-60183-062-9

ISBN-13: 978-1-60183-173-6
ISBN-10: 1-60183-173-0

Printed in the United States of America

This book is dedicated to my Mom,
who always believed in me . . .
even when I didn't.

ACKNOWLEDGMENTS

Writing may seem like a solitary sport, but it is not. I have much to be grateful for and a lot of people to thank. Without the love and support of some very special people, my dreams would still be just dreams.

I'd like to thank my editor, Alicia Condon, for believing in my warped imagination and making me seem like a much better writer than I really am! Her attention to detail is mind-bogglingly wonderful.

My fantabulous beta readers, Kristy, Susan, Kim, Jennifer G, Jennifer M, Jim, and Candace—without you guys, I never would have finished! An extra shout-out to Kristy, who has read every word I've written at least twenty times. (Please note, my friends, you all show up in my book.)

A special thanks to Monette Michaels and JM Madden. Your generosity and talent blow me away. JM, thanks for holding my hand and supporting the big fat hairy lie that turned into my first published book!

Kris, without you I would have no website, Facebook, newsletter, etc. You taught me much more than just how to cut and paste, and thank God for that! Love you!

I would be remiss if I didn't thank two of my favorite authors who humbled me with their cover quotes. Michelle Rowen and Lexi George, you both rock and I am forever your fangirl!

And last but not least, thank you to my family. Nothing would be any fun without you crazy people. My husband, who's *way* hotter than any hero I could ever write, and my noisy, funny, wonderful kids. You guys make everything worth it.

Chapter 1

"If you handcuff a woman to a headboard, you need to use fur-covered cuffs. Otherwise you'll rub all the skin off of her wrists during rough sex, and she'll bleed like a motherfucker. Blood is just not sexy unless you're writing paranormal." The gal with the lesbian haircut delivered that little nugget with gusto.

What in the hell am I doing here? I'm going to kill Oprah. Does anybody actually listen to her "if you can visualize it you can do it" crap other than me? Becoming a famous romance novel writer had sounded like such a good idea the other day. The simple fact that I couldn't really write had seemed beside the point . . .

My best friend and roommate, Kristy, accused me of pulling a Sunshine Weather Girl again, referring to my embarrassing and very recent attempt to become a meteorologist. Kristy's reminder was a low blow. I didn't like to think about that. Clearly showing up at the news station for a month straight wasn't the way to become the new weather girl. It had resulted in a restraining order, six hours in the pokey, and a feature story on the six o'clock news. My mother told all her friends I was adopted . . . I wasn't.

So here I stood, in the poorly lit back meeting room of the downtown public library, with ten or so women who looked like seventy-year-old church ladies. Why do women in the Midwest think that really short hair shaved up at the back of the neck is a good look? I found out the bondage gal's name was Sue, but she went by Shoshanna LeHump. Quite the little fireball, she was dressed entirely in lavender fleece. She explained her husband had threatened to divorce her if she continued to write that garbage under her real name. Her words, not mine. I didn't know if I was more shocked by her pen name or the fact that she was married.

I glanced around the room hoping to spot Evangeline O'Hara, the famous *New York Times* best-selling author. She wrote a mean bodice ripper and was the main reason I'd joined this group. I hoped she'd like my ideas and mentor me to stardom. Of course, ideas were a slight problem at this point, but I would continue visualizing like hell.

I was looking forward to discussing Evangeline's books with her, until Kristy, not unkindly, had reminded me I hadn't read any of them.

"Turkey Noodle Dooda Surprise served with Tater Tot Casserole can really get your amorous juices flowing," the one who called herself Nancy gushed. Her floral caftan reminded me of Hawaii. The quintessential grandma had no last name. Apparently she had legally changed her name to Nancy . . . you know, like Cher or Beyoncé or Gaga.

"I'm sorry," I interrupted. "I thought this was a romance writers' meeting." My insides clenched. This couldn't be right. I must be in the wrong room, or hopefully the wrong building.

"It is," Shoshanna LeHump said. "Nancy writes romantic cookbooks!"

"Oh, aren't you a lovely thing." Nancy smiled and squeezed my hands. "Are you a cover model?"

"Um, no. I'm actually a, um . . . writer," I white-lied. I do write things. I'm a CPA, for God's sake. I just happen to write numbers instead of words.

"Shoshanna," Nancy called out to the handcuff-loving porno granny, "we have a new writer!"

"Fucking awesome," the Shoshanna woman yelled back, giving me a big thumbs-up.

Shit, this was not turning out the way it was supposed to. These women were very sweet; they'd all hugged me when I arrived like I was a long-lost friend. Okay, that was a little unsettling, but as well meaning as they were, I didn't want a Bunko group of grandmas who cussed like sailors . . . I wanted Dorothy Parker and the Algonquin Round Table, where we would drink wine and chuckle at our own witty brilliance. Speaking of witty brilliance, where in the hell was the Queen of Bodice Rippers? I wasn't sure how much more information my brain could hold about bondage, whippings, and hot dishes before it would explode.

"Excuse me," I said, interrupting Shoshanna LeHump's in-depth explanation of the benefits and sanitation of butt plugs. "I thought Evangeline O'Hara was a member."

The room went silent. Everyone stared at me like I'd grown three heads. All of the lumberjack-looking softball-playing grandmas narrowed their eyes at me.

"Are you friends with that viper bitch whore from hell?" Nancy, the storybook granny, inquired kindly. Her words and her tone did not match. Clearly I'd heard her wrong, but on the off chance I hadn't, I refused to ask her to repeat herself.

"Um . . . no," I whispered, a little bit scared. "I've never met her. I just thought she was a member."

Everyone's smiles returned when they realized I wasn't best buds with the viper bitch whore from hell. These seniors had some amazing vocabularies. I made a mental note not to get on their bad side.

"Oh, thank God," Shoshanna LeHump grumbled. "I was worried that stinky hooker sent a spy in to steal more of our ideas."

"What do you mean?" I asked, shocked. What kind of ideas would a New York Times best-selling author steal from a group of old ladies writing about butt plugs?

"She's a criminal," Poppy Rose Petal yelled. *God, I hope that's her pen name.* She was a big-boned gal with a blinding fuchsia neck scarf, trim khakis, baby pink sweater, and loafers . . . with a shiny penny in each. "That last book she wrote was Shoshanna's idea."

"That's true," Ms. LeHump, the handcuff expert, ground out angrily. "The bus tour across Russia was my baby and she stole it. Of course, my bus is a rolling S and M club for amputees, but the basic premise is the same."

It was time for me to get out of there. If Evangeline O'Hara was even one-fourth as bat-shit crazy as the rest of these gals, I needed to make a break for it.

"So," Poppy the flower woman asked, "Rena, what are you writing?"

"Well . . . um—" What in the hell was I going to say? I didn't want to give away any of my brilliant ideas. Wait . . . I didn't actually have any ideas. Time for a butt-yank explanation. Not to be confused with butt plug. "It's a romantic comedy about a schoolteacher and um . . . a bus driver." In my nervousness I spoke a little louder than I'd intended. Evidenced by several of the old girls discreetly covering their ears. Shit.

"Sounds great," Nancy exclaimed. My God, could she be nicer? "What's the plot?"

"The plot." What was the plot? That was an excellent question. "Well, it's a forbidden love . . . because he's a former convict and um, they vow to have sex in every room in the school."

"Fantastic," Shoshanna LeHump yelled, slapping her thighs and doing what looked like a drunken Irish jig. "Are there any threesomes or girl-on-girl action?"

"No." I bit the inside of my cheek to keep from laughing. "That hadn't occurred to me."

"Well"—she winked at me—"a little girl-on-girl action can really spice up a story."

Was she hitting on me? I couldn't tell. It seemed like she was, but she's married. I'm fairly sure she had used the word *husband* at one point between her diatribes on cock rings and lubricants. To avoid that train of thought, I continued on with my big fat hairy lie of a plot.

"Anyway, it turns out he was unjustly accused of a mass murder during a hurricane and spent the last five or ten years in prison. Maybe it was seven years . . . I can't remember exactly. Then he dug his way to freedom, using a spork, right before his sentence was overturned, but now they want to put him back in prison for breaking out. You see, he didn't know they were going to let him out of the pokey. That's why he tunneled to freedom." I sucked in a deep breath and scanned the room for alternate exits. Maybe I could slip out when they weren't looking . . .

"Oh my God," the Rosebush Petal woman said, "that's incredible. How does he meet the teacher?"

"Of course," I stammered, "the teacher. So he dyes his hair and gets his teeth capped. He had a gap between his two front teeth because his parents couldn't afford braces when he was a child, and he steals an identity. He goes to the school and gets a job as the bus driver after about four interviews. He's really worried about the background check because he doesn't know all that much about the person he stole the identity from."

"Intrigue, that's good." Nancy nodded her approval.

"Thanks," I said, smiling. Her genuine kindness and encourage-
ment made me feel like an ass for lying, but I was already in too
deep. "Then he sees the teacher across the playground during third
period and it's love at first sight."

"Does she have big boobs?" Shoshanna LeHump asked.

"Um . . . yes. Yes, she does." I sucked my bottom lip into my
mouth and put on my serious face. She had definitely been hitting
on me.

"Wait—" My potential girlfriend stopped me. "I thought you
said romantic comedy. Where's the funny part?"

"Oh, the funny part . . . right." What is the funny part? Shit, shit,
shit. "The funny part is when they . . . um, have, you know, sex in
all the classrooms. Chalk and erasers get in the way, mayhem en-
sues. The fire alarm goes off. The chairs are too small . . . Stuff like
that." I was sweating now. I wasn't sure how much more crap I
could come up with.

"Does he have to go back to prison?" a rather rotund gal with
kind eyes and no eyebrows named Joanne asked. She clearly had a
violent relationship with her tweezers. More impressive was her
purple Minnesota Vikings sweat suit. It made her look like a giant
grape.

"No, no, he doesn't," I said with finality, hoping we'd move on
to someone else.

"Does the teacher ever find out about his past?" Nancy inquired.

"Nope." I smiled. "I'm going for that ambiguous feeling. Kind
of like real life."

"Fucking brilliant," Shoshanna bellowed. "I still think you
should consider a little threesome action. Maybe with the principal
or one of the lunch ladies."

"You might be right." My enthusiasm sounded forced, but I
hoped if I agreed, she would shut up.

"You should listen to LeHump," Poppy the Plant said. "She
made three hundred thousand in sales last year alone."

"What?" I gasped. I had no idea so many people wanted to read
about sticking things in their butt. As impressed as I was with that
number, I couldn't possibly add a scene with the teacher and the
bus driver and the lunch lady. It wasn't true to my vision. *What am
I thinking? I have no vision. I just pulled the most ridiculous premise out of my rear end and now I have a vision?*

As I silently contemplated the merits of a threesome with the lunch lady, the mood in the room changed abruptly. The tension grew thick and the hair stood up on my arms. The women scurried around like ants in a rainstorm. What was going on? Were they offended that the bus driver didn't come clean about his past? I could change that part. Maybe he should tell her . . . After all, he's not really guilty of killing anybody. I mean, he did steal an identity, but he found the driver's license in the garbage in back of a fast food restaurant when he was scrounging for burgers. He was starving, for God's sake . . . couldn't they understand that?

"She's here," Nancy hissed. All eyes flew to the door.

"Who's here?" I whispered urgently. My breakfast doughnut was threatening to make a reappearance. Why in the hell didn't I leave at the first mention of bondage? I was scared to death and I had no idea why.

"The skanky, book-stealing, bottom-feeding slag," Shoshanna LeHump said quietly. "Don't look her in the eye—she'll suck out your soul."

"Put Rena behind you," Nancy frantically barked to Shoshanna. Her muumuu flowed wildly around her, making me dizzy. "The smelly skank-hole always goes for the new ones. Protect her!" she hissed.

LeHump shoved me behind her. She was strong for such a tiny thing. I was starting to hyperventilate. What in the hell had I gotten myself into?

A small almost inaudible whimper rippled through the room as she entered . . . Ladies and gentlemen, Evangeline O'Hara was in the house.

Chapter 2

An eerie hush fell over the room. I could feel Poppy the Azalea Bush trembling next to me and Joanne was picking at her face where her eyebrows used to be. Nancy and LeHump held their ground, but they were half the women they had been only five minutes ago. We stood huddled together like a herd of cows. There was a lump in my throat and my heart was bouncing around in my chest like a Ping-Pong ball; I knew everyone could hear it. What in the hell was happening? With extreme caution, I peeked out from behind Shoshanna's head.

What the fuck was that? That couldn't possibly be Evangeline O'Hara. Could it? My God, the picture she used on her website had to be at least thirty years old . . . maybe forty.

She prowled the room like a panther . . . with a limp. It had to be the shoes. I'd seen shoes like that only in magazines. They were so high, I didn't know how she didn't teeter off. Her body was skeletal thin. But her boobs . . . her boobs were ginormous and didn't move as she circled the mound of terrified women pressed together in the middle of the room. She was draped in turquoise silk. The same color as her eyes. I'm positive she slept with them open, not by choice . . . by necessity. They'd been lifted to her eyebrows. She looked like she'd just come out of a supersonic wind tunnel; her face was yanked back as tight as a drum. There wasn't a line on her forehead or around her eyes or mouth, but her neck resembled a flesh-colored rotten prune. Clearly her vision was impaired, because if she got a gander at her neck . . . Hoo Betty. My guess was that misplaced pride in her frighteningly abundant cleavage blinded her to the saggy neck.

There's just something inherently wrong with an eightyish-year-old woman sporting the triple-D bosom of a twenty-year-old centerfold model. Although to be fair, she was kind of cadaver-ish chic, similar to Cher.

Her mouth was a train wreck. It was a cross between a fish and a duck, and it didn't quite close. Between the mouth and the eyes, she appeared to be in a constant state of surprise. Her plastic surgeon should be shot. I idly wondered if food fell out when she ate, although it didn't look like she ate much. I couldn't look away. I pulled on my bangs, forcing my eyes to the floor, trying desperately not to make eye contact. There was no doubt she could suck out a soul.

"Hello dahalllings," she purred, and her voice was a mix of Harvey Fierstein and Marilyn Monroe. Her bodyguard, a big burly man in a black suit somewhere in his fifties, quickly put his arm out to steady her as she almost tumbled off her designer stilettos. "Shoshinka, my love, how are we doing today?"

"Fine," Shoshanna growled, "until about three minutes ago. And my name is Shoshanna."

"Of course," Evangeline laughed. Her laugh reminded me of ice breaking off trees after a horrific winter storm. Deadly. "You have such an amusing sense of humor, Shoshushu."

Shoshanna's body tensed like a coil about to spring. I gently put my hand on her back to calm her. Her small body shook beneath my touch. Why were these women so scared, and why were they taking this mean old biddy's crap? I held my breath, watching in fascination as Evangeline's bulging eyes scanned the crowd. Nancy pushed me down so the scary hag wouldn't see me. Their protectiveness confused and touched me. Their fear was palpable, but my own terror began to ebb away . . . replaced by anger.

Five minutes ago this room was filled with joyful, kind women who had passions for butt plugs and dishes made with cream of mushroom soup. They'd taken me in and hadn't laughed at my book idea, and it certainly wasn't much of an idea. Although with some work . . . Focus, I needed to focus. I needed to save these women. These gals were protecting me. They didn't even know me and they'd thrown their bodies in front of mine so the viper bitch whore from hell (Nancy's words, not mine) couldn't eat me.

My sense of justice had gotten me in trouble before, but that was baby stuff compared to what was about to go down . . .

"So girls—" Evangeline took a seat with a lot of help from her bodyguard. I knew my eyes should be trained on the floor like the rest of the group, but I couldn't keep myself from looking. I wish I had. Her silk sheath hiked up during her descent to the chair, exposing an ungodly amount of spray-tanned, pickled thigh. She crossed her toothpick legs, and I realized with sickening clarity that she was going commando. I bit my lip to tamp down my gag reflex, but I knew it would be weeks before I had an appetite again. "I'm curious if anyone has any new ideas."

She waited.

And waited.

"I bet you are," Shoshanna muttered under her breath.

"What was that, Shorunka darling?" she asked, grinning evilly. "I thought I heard something unpleasant."

"It must have been your conscience, dear." Nancy smiled, speaking in a loving tone.

"I don't think she has one," Rosebush Flower Petal burst out, her voice sounding fragile and shaky.

"I don't think she has one," Evangeline mimicked Rosebush Gal with an evil hiss. "Well, she doesn't. And all of you stupid, unattractive old women should know that by now, so cough up the ideas," she shrieked.

Eyebrow-less Joanne was hyperventilating behind me and Flower Power seemed seconds away from fainting. This would have been funny if it wasn't real, but it was . . . very real, and these lovely, albeit strange, older gals were terrified. If these ladies couldn't stand up for themselves, I'd do it for them . . .

"I have an idea." I shimmied my way out of the huddle and stood in front of her. Holy shit, up close she looked like a wax figure from Madame Tussaud's Museum.

"No, Rena, no," Shoshanna moaned in agony. An icy blast of fear shot through me at Shoshanna's tone, but I figured if I gave Evangeline my idea, maybe she would leave, and my cute little ladies could have fun again.

"Ah, what have we here?" Evangeline eyed me from head to toe. She enviously fingered my long blond hair and winced at my snow boots. "Some new blood. How lovely of you ladies to bring me a gift. Especially one so breathtakingly beautiful."

Good God, are all these old women lesbians?

"She's not for you," Shoshanna said through clenched teeth, stepping forward to stand next to me. "She's not even a writer."

Ouch, that stung. Of course Shoshanna was correct, I'm not a writer. I knew she was trying to save me from the plastic surgery experiment gone awry seated in the chair, but I wish she had come up with a less hurtful defense. I put my arm around my little bondage-loving new buddy in solidarity and to let her know I was fine.

"I'll be the judge of that," the viper spat, pushing Shoshanna away from me with the pointed toe of her shoe. I quickly averted my eyes to avoid the peep show she insisted on performing. "What's your name, pretty girl?" Evangeline asked in a silky voice.

"Rena," I could hardly raise my voice above a whisper. Maybe this hadn't been such a good idea.

"Rena what?" she pried. The bodyguard took out a pad and pen from his breast pocket.

"Rena Gunderschlict." There was an audible groan of dismay from the pile of ladies behind me. I knew my last name was awful, but I didn't think their reaction was to my name . . . it was the fact I'd given it to the idea-stealing hag.

I experienced a surge of panic as the bodyguard wrote it down on his pad. He was formal and official, causing me a hellacious flashback to my recent arrest downtown at the news station after my pathetic attempt to become the new Sunshine Weather Girl.

"So, Rena, my dear," her strangely hypnotic voice urged me on, "what's your idea?"

There was no way in hell I was going to tell her about the teacher and the convict bus driver. I wasn't sure if the girls were blowing smoke up my butt about my story or if it's a best-seller in the making. Just in case, I wasn't giving it to the walking Botox experiment. I'd simply have to yank another one out of my rear . . .

"Well . . . um . . . there's this pirate," I started.

"Yes?" In her excitement she leaned forward, giving me an unfortunate view of the perky round globes attached to her eighty-year-old bony chest.

"Yep, a pirate," I said, looking everywhere except at Evangeline's bosom. I rocked back and forth in panic, having no idea what was going to come out of my mouth. "And he kidnaps these beautiful twins during an earthquake. It was about a four or so on the

Richter scale. He's never seen anything as gorgeous as these young women in his life." I glanced over at Shoshanna, who discreetly moved her hands to her breasts. "They had ginormous breasts."

"Ahhh, yes," Evangeline cooed. "Tell me more."

"Right, so . . . he steals them in the middle of the night from their mansion in Sydney, Australia. Once he gets them on the ship, he realizes they're conjoined." I stared at the ceiling, praying for divine intervention, or a power outage.

"Holy shit," Shoshanna choked.

"Be quiet, Shoshoodoo," the viper hissed. "Continue," she demanded.

"At this point he realizes he only loves one of them. The other one is a total bitch."

Evangeline clasped her hands greedily. "What's her name?"

"Whose name?" I asked.

"The name of the one he loves." She rolled her eyes at my stupidity.

That was really alarming. Bulging eyeballs with permanently open lids should not be permitted to roll. Ever. "Oh, her name is, um . . . Shirley, but it just so happens that the pirate is a time-traveling vampire warlock."

"I've never heard of that." Intense astonishment touched her waxy face.

"Of course you haven't," I stammered. A wave of apprehension swept through me, and I started to sweat. "There's only one in existence."

Her head whipped around to her bodyguard, "Are you getting all this, Cecil?" He nodded his huge head and kept writing.

Cecil? His name was Cecil? That so didn't work for me. He looked like a Butch or a Rocky. "So . . ." I had no idea what was going to come out of my mouth next. I needed to wrap this baby up or I was going to pass out from anxiety. "The pirate—"

"What's his name?" the pantiless meanie asked.

"Um . . . Dave, his name is Pirate Dave. So Pirate Dave time-traveled to the future with the conjoined twins to John Hopkins Hospital."

"What year?" she asked, reaching out to touch me with her claw.

I backed away, feigning deep thought. "1974."

"Why 1974?" She sounded bewildered.

"Pardon my rudeness, but if you keep talking, I will never finish." I made eye contact and held it. She narrowed her eyes. I narrowed mine . . . and waited.

"Fine," she snapped, "I'll be quiet."

"Good. Anyway, Pirate Dave held his massive sword to the surgeon's neck and demanded that he separate the twins. So the surgeon did and Dave gave him three bags of gold and some Elvis trading cards he found when he visited the 1950s. He magicked up some limbs for his love and her bitch of a sister because . . . um . . . it would be too hard to live a regular life, you know, missing half a torso and arms and legs and half of your butt and . . ." I stopped. The entire room watched me, mouths agape. I didn't take that as a good sign . . . I skipped the rest of their physical description. "So they time-traveled back to the year they were from."

"What year?" Evangeline bounced up and down with excitement. Her boobs did not.

I paused and gave her the evil eye. Her bouncing stopped and she looked passably contrite. "Sorry," she muttered.

"The year was 1492. The very same year that Columbus sailed the ocean blue. But what most people don't know is that Pirate Dave discovered America, not Columbus . . . not Leif Erickson."

The crowd gasped. *I can't believe they're buying this shit. I wonder how far I can go . . .* "If you think about it, it makes perfect sense. Pirate Dave is a time-traveling vampire warlock. He's already been to America in the future a bunch of times and he knows exactly where it is. He doesn't want to take credit for the discovery because he likes being a pirate too much. He garners great enjoyment out of kidnapping beautiful women and having sex with them. He has a medical problem that causes a constant erection and he has to have sex four to six times a day."

"Is this based on a true story?" Evangeline inquired.

"Yes, yes it is." I nodded, biting the inside of my cheek so hard I drew blood.

"I thought so," she said, impressing herself with her vast knowledge of history.

"So when they got back to the ship, Pirate Dave and Shirley started to have sex on the deck of the ship while everyone watched. They were so in love, they couldn't wait to ravish each other and they were so into each other, they didn't even realize anyone was watching."

"How romantic." Evangeline was breathing hard; her left hand cupped her right breast.

Ewwww, she was turned on. I was going to shower for a long time that night.

"Then they lived happily ever after. The end."

"Wait," Evangeline shouted. "What happened to the bitch sister?"

I hesitated. What in the hell happened to the evil sister? Shit. "She . . . um, tried to kill Pirate Dave and Shirley while they were having intercourse on the deck, but the crew got so mad they threw her overboard. They were all voyeurs."

"Did she die?" a high squeaky voice asked. Who in the fuck said that? Cecil? Cecil sounded like a ten-year-old nerd before puberty. His voice did not match his body. He and Evangeline were quite the pair.

"That's for me to know and you to find out in the sequel," I said. As if.

"What's the sister's name?" Cecil asked.

What the hell was it with these people and names? "Laverne, her name is Laverne."

Cecil gave me a big shit-eating grin. "Laverne and Shirley? You named them Laverne and Shirley?"

If he wasn't connected to the viper bitch whore from hell, he might just be okay . . . but he was with her, and therefore he was the enemy. "Yes." I couldn't help but return his grin. I could hear the stifled giggles from behind me. Evangeline looked confused and pissed about being left out of something.

"What are you idiots laughing at?" she snapped. "This is based in truth. I remember reading all about this in high school. Rena has no imagination! She just looked up facts and is trying to make you think she's created a masterpiece." Her voice was shrill.

My God, she was stupid and evil, never a good combination.

"Jeeves—" She unconsciously grabbed both of her breasts and her eyes got glassy. The images she was embedding in my brain would take years of therapy to remove . . . and I thought his name was Cecil. "We've not done a paranormal yet. They're very popular right now," she hissed with excitement. "This will be my crowning glory! I will be bigger than Jackie Collins!"

Cecil-Jeeves nodded and continued to write. Wait . . . was it really a good idea? I basically just coughed up a hairball of idiocy and she planned to turn it into a *New York Times* best-seller? You know, maybe it was good. The whole time-traveling vampire warlock thing hadn't been done yet. I'd just come up with the next big thing and this over-Juvédermed shrew was going to steal it. I'd never read a romance novel about conjoined twins. It was a huge market that had never been tapped. I had just come up with the new *Twilight,* and it was slipping through my fingers. This would make a riveting movie. What in the hell was I thinking, giving my entire future away like that? The whole separation of the twins and the murder plot was truly inspired. There was absolutely nothing like it out there. Thank God I hadn't told her about the teacher and the convict bus driver—that would be a hit for sure. She was going to steal my story and make millions off it. My millions. Damn it, that was not going to happen.

"There's just one little problem," I replied sharply, cutting into her Jackie Collins fantasy. "It's my idea and I'm writing the book."

Evangeline's nostrils flared with fury and she glared at me. The little ladies gasped and without even seeing them, I knew they had huddled closer together in abject terror. Cecil-Jeeves raised an eyebrow and Shoshanna swallowed a laugh that ended up sounding like the first gag of someone throwing up.

"You're right, Rhonda"—Evangeline's voice was like honey—"but you're a nobody. Never been published. Sholulu here says you're not even a writer."

It was funny how she couldn't remember anyone's name, but she could recall every word they said. I had a bad feeling Shoshanna's comment would come back to haunt me.

"When I said that"—Shoshanna leapt to my defense—"I was simply referring to her unpublished status . . . at the moment."

"Of course you were, Shoshanka." Evangeline had turned on a dime. She now sounded sane, rational, and sweet. WTF? "Reba, darling—" She smiled and extended her claws to me. I so did not want to touch her, but politeness dictated my decision. I gingerly took her hands. I'm a good Midwestern girl, after all. Her hands

were ice cold, and I tried to block out the fact that they'd been cupping her bosom only moments ago. "You're right," she continued
gently. "It is your idea and it's brilliant. I'd like to offer you something . . . something rare and special. Something I offer to no one.
Would you like that, Rona?"

"I don't know," I answered, half in anticipation, half in dread.
The room had become so quiet, I thought everyone had left. Nope,
they were still here, they'd just stopped breathing. So had I.

"I'd like to mentor you on your book," she purred.

My ladies gasped. I don't know if it was in envy or horror. Although, if I was a gambling girl, I'd put my money on horror. I noticed Cecil's jaw clench. He continued to write, but his body
language suggested anger. What was that about? Was he jealous?
Ew, did he have a thing going with her and didn't want to share? I
needed to stop this line of thought before my gag reflex kicked in.

"I don't know . . ." I started.

"We will write together," she quickly interjected. "You and I
will share co-author credit. I already have an agent, a publishing
house, publicity team, website, and a fan base of millions. You
would be a shortsighted fool not to take me up on this . . . That is,
unless you're not really an author," she challenged, watching me
carefully.

I was still freaked out that she liked the pirate idea. Was she
brain damaged? Even though I loved the idea of being a rich
and famous author, I wasn't sure selling my soul to the devil
was the best way to go about it. I knew deep down inside that
the Pirate Dave–Laverne and Shirley conjoined twins concept
sucked. And while I was being brutally honest with myself, the
bus driver–teacher thing was pretty horrid, too. Shoshanna was
right I'm not a writer. I'm an accountant. I just wished there was a
little more excitement in my life . . .

"Um . . . thanks for your interest, but no. I already have a job,
and I am saving my vacation days for a trip to see the Tommy
Bartlett Show at the Wisconsin Dells." Oh my God, did I just say
the Tommy Bartlett Show? The cheesy water show with the skiing
squirrel? Yes, I did . . . I had just revealed my total inner dork. Why
didn't I lie and say Aruba or someplace sexy?

I began biting my cuticles in panic. I didn't belong there. All these women, eyebrows or not, were authors . . . real authors, who could actually write. Not young, bored-with-their-life girls who were desperately searching for something to feel passionate about. That being said, I wasn't about to let the skanky witch have my idea. I'd give it to one of the girls there. Shoshanna would love it; there could definitely be some girl-on-girl action in this one. Although the conjoined twins thing made it a bit complicated. I noticed everyone in the room was breathing again and Cecil's jaw had relaxed. Everyone seemed happy, except the viper bitch whore from hell.

"I'll pay you," she spat. "I'll pay you ten thousand dollars a week for three weeks." The happy relaxed atmosphere in the room disappeared abruptly. My stomach clenched and I felt dizzy. That was a shitload of money. "You'll be at my home every day from eight in the morning till five. We will write the book. We will split the profits fifty-fifty and then you will be free to go to the Tommy Bartlett Show," she sneered.

Damn it to hell, why had I mentioned the Tommy Bartlett Show? That would be hard to live down . . . God, I could make more than half a year's salary in three weeks . . . if I sold the witch my soul. I'd done plenty of stupid things for free; why not do something massively stupid and make a butt load of money doing it? Could I stand being around her for that long? I was a little curious to see if food dropped from her mouth when she ate . . . I could probably see her without makeup. No, that would induce nightmares. Shoshanna took my hand.

"If she goes, I go with her," she said in a steely tone.

"Delightful," Evangeline trilled evilly, "that makes me very happy, Shrilanka. I'll see you both on Monday." She stood with an enormous amount of help from Cecil or Jeeves or whatever his name was and sauntered out of the room.

"Wait," I gasped when I found my voice, but she was gone. "I never said I would do it. Shit, shit, shit." I paced the room in anxiety. "Shoshanna, I can't go work with that thing." My cuticles found their way back to my teeth.

"Relax, Rena, I'll be with you. I wouldn't leave you alone with that heinous cow bitch from the underworld. Do you really have vacation time?" LeHump asked and I nodded. I couldn't speak because my mouth was full of fingers. "Good, then you can make a bunch of money and we can get our lives back from that skank." Shoshanna rubbed her hands together with glee. "This could kill two birds with one stone."

"What in the hell are you talking about?" I was still in shock that by not speaking up I might have fucked up my life for the next three weeks, although I'd be richer for it.

"The first bird is the money for you," Shoshanna explained excitedly; then she began to fidget. "Rena"—LeHump's fidgeting increased—"I don't want you to get offended by what I'm about to say . . ."

"Okay," I said, feeling a little nauseous and bracing myself to be heartily offended.

"We could effectively end her career with that paranormal Pirate Dave–Laverne and Shirley story. It's the worst pile of shit I've ever heard," she exclaimed with intense pleasure. "We help her write it, take absolutely no credit . . ."

"Like she would have given you any credit anyway," Nancy chimed in.

"True—" Shoshanna was on a roll. "The toothpick with knockers takes full credit, gets it published, and goes down in flames!"

"This could solve all of our problems," Petunia Tree Bush yelled, eyes blazing with joy.

"Possibly," Nancy said cautiously, "but it could backfire."

"How could bringing her down with conjoined twins and a time-traveling vampire warlock with erectile dysfunction backfire?" Shoshanna was confused. Clearly she thought my story was a no-brainer career killer.

Fine. I knew it wasn't a good idea, but to have it paraded around as the crowning jewel that could bring a career down in flames was humiliating. More so, because I knew it was true. And what was this backfire talk? I felt the heat crawl up my neck and I bit my bottom lip so I wouldn't cry. It didn't work.

"Oh dear heavens," Eyebrow-less Joanne, the purple grape, grabbed me in a bear hug and rocked me back and forth. "LeHump, you made her cry." She held me in a vise-like grip and I was having a hard time breathing. These ladies were strong.

"Oh fuck," LeHump was distraught, "Rena, I'm so sorry. Were

you serious about that story? I had no idea. I thought for sure you were making that pile of crap up as you went along." LeHump started to cry. "I feel awful," she sobbed.

They all started to cry. The room was filled with snot-nosed, weeping seventy-year-olds . . . and it was my fault. The viper whore bitch from Hades had nothing on me. I brought an entire roomful of sweet women to tears and because of Joanne's stranglehold, I couldn't breathe well enough to tell them it was all right.

"Can't breathe," I wheezed, trying to extricate myself from my comforter.

"Jesus Christ on a cross," Poppy Bush shrieked, "you're killing her!"

Joanne screamed, dropped me to the floor, and started to wail. Holy hell, this was worse than speed dating for Lutherans. I landed on all fours at her feet. I felt light-headed and had to remain in the doggie position for a few moments before the dizziness subsided.

"It's okay, guys." I struggled to my feet. "It's okay," I repeated. "I did pull it out of my ass and I knew it sucked . . . it's just hard to hear somebody else say it out loud." I drew in a huge shaky breath and wondered if Joanne had crushed my lungs. I dropped into the chair that Evangeline had vacated minutes ago as all the ladies nodded in understanding.

"I feel like a douche bag," Shoshanna groaned, her shoulders slumped; she wiped her tears on the sleeve of her lavender fleece pullover.

"You're not a douche bag," I said, the beginnings of a smile pulling at my lips.

"I'm a total douche bag," she muttered, running her hands through her hair and making it stand up on end. "A thoughtless stinky douche bag."

"I'd say you're just a douche, not a douche bag." I giggled at her description of herself and the scary hairdo.

The rest of the girls began to smile and chuckle. Shoshanna grinned at me gratefully and took my hand. "I really am sorry. I have a malady called diarrhea of the mouth. I am insensitive and loud and . . . I'm sorry. It's not that bad of an idea. With some work . . ."

"Stop," I laughed, smacking her little hand. "I'll be more hurt and insulted if you lie to me. The idea sucks and if you guys want me to feed it to her, I will. God knows I could use the money, but how will we get away with this? She's got to know the idea is awful."

"Are you kidding me?" Joanne couldn't control her burst of laughter. "You think she has taste? She's under the very mistaken assumption that her plastic surgeon is a genius!"

"Joanne's right," Poppy Rose Vine laughed. Her voice was rich and warm, almost masculine. She was anything but, with her trim bod and pink feminine clothes. "She thinks she looks forty!"

"She's smokin' crack," I laughed. I twisted my hands and racked my brain, but I couldn't for the life of me remember Poppy's whole name. I don't know why, perhaps it's because it doesn't fit her. "What's your real name, Poppy?" I asked, wondering if it fit her any better. A blush covered her face, and I noticed she could use a really good lip wax. "Um . . . ," she stammered, looking around for support. Had I gotten too personal? "I've changed it several times"—she smiled shyly—"but lately I've been going by Harriet. It was my mom's name."

"It's lovely," I told her. She was fragile for such a big gal. She was by far the largest of the women. Not fat, just big boned and strong. Harriet was easy to remember. It didn't really fit her either, but it was better than all the floral names I had running around in my head. "May I call you Harriet?"

"Yes, you may," she paused, "but would you mind terribly calling me Poppy Harriet?"

"I think that could be arranged." I smiled. God, I felt like I'd known these women forever. What was that about? "So, back to the matter at hand," I rallied my newfound troops. "If she's going to buy a time-traveling vampire warlock with a permanent hard-on who likes to have intercourse with recently separated conjoined twins that he had to magic up some body parts for, what else do you think I can get away with?"

My posse of gals grinned evilly, and we started to plan.

Chapter 3

After the meeting, Shoshanna walked me to my car, letting me know what to expect Monday morning. Thank God she did. Damn thing was totally dead.

"Son of a bitch," I groaned, banging my head on the steering wheel.

"Don't worry about it, Rena, I'll drive you home," LeHump offered.

I glanced up at Shoshanna. There she stood, bundled up in a lime-green down coat with a Minnesota Vikings matching hat, glove, and scarf set. Her snow boots were blue with hot pink polka dots. Never had I seen an ensemble so hideous and so lovely at the same time. First impressions aren't often wrong, but they can be. I had definitely been wrong about LeHump. She might write porno and have a bad haircut, but she also had a huge heart and I don't think she had been hitting on me. I think she was just weird.

"Where do you live?" I asked.

"New Hope. Where do you live?"

"Saint Paul," I sighed. I was going to be cabbing it, or possibly even worse . . . bussing it. Shit. New Hope was thirty minutes in the opposite direction from my house, and I lived a half an hour from where we were. There was no way I could let her drive me home.

"That would add an hour onto your trip. I can't let you do that." I smiled and squeezed her purple and gold clad hand.

"It's no fucking biggie. My sister lives in Saint Paul. She'll be thrilled if I stop by. She owes me money. Plus I need to get you a little more up to speed about the slag."

"Shoshanna, it's really too far."

"Bullshit. Just hang on a second. I need to move my computer and baseball bat out of the front seat."

Shoshanna was not taking no for an answer, which was very sweet . . . I thought. The baseball bat concerned me, but I figured if she was going to kill me she would have already done so in the parking garage. There was no one in sight and no security cameras anywhere.

I grabbed my tote and my purse and hustled over to Shoshanna's sky blue minivan. I could have called AAA, but I didn't have enough body fat to sit in subzero temperatures for three hours and wait for them. As it was, my snot was freezing as I walked the thirty feet to Shoshanna's soccer-mom-ish mode of transport. I needed to move to a warmer climate.

"Get in. It takes a while for the heat to work in this piece of shit, but when it kicks in, you'll sweat like a fat whore at confession."

"Do you eat with that mouth?" I grinned, shaking my head and searching for the seat belt. The car was a pigsty.

Shoshanna cackled with glee, "You bet I do! Are you going to remember all the new stuff you came up with?"

"It would be very difficult to forget the part about the three-way between Pirate Dave, Leif Erickson, and Christopher Columbus," I choked out, still searching for the seat belt.

"That's some good stuff there, Rena. I don't think I could have come up with that one myself. You have the scariest imagination I've ever had the pleasure to witness."

"Um . . . thanks." A compliment is a compliment no matter how insulting.

"The part that really gets me is when the pirate with scurvy and no fingers on his left hand tries to sew the twins back together. That is just fucking gross."

"Is it too gross?" I worried. Maybe that was going a little too far. I had gotten kind of carried away, but when Poppy Harriet's soda flew out of her nose, I couldn't stop myself. Maybe I should try stand-up comedy . . .

"Absolutely not!" Shoshanna bellowed. "I'd go even a little farther. Give him lice or severe halitosis, a clubfoot maybe."

"LeHump, that's gross."

"You're right—" She grinned sheepishly. "I don't have it like you do."

"I'm not real sure that coming up with plots that can bring careers down in flames is 'having it,' but thank you." I still couldn't find the damn seat belt, but I did find a few rock-hard fries and what may have been a cheeseburger during the 1980s. "LeHump, your car is disgusting."

"I've been meaning to clean it out. What in the hell are you digging for?"

"The seat belt."

"Oh." She shrugged guiltily. "I cut them out. Everybody's doing it."

"Oookay." I didn't have a comeback for that one, so I simply smiled and nodded. She is nuttier than my Aunt Phyllis, who is convinced there are little people in her TV. I was beginning to wonder about her sanity, as well as my own for getting into her car.

I told her where I lived and she proceeded to drive like a bat out of hell. I prayed the entire time. I wasn't particularly religious, but when my life was in danger, I figured it couldn't hurt.

"So, we'll probably do some light housecleaning and possibly bathe her turd-laying, skank-breath rat dogs. Bring your lunch because the viper bitch doesn't keep food in the house. Oh, wear sweats, but bring a nice outfit. She likes to make us run errands. Don't ever say no to an errand."

My mouth was agape and an icy chill ran up my spine. "Are you serious?" What had I gotten myself into?

"As a heart attack." Shoshanna made a gagging sound. I thought she was going to vomit. "Once Joanne refused to drive in a blizzard to get gourmet treats for those shit-eating canines and Evangeline made her scrape her bunions for an hour. That's the day Joanne started pulling her eyebrows out."

"I thought maybe that was a fashion choice."

"Oh, God no. She had wonderful bushy eyebrows before the bunion incident."

I wasn't sure I would put the words *wonderful* and *bushy eyebrows* together, but I also wouldn't be caught dead in a lime-green coat driving a light blue minivan. Then again, who was I to judge? I'd been tapped as the girl with career-destroying ideas.

"Okay, sweats, nice clothes, lunch, and never say no to an errand. I got it. Will we do any writing?" I put my feet up on the dash, hoping it might break the blow from the accident we were sure to have. She'd already run two red lights and flipped off more drivers than I did in an entire month.

"We'll sit down with Cecil and dictate to him. She sleeps most of the time when she's not having procedures done or yelling at us." LeHump leaned over to turn the heat down and almost swerved into a convenience store.

"Shoshanna," I shrieked. I saw my life flash before my eyes and was thankful I was wearing nice underpants. I would hate to die in holey granny panties. My mom would shit a brick.

"Sorry"—she grinned—"I was getting hot. So anyway, like I was saying . . ."

"Wait." I cut her off. This was not making sense to me. "Why are you guys all doing stuff for her? Does she pay you?"

Shoshanna shifted uncomfortably in her seat. "Not exactly. Let's just say it's a business arrangement."

"Well that's fairly cryptic," I deadpanned.

"I love that word," LeHump gushed. "Don't you love that word?"

"Sure." I raised my not bushy brow sarcastically. "Do you also like the word 'avoidance'?"

"Love it," LeHump laughed. "It's my favorite."

"Holy fuck." Shoshanna grabbed my arm and yanked me to a halt as we rounded the corner to walk into my building. "Smokin' hot butt dead ahead."

"Oh my God," I gasped. She was right. It was a little creepy to have someone my grandparents' age ogle the behind of a thirty-ish-year-old guy, but she was correct. It was the finest ass I'd ever seen.

"He's going into your building," she hissed, hopping up and down with excitement.

Mr. Sexy-ass used a key and went in. That meant he lived there. *That amazing ass lives in my building!* From the back he was Adonis. Unless he was sporting a unibrow and no teeth, my guess was he was hot from the front, too. "You know he's probably gay," I said pulling Shoshanna toward the front door just in case we could get another glimpse. No such luck.

"I don't think so. That ass looked very straight to me," she said. I refrained from asking why she thought that. I was more afraid of her answer than the thought of the butt being gay.

Shoshanna came up to my apartment to use the loo. It was the least I could offer, after she'd gone so far out of her way for me. I was grateful for the ride, but even more grateful to still be alive. In a mere matter of hours Shoshanna had grown on me . . . kind of like a fungus. A nondeadly, sweet-smelling, insane fungus. I liked her and actually looked forward to spending time with her in the next three weeks, despite the scary circumstances. There was no telling what would come out of her mouth. I enjoyed not being the only loose cannon in the room.

"Oh my God!" Kristy gasped. "Professor Sue?"

"Kristy!" LeHump shouted joyously, embracing my roommate in a bear hug. "How are you? I haven't seen you in years. What are you doing now? I still remember that thesis you wrote on women's roles throughout religious history. One of the best goddamned papers I ever read."

Kristy blushed furiously and preened under LeHump's praise. What in the hell was going on here? LeHump was a porno writer, not a professor . . . Wait a minute. Was LeHump the famous "Professor Sue" I'd heard about ad nauseam from Kristy's college days? No freakin' way.

"Shoshan . . . Sue, you know my roommate?" Damn, I'd almost blown her cover. I was very curious as to her real last name, but asking didn't seem appropriate at the moment

"Know her? Know her?" Shoshanna yelled. Dang, she was loud. "Not only do I know her, she was one of the best students I ever had!"

Kristy looked positively orgasmic and I was flabbergasted. Had I moved into an alternate universe? The sum so did not equal the parts. I thought today couldn't get any weirder.

I thought wrong.

"Rena," my starstruck roommate gushed, "this is *the* Professor Sue. One of the most respected and sought-after professors of women's studies in the country. Her work has been published worldwide."

I glanced at Shoshanna/Sue. The irony was almost too much to bear. She winked and put her finger to her lips. I got it . . . Clearly

Kristy was not referring to the butt-plug trilogy or the contortionist sex-slave series LeHump had regaled me with when she wasn't trying to run us off the road during our thirty-minute ride from hell.

"I didn't realize you had a day job." I grinned at LeHump, shaking my head and removing my snow boots. She smirked and gave me a thumbs-up. She was crazy.

"Where's the john? I'm about to pee in my pants!"

"Down the hall and to the left," I interjected quickly. LeHump had no manners or social graces and while I liked her, I wouldn't put it past her to relieve herself on my kitchen floor. *I am so not cleaning that up.* I yanked her coat off and shoved her down the hall.

Kristy ran around the kitchen like a chicken with its head cut off, pulling open cabinets and sniffing things she pulled from the fridge.

"Hey, we have a new neighbor with a rockin' hot ass."

"I have no time to discuss body parts. Help me," she hissed frantically, slapping cheese and crackers on our best platter. "Damn it," she muttered, staring at the green mold on the corner of the hunk of cheddar. I grabbed a knife and cut it off.

"Voilà!" I curtsied and tossed the offending cheese in the trash. "My Aunt Phyllis taught me that."

"Isn't she the one with people in her radio?"

"TV, not radio."

Kristy rolled her eyes, "That certainly makes all the difference." She stopped moving and I watched her brain go into rewind. "What do you mean, you saw the neighbor's ass?"

"We have a new neighbor named Mr. Asstastic." Fully clarifying I hadn't humped the new neighbor.

"Did you introduce yourself to his ass?" she asked, rearranging the hors d'oeuvres on the platter.

"Hell no. I never even saw his face."

"His face is good. I met him earlier, but I didn't get to see his ass. When you see his face, you'll jump him. Hell, when he sees you, he'll probably jump you first." I rolled my eyes and she fussed some more with the tray. "Is this classy enough?"

"Trust me, Sho . . . Sue will love it. I've been in her car." I went for some crackers, only to get my hand slapped down by Kristy. "So, she's really a professor?" The paradox was mind-boggling.

"Not just a professor, she's one of the foremost authorities on women's studies in the United States. There are waiting lists to get into her classes at the U. Oh my God." She froze. "Is Professor Sue in your writing group?"

Hmm, how to answer that without giving up LeHump's passion for all things anal? Thankfully I didn't have to.

"You bet I am!" Shoshanna loudly informed us as she marched directly to the cheese, cut herself a few slices, and shoved them in her mouth. "I love cheese." She grabbed a handful of crackers and made herself comfortable on the couch. I guess she was staying.

"So Kristy, I hope to the great God Almighty you are using your amazing brain to make the world a better place." LeHump put her little feet up on the coffee table. "You guys got anything sweet?"

"Yes, doughnuts. And get your damn feet off the table. Do you live in a barn?" I grabbed a box of powdered sugar minis and tossed them to her.

"Rena!" Kristy screeched at decibels that could result in hearing loss. Her mortification made her eye twitch. Not a good look. "I'm so sorry, Professor Sue, for Rena's horrific, disgusting, appalling behavior. Please, put your feet anywhere you like." She shot me a look of death.

Shoshanna/Sue LeHump chuckled and dug into the doughnuts. "Oh Kristy, Rena's right. I tend to fall on the side of uncouth. I could use a good handler to keep me in line."

I made a face at Kristy and I literally felt her need to slap me. She wouldn't dare, not in front of the legendary Professor Sue Whatever-her-last-name-was.

I decided to make nice with my roomie. Last time I pissed her off, she froze all my bras. Very high school, but very effective. "Kristy started a nonprofit literacy program at the battered women's shelter," I explained to LeHump proudly. "It has a daycare, and she's helped hundreds of women get their GED and find jobs."

"Goddamn it!" Shoshanna shouted, diving for Kristy and bear-hugging her for the second time in less than twenty minutes. "I am so fucking proud to call you my student! You are helping women help themselves. You are my hero!"

After a bunch of crying, pride on Shoshanna's part, joy on Kristy's, and, if I'm being totally honest, a little jealousy on mine, we all settled down and finished off the buffet of doughnuts, crackers, and cheese. Shoshanna finally decided to hit the road, but not before we filled Kristy in on our project with Evangeline.

She screamed in horror upon hearing my plot and laughed so hard she had to run to the bathroom to pee. Maybe I really should consider a career in stand-up comedy. I could pack a house with urine and all kinds of other liquids expelled through the nose. As I daydreamed about being a famous comedienne and hanging out with Stephen Colbert, I idly wondered if Shoshanna would carry the baseball bat into her sister's house to get her money back. I didn't for a moment believe she'd use it, but she did have a bizarre flair for inappropriate drama.

"Rena, don't bother bringing your lunch on Monday. When I was on the crapper, Nancy called. She's going to stop by and bring us something to eat. She wants to make sure that we're alive."

That didn't sound good. The alive part and the Nancy lunch part. "Will it have cream of mushroom soup in it?"

"Definitely." Shoshanna grinned evilly as she walked to the door. "Just bring a couple of snacks!" She winked and left.

We sat in silence for two minutes and forty-seven seconds. Kristy in heaven and me in shock.

"I can't believe Professor Sue was in our house, and she's proud of me."

"I can't believe she's a professor." I shook my head in disbelief and went scrounging for some chocolate. Nothing. I could find no chocolate. Damn.

I didn't need it after the carb fest I'd just indulged in, but I wanted it. My voracious appetite was demanding it. "Don't we have any candy around here?"

"You ate it all last night."

Dang it, she was right. If it wasn't so cold outside I'd walk to the corner and buy six candy bars. Occasionally the subzero temps were a blessing in disguise for my ass. I decided to go to bed before I ate something unforgivable. Plus, I couldn't handle any more weird.

"Are you going to go for Casssssanova?" Kristy grinned.

"No, but I may bring him a casssssserole," I giggled.

"I was thinking you might want to do some matrasssss wrassssssling with him and his fine tushy."

"That sounds a little too sasssssy for me," I laughed and punched her in the arm before we got so assed out, we couldn't stop.

"Why don't you ask him out?" she said, pulling her legs up underneath her on the couch.

"No, I've only seen his butt. That would make me shallow. Why don't you ask him out?" I cringed at the thought of the ass I considered mine, on my couch watching bad reality TV with my roommate. What in the hell was wrong with me? I needed to get laid in the worst way. Soon.

"Nope," Kristy said. "He's not my type, too built and too bad boy. Looks like a lawbreaker. He's totally your type. You are so going to drop your panties when you see his face."

I rolled my eyes. Hell, I was ready to drop my panties for the butt . . . "Don't think so. I don't need anyone else with a rap sheet, no matter how fine his buns are."

"I realize you've been traumatized by your questionable taste in men," she giggled, "but this guy is sexy."

"Whatever. Good night," I muttered, determined to get Mr. Wonder-Butt out of my head. "Oh yeah, what's Professor Sue's last name?"

"Lumpshclicterschmidt."

WTF? I almost choked on my own spit. Just when I thought the weird had left the building . . . That was by far worse than my last name; it was the worst last name I'd ever heard in my life. No wonder she went by Professor Sue. I grinned as I thought up ways to use my newfound info about LeHump to make our time together more fun. I truly hoped being armed with her last name would give me a little leverage in the "you have to shave her bunions" department, but with LeHump, who knew?

I crawled into my bed fully clothed and shut my eyes. *Are you there God? It's me, Rena . . . please let tomorrow be a little less eventful than today.*

After the most bizarre Saturday of my life, Sunday was a breeze. Even brunch with my parents, Aunt Phyllis, my newly pregnant younger sister—the doctor—and her boring lawyer husband didn't faze me. Normally being within ten feet of my overachieving younger sibling made me want to slap her, but today she didn't bother me. Even the questions about my love life didn't make me want to chew glass and swallow it . . . because I lied.

Apparently I'm dating a really rockin' guy I met at the library on Thursday. Named . . . um, Jack.

"So what does he do?" Mom asked excitedly, separating her

eggs from her bacon and hash brown casserole. She can't stand it when her food touches.

"He's in, you know, like communications and stuff," I muttered, quickly shoving pancake into my mouth to avoid speech. Why did I lie? It was so much harder to keep track of all the bullshit I kept spouting instead of sticking to the truth. My sister Jenny grinned evilly, enjoying my sudden discomfort. I grinned back enjoying her big butt and dark roots. Now that she was pregnant, she couldn't dye her hair. It pissed her off royally that I was a natural blonde and hers came from a bottle. I was sure I'd get karmically kicked in the ass for taking pleasure in my sister's shortcomings, but aside from her wide ass, which she inherited from Aunt Phyllis and her skunk hair, she was perfect. I was the fuckup, but at least I had a good rear end.

"How old is Jack the communicator and stuff?" she smirked.

"Thirty-fiveish. When's the baby due?" Maybe turning the tables back to her favorite subject—herself—would get her off my fictitious boyfriend Jack.

"October. Why didn't you invite him to brunch, Rena?"

I chewed a new wad of pancake I'd shoved in my mouth and stared at her. She hated that.

"Is his last name Snuffleupagus?"

God, she was a bitch. "As a matter of fact, it is," I bit out sarcastically, "and I didn't invite him because he's in Russia doing . . . um, work." Shit, shit, shit. Well, if that didn't sound like a big fat hairy lie, I didn't know what would.

"How exciting!" Aunt Phyllis gushed. "Does he have a TV?"

"Oh, Jesus," my dad mumbled. He had a fairly low tolerance for Aunt Phyllis's eccentricities. Jenny's husband, Dirk, ate and pretended he didn't know us.

"I don't know. I haven't been to his place yet," I murmured, praying this conversation would end.

"Well, if it turns out he owns one, have him come talk to me," she said.

Mom's brow furrowed with worry. "Phyllis, I don't want you sharing your crazy ideas about people in your TV with Rena's beaus. She has enough problems keeping a man without them knowing how crazy we are."

My mother and Aunt Phyllis took my single status personally.

I'd sworn off dating for a while. I didn't understand why it was such a big deal. My Aunt Phyllis repeatedly told me she would still love me if I decided to be a lesbian. Sweet Baby Jesus, if it were only that easy. Hence the mythical boyfriend . . . Jack.

Being single in my family had gotten dangerous. I hadn't had a date in two months, unless you counted the hostile takeover of three hours of my life last weekend. I thought I was going to poker night at the church with my mother and Aunt Phyllis. They'd lied. It was a singles mixer for Lutherans who couldn't find dates without help from Jesus.

"Mom, don't worry about it. Jack likes insane people," I muttered, reassuringly patting my aunt's hand.

My sister laughed, so I leaned forward, ran my fingers along my natural blond roots and started humming "I Like Big Butts."

"Mom, do you hear her?" Jenny hissed, pointing her butter knife at me.

"Rena, don't incite your sister. She's hormonal and she can't do anything about her hair stripe, so don't be mean."

Jenny turned a very unbecoming shade of purple. She gave me the finger, pulled her beret out of her purse, and plopped it on her head, effectively covering her stripe. I had to think her bedside manner sucked. Dirk kept his head down and ate faster than I thought humanly possible.

"What about the aliens in my toaster?" Phyllis inquired as if she were speaking of something as mundane as the weather.

"For God's sake Phyllis, do you have Martians living in your toilet, too?" Dad snapped.

"Yes, sometimes," she replied.

That was new. I wondered if the sock gremlins in her dryer would come up. Crazy didn't just run in my family . . . it stopped and strolled and hung out. And I was fairly sure it had taken up permanent residence at Aunt Phyllis's. I listened while everyone shot down all my poor aunt's hypotheses and quietly made my escape before anyone remembered to interrogate me about my new love, Jack the Communicator, any further.

Chapter 4

The Lake of the Isles was one of the ritziest areas in Minneapolis, so of course Evangeline O'Hara resided there.

At exactly seven fifty-one a.m., I pulled up to a gorgeous turn-of-the-century Georgian Revival. I'd had to borrow my Aunt Phyllis's butt-ugly car. God love her, she had explained at length about the little green men living in her gas tank. After swearing on a stack of Lutheran Bibles that I wouldn't let any harm come to them, she loaned me her automobile. My own cute little car was permanently dead. Dad had pronounced her death after looking under the hood at the parking garage yesterday after brunch. Apparently changing your oil is an important aspect of keeping a car running. Lack of oil, for those of us who didn't know (mainly me), can burn out your engine. All of a sudden the thirty thousand Evangeline was going to pay me was necessary. I needed a car . . . fast.

The portico at the entrance of her mansion was stone, flanked by two enormous statues that bore a disturbing resemblance to Evangeline . . . right down to their enormous racks. The house was grand and the lines were graceful, but the entire effect was destroyed by the sheer number of naked statues blanketing the front lawn. It was obscene. And quite honestly, I wondered if it was legal. This was Minnesota, for God's sake . . . Land of the hot dish, mosquitoes, and hard-core Lutherans.

Minutes later, Shoshanna arrived in her minivan and parked behind me. The glare of the morning sun made her lime-green coat glow, causing me to squint in pain, but her shit-eating grin calmed my jangled nerves.

"You ready?" she grunted, trotting over to my car.

"No."

"Great," she laughed. "Let's go."

As we made our way through the naked wonderland, Shoshanna whispered, "You think these are bad? The ones inside are fornicating."

"I can't wait."

Cecil-Jeeves let us in, wearing his requisite black suit and frown. He eyed us skeptically and then abandoned us in the foyer. And what a foyer it was. The tackiest, most expensive, nouveau riche disaster I'd ever seen. Pink marble floors with deep rose velvet covering the walls. The windows had to be twenty feet high, with mounds of baby pink silk raining down to the floor. Not only was it baby pink . . . it was bejeweled baby pink. Someone had spent months putting tens of thousands of rhinestones all over the curtains, and the effect was stupefying. I felt like I was in a Vegas bordello.

But the statues . . .

Shoshanna was correct. They were definitely fornicating, and it wasn't pretty. I saw some things I didn't know were possible. I did catalog a few positions away for future research with my imaginary boyfriend Jack Snuffleupagus.

"Is this for real?" I whispered.

"The whole fucking house is pink and if it's not a statue of people screwing, it's a painting or a hand towel or a lamp depicting some weird sex act. Or someone getting spanked."

I tried unsuccessfully to hold back my laughter. I had stepped into another dimension and was so grateful I wasn't alone. No one would ever believe this without seeing it.

"It's foul." Shoshanna wrinkled her nose in disgust.

"I thought you wrote about stuff like this," I said, referring to one of the statues I couldn't quite figure out. The man was holding a whip in one hand and his member in the other. The buck naked woman standing next to him did not look pleased. I wasn't sure if it was because of the whip or the fact his wiener was extremely unimpressive.

"Hell no! I write about consenting adults who enjoy bondage, domination, and sadomasochism. My erotica is all about the empowerment of women. All of my dominants are women. Of course they like butt plugs, cock rings, furry handcuffs, and the occasional pair of ass-less leather chaps, but it's all in the name of the big O. The women call all the shots in my novels, but they are concerned and attentive to the pleasure of their submissive men. Big difference. Plus," LeHump added wickedly, pointing to Mr. I-Carry-a-Whip-to-Make-Up-for-My-Small-Penis, "I'd never write a guy into my book with a pecker the size of a miniature sweet pickle."

"I truly wish I didn't know any of that." I shook my head and pondered how long it would take to forget about this particular conversation. I'd put my money on years . . . like, ten.

"Hello ladies." Evangeline stood at the top of the ornate curved staircase. What on earth was she wearing? It looked like a turquoise lace peignoir set . . . heavy on the lace. Her bosom was tremendous; it looked far bigger than it had on Saturday. Was that possible?

"How do I look?" Evangeline purred. It was creepy.

"Like a hooker well past her prime," Shoshanna grinned, leaning on Tiny Package Whip Guy.

"Shut up, Shopoopie, and get off my masterpiece. That Italian sculpture cost more than twenty years of your salary," she hissed as she wobbled her way down the stairs.

Where in the hell was Cecil-Jeeves? I had horrific visions of Evangeline tumbling down the stairs and landing dead at our feet. Orange was not a good color for me, and I was not going to prison for a death I hadn't caused. It was bad enough that I'd spent six hours in the pokey for trying to follow my dream of being the new Sunshine Weather Girl. If someone had let me in on the fact meteorologists actually went to school for that crap, I wouldn't have been so persistent. I had thought all I would need was a great smile and a cute wardrobe. Live and learn.

"Did Belvedere give you the list?" Evangeline inquired, thankfully making it down the stairs in one piece.

I was not mistaken; her bosom was larger. As in, look at my boobs . . . they are almost level with my collarbone. The visual was so shocking, I couldn't look away.

"Impressive, aren't they?" she asked seductively.

"Good God, they're bigger," I gasped. Shit, had I said that aloud?

"Thank you for noticing, Rhoda. It's a new procedure from Bulgaria. No surgery, just some Silly Putty and a pump. It's not legal in our country, but I have my sources," she informed us slyly, running her hands lovingly over her obscene boobies.

"You pumped Silly Putty into your chest?" I felt a little woozy. She was deranged and probably going to die. Silly Putty was meant for stretching and putting into your sister's hair so she screamed bloody murder and had to get it cut out . . . not to make your boobs bigger. Shoshanna stood beside me . . . stunned to silence. Probably a first for her.

"Of course it's not Silly Putty from the toy store, you imbecile," she sneered. Her bulbous lips made a sneer—one of the most frightening things I'd ever seen. "It's a highly secret compound discovered in Newark, New Jersey, and manufactured in Bulgaria. Only those with means can afford such quality."

"I think she meant those that are mean," Shoshanna muttered under her breath.

"I heard that, Sholumpy. Since Alfred can't seem to do anything right, I'll just explain to you what I need done today," she said sweetly.

My gut dropped and a chill skittered up my spine. Evangeline was anything but sweet.

"The babies need their teeth brushed and their anal glands expressed, I need someone to run a package to the news station, and my breasts need to be massaged. If they're not manipulated every half hour today, they'll harden. And that's out of the question. I paid fifty thousand dollars for my bosom and it shall remain supple and beautiful."

My stomach roiled and I almost threw up a little bit in my mouth. She wasn't joking. My gag reflex precluded me from squeezing anal glands, so touching her breasts was . . . was, um . . . probably the most repulsive thing I could imagine. And I had a very well-honed imagination. The news station thing didn't sound bad, unless it was WMNS. I wasn't allowed within five hundred feet of that one. But if I went to the news station Shoshanna might have to touch those horrible soccer balls protruding from Evangeline's chest.

"Rena will go to the news station," LeHump informed the hag, trying to save me yet again. "I'll brush the skank dogs' teeth. Cecil can express their glands unless you'd like me to puke all over your house, and you can play with your own tits. It's not my bag."

The witch narrowed her eyes and much to my and LeHump's great surprise, accepted the terms. "Fine, Shobooboo, we'll do it your way. Rollo, you will take a package to WMNS. You will take it to the production offices on the main floor and get written confirmation of receipt. Do you understand me, Rula?"

I said nothing, I had no idea what to say. Sharp tingles of panic began dancing in my chest. I couldn't go there . . . I had a restraining order against me. If I stepped within five hundred feet of the WMNS building, I would be breaking the court order and could end up in jail. I started to sweat, little droplets of fear and shame dotting my upper lip and forehead. Should I just come clean and explain why I couldn't do it? No, I'd just offer to massage her boobs . . . fuck, I couldn't massage her boobs. I could barely look at them. Touching them would scar me for life. Maybe if I got a nose plug and a blindfold I could squeeze her dogs' anal glands. I didn't even know exactly what that meant, but with the term *anal* involved, I assumed it would smell bad. My gag reflex was real, and I knew anything that had to do with butt smells would set it off with a vengeance, causing me to hurl repeatedly. Of course vomiting gave me migraines, and migraines led to me lying in darkened rooms for days on end. I didn't have time for any of this shit, but I needed the thirty thousand bad. Cars didn't buy themselves. Butts, boobs, or the pokey. How in the hell did I get into these messes?

I knew what I had to do.

"I'll massage your hooters," I whispered, horror and fear clinging to each word.

"Oh Sweet Baby Jesus, no," Shoshanna shouted, grasping Tiny Penis Man's whip for balance. My volunteering for the heinous chore clearly made LeHump's knees buckle.

I quickly whispered to Shoshanna, "I can't deliver the package. I'll explain later."

LeHump stared at me as if I'd lost my mind. I'm fairly sure I had, but when it boiled down to going to jail or touching the scariest boobs I'd ever seen . . . the answer was clear. Boobs.

"I don't think so." Evangeline smiled, and something odd colored her tone. "Shodunky has a point—I do believe I'll enjoy playing with myself all day. It's clear to me, Ruby, you harbor lesbianic tendencies and want to caress my bosom, but I've decided to deny you that pleasure. If you'd like to keep this job and earn the obscene amount of money I've offered you, you will leave this room immediately, change your clothes, and go." She held the package out and watched me closely.

Lesbianic tendencies? WTF? She should be so lucky. Something didn't feel quite right, but with everyone staring at me, I had no time to figure it out. I supposed if I kept my head down and moved quickly through the lobby of WMNS I could get away with it. I'd keep my hat pulled low and tuck all my hair into it. My dressy clothes included an awesome cashmere turtleneck sweater. If I pulled it up over my mouth, between the hat and the sweater, my face would basically be covered . . . I could do this!

"Fine," I said, throwing my shoulders back, ready to dive into the Fourth Circle of Dante's Inferno. That would be the Circle of Greed. I had turned into a whore. I was risking jail time to make thirty thousand dollars because I needed a car, and I was terrified of a woman sporting bowling balls on her chest.

I grabbed the package out of her hands, picked up my bag, and turned to leave, only to find Cecil-Jeeves blocking my way.

"I'll take it, Rena," he squeaked out in his prepubescent voice. "You stay here."

I knew this game. I had a sister. He was so not going to get out of butt gland land by pretending to be concerned about my mysterious stress at going to the news station.

"Absolutely not," Evangeline spat, giving Cecil a hostile glare. He immediately shrank back and lowered his eyes. "Ruthie is going and I will hear no more about it." Her face was a glowering mask of rage. I had never seen anything so frighteningly unattractive in my life. This was the weirdest place ever . . . and I knew weird.

"Take her to the powder room to change," she seethed, "and do not speak to her. Do you understand me, Kato?"

"Yes," he whispered, appearing scared out of his gourd.

I was completely confused about their relationship. I'd thought he was her bodyguard and possible lover, but he now seemed more like a servant. A horribly treated houseboy with a plethora of butler names. I found myself feeling sorry for him, but that didn't mean I trusted him. He gently took my arm and led me away. I went into the powder room to change and when I came out he was gone. Everyone was gone. I checked myself in one of the many full-length mirrors placed around the foyer and was pleased with what I saw. My super cute plaid woolen miniskirt looked hot with my tight black turtleneck. My knee-high black boots made the out-fit kick-ass, not that anybody would see it . . . I planned on staying very covered up the entire trip.

Glancing around the pink hellhole, I wondered again what I'd gotten myself into. No time for thinking . . . I grabbed my purse and the package and headed out to do one of the stupidest and most illegal things I'd knowingly ever done.

Chapter 5

The WMNS lobby was nuts, people everywhere . . . like Grand Central Station, but that was a good thing. More people, less chance of being noticed. Several businessmen in suits glanced curiously at me, some with pity at my obvious lack of fashion sense. If I got one more gawk, I was going to lift my middle finger. *Shit, that's probably not in my best interest. Do not draw attention . . .* I suppose the hat-turtleneck-face-covering style statement was a little unusual. I wrestled a tiny bit with my vanity. I knew I looked like a freak, but the choice between fashion victim and inmate was a no-brainer.

The sickeningly familiar lobby was enormous. The ceiling rose about five stories up and a fountain dominated the center of the room. Very modern, very stark. Not very Minnesota. There were two fancy restaurants and a coffee shop that was kind of a dive. I quickly hustled past the coffee shop. I knew all the guys who worked there. We'd become buds during my monthlong disastrous attempt to become the Sunshine Weather Girl. They were the cutest, hairiest little men I'd ever had the pleasure to know. My buddies had been pulling for me to get the job and were possibly more devastated than I was at my arrest. All I needed was for one of them to run out here, recognize me, and scream my name. There was a gymnastics meet going on in my stomach and my mouth felt like the Sahara Dessert.

I could do this . . . head down, deliver package, get receipt, get the fuck out. The receipt part was worrisome; I didn't want to make eye contact. In the car on the way over I practiced accents. My New York sounded like a mentally challenged woman—that was out.

My Southern sounded equally horrific, so I decided on British. It was bad, but not quite as bad as my German. My Italian was pretty good, but in order to do it well, I had to do it loud and use tons of gestures. I figured that would draw too much attention. All my accents sounded a little off due to my turtleneck-covered mouth, but that couldn't be helped.

After bashing into eight people, I realized keeping my eyes glued to the floor was a bad idea. I covertly glanced around, looking for security . . . not a one. Thank you, Jesus. Just regular people, working and minding their own business. The preppy business guys, the twentysomething gals with short skirts, pantyhose, and stilettos flanked by the fortysomething gals in pants, sensible flats, and big bunions from their own high-heel-wearing twenties. Just normal, everyday, boring, run of the mill . . . Holy Mother of God! *He* is not normal.

I stopped dead in my tracks. Ten feet away stood the most beautiful man I'd ever seen in my life. More beautiful than my new neighbor, Mr. Fine-ass. I felt light-headed and realized I'd ceased to breathe. Sandy blond hair, full lips, eyelashes that belonged on a girl, and a build like a brick shithouse. He didn't fit in here. His jeans and dark gray T-shirt covered by a rockin' black leather bomber were hotter than hot. He was holding a folder and kept glancing at it. No ring on his left hand. Aces! He looked about thirty-five or so. Absolutely perfect. With my luck he was probably gay.

What the hell was wrong with me? I wasn't here to pick up guys. I was here trying not to get arrested. My brain knew that, but all my girlie parts were screaming something else entirely. There was no security guard in sight . . . maybe, just maybe . . . No, absolutely not. I couldn't take the chance of going back to jail. It wasn't a parking violation; it was a restraining order, for shit's sake. But if I didn't show myself, there was no way my future husband would notice me. I was covered up like a fashion-impaired nun. Maybe I could remove the disguise just for a minute . . . make eye contact, ask him to marry me, and then finish what I came for. No, wait, maybe I'd deliver the package first and then tackle him to the ground and have my way with him . . . No, wait, what if he left while I was delivering the goods? And what if I got arrested before he noticed I was alive? Jesus Christ, I needed to get laid. This was the second stranger I'd considered marrying in two days and I'd only seen the other one's butt.

Damn it, damn it, damn it. The tingling in my nether regions was fogging my brain and self-preservation skills. What if he was my soul mate and I walked away and ended up a shriveled old sex-starved maid? What if I was denying myself the best, most mind-blowing orgasms imaginable? What if I revealed myself and he didn't like me and some undercover security dork arrested my ass? Or what if he fell instantly in love with me and the same said security dork from the previous scenario came up and arrested my ass?

What was happening to me? Had I jumped into the deep end of my own cheesy romance novel? I felt squooshy and short of breath. My lady bits were on fire, and I might possibly be in heat. I didn't even know this hunka hunka burning love . . . I hadn't made eye contact, yet I was picking out china patterns in my head. WTF? Was love at first sight real? I hadn't been this whipped up about a man in . . . well, ever. That wasn't exactly true, I had been fixated on my neighbor's ass since I'd seen it with Shoshanna, but he could be ugly or married. This one was hot, and wasn't wearing a ring . . . I was going to go for it. I would not go through my life wondering what if . . .

In a move of gargantuan stupidity, I peeled my turtleneck off my mouth, yanked the hat off my head, and let my long, naturally (eat that, Jenny) blond hair spill over my shoulders. I considered taking off my coat to show my boyfriend my fine derriere, but my hat in one hand and the package in the other made that move an impossibility. Of course I did unzip my coat to reveal my frontal assets. I mean, if you're gonna go there, you may as well go.

My heart thundered in my ears as I moved toward my intended. I was drawn to him like a moth to a flame, like Simon to Garfunkel, like my Uncle Sven to a case of beer . . . Crap, I feared what would fly from my lips when I spoke to him.

Who cares? I promise I will refrain from potty words till the third date. Lethimlikeme, lethimlikeme, lethimlikeme. I swear to everything chocolate, I will love him, cherish him, and have sex with him on a daily basis, but I won't pick up his dirty socks and underwear. Oh, and I'll occasionally cook, but I'd prefer to eat out.

I took a deep breath and moved stealthily toward my lover. A sense of urgency drove me toward him . . . Just as I was about to ask for his hand in marriage or, at the very least, a quickie, he looked at me.

And the world stopped.

Holy Brad Pitt, Johnny Depp, and Robert Redford (when he was young). My husband-to-be was H-O-T, hot. His eyes were the most gorgeous blue gray. The chemistry that burned between us was palpable and my entire body felt steamy hot. He stared at me and my heart began to hammer in my chest. His eyes traveled from my head to my toes, lingering briefly on my bazooms. I had never been so turned on in my life. I fought an overwhelming need to body slam him and shove my tongue down his throat. Thankfully he seemed to be having the same issues. His body language implied he would happily be my sex slave.

"Hi there," Mr. Sex-on-a-Stick said in a husky voice that made my knees buckle. He grabbed my hand to balance me, and I swear electricity shot up my arm. The left side of his mouth curved into the hottest crooked grin I'd ever seen. I was a goner . . .

"Hi yourself," I giggled. Really? Did I really just giggle? Shit. "I just saw you and I, um . . . was wondering if you, well, you know . . . um . . ." Eloquent much?

"Can I help you out there?" he laughed.

Christ, he was even hotter when he laughed. "Um, yes. English seems to be my fourth language today."

"Well in that case, you're doing pretty good." He smiled, watching my mouth intently. My tongue darted out to lick my dry lips and his smile grew wider. *Ilovehim, Ilovehim.*

"Do you work here?" I asked, putting my best flirt on.

In a move that I knew looked good on me, I went to flip my hair and somehow nailed myself in the cheek with the package. Dang it, not smooth.

Shit—the package. I quickly scanned the area for security. Nothing.

"You okay?" Mr. Hotpants asked, gently running his fingers across my cheekbone. More electricity shot through my body, and I leaned into his hand.

I am no ho-bag, but I'd never been so taken with someone in my thirty years. Time to get down to business. "Do you have a girlfriend?" I narrowed my eyes and assessed him.

"Nope. Boyfriend?"

"Nope," I grinned. "Married?"

"No, you?"

"Absolutely not. Never have been."

"Me neither."

His closeness was like a drug. He smelled beyond delicious, like clean laundry and soap and man. I was very close to asking him to marry me, but I wasn't quite done with my interrogation.

"How long was your longest relationship?" I asked. No way could he father my two unborn children if he had commitment problems.

"A year and a half. She left me for another guy."

Was she on crack? "Mine was two years. He was more into his job than me."

"Stupid man, but hopefully his loss will be my gain."

Oh. My. God.

"I don't want to be forward"—he tilted his head to the side, his breathtaking gaze bored sexily into mine—"but can I buy you a cup of . . ." He trailed off. His eyes got wide and he appeared to have swallowed a lemon. "Oh, hell no," he muttered, looking down at his folder. "Please tell me your name isn't Rena Gunderschlict."

Panic like I'd never known rushed through me. I had no idea why he didn't want me to be me, but I had a bad feeling I was about to find out . . . and I wasn't going to like it.

"Why?" My voice seemed to be coming from a hundred miles away.

"Just please tell me you're not Rena."

"I can't," I whispered.

He looked up to the heavens and ran his big hand through his hair. As terrified as I was, I was jealous of his hand. I wanted my hands in his hair, but as much as I wanted that, my instinct told me to run. Something was off . . . very off.

Still staring at the ceiling, he muttered, "Goddamn it, I hate my job."

"Are you okay?" I asked. I knew I truly loved him, or at least seriously lusted him, when I actually forgot about my own impending shit storm and worried about his.

This time when his eyes met mine they were mortified and apologetic. Apprehension swept through me and a lead weight settled in my stomach. He slowly pushed back his bomber jacket and revealed a badge . . . and a gun. "Rena Gunderschlict, I'm placing you under arrest for breaking your restraining order. You have the right to remain silent. Anything you say can and will be held against you in a court of law. You have the right to speak to an attorney. If you cannot afford an attorney, one will be appointed to you. Do you understand these rights?" I mutely nodded my head as the love of my life continued to rip my heart out. "I don't want to handcuff you, so please follow me out to my vehicle."

Of course he was a cop . . . Fuck. Fuck. Fuck.

My walk of shame was compounded by my little hairy friends from the coffee shop. Vito and Angelo spotted me and the hunk who was about to ruin my life.

"Rena!" Vito screamed, shoving startled customers out of the way to get to me. Mr. Hottie's hand went to his gun.

"They're my friends," I quickly interjected before he blew two sixty-year-old little hairy guys away for no reason.

Vito, with Angelo on his heels, ran to me like an excited puppy. God, I'd missed them.

"Did you finally get the weather girl job?" Vito screeched, squishing my face. "I made white chocolate apricot scones this morning. You will come in and have one," he demanded.

Angelo smiled slyly. "Looks like our little girl has something to tell us." He nudged Vito and started winking repeatedly at what he assumed to be my new man friend.

"Um, guys, I can't hang right now. I'm a little busy."

"Did you get the job?" Angelo asked, still winking obscenely at the cop who he clearly thought was my boyfriend. I wish.

"No, I didn't get the job."

"Ba Fongool to the slut they hired. I spit in her coffee every day," Vito informed me and anyone within a hundred feet. This was a new kind of loyalty. Kind of gross, but kind of great.

"Guys," I whispered, nodding surreptitiously to the freedom-destroying sexy bastard standing next to me, "I'm actually under arrest."

"Again?" Angelo gasped. He quit winking at my boyfriend and gave him the evil eye.

"Shame on you, big man," Vito hissed. "She is no criminal! Have you seen her ass?"

Oh. My. God.

"Rena"—Angelo cut Vito off before he started waxing nostalgic about my other body parts—"did you break the law?"

"Kind of," I muttered, "but it wasn't my fault this time."

"Did you hear that, Mr. Big-Meany-Police-Man? It is not her fault! No one who has a rack as stupendous as she does should ever be arrested," Angelo concluded, making me want to die.

"Um . . . guys, you're not really helping here." I stole a quick glance at Mr. Big-Meany-Police-Man, who to my shock seemed amused.

Angelo stood up to his full five-foot-two height. "Rena, do you want me to kick his ass?"

"Um, no."

"We will visit you in the big house," Vito whispered loudly. "We have connections." He winked at me spastically.

"Thanks guys." I grabbed Mr. Hot Cop by the hand and dragged him away before my little friends started informing all who wanted to hear how they were "connected."

His big hand was warm and slightly calloused. He was as stunned as I was that I'd grabbed him. I tried to extricate my hand, but he held on tight and led me out of the building. Little shocks vibrated through my body and I cursed the situation. *Why do I have to have the hots for an undercover detective who is carting me off to jail?*

We walked out in to the subzero temps and directly to a waiting car. He was parked illegally in front of WMNS. He politely opened the front passenger door of his vehicle and waited for me to get in.

"Aren't you supposed to put me in the back, in case I try to kill you or something?" I asked, trying to recall the procedures on *Law & Order.*

"Just get in the car, Rena," he said gruffly.

I did. He was arresting me and all I could think about was what his lips would taste like and if he could bench-press me. And his butt . . . oh my God, what a butt. It was even better than my neighbor's. Talk about inappropriate thoughts. He got in, started the engine, and we began our twenty-five-minute drive to hell.

I felt him staring as I kept my eyes trained ahead. Why, why, why couldn't I have met him somewhere else? Anywhere else. Every so often I peeked over and had mini orgasms at the way his thigh muscles were flexing in his jeans.

"May I ask you a question?" my evil captor inquired. Damn, his eyes were pretty.

"Is this the stuff that can and will be held against me before I'm thrown in the pokey?"

He laughed and shook his head, "No, Rena, it's off the record."

God, the way he said my name made me lose brain cells. Did I have that disease that kidnap victims get? The one where they get the hots for their abductors? Of course he wasn't a kidnapper and I was a soon to be convicted felon . . . not a good first date and definitely not a good way to start a meaningful relationship or even a meaningless night of debauched sex. I couldn't stop imagining the strong hands gripping the steering wheel, gripping my butt. Shit.

"Is off the record legal?"

"Nope, but you can trust me."

"Why should I trust you?"

He looked over and shrugged. "Something seems a little off about all this."

Hmm, what did I have to lose? Maybe if I could explain my predicament, he might let me go . . . "Okay, well, seeing as how I'm leaning toward a life of crime, I may as well take you down with me."

"You may as well," he grinned.

My tummy flipped and for one brief moment I considered throwing him against the car door and crawling on top of him. Thankfully I had my seat belt on. It stopped my involuntary forward motion and reminded me to ignore my inner slut. It also stopped me from causing an accident . . . he was driving, for God's sake. I had a really hard time believing this was standard police procedure, but he was so cute and how much more trouble could I get myself into?

My Prince Charming continued, "Why were you at the news station when you have a restraining order against you?"

"Because I couldn't bring myself to massage her boobs."

"I'm sorry, what?" He pulled the car over, turned it off, and stared at me.

"That didn't come out exactly right," I muttered as he continued to gape at me like I was insane. I took a huge breath and let her rip. "My car died because I didn't put oil in it, and I need a new car because I'm driving my Aunt Phyllis's butt-ass-ugly clunker with little green men living in the gas tank. I'm an accountant, but I joined a group of seventy-year-old women who write porno. You know, butt plugs and furry handcuffs and edible body suits . . . I have no talent as a writer, but lack of talent has never scared me. So as it turns out, I do have a talent for coming up with hideous ideas for romance novels and there's this horrible skank woman who's been stealing ideas from the cute little bondage writing ladies for years. Anyway, skank woman is famous and has had more plastic surgery than Cher, Kenny Rogers, and Sylvester Stallone put together. She thought my ideas were great, which makes me think she's smoking crack, but that's beside the point. She hired me for three weeks at ten grand a week to give her my ideas. The little sex ladies think my ideas will bring her career down in flames. At first I was upset that I sucked so bad as a writer, but now I'm okay with it. I want to help the little ladies and like I said, I need a new car."

He was shell-shocked. "Um, Rena . . ."

My man-candy was at a loss for words. He pressed on the bridge of his nose with his thumb and pointer finger, clearly trying to ward off the headache that I was sure I'd just caused.

"Rena, that is the strangest and most confusing thing I have ever heard, but nowhere in that frightening diatribe did you answer my question or explain your bizarre um . . . massage issue."

"Oh, right. I was at WMNS to deliver a package for Evangeline O'Hara, the book-stealing, frozen-faced, scary-knockered hag that I'm doing the three weeks of work for."

He opened his mouth to speak and nothing came out, so I continued.

"I didn't really have a choice. My options sucked. I could either squeeze her rat dogs' anal glands, massage her newly enhanced with Silly Putty boobs from Newark, New Jersey, or deliver a package to WMNS. I figured if I kept my face covered, I could be in and out of there and no one would be the wiser."

"Oh my God," he laughed, shaking his head in disbelief.

"Right? I mean, I wasn't about to touch her boobies—they start all the way up at her collar bone. I have a very active gag reflex, so butt gland squeezing was out. Do you see how breaking the law was my only option?"

"Actually, I kind of do."

"So you'll let me go?" I tilted my head and gave him my best sexy look. His eyes flashed and he white-knuckled the steering wheel. He was definitely affected . . . so was I.

"You're killing me here," he groaned. "Rena, I can't let you go. Dispatch already knows you're in my custody. Trust me. If I let you go, they will assume you escaped . . . life will get much, much worse for you."

"How can it get much worse than this?" I muttered, wondering who I'd fucked over in a past life.

"Look, I'm going to take you in and we'll get to the bottom of this."

"So you think I'm innocent?"

"No, you did break your restraining order, but . . ." He paused, considering his words carefully.

"What?"

"How many people knew you were coming down here?" he asked.

What was he getting at? "Three. The Boob Monster, her butler slave, Cecil-Jeeves, and my friend Shoshanna LeHump."

"Shoshanna Le what?"

"Hump. And don't laugh," I warned, narrowing my eyes, "her real last name is far more appalling than that. Why does that make any difference?"

"Because someone called in a tip to let us know you'd be there."

"What?" I shrieked. That little bastard Cecil-Jeeves. I knew he was jealous, but I had no idea how far he was willing to go to bring me down. His body language at the writers' meeting should have tipped me off. I was going to kick his prepubescent-voiced ass . . . right after I served two years in the pokey. Wait! He'd offered to go in my place . . . was that guilt? Or was this the work of the Boobies from Hell? I'd bet my sanity, which was quickly disappearing, that it wasn't Shoshanna. She was my friend, and I knew too much about her secret life for her to be so stupid.

"Do you know who would do that?" he asked, starting the car back up.

"Not for sure." I answered in a shaky voice. I wanted to cry.

"It's okay, Rena; we'll figure this out."

"Are you this nice to all the women you arrest?" I sniffed.

He took a long pause and looked at me through hooded eyes. "Nope."

I liked his answer even though I kind of hated him for being the instrument of my impending incarceration. Wait, I didn't need anyone to fuck up my life. I was doing an outstanding job of that all by my lonesome. "Why are you being nice to me?"

"I'm not exactly sure, but I'm positive I'll end up in a lot of trouble for it," he said with a grin.

"I'm sure you will." I grinned back. "Can I ask you a question since you seem to know so much about me?"

"Shoot."

"What's your name?"

"Jack."

Of course it is. I sighed and wondered if his last name happened to be Snuffleupagus.

Chapter 6

The police station was a circus and I was the center ring act. I got recognized by police and perps galore from my weather girl debacle. I even signed a few autographs before Jack the Hottie took me by the arm and led me to a private room. The room was cold and in need of a good scrub down. The fluorescent lighting was harsh and unfriendly. It reminded me of the interrogation rooms on *Law & Order*. I kind of hoped he would frisk me, but no such luck. He paced back and forth and I watched.

"What are we waiting for?" I asked.

"My sergeant. I was instructed to take you to this room."

His agitation was making feel queasy, but the way his ass filled out his jeans was making me horny. I contemplated giving him my number, but there was probably a law against that, and I was batting a big hairy zero right now.

"I'll be right back," Jack muttered. "Stay here."

Like I had anywhere to go . . . He left the room and took all my confidence with him. It was the first time today I truly felt scared. What the hell had I done? Was I actually going to go to jail for real? I shuddered at the thought. Did it make any difference that I wasn't trying to be the weather girl anymore? I supposed not. I'd broken the law . . . Shit, shit, shit.

Moments later a beady-eyed Santa in a police uniform entered the room. He stood about six-foot-three and he didn't like me . . . at all. The rosy-cheeked, white-bearded cop gave me a hostile stare. "You're in a lot of trouble, young lady."

I flinched at the tone of his voice. This was so real, and I was so fucked. "I'm sorry Sant . . . um officer," I stammered. Damn it, I'd almost called him Santa. "I know it doesn't make any difference, but I wasn't trying to become the Sunshine Weather Girl. I got a new job and I was trying to . . ."

"Can it," he spat, glaring at me with an ugly frown on his Santa face. "None of that matters. The judge won't care why you were there. You weren't supposed to be there. Period. You're looking at two years minimum."

His stare drilled into me as his words blasted through my brain.

"Can I at least explain myself?" I swallowed hard, trying not to cry. My mother was going to disown me. And my sister, she was going to love this . . . forever. Why oh why didn't I just rub the boobs?

"Do you want to call your lawyer?" Santa asked indifferently.

My lawyer? I didn't have a freakin' lawyer. My mind reeled with confusion. The only lawyer I knew was my boring brother-in-law Dirk. I sure-as-fuck was not calling him. I pinched myself hard, praying this was a nightmare. Ouch . . . not a dream. "Well, um . . . I don't really have a, you know, a lawyer."

Father Christmas shook his head in disgust. Before he could further explain to me what a stupid ass I was, the door to the interrogation room opened and a little person walked in. He stood about three feet tall. He wore a police uniform and had blond side-swept hair and slightly bucked teeth. His face was round, his cheeks were pink, and his eyes were huge. I gripped the arms of my chair in terror . . . He looked exactly like Herbie the Dentist from the Christmas special *Rudolph the Red-Nosed Reindeer.*

Sheer black fright swept through me and my body began to shake. I bit down on my tongue, the inside of my cheek, and my bottom lip to tamp down the hysterical laughter that was threatening to escape. Cackling at a little person, regardless of his likeness to Herbie the Dentist, was not going to endear me to anyone. Especially Santa. I tried to look away, but I couldn't. Herbie the Cop-Dentist watched me chew on my mouth warily as he took his place next to Santa.

"Is she all right?" Herbie asked Santa, handing him a piece of paper.

"No clue, don't care," Santa replied callously. He read the note with his beady little eyes.

I wondered if it was from Yukon Cornelius. That did it . . . My body was no longer my own. I became possessed by the Inappropriate Laughing Monster. I could not, for all the money in the world, control myself.

To disguise my disgraceful behavior, I threw myself down on the dirty linoleum floor and groaned in between peals of hysterical guffawing. I prayed it looked like I was upset and crying. I beat the grimy floor with my fists, hoping to cause myself some pain. If I broke a few fingers or knuckles I was sure I could manufacture some real tears. I peeked up to see if the Christmas Boys were buying it. I couldn't say for sure, but they were definitely alarmed.

"Should I get a straitjacket, Sergeant?" Herbie whispered.

Sergeant? Santa is Jack's sergeant? Crap.

"No, she's going home. All charges are being dropped," Sergeant Santa groused with disgust. He held up the piece of paper Herbie had given him and flicked it disdainfully. "Apparently the little lawbreaker has friends in high places."

WTF? I don't have any friends in high places . . . Did Jack do something? That made no sense. Could he get my charges dropped? Sweet Baby Jesus, did they call my parents? Wait, my parents don't have any pull. Mom's a librarian and dad's a dentist . . . like Herbie. Oh fuck no . . .

I quickly clawed my arms to suppress the wild surge of laughter that wanted freedom from my throat. I'd be a bloody mess by the time I left here.

"You are a very lucky young woman," Santa sneered. "A paragon of virtue has come to the station to plead your case. This person is taking full responsibility for you. You owe this person your life. Without Evangeline O'Hara, your ass would be in jail."

I no longer needed to laugh. I felt like I'd been plunged into the Arctic Sea during January. My stomach clenched and my breathing became erratic. What in the hell was Evangeline doing here? Shit, shit, shit. Had Jack called her? Had Cecil-Belvedere-Kato admitted his guilt? That doesn't seem right . . . Maybe Cecil-Alfred-Benson had admitted guilt and she got pissed because she still wanted my idea. It would be difficult to collaborate from the pokey. That had to be it. She didn't have one compassionate bone in her skinny body . . . or maybe she did. *Why am I always such a bitch? Maybe she's not as bad as I think.*

"Follow me," Herbie the Dentist barked, knocking me back to reality. I idly wondered if he'd gotten his uniform from a children's costume store.

Santa and I followed Herbie down the hallway to another room identical to the one we'd just vacated. It might have been a tad bit cleaner, but not much. The major difference in the room was the company. Evangeline was perched on the table looking like the cat that had eaten the canary. Her outfit would have been slutty on a teenager; on her it was positively gruesome. She wore a teal miniskirt, a purple midriff-baring net top, a teal bra, and thigh-high stiletto boots. My mother would have beaten my ass if I tried to walk out of the house in that. I prayed that Evangeline wasn't going commando again, but just in case, I kept my eyes trained on her face.

Cecil the Betrayer stood behind her and my fantasy boyfriend Jack leaned against the wall on the other side of the room.

"Oh my sweet darling," Evangeline cooed, "Are you all right?"

"Um, I think so," I muttered, confused and wary of her loving manner.

"You should have told me you had a restraining order against you! I never would have sent you to the news station had I known, you silly girl," she purred.

"Oh, okay."

"Aren't you going to say thank you?" Santa demanded, leering at Evangeline.

"Oh, Gerald darling, aren't you just ever the gentleman," she tittered, leaning forward to give Santa-Gerald a better view of her knockers.

"Thank you," I mumbled contritely, still trying to figure out what was going on. "How did you know about this and how did you get the charges dropped?"

"That is no way to show your gratitude," Sergeant Santa-Gerald growled, clearly affronted that I wasn't on my knees before her majesty. "By the way, little missy, if she changes her mind, your ass is going to jail."

Something felt so wrong about this. I couldn't put my finger on it, but my stomach churned with anxiety.

"Gerald, my sweet," Evangeline coyly crooned, sounding a little like a wounded cow, "you're such an alpha male. Let's go to your office and finish the paperwork."

Santa blushed furiously and quickly grasped Evangeline as she almost took a tumble off the table. Moving in general seemed to come with a whole set of issues for her.

"Stay with the perp," he snapped at Jack.

"Yes, sir."

Santa and Evangeline led the entourage from the room. Herbie held the door and Cecil brought up the rear. Before he left the room, he turned back.

"I'm sorry," he whispered.

"For what?" I asked, wanting him to admit his guilt in front of Jack. Why? I don't know. It didn't make any difference now . . .

"For you," he replied and left the room quickly.

What in the hell did that mean?

The silence in the room was loaded. I wandered over to the table and sat down, careful to avoid the area where Evangeline had been seated. Knowing Bionic Boobs, I'm fairly sure she wasn't wearing panties. I swallowed back the bile that had risen in my throat. I was still unsure whether Jack had called Evangeline. Again, it really didn't make any difference. I'd never see him after today anyway. Why did that make me feel queasy? I stared at everything except for the beautiful man leaning against the wall. I was so embarrassed and ashamed . . . and embarrassed. I struggled to find my voice. I could feel his eyes boring into me. I wanted to say something witty and sexy and self-deprecating . . . something he'd always remember.

"Do you realize your Sergeant looks like Santa and his sidekick looks like Herbie the Dentist?" Oh fuck, did I just say that? It would have been an opportune time to shut up, but knowing when to stop had never been my forte . . . so I kept talking. "Do you see why I couldn't touch her boobies? They're ginormous and disgusting. I would have been scarred for life. I suppose some guys like huge knockers, but those suckers are rock hard. She could kill someone with those things. But like I said, some guys like 'em big. Do you like big ones?" I slapped my hand over my mouth before I uttered something more awful than what I'd already said. I couldn't for the life of me imagine what that would be, but I was taking no chances.

I stared at the floor wishing I could melt like the Wicked Witch of the West. I was so mortified I started getting mad at him. Reasonable? No. Legit? In my mind, yes. If he would just speak, I might not continue to make such a gaping ass of myself.

"Please say something or I'm going to jump off the conversation cliff, never to be heard from again," I whispered, still staring at the floor.

"Rena, I want . . ." Jack started only to be cut off by the ungodly, horrifically timed reentrance of Herbie the Dentist.

What did Jack want? Did he want me? Did he never want to see me again? Did he want to bump uglies and father my children? Maybe fathering my children was moving too fast . . . maybe a weekend of sweaty screaming sex would be a good place to start. Damn it, now I'd never know because of the reappearance of a three-foot animated cartoon character in a police uniform. My fingers itched to pull Herbie's little dentist head off.

"You're needed in Interrogation Room Four. Now," Herbie informed Jack smugly. He definitely had a Napoleon complex.

Jack eyed him silently and Herbie fidgeted under the scrutiny. Mr. Hunky Pants slowly pushed himself off the wall and approached the table I was sitting behind. My pulse raced as I caught a whiff of his sexy scent. He stood in front of me, bent down, placed both of his big hands on the table between mine, and stared straight into my eyes. I thought I would faint.

"Rena, you need to be a good girl. Can you do that?"

My eyes were glued to his lips, watching them move. I knew he'd just asked me something, but I had no idea what. I felt tingly all over, and I flexed all the muscles in my arms to keep from reaching out to touch his beautiful mouth. God, what in the hell was it with this guy? He made me feel like an animal in heat. I looked down at his hands. They were huge. I wondered if that meant his . . .

"Rena?" he chuckled, cutting off my pornographic train of thought. He was totally aware of what he was doing to me. "Look at me."

"I can't," I muttered. "I'm afraid I'll jump you and get rearrested for accosting an officer."

He threw his head back and laughed, sending delightful little chills all through my body and right down to my panties.

"What's going on here? You're supposed to go to room . . ." Herbie babbled, crossing the room toward us and fucking up my chi.

"Stay!" Jack barked at the little man like he was a dog. Herbie did. I heard him shuffle back to the door. Damn, Jack definitely had some authority here. Lordy, that's hot. He shifted his attention back to me and leaned in closer. "I told you to behave. I don't want to have to arrest you ever again."

"Um . . . okay."

I felt him slide something under my hand. He leaned in even closer, his mouth by my ear, and whispered, "Although I wouldn't mind handcuffing you."

Oh. My. God.

If I hadn't been sitting in a chair, I'd have been in a puddle on the ground. I have never ever, ever wanted to straddle and ride someone so badly in my entire life. If Herbie the Dentist hadn't been in the room I might have stripped naked and let my inner slut loose. That would have looked really bad on the six o'clock news.

Jack stood up, grinning at me. He winked, turned, and sauntered out of the room. I peeked under my hand and realized he'd slipped me his card. *Ilovehim, Ilovehim, Ilovehim.* I briskly shoved it into my pocket.

Herbie ran to my table on his tiny little dentist legs. "He's gay," Herbie informed me triumphantly.

"Really?"

"Yep"—he sucked in his gut and stood up taller—"but I'm not." He waggled his eyebrows and grabbed his package.

It was all I could do not to gag-laugh. I closed my eyes and sucked in an enormous breath. "That's wonderful . . . that you're not gay. I'm sure you'll make some unsuspecting girl very unsettled someday, but here's the thing . . . I'm a lesbian. So while I'm flattered by your outstanding posture, your acrobatic eyebrows, and your crotch handling, I prefer vaginas."

"Really?" Herbie asked dejectedly.

"Really," I assured him.

Chapter 7

Much to my great embarrassment, twenty minutes later I found myself sitting in the backseat of a garish hot pink sedan with painted caricatures of Evangeline and her boobs on the hood and the doors. Cecil had donned a chauffeur's cap and aviators. He drove silently. Unfortunately the evil hag didn't pick up on his cue.

"So Ruth, it looks like we have a little situation here," she purred, massaging her bosom.

"What situation?" I stared out the window, wondering if thirty thousand dollars was enough money to watch an old woman fondle herself. I reminded myself I needed a car. Thirty thousand could buy a brand-new car . . . I'd never had a new car before. I supposed as long as she was wearing clothes, I could tough out the boob handling.

"Well, according to the police, if I decide to press charges, you'll go to jail."

"For what? What do you have to do with my restraining order?" I shook my head and began demolishing my cuticles again. At this rate, the confusion I was feeling would cause me to chew my fingers off in the next five minutes.

"Dahalling, I have nothing to do with your restraining order. That's all on you." She smiled . . . kind of. Her lips didn't allow for much give.

"What are you talking about?"

"Rhoda, surely you know," she offered mildly.

"No, Ester, surely I don't know or I wouldn't be asking," I shot back, casually trying to hide the dread threatening to consume me. I shoved my hands under my butt. I would not give her the satisfaction of watching me amputate my fingers. Something was so wrong; I just had no idea what it was. I could have sworn Cecil snorted. I was sure he enjoyed the Ester thing, considering she called him something different every time she spoke to him. I wondered if his name was even Cecil.

Evangeline's bulbous lips thinned and her nostrils flared. She didn't like the name game being played on her. Tough shit, I'd had about enough. In a moment of utter clarity, I decided being a greedy whore was a stupid move. Thirty thousand dollars wasn't enough to sell my soul. I'd take the fucking bus to work for a year while I saved up for a car. Or maybe Aunt Phyllis would loan me a down payment if I offered to babysit the aliens and Martians inhabiting her abode.

God, I felt so much better. My need for self-mutilation all but disappeared. I put my raggedy hands back in my lap and felt a hundred pounds lighter. I turned to the evil queen to quit and was struck dumb. She had her hands down her shirt and was massaging for all she was worth. There were no words . . . I decided to wait and quit when we got back to her house. Two reasons: I was a little afraid she might put me out on the highway, and I was scared if I opened my mouth I would vomit. I noted that Cecil didn't use his rearview mirror much; I guessed using the side mirrors offered less chance of witnessing unspeakable behavior from his boss.

Still clueless in the pressing charges department, I tried again. I knew in my gut this was important. Staring at the back of Cecil's head, I broached the subject, praying she was done with her deep-tissue massage.

"So Evelyn," I taunted. What did I have to lose? I was quitting. Cecil's shoulders shook and a frisson of joy buzzed through me. His life seemed just awful; it felt good to make him laugh. "What exactly are the charges you could press?"

"Why, stealing, of course." Her eyes pinned me to my seat.

WTF? "Stealing what?" I gasped. "I didn't steal from you." The blood left my face as it dawned on me that this was very likely the missing puzzle piece I couldn't put my finger on.

"Of course you did, my pet," she leered. "Three hundred and seventy-five thousand dollars' worth of jewelry was in that box you stole from me. Thank God you had a restraining order against you or you might have gotten away with it."

Shock didn't even begin to cover the feelings that overwhelmed

me. Rage and nausea consumed me and my brain worked in over-
drive. I shook like a leaf and my mouth was filling with saliva,
making chewing on my cuticles impossible. Throwing up on her
right now seemed like a fine idea. Why in the hell would she frame
me for stealing? What did she have to gain? Fuck, did Jack think I
was a thief? He'd never marry me now. This was by far the worst
day of my entire life. Who knew karma for being greedy would
kick me in the ass so hard and so quickly? I should have quit while
she was kneading her rack, but somehow I didn't think that would
have made any difference. Fuck, shit, fuck, fuck.

"Cat got your tongue, dear?"

I looked away from her. I would not let her see me cry. Everything was careening out of control and I had no idea why. My chest
tightened and the ringing in my head was making me dizzy. I'd
been set up. She knew about the restraining order, and she'd loaded
me down with jewels. She had to have been the one who'd tipped
off the police, or maybe it had been Cecil . . . They were clearly in
on it together, but what did they hope to achieve?

"So here's how I see it, Ruba, you owe me. You owe me your
life, so I don't owe you anything." She readjusted her repulsive
bosom, grabbed my chin, and made me face her. "You will work
for me for free. There will be no thirty-thousand-dollar payment.
You will give me all of your ideas for the rest of your natural life,
and you will tell no one about our little arrangement or your pretty
little blonde self will spend the next three to five in the slammer.
Are we clear, Rita?"

"You're a bitch," I hissed.

"That's already been established, my sweet," Evangeline trilled
joyously. "Cecil, drive through the Dairy King. I want a Chocolate
Doozy Parfait to celebrate. Ramona, would you like an ice cream?"

I turned away, refusing to answer her. I wanted to kill her, but
Cecil was in the car and I figured a witness was a bad idea.

"Fine, be that way." Evangeline pouted. "Cecil, you may get
yourself a little something as long as it doesn't cost more than
ninety-nine cents."

My fingernails dug into my palms as I struggled with the impulse to slap her into unconsciousness. Was this how she got all the
little old ladies to be her slaves? Was she blackmailing everyone?
She had to be . . .

"Reva, I can see your brain wheels turning and I want to be very explicit. You are to tell no one about our new modus vivendi. No one, especially not the little freak waiting for you back at the mansion. No. One. If you do, I will ruin your life and the lives of all your little writing friends. Not only that, I will see to it that your roommate's shelter is put out of business and your father's dental practice is sued repeatedly until he is bankrupt and destitute. Are we crystal clear?" She smiled, basking in the knowledge of her power over me.

"We're clear," I ground out through clenched teeth, hatred lacing my words. My fingernails dug into the skin of my palms. Warm blood began seeping into the creases of my balled-up fists and the bile in my stomach reached my throat. There was very little I could do to her on purpose, but if it looked like an accident . . .

"Shall we shake on it?" I whispered, giving the viper bitch whore from hell my most innocent look.

"Of course! I knew you would see it my way. We will have such a wonderful time together, making me the most successful and richest author in the world. J. K. Rowling can kiss my ass!"

She extended her claw and I grabbed it firmly with my bloody one. I grabbed her forearm with my free hand, smearing my blood up and down her toothpick arm with glee, making sure to drip on her skanky outfit. I watched with delight as she shrieked in disgust, knowing the best was yet to come . . .

"I don't feel very good," I moaned, tightening my grasp on her arm. I needed her to be in good range for the thank-you I was about to bestow on her. Literally.

"Oh my God, oh my God," Evangeline yelped, trying desperately to free herself.

"I'm so sorry," I gasped, trying not to grin from ear to ear. "My stomach is just . . ."

I reared back and let her rip. Normally I despise throwing up, it tends to give me migraines, but sometimes you have to suffer for the good of mankind. This would definitely make the world a better place. I had a moral obligation.

I opened my mouth and projectile-vomited on her from head to toe. The more I retched, the more I had to retch. It was a disgusting self-fulfilling prophecy. Her howls and screeches were music to my indebted ears. Her hair was covered and her net top held my gift beautifully. I noticed I'd successfully filled her thigh-high boots. My aim was outstanding.

"I'm so sorry," I choked out, wiping my mouth and my bloody hands with a clean section of her mink coat. "I think the excitement of helping you attain mega-stardom was too much for my system." I lowered my eyes and looked away. "Please forgive me, Your Greatness."

She was actually confused. Her intelligence level was subpar at best, and she thought I was being honest. I filed this info away for future reference.

"Um, well . . . that's okay," she moaned, trying to remove my gift, but only succeeding in rubbing it in more. "You will never do this aguuun," she gagged on her last word.

"I'll try not to, Your Excellency, but I have a very active gag reflex and it goes off at unexpected moments."

"Yes, well then, you need to work on your aim. Next time you will zero in on Cecil, he's quite worthless."

I had to agree with her on that. I would make sure I saved some of my wrath for him. I knew vomiting on people was not going to be my new weapon of defense; I wouldn't be able to handle all the migraines that would accompany it. But Cecil . . . Cecil would soon get a taste of my evil genius.

"Forget the Chocolate Doozy Parfaaauhh," Evangeline gagged. "Take me home, Jahhves."

I popped a piece of gum into my icky mouth, turned back to the window, and opened it. The subzero temperatures felt good on my overheated skin, plus the smell was bad with a capital B. I knew she had me, but I also knew I had her. If I had been determined to bring her career down before, now I was obsessed. Her threats against my family and my friends raised this game to a whole new level. I would rely heavily on her stupidity and greed. Shit, my own greed was how I got here in the first place . . . She was going to get the story of a lifetime. Not only would there be conjoined twins and time-traveling vampire warlock pirates with erectile dysfunction, there would be halitosis, clubfeet, lice, pirates who preferred animals and blow-up dolls, venereal diseases, dirty fingernails, cannibalism, and flat-chested women. She was going down.

Chapter 8

"So, can you read that back to me?" I asked a crimson-faced Cecil.

I wasn't sure if he was appalled, embarrassed, or simply grossed out. Shoshanna seemed stupefied and I was on a roll.

After getting back to the mansion, I'd brushed my teeth, put my sweats back on, and began my guerrilla warfare. I was going to take the bitch down and no one was going to stop me.

"Are you sure this is what you meant?" he asked.

"Oh yes, very sure. Now read it," I barked.

"But is this the beginning?" he whispered, thinking if he spoke quietly he might escape my crazy.

No. Such. Luck.

"Yes, it's the beginning," I rolled my eyes. "The book will be written in a series of nonconsecutive flashbacks and flash-forwards to signify the time-traveling element. It's the new thing that the buying public doesn't realize it wants yet. Read it."

Cecil fidgeted uncomfortably and Shoshanna rocked back and forth, trying not to cackle. We were holed up in a disgusting mauve pink office littered with fornicating statuettes somewhere in the Monster Mansion. Evangeline was cleaning my vomitous gift off, but still had the wherewithal to demand we begin working before she retired to her dungeon. Thankfully, I had no alone time with Shoshanna. It would be very difficult to hide today's events from her, but I would. Too many lives depended on my silence. I might be a loose cannon, but I was a loyal friend and daughter. No one fucked with my people. And if they tried . . . they would pay.

Evangeline was about to pay through the nose.

"Read it," I snapped.
Cecil blanched, but he read.

*"I have a date with Mork and Mindy," Pirate Dave told
Shirley, looking down at her with pity.*

*He yanked on his plaid breeches and ran his hands
through his greasy hair. He picked several lice from his
chest fur and smashed them with his bare hand. He briefly
considered bathing, but decided against it. A manly smell
was something he prided himself on. Besides, he had bathed
two weeks ago last Sunday.*

*"Whatever do you mean, my cocksman extraordinaire?"
Shirley screamed, confused by his behavior. She shoved her
ample bosom back into her corset and fluffed her fiery red
curls. She had just performed thirteen disgusting sex acts
for her lover. How could he not be satisfied with her
acrobatic performance?*

*Pirate Dave glanced over at the formerly conjoined twin
and realized, much to his surprise, he'd been more attracted
to her when she was attached to her bitch of a sister,
Laverne. He wondered if Captain Hook could sew them
back together . . . His warlock powers would not work on
such a major feat as rejoining separated conjoined twins.
Maybe he could time travel back to 1974 or possibly 1983
and have Johns Hopkins Hospital rejoin them. After all,
they'd been the scurvy bastards who'd separated the twins
in the first place. It mattered not to him that he had
demanded the operation. He was a pirate and pirates were
known for changing their minds, if not their underpants.*

*"My well-hung love, have I offended you?" Shirley
shrieked. "Is there something you want me to do?"
she bellowed.*

*Pirate Dave slapped his hands over his ears. Goddamn if
she wasn't the loudest harpy he'd ever heard. He was sure
his eardrums were bleeding after having spent the last
twenty-six hours humping her. Her rack was beyond
stupendous, but the voice . . . The voice was enough to make
a man want to cut his own testicles off with a butter knife.*

Cecil finished reading to complete and utter silence. He popped his neck and stared at the ceiling. I bit my lip and lowered my head. I knew if I made eye contact with Shoshanna I would lose it.

"Would you please read the next section?" I politely inquired a mortified Cecil.

"Was that a chapter?" he asked.

"Yes, we are going to do something new with the chapter system."

Shoshanna and Cecil waited to hear exactly what we were going to do. I wondered the same thing myself . . .

"We won't have chapters, per se. Just . . . um, vignettes, about four hundred and ninety-six or ninety-eight of them. Possibly six hundred. The table of contents will be a bit long, but whatever." I grinned at a pale Cecil and a delighted Shoshanna. "Cecil, please continue."

"Ooookay," he muttered.

Laverne bitch-slapped Captain Crunchy, knocking out two of his gold teeth. She was tired of playing second fiddle to his blow-up doll Susan. He screamed like a little girl, grabbed his plastic lover, and left. What was a formerly conjoined twin to do? Life without her sister, even though she hated her, was lonely.

Laverne smoothed her wild red locks and gingerly scratched her nether regions. That bastard Long Dong Silver had definitely given her something. Long Dong was soon to be dong-less. She made a mental note to call Dr. Smee and get some antibiotics. Thank God for time travel. Meds like antibiotics hadn't even been invented yet, but thankfully the shit-ass vampire warlock had had the forethought to get the good stuff. It would suck to die from screwing.

Why Pirate Dave had chosen her sister over her, she would never understand. Shirley's voice was like nails on a chalkboard. Of course, Shirley was nice and had bigger tatas, but the voice . . .

Laverne paced her small stinky cabin on the ship and made new plans to off her sister and Pirate Dave. If Pirate

Dave didn't want her, he didn't deserve to live. She felt better now. She decided to behead them on Saturday at the bingo tournament. She figured since he was a vampire, beheading would be a sure form of death. She pondered forcing him to turn her into a vampire before she decapitated him. Living for all eternity would mean she could screw hundreds of thousands of men. Hmmm.

"I will become the first female captain ever!" Laverne hissed to no one in particular since she was alone. Again.

She wondered if more people might like her if she became a captain . . . No matter, she would demand everyone like her and she would castrate anyone who defied her. She took a deep cleansing breath and congratulated herself on her outstanding scheme.

Little did she know, Calico Andy the Mind Reader was standing outside her smelly abode and knew of her dastardly plans! He'd been trying to get into Laverne's pants for two weeks and three days, only to be shot down due to his small man-package, dirty fingernails, and halitosis. He chuckled to himself, realizing she would soon be his. Blackmail was a beautiful thing . . .

Again, my story was greeted with silence. Eerie silence.

"So Cecil, what do you think?" I crossed my arms over my chest and gave him a hard stare, daring him to insult my masterpiece.

"I think it's um, it's . . . uhhh—" He fumbled for words that wouldn't induce my wrath. I almost felt sorry for him, but I kept reminding myself what a rat bastard he was.

"I think it's thought-provoking and sexy in a realistic, somewhat unclean, fucked-up way. Definitely a hit with the twenty-five to forty-three-ish demographic," Shoshanna chimed in, clearly trying to tamp down the hysterics threatening to explode from her little self. "It's different from anything I've ever read or have ever in my life wanted to read, but hey, the way of the future is the way of the future." She gagged on her laughter and excused herself to the bathroom.

I eyed Cecil warily. I didn't want to go too far too quickly. I needed to ruin Evangeline, but Cecil couldn't be in on the joke. He was on her team and I couldn't forget that. It didn't matter that she treated him worse than a dog . . . he was still the bad guy.

"That will be all, Cecil. My creative juices come in spurts and I'm very tired from all the action today. Thank you, you may go."

He stood up reluctantly. I knew in my gut he wanted to say something, but he stayed silent. That was probably better for both of us. I could not under any circumstances feel anything for him.

I turned back to dismiss him again, but he was gone. I collapsed onto a hot pink poor excuse for a couch and shoved my hands into my pockets. I pulled my knees up to my chest and tried to become as small as I could. Disappearing wasn't an option, but oh, how I wish it was. I hated my life, and I hated the bitch who now controlled it even more.

What the hell was in my pocket? I pulled out a card and my hand began to tremble. Jack . . . the man of my dreams. The cop. His card lay crumpled in my hand. There was no way I could call him. He thought I was a thief and a restraining-order-breaker. It didn't matter that the chemistry was out of this world and that I would probably step in front of a train to save his life or that I was already half in love with him, and I couldn't get the image of him handcuffing me to my bed out of my brain . . . it wasn't meant to be. Ever. Crap, crap, crap.

Hell, how many lives besides my own could I ruin in one day? I would not take him down with me. There was still a fine chance I might do some bodily harm to Evangeline and get arrested again. A cop can't date, have sex with, or marry a convicted murderer.

Out of all the things that had gone wrong today, one of my biggest regrets would be never seeing Jack again. I slowly shredded my future, ripping Jack's card into tiny pieces. Just in case I was tempted to put it back together, I swallowed it. Of course I gagged and almost threw up again, but there was nothing left in my stomach after my earlier performance. I flopped back on the couch and proceeded to give in to the need that had been pressing on me for hours . . . I cried. Hard.

Thankfully it took Shoshanna about a half an hour in the bathroom to pull herself back together. Clearly my story had affected her deeply or she'd peed in her pants and had to let them air dry. Regardless, that reprieve gave me enough time to sob my heart out and freshen back up. I couldn't let my little LeHump know that anything was amiss.

"Are you hungry?" Shoshanna asked upon her return, plopping herself down next to me and putting her feet up on the pink marble coffee table.

"Actually, I am," I laughed, surprising myself. Usually when I'm distraught I can't eat, but I suppose emptying my stomach earlier made me hungry. I placed my feet on the ugly coffee table next to my little buddy's.

"Good. Nancy, Joanne, and Poppy Harriet will be here in about five minutes with lunch. I can't guarantee it's edible"—she grinned—"but it will be made with love."

"I thought only Nancy was coming."

"Yeah, but after I told her about the weird morning, they all decided to come and make sure you're okay . . . Are you okay?"

"Um, yes . . . I am."

I gave Shoshanna a smile and squeezed her hands. What I really wanted to do was curl up next to her and bawl, but there was no time for self-pity. I'd made my bed, and I would lie in it. Alone. For the rest of my life. Shit.

"Would you like to explain why the evil sow was covered in vomit and why you left alone and came back with the silicone skank and her evil henchman?"

It was going to be difficult to pull stuff over on LeHump, but since her life, mine, and several others depended on it, I had no choice.

"Yeah, but can it wait till the girls get here? I don't want to tell this one twice."

"No prob. Hey, that was one hell of a story you pulled out of your ass," she said, grinning.

"Thanks. Unfortunately it's beginning to come naturally."

"Well, it made me pee my pants. Literally." Shoshanna shouted gleefully, "I can't wait for the upchuck story."

"Yeah, me neither," I muttered.

I still had no idea what I was going to say. All I knew for sure was that I wouldn't be telling the truth. Hell, I was going to have to keep a notebook full of all the lies I told or I was going to be in some deep shit.

On cue the ladies arrived, bearing a scary tuna hot dish, snickerdoodles, chicken wild rice soup, and wine in a box. Nancy spread out the Minnesota-style feast on the ugly pink marble coffee table, pulled out her robin's-egg-blue travel dishes, and we all dug in. I avoided the crumbled-cracker-covered cream of mushroom tuna concoction and stuck to the wild rice soup, snickerdoodles, and wine. Which, by the way, wasn't half bad.

Kristy would be appalled that I drank wine from a box. She was a wine snob, but I'm sure when she found out Professor Sue liked it, it would become her new favorite thing.

I noticed all the gals, except Nancy, sniffing their food cautiously before eating it. They appeared to sniff only when Nancy wasn't looking. What in the hell was that about? I almost laughed when Shoshanna gave Poppy Harriet and Joanne the thumbs-up, clearly the cue that the food was edible, or at least not poisonous.

"Love the plates, Nancy," Joanne enthused with a mouthful of Tasty Tuna Surprise.

"Two twenty-five last fall at a mega yard sale," Nancy informed our lunch bunch proudly.

"Two hundred and twenty-five dollars?" I choked out, examining the scratched blue plastic plate with shock.

"Oh, sweet holy mother of baby Jesus, no!" Nancy laughed. "Two dollars and twenty-five cents for a set of sixty."

"You are the bargain queen, my friend," LeHump yelled, helping herself to more wine in a box. "Oh shit, I forgot to tell you guys . . . I'm getting divorced," she announced, holding up her blue plastic coffee cup of merlot.

"Congratulations!" Poppy Harriet squealed. "Did Kevin meet someone?"

"He did," Shoshanna said proudly. "A nice young man named Steve. Steve has a job and doesn't seem to be a man-whore."

"Will the divorce take long?" Joanne asked, with a mouth full of snickerdoodle. "Maybe you should go to Mexico. I hear they can do one in twenty minutes."

"Shoshanna, you must be so proud. He's such a good boy. Do you think they'll adopt?" Nancy inquired as she spooned a heaping pile of Tuna Surprise onto my plate. It looked suspiciously like my earlier gift to Evangeline.

"No clue, but Kevin would make such a good daddy and I'd love to be a grandma. God knows Sue Junior doesn't want kids. Last week she told me she didn't think our DNA should be passed on. She's such a bullheaded bitch."

"Like mother, like daughter," Poppy Harriet laughed.

"Yeah," Shoshanna chuckled, "but I think she's a lot more like her daddy, Herm. Talk about a great lay ... In his day that man could go six times in one night! He would be so damn happy for Kevin."

"Are you positive Steve isn't a man-whore?" Joanne nervously ran her fingers over her nonexistent eyebrows.

"Kevin feels quite confident, and they've been dating for nine months."

"That's all well and good, but his last boyfriend, Timothy, turned out to be a stripper and a hooker," Joanne huffed. "Do you want me to do a background check on this Steve character?"

"That's not a bad idea." LeHump nodded to Joanne.

"All I can say is thank God! That's one less thing the Botox Bitch has on us!" Poppy Harriet trilled.

"Harriet!" Joanne hissed.

They all froze. It was like Joanne had thrown ice water on all of them. No one would make eye contact with me ... then they all started talking at once.

What the fuck is going on? Am I in the twilight zone? I am confused and grossed out and ... confused. I have absolutely no idea what my insane gal pals are talking about and I'm afraid to ask ... but asking questions I don't want the answers to is a talent of mine.

"All of you need to stop talking," I said, standing up and moving away from the lump of tuna bile on my plate. "I am so fucking confused, I'm dizzy. First I mistakenly think Nancy paid an obscene amount of money for plastic dishes, then I think I just heard that Shoshanna is married to a gay man named Kevin who found himself a non-man-whore named Steve, so he wants a divorce. And her baby-daddy Herm sounds like he might have erectile dysfunction like Pirate Dave. Why on earth did you kick someone who can get it up six times a night to the curb for a gay man who's looking for a non-man-whore? And why did Kevin date a stripper-hooker while he was married to LeHump? And why in the hell was he or is he married to LeHump? And what does the viper bitch from hell have to do with any of this?"

"Oh dear," Nancy giggled, tucking her neat gray bob behind her ears, "I suppose this conversation does sound a little odd to someone without the backstory."

"You think?" I shook my head in disbelief.

"May I?" LeHump asked, clearly offering to explain.

"Please do." I sat back down. Nancy handed me my plate and a fork. Shit, I couldn't eat Tasty Tuna Surprise, no matter how sweet Nancy was.

"Herm, or Mr. Wonder Pecker, as I used to call him, died about six years ago," she said.

Did she just say Mr. Wonder Pecker? My Pirate Dave stories were beginning to sound tame compared to LeHump's real life.

"Of gallbladder complications," Nancy chimed in. "He was the love of Shoshanna's life."

"He was. We were married forty-four years"—LeHump smiled fondly—"and I miss him every day." She paused and looked to the heavens. As cheesy as the moment was, my eyes welled with tears. "So anyway, our gay neighbor Kevin was going to get deported back to Canada because his work visa had expired. Herm, besides being Superman in the sack, was slightly psychic and had a feeling he was going to die. He suggested Kevin and I get married when he kicked the bucket. I told him he was full of shit, not about marrying Kevin—I had no problem marrying a gay man as lovely as Kevin so he could get a green card. Herm was full of shit about dying."

"Unfortunately, he wasn't," Poppy Harriet whispered.

"He wasn't," Shoshanna agreed. "So after Herm's funeral, Kevin and I got married."

"Oh my God, do a lot of people know about this?" I was so shocked, I mindlessly took a bite of Tasty Tuna Surprise. It was pretty good.

"Hell no," Shoshanna laughed, "only the women in this room and Kevin. And I suppose Steve knows."

"That's not exactly accurate," Joanne huffed.

"Accurate enough," Shoshanna cut her off.

A confusing awkward silence filled the room, broken abruptly by Poppy Harriet's sobs. The gals surrounded her quickly, stroking and cooing.

"What's wrong?" I asked, momentarily forgetting LeHump was married to a homosexual as I wedged my way over to Poppy Harriet.

"It's her taxes," Nancy whispered.

"Her taxes?"

"The IRS is after her. She wouldn't do well in jail," Nancy explained.

I wasn't sure why the IRS was after Poppy Harriet, but I was fairly sure I could help.

"Don't cry," I told her, taking her rather large hands in my own. "I'm an accountant. I can fix it for you."

"Oh my God," Joanne yelled. "You don't have to go to prison. Let Rena help you."

"I can't," Poppy wailed. "You know why I can't," she cried, pointing an accusing finger at Joanne.

My bruised ego had now been beaten to a pulp. Did these crazy old ladies think because I sucked as a writer I sucked at everything? I might not ever be the Sunshine Weather Girl and I was positive I would never be a *New York Times* best-selling author, but I sure as hell was an excellent number-crunching nerd with a CPA license to show for it.

"Look." I put on my brook-no-bullshit voice. "Clearly you all think I'm mentally challenged because of the disgusting stories I tell, and I may be, however I'm a damn good CPA and I insist on helping you. I will not take no for an answer."

A round of eyeballing began and I watched in fascination as they seemed to communicate telepathically with each other. WTF?

"You have no choice," Shoshanna said to Poppy Harriet.

"But . . ." Poppy's tears continued to flow.

"No choice," Joanne echoed.

Poppy Harriet's shoulders fell, and she quickly and neatly popped every knuckle in her big hands, including her wrists. Gross. A sinking feeling whizzed through me briefly as I pondered the possible financial trouble she'd gotten herself into, but short of her never having paid taxes in her seventy-some-odd years, I was confident I could help.

"Have you ever paid taxes?" I asked, praying she'd say yes.

"Um, yes, but I've changed my name quite a few times, and they won't believe I am who I am," she sniffed.

"That will be easy." I smiled. "I'll come over Saturday morning and we'll work it out."

A silent round of telepathy replayed between the gals, and I wondered what part of the story they'd left out. No one was talking. I assumed I'd unravel the mystery Saturday morning.

There was no way out of an explanation of the day's earlier activities, so I lied. After a brief and totally untrue version of the vomit story centering on some bad cheese, I conned Shoshanna into driving me back to my aunt's alien-infested car and went on my merry, lying-sack-of-shit way.

Chapter 9

I sat forward on the floral, plastic-covered couch, careful not to squash any aliens or gremlins. Being unable to actually see the magical beings put me at a slight disadvantage, but I figured if I perched on the edge of the cushion and sat very still, there was a fine chance I wouldn't kill or maim anything.

"So, um, Aunt Phyllis, thank you for loaning me your car these past three days. It drives like a dream and the little green men didn't give me any trouble." God, I sounded as crazy as she did. I swallowed my pride and decided to get right to the point. "I'm in a bit of a financial bind, or deficit, if you will." I sat up straighter and put on my CPA voice. I figured a little professional speak might be a good idea. "And I was wondering if it would be okay if I, you know, um, borrowed a couple thousand dollars for a down payment on a car. I'll sign a loan agreement and pay interest. We can put a time frame on the repayment and . . ."

"Stop right there." She smiled, while arranging cookies along the outer edges of her antique coffee table. For the Martians, I presumed. "The answer is no. Would you care for a cookie? They're gingersnaps."

"No, thanks."

My heart sank to my stomach and I slumped back, uncaring if I squashed an invisible troll or two. Aunt Phyllis was my only shot besides my parents. And the folks were beyond a last resort. Their disappointment in me and the fact that perfect, pregnant Doctor Jenny would be sure to find out made that choice a very bad one. I'd rather chew glass and swallow it before I gave my sister an opportunity to hang my shitty personal financial skills over my head.

My being an accountant would only intensify her joy to the point I might have to kill her.

Of course killing her could result in my being arrested by Jack again . . . Damn, just thinking about him set my panties on fire and made my heart hurt. I needed to block him out, the same way I did the scale after a date with ice cream and French fries, or Kristy, when she watched Housewives of Whatever marathons.

I picked up a gingersnap and shoved it in my mouth, hoping the chewing would disguise the crying that was sure to burst forth any moment.

"I like chocolate chip cookies," Aunt Phyllis mused, "but the little people in the TV prefer the gingersnaps or macaroons."

"That's interesting." I nodded, biting back the snarky reply that hovered on my lips. Normally I adored my aunt, but right now the selfish, desperate part of me hated her.

As a child, I loved listening to the stories about all the oddities inhabiting her home. Now, I worried if someone outside the family actually listened to her for more than ten minutes, they'd have her committed.

"So anyway, dear, there will be no contract or interest or time frame. I'll just give you the money. You and your sister will get it all when I die, so I may as well enjoy watching you spend it while I'm alive."

Now I did start to cry. "Oh my God, I can't just take your money. I'll pay you back."

"Don't be silly. I have several hundred thousand sewn into my mattress, not to mention the half million your late Uncle Carlton forced me to put in the bank. God rest that son of a bitch's non-believing, womanizing soul."

"Wait, what?" I gasped.

"Oh, you know I never trusted banks. They're full of money-grubbing cyborgs, and if you believe the Internet, zombies are running Wall Street."

"I'm pretty sure there's a lot of misinformation on the Internet, Aunt Phyllis."

"Of course there is. People like me know how to weed out the truth from the lies. Come with me, sweetheart."

I followed her to the guest bedroom, via the kitchen, where she selected a large, sharp carving knife from the butcher block on her peach Formica countertop. I felt quite sure she wouldn't murder me, so I continued to trail her.

"Would you be a dear and remove the quilt from the bed? I'm rather fond of it," Aunt Phyllis requested as she flexed her muscles and bent over to touch her toes. WTF?

"Sure. Do you want me to take the sheets off, too?" I asked, removing the Daisy Star quilt from the bed. Aunt Phyllis was a Minnesota State Fair quilting winner, and that's no small thing. Quilting is serious business in the Midwest. I had one of her rosebud quilts on my bed. I wouldn't trade it for all the money in the world. Although if someone offered me a car . . .

"No, they're old, and I think I may have had these when your cheating bastard uncle was still alive. In fact, I believe I'll pretend I just caught your uncle screwing the neighbor on the bed. This will be fun."

"Um, okay."

This was getting weird and disturbing. Aunt Phyllis seemed delighted to playact mortally wounding my long-dead uncle and his concubine from down the street.

"Stand back," she warned. "This could get messy."

"Right." I moved to the doorway, in case I needed to make a run for it.

My Aunt Phyllis, who must have been a ninja warrior in a prior life, pirouetted, arched back, and hurled the carving knife toward the bed. With a bizarre and alarming grunt that sounded vaguely like "take that you unfaithful bastard ass-wipe," she split the mattress clean in half. Money exploded from the feathers that flew around the room. I walked to the bed in a daze.

"Holy shit, Aunt Phyllis." I held up a hunk of hundred-dollar bills that she had chopped in two. "I think you just destroyed a couple thousand bucks."

"No, you can tape it. It'll still work. Besides, there's more. Every mattress in the house is loaded. Here."

She handed me an obscene wad of cash, far more than a down payment. She then pulled an old purse down from the top of the closet and filled it to the brim.

"I can't take all this," I stammered, trying to hand it back to her. "There's got to be twenty or thirty thousand dollars here."

"You can and you will," she said, shoving it back into my hands. "I earned that money by keeping my mouth shut while your Uncle Fucker gigoloed his way through the cul-de-sac. I want you to have a new car and if it makes you feel any better, you can start accompanying me to my Bigfoot Is Alive and Well in Minnesota meetings. You can drive me."

"Okay." I was in shock. Shock that she was giving me all this money . . . shock that she'd renamed my Uncle Carlton Uncle Fucker . . . shock that she had hundreds of thousands of dollars in all the mattresses in her house . . . shock that my long-deceased uncle had fornicated his way through the neighborhood . . . shock that I was going to become an active participant in the Bigfoot subculture.

"Come on, dear, let's go have some cookies before the people in the TV eat them all."

"Okay."

Re-perched on the sofa, I tried to find a polite way to decline the disgusting little gingersnaps that lined the coffee table.

"What do you think of Evangeline O'Hara?" Aunt Phyllis asked, pouring lemonade into mismatched Twins baseball mugs.

My mom must have told her I was working for Evangeline. Crap, the color drained from my face. "Well . . ." I decided to be diplomatic. I didn't want to tell her that the past three days of my life had been some of the worst I'd ever had. Or that I'd cleaned seven of her bathrooms on my hands and knees. Or that without my friend Shoshanna, I would be in jail right now because I would have choked Evangeline to death. I didn't want my aunt to worry or, God forbid, show up at the mansion to give Evangeline a piece of her questionable mind. The only good part of the week was that the Viper had loved the appalling story I'd been feeding Cecil daily. "She's okay."

"Hmmm." Phyllis pursed her lips. "Last time I saw her at the bridge tournament, she looked like a reality show contestant for plastic surgery addiction."

I choked on my lemonade.

"Not to mention," my aunt went on, "she was a royal bitch."

"I didn't know you knew her." I busied myself rearranging the gingersnaps into a new formation.

"Oh, I know her all right, known her for years. She was there for salmonella-gate."

Salmonella-gate had been a big deal. A couple of years ago, two hundred ladies playing bridge had been poisoned by spoiled Turkey Noodle Dooda Surprise at their annual Christmas party. It actually made the national news. Thank God no one died. The caterer disappeared, never to be heard from again.

"I have to say, as sick as I was, it was wonderful to watch that bag of bones throw up all over her mink coat," Aunt Phyllis chuckled fondly. "She actually tried to fuck your uncle, but he declined. That's one of my only good memories of that bastard."

Of all the random things . . . It shouldn't surprise me that Aunt Phyllis played bridge with the Viper Bitch. Thank Jesus, Phyllis's last name was different from mine. I wanted no connections made. It was a bit difficult to wrap my head around Evangeline hitting on Uncle Fucker. The visuals were too alarming to process. I'd pretend I'd never heard it, like that was going to work. Everything was starting to connect, and that was a bad thing. My family did not need to know anything more than what I chose to tell them about my life, and that was going to be nothing.

"I forgot to tell you," Phyllis giggled. "Your mom and I stopped by your apartment building yesterday and met your boyfriend. He's quite the looker."

"I'm sorry, what?"

"Jack. We met your new boyfriend Jack the Communicator."

Oh my God. Jack was at my apartment building? What in the hell was he doing there? Was he investigating me? I bet he thought I was a jewel thief. That son of a bitch.

"He's a lovely man," my aunt gushed. "He asked all kinds of questions about you once we told him who we were. I told him all about the time when you tried to be a Cirque du Soleil performer and ended up in traction in the emergency room."

"Did you mention I was nine years old at the time?" I felt the heat creep up my neck and land squarely on my face.

She looked confused for a moment. "I'm not sure I remembered that part."

That's just fucking great. The hottest man alive is snooping around, trying to build a case against me so I can live out the rest of my pathetic life in the slammer. I am so glad I ate his card. He doesn't like me . . . he wants a promotion. He wants to nail the

perp, and not the way I want to nail him. If I ever see him again, I
will rip him a new one. One that will impede sitting.

"Rena, I want to have a heart-to-heart. I don't want to see you
ho your life away like your uncle did. I don't know how many men
you're juggling at the moment, but Jack is not a communicator.
He's a cop. And his last name is not Snuffleupagus. You really
must keep your male suitors straight."

"Right," I muttered, making a gingersnap pyramid. "We actually
broke up before I came here today."

"Oh my God, that's terrible. He has an ass you could melt butter on."

I stared hard at the cookies, trying to let go of the knowledge that
my aunt had seriously scoped my ex-not-really-boyfriend's butt.

"Don't worry your pretty little head," she continued. "You two
lovebirds can work it out Saturday night."

"What are you talking about?"

"Your mom invited him over to their house for family dinner on
Saturday," she bubbled, swatting at imaginary people flying through
the air.

"You've got to be fucking kidding me," I gasped. That was awful. Was he pretending to be my boyfriend so he could take me into
custody in front of my entire family? I had judged him so wrong. I
was flabbergasted that I'd considered letting him father my children. He was probably married, for Christ's sake.

"Rena, watch your language," Phyllis admonished.

"Why? You just renamed Uncle Carlton Uncle Fucker."

"I did, didn't I?" she laughed. "Well, he was. I have at least six
slutty neighbors that can back me up. Or maybe it's five . . . Hilda
died of something random last spring."

"Natural causes?" I asked, hoping it wasn't from a carving knife
wound. My aunt is a little kooky, but I'm fairly sure she's not a killer.

"Explosive gas."

I wanted no more of an explanation than that. Explosive gas was
good enough for me. Saturday was two days away . . . I needed to
go home and plan Jack's demise, preferably before he showed up
at my parents' house. I kissed my aunt, thanked her profusely for
the money, and headed home to look at cars online, praying the rest
of the evening would be boring.

Chapter 10

My date with myself was going well so far. Kristy had gone to Wisconsin to visit her grandma for a few days, so I had full control of the TV remote. It was perfect. No Evangeline, no little green men or gremlins, no geriatric gal pals who are married to gay men, no assholes masquerading as sexy cops . . . Just me, myself, and I. A nice boring evening at home, dim lights, citrus-scented candles, a *Hoarders* marathon on A&E, and a huge bowl of black raspberry chip ice cream.

Speaking of hot cops, I needed to find Jack and un-invite him for Saturday. Eating his card had been a bad idea. It had seemed like such a smart move at the time. Now I was screwed. There was no way I was stepping foot anywhere near the police station. Having no clue how to solve that little dilemma, I decided procrastination would be the wisest course. I would let nothing come between me and my ice cream.

Although Jenny's reaction to my having the hottest (albeit fake) boyfriend in the universe might be worth being cuffed in front of my entire family. Maybe I could strike a deal and he'd agree to arrest me after dinner . . . Fuck it and fuck him. I would meet him outside my parents' house and tell him to leave. If he wanted to take me into custody for being a jewel thief, fine. At least my family wouldn't see it happen. Done. I was glad all of this had happened. It strengthened my resolve to stay away from cops. Thankfully the burning desire to see my neighbor's face was gone, too. Jack had very effectively taken the shine off dating any cop or man for the rest of my life.

I looked down at my T-shirt and smiled. I'd dressed up for my date. My Captain Crunch T-shirt made me happy. The small fact that the Captain and his blow-up doll Susan made an appearance in my career-destroying story was pure bonus.

The T-shirt was obscene. Tight and sexy and worn out in all the right places. I'd had it since middle school and it was my favorite piece of clothing. Paired with a comfy pair of jeans that sat low on my hips and with my hair twisted into a cute, messy ponytail, I felt relaxed and calm. Kristy called this my jailbait hooker look. I thought it was hot even though I'd never go out in public like that. A knock at the door yanked me back to reality and scared the hell out of me.

"Son of a bitch," I told my ice cream, "who's knocking on my door at 9:30 at night?" The gay couple downstairs worked the night shift and the gal next door was a bit of a recluse. Maybe it was Mr. Asstastic from downstairs . . . God, I just wanted to be left alone. "Who is it?"

"It's Jack."

"Jack who?" I asked.

"Jack Snuffleupagus."

I couldn't help laughing. My mother and aunt had obviously clued him in on his fictional last name. He might have a sense of humor, but he was still the enemy. I couldn't let his assorific behind, hot bod, and beautiful face cloud my judgment. What in the hell was he doing here? How did he get into my building? I was so not ready to do hard time. "Do you have a search warrant?"

"Um, no. Should I?" He sounded confused. Good. I planned to keep the bastard on his toes. I would not go willingly and I wouldn't open the door.

"Why are you here?" I asked warily.

"Because I want to see you. You didn't call me." I could hear the smile in his voice.

"I ate your card."

"I'm sorry, what did you say?"

"I. Ate. Your. Card."

There was a long pause. I realized I sounded as insane as my Aunt Phyllis. That wasn't such a bad thing; maybe he'd run away.

"Did it taste good?" he asked.

"No."

"Rena, open the door."

"Are you going to handcuff me?" I demanded.

"Not unless you want me to," he laughed. "Rena, open the door, please. It's a social call."

Social call, my butt. I yanked open the door, ready to give him a piece of my mind, and was rendered speechless. I'd seen many pretty things in my life, but nothing as stunning as the man standing in my doorway. Shit, shit, shit. How could he look better than I remembered? His faded jeans weren't too tight or too loose. His long-sleeved henley amplified his muscular chest and arms and the color matched his gray-blue eyes. It wasn't fair. It didn't matter how good-looking he was, it couldn't erase the fact that he wanted to throw me in the slammer and ruin my life.

He stopped in the doorway. His eyes got large as he took in my outfit. Good. He could see what he would never have. I noticed he moved in a few steps, making it impossible for me to slam the door in his face without breaking his nose.

His eyes were glued to my chest, which was being firmly hugged by Captain Crunch and no bra.

"Um, hello," I snapped, jolting him out of his boob fantasy. "My face is up here."

He had the decency to look embarrassed, but that didn't stop his appraisal. His eyes traveled lazily to my neck, my lips, my eyes, lingering everywhere they passed. Delight and something I couldn't define flashed in his gorgeous eyes. I felt a little light-headed . . . I realized I had forgotten to breathe.

"Hi Rena." He grinned and stepped toward me. "I've been thinking about you."

"Really?" I lifted an eyebrow and backed up into the wall. "I haven't thought about you at all, not once . . . not even a little bit . . . at all . . . ever." I shoved my hands behind my back so I wouldn't grab him and yank him to me, or worse.

"You haven't thought about me once?" He made a sad face. His eyes were anything but sad. They were come fuck me, bedroom eyes.

Shit, I was in trouble.

"Nope, not once." I tried to back up some more, but a wall is a wall. If he didn't stop looking at me like that, my inner slut would take over and I'd ride him like a cowboy. "So are you here to arrest me?"

He stared at me in confusion. "Are you serious?"

"Of course I am, you idiot."

The expression on his face clearly evidenced that not many people call him an idiot. Bizarrely enough, he seemed to enjoy it. That was a good thing because I had an arsenal of things I planned on calling him.

"Did you do something else illegal?" he asked, trying unsuccessfully to keep his eyes glued to mine. My tatas were apparently too much of a distraction.

"No, I did not," I huffed. His intense concentration on my body set off fireworks in my stomach, not to mention that my lady bits were dancing up a storm in my panties. He needed to leave. Now.

"It was lovely seeing you again. Sorry you have to go so soon," I chirped trying to push him toward the door, but six-foot-two of solid muscle is not easy to move.

He laughed. God, he was so sexy when he laughed. I couldn't think straight when I was near him. Thank Jesus, I had the wall to hold me up. He moved closer and stopped inches from me. My insides started to tighten.

"You're a mystery," he said running a finger along my bottom lip. I leaned forward with a burning desire to take that finger into my mouth and suck on it. What the fu . . . ? I was beginning to think I might have inherited some of Uncle Fucker's ho-bag tendencies.

I pressed myself back up against my friend, the wall. I was hoping to put more than just a few inches between us. This man, this Jack, this cop, was making me consider things I'd never imagined doing in this lifetime. Evangeline's fornicating statues came to mind.

He moved even closer. I closed my eyes, praying that if I couldn't see him, the need to knock him to the ground and have my way with him would disappear. Maybe, just maybe, if I couldn't see his lips and his eyes and the sexy stubble on his cheeks, my body would relax and the pressure between my legs would lessen.

No. Such. Luck.

Damn, he smelled good. I opened my eyes to find the object of my desire and possibly the instrument of my incarceration a simple breath away from my lips. His eyes were intense. He put his hands on the wall on either side of me. Successfully, but loosely, trapping me. I knew I could get away if I wanted to . . . I didn't want to. God, I hadn't been this turned on in like . . . ever.

"Is this normal police procedure?" I whispered.

"Nope." He grinned.

"Then what is it?" Was that my voice? I sounded like a freakin' phone sex operator.

"This is me, Jack, wanting to get to know the most gorgeous, sexy, and possibly craziest girl I've ever met in my life."

"Oh, okay then."

He slowly bent his elbows, his eyes never leaving mine, until his chest was pressed against my breasts. I felt my nipples harden. His eyes flashed with delight and the corner of his mouth lifted into the sexiest smirk I'd ever seen. I was very sure he no longer wanted to arrest me.

"Is this okay?" he asked.

"Um, yes," I muttered, positive he could hear my heart bouncing around in my chest.

He was so close I could taste his breath and it tasted good. If he pressed himself against me any harder, I was liable to have a very loud, screaming orgasm. He smiled as if he knew what I was thinking.

"I'm not sure Saturday night is such a good idea," I mumbled.

"No?" he whispered into my mouth. "I think it's a great idea."

To my horror, my tongue darted out and ran slowly over my lips. He smiled evilly and made the sexiest sound I'd ever heard. The blue of his eyes intensified. *Help me, Jesus.*

"I think it's a bad idea," I gasped. If he didn't back off soon, I wouldn't be responsible for my actions. I didn't think he'd take issue with what I wanted to do to him, but even I knew screwing the guy that could take my freedom away was probably a bad move.

I wondered if I just kissed him once, if he'd leave it at that. Somehow I didn't think so. He so did not seem the type to kiss and run. He seemed more of a kiss and kiss and kiss guy . . . starting at my mouth, then my neck, then lower and lower and lower and . . .

"Are you still in there?" Jack snapped me out of the porno playing in my head with a twinkle in his eyes, leading me to believe he could tell what I was thinking. Shit, was he one of those psychic cops?

"Still here," I murmured.

"Excellent. I'd hate to lose you now. We're just getting to the good part."

My knees buckled as he nipped and kissed my neck. He grabbed me as I started to melt into a puddle at his feet. The entire length of his body was pressed to mine. And let me tell you, it was one hell of a body. Every long, hard, muscular inch of him.

"Oh my God," I whimpered, grasping his broad shoulders and pressing back against this man I barely knew. Who, until two minutes ago, I thought wanted to take me to jail. Maybe he had a weird fetish for lawbreakers . . .

"You are wild and beautiful and totally disrespectful," he whispered, running his tongue along my earlobe. He continued to speak softly, and I continued to lose brain cells. He ran his lips over my jaw and back to the corner of my mouth. I shuddered and almost passed out.

His eyes bored into mine with an intensity that scared the hell out of me and turned me on at the same time. "I think your outfit is kinda hot," he said, grinning.

"Just kinda?" I let my inner slut out and put my best flirt on.

"Just kinda, definitely, absolutely hot." He was a pretty damn good flirt himself.

He placed his hand on the small of my back, trapping me for real. No getting away this time, not that I wanted to. I threaded my hands through his thick blond hair, cupped the back of his neck, and pulled his lips to mine. He teased my mouth with the tip of his tongue, licking along my lower lip before he slanted his mouth across mine and turned me to jelly. He parted my very willing lips with his tongue and took his slow sweet time. His body against mine sent a warm heat coursing through me, making my girlie parts sing. Loud. Kissing him was better than any sex I'd ever had.

Sex with him would be . . . God, I couldn't even . . . I bet it would be better than black raspberry chip ice cream. Legs, I couldn't feel my legs. Oh God, I couldn't . . . He tasted so good. I kept trying not to notice, but he was determined to remind me. His hands moved to my bottom, grinding me against an erection so impressive, I felt light-headed. This guy was killing me.

My wisp of silk panties were now soaked and my body had grown its own brain. My inner slut was having a gymnastics meet in my nether regions and I prayed silently Jack had condoms in his wallet. I really, really wanted to get him naked and make him see God.

My traitorous body was writhing all over his and the gorgeous cop was having a difficult time maintaining control. God, that's hot. But more alarming than what I was doing was what I was thinking. *I want him to be mine. That's right, I want to marry him, bear his children, and fuck him into unconsciousness every night for the rest of my life. I want to sink into him and claim him as mine. Mine, mine, mine. No one else can have him. Ever.*

WTF? Had I lost my mind? In the span of an hour, I'd gone from wanting to kill him to wanting to kill any girl who so much as looked at him. I needed therapy and my inner ho-bag needed to be bitch-slapped.

Jack pulled back with supreme effort, putting some distance between us. His breathing was ragged. That's nothing; I couldn't even remember how to breathe.

My lady bits informed me it was time to throw him to the floor and ride him blind. Neither me nor my nether regions cared if the entire building heard us. But wait . . . I couldn't. Because he was talking . . . Why was he talking? What in the hell was wrong with him?

"I am completely undone by you. I've never wanted anyone so badly in my life."

"Then what the hell are you waiting for?" I demanded. Fuck, did I say that out loud? Yes, I did.

"I want you for more than one night."

Wasn't that my line? Was Herbie the Dentist Cop right? Was Jack gay? No way. The gun he was packing in his pants was clear evidence to the contrary.

"We are going to get to know each other first," he continued.

"Well, it's probably a good thing that we didn't, um . . . you know, do it," I replied flippantly.

"Why's that?" He tilted his head to the side and smiled. I almost forgot my name.

"Because I don't date cops."

"Really?" He grinned.

"Yup, I don't like them."

Before I even saw him move, he was back up in my face, his body grinding into mine. *Can't think, can't think, can't think.*

"We'll see about that, Rena."

He leaned in and gently pressed his lips to mine. My eyes fluttered shut and all my resistance melted away. He deepened the kiss, then pulled back.

Embarrassingly, I gasped at the loss, but did enjoy watching Jack struggle with himself. I hoped he got a raging case of blue balls.

He ran his fingers lightly across my collar bone and down my arm. His sexy smirk was firmly back in place. "I'll see you on Saturday."

Before I could get a word out, he was gone. I sank to the floor and dropped my head into my hands. Shit. I was in lust with the enemy and he wouldn't even screw me. He wanted to know me better . . . that couldn't possibly turn out well.

I crawled over to my now melted bowl of ice cream and realized I still had no idea how he'd gotten into my building. Maybe he was friends with the guy who'd moved in downstairs. Maybe they had butt contests . . . standing in front of the mirror in their underpants, trying to figure out whose butt was hotter. I'd seen both and I'd have to call it a draw. I giggled at the thought of two hot guys in their underpants comparing asses. As hot as Jack was, I still didn't trust his motives . . . Shaking my head and trying to remove him and what could have happened from my brain, I went in search of Vinnie the Vibrator. My lady bits would bitch at me all night if I didn't comply with their demands. So much for a boring evening . . .

Chapter 11

Pirate Dave grabbed his throbbing tallywhacker in agony, raised his eyes to the heavens, and screamed for all he was worth. "Why me? Why have I been cursed with a johnson that won't go down?"

So caught up in his own angst, he squeezed his winkie for all it was worth. "Goddamn," he yelped, letting go of himself and running in circles like his feet were on fire. He shook his fist at the sky and cursed up a storm. "Poseidon, you fat bastard, if I ever die, your jiggly ass is mine. I know you're up there laughing, you porcine motherfucker," he screeched.

As his rant at the obese god escalated, the horizon filled with a blazing purple light and a shape-shifting, fairy-like blind troll dropped out of the sky and landed smack on top of Pirate Dave, giving him a minor concussion.

"What the fuck?" Pirate Dave yelled, throwing the sightless troll twenty-seven feet away from him. "Who are you?"

The shape-shifting, fairy-like troll got up and brushed himself off. He was pissed. "Well, you idiot, I'm supposed to be your blind magical fairy troll, but after a reception like that, I think I will become your archenemy," he huffed, in a teeny-tiny squeaky voice.

"I'm over here," Pirate Dave offered, as the blind troll had been speaking to air.

"Oh, sorry."

"No biggie."

The blind troll fairy turned forty-five degrees to his left and continued. "Poseidon said you were a dick, but . . ."

"Dude," Pirate Dave cut him off, "you need to turn about twenty-two degrees to your right."

The blind shape-shifting fairy-like troll's face burned crimson with embarrassment. "Is that better?" he asked as he made the adjustment.

"Yep."

"Thanks. Now as I was saying, Poseidon said you were a dick, but he didn't say anything about how stinky you are."

"That's my manly smell," Pirate Dave haughtily informed the troll. "Plus, I'd guess your sense of smell is pretty sharp considering you can't see a goddamn thing."

"True. So what is your problem?"

"My salami won't go down. No matter how many beautiful large-breasted women I bed, no matter how many sheep I befriend, no matter how many times I yank my pud, no matter . . ."

"I get it," the blind fairy troll interrupted. "I can help you with that."

"You can?" Pirate Dave was ecstatic. "If you can help me, I will restore your sight. I am a time-traveling vampire warlock, after all," he boasted.

"That sounds fair." The little troll nodded his bulbous head. "Go ahead and give me back my vision and then I will take care of your wanker. It would be far wiser if I could see before I deal with your skin flute."

Pirate Dave readjusted his rock-hard electric eel and lifted his arms in the air. The blind troll almost passed out from the foul odor wafting from the pirate's pits, but he plugged his nose and went with it. He'd been blind for twelve thousand years. He'd wade through a pile of poop to get his sight back.

Pirate Dave dirty danced and swore profusely. Warlock spells tend to be vigorous and profane. Sweat poured from Dave as he bounced up and down like he was having an epileptic fit. The troll learned seven new swearwords. He tucked that info away for future use. Pirate Dave finished and the blind troll was no longer blind.

"It's your turn now," Pirate Dave bellowed. "You will make the problem with my pork sword go away. Now!"

The troll peered over at Pirate Dave. He was ridiculously handsome in a big, macho, hairy, smelly way. The troll, not one to welsh on a bargain, giggled and turned to the left three times, hopped on his right foot, then his left. Lightning split the sky and a huge wind whipped viciously across the deck of the ship. Three deckhands were blown to sea, never to be heard from again. Pirate Dave didn't care, he just wanted freedom from his ding-dong. He was tired of his life being dictated by the randy desires of his love muscle.

"It is done!" the little troll screamed, laughing maniacally.

Pirate Dave realized the obscene pressure between his manly hairy thighs was gone. A huge grin split his face. His life was his own again. He was free!

He looked down at his lack of erection and froze. Icy fear ripped through his body, causing temporary paralysis, and he screamed like a little girl. He no longer had a hard-on . . . because he no longer had a penis.

"Holy shit," Shoshanna choked, "you castrated the hero."

"Yes, I did," I replied smugly. I couldn't tell if Cecil was trying not to laugh or cry. He buried his head in his hands and rocked silently back and forth.

Evangeline slapped her frosted mauve claw down on the table in our icky pink office and began her tirade. "You cannot have a hero who can't woo and have sex with the large-breasted heroine," she shrieked.

"I didn't say he couldn't have sex anymore." I pulled my feet up on the couch Indian style and waited for her to combust.

"She didn't say that," Shoshanna agreed.

"Shut up, Sudoku," the Botox Bitch hissed. "How can a man have sex without the proper plumbing? Cecil," she shouted, knocking him out of hiding. "You're a man . . . well, kind of," she sneered. "Can a man have sex without an organ?"

Cecil colored fiercely and his hands clenched into fists. I was missing something about their relationship. Something bad. "I'm not sure," he said quietly. "It's Rena's story. If she says he still can, then he still can."

"It's not Rena's story, it's mine," Evangeline ground out between clenched teeth. "I won't remind any of you of that again. If you make that necessary, I will destroy you and everything you hold dear. Am I clear?" She pointed her nasty claw at us and waited.

We nodded. I had never hated anyone so much in my life.

"So," she purred, "Rika, if the hero has no equipment, how does he satisfy the heroine?"

That was actually a good question, but in the land of "I'm going to destroy your career," there's always a perfect answer. I simply needed to take a breath and start talking. Not knowing what would come out hadn't been a problem yet . . . "He's a vampire," I stated, as if that would solve it.

"So?" she shot back.

"Clearly you don't know the rules of the vampire." I stayed in my casual pose on the couch and spoke condescendingly to the skank.

"Yes, I do," she insisted, examining her manicured claws.

"I beg to disagree. If you knew the folklore of the magical undead, you would know that if you cut something off of a vampire . . . um, two will grow back in its place."

Shoshanna stood on shaky legs and excused herself to the bathroom. I was fairly sure she had just peed herself again. Quite honestly, I almost peed myself after that new nugget of information flew out of my mouth. Cecil went back to rocking.

"Yes, yes." Evangeline's eyes sparkled with excitement. "I had forgotten about the double regeneration of the Blood Drinkers. I read about that in *National Geographic* a while back."

"Of course you did." I smiled sweetly.

"I did," she barked. "You think you're so smart, but you're not."

"Then you must also be aware that a vampire, especially a time-traveling warlock vampire, can self-combust into a gooey green globule if he doesn't masturbate regularly."

"Don't be ridiculous," she said, "everyone knows that. I've known that for years."

"Good, then we should talk about product placement."

"Product placement?" She seemed confused.

Cecil's head shot up. I could swear he looked at me with admiration in his sad eyes, but I had to be mistaken. He was on her team and I still worried he'd clue her in. I ignored him and turned to my nemesis.

"Yes, it's similar to what they do in the movies. I figure you could make a fortune by advertising within your books. It's never been done. You will be on the cutting edge." I didn't bother to mention that it was the cutting edge of obscurity and ridicule. I didn't feel that was necessary information at this time.

"How is it done?" Her greedy, permanently open eyes got alarmingly wider.

I sucked in a quick breath and tried to squash down the fear that looking at her ignited in me. "We add things like, 'The pirates ate a bucket of Bucky's Fried Chicken and washed it down with a Smeerbeer followed by some Dancin' Donna Donuts and some orange Yummyade.' Stuff like that."

"But I've never heard of any of those products."

"You've gotta be kidding me," I said leveling her with a look. She grew uncomfortable and fidgety under my surprised stare.

"Oh, silly me," she said tapping her brainless head, "Of course I know those products. I use them all the time! But how did they get all those things? They live in 1492."

Shit. "Yes, well . . . that's why I added the time-traveling element. Pirate Dave can, um, pop back and forth to the future and go to drive-through windows of different restaurants." I stared up at the ceiling, waiting to be busted.

"Does he know how to drive?" she inquired.

"Yes."

I'd gone too far. The silence in the room was ominous and I started to sweat. Damn it, maybe I should have stopped at the double penis thing . . .

Evangeline stood and began to wobble her way around the room. I fully expected her to strike me at any moment. I tried to make myself as small as possible. Her eyesight seemed pretty bad . . . maybe she'd miss.

"Brilliant," she roared, scaring the hell out of me. "I will be the richest, smartest, most sought-after author of this century and the next. I will give you a list of the products that shall be in the story."

"Oookay," I stuttered. "You should probably give me about three hundred or so and I will insert them everywhere."

"I was thinking more like five hundred."

"Even better." I nodded solemnly.

"Yes, well, I am an experienced businesswoman. I wouldn't expect someone like you to understand the importance of quantity."

"I am learning so much from you. Thank you." I bowed my head in reverence and so she wouldn't see the shit-eating grin on my face.

"You're welcome. Cecil," she snapped, "you will escort me to my chambers and I will develop a list so the hired help can continue crafting my story."

"Very well, Madame," he said. He took her bony arm and they left.

I collapsed on the couch in a fit of giggles until I heard Shoshanna talking to herself out in the hallway . . . only her conversation wasn't one sided. She was being dressed down by Evangeline. I moved quietly to the door. I would take that bitch out if she hurt LeHump.

"So you think you're free now that your illegal, gay, Canadian, terrorist ex-husband has a green card," the Viper laughed. "Well, I'm here to tell you, you're not."

"Canadian terrorist is actually an oxymoron," Shoshanna informed her.

"What did you call me?" Evangeline shouted.

"Oh my God," I heard Shoshanna mutter. "Generally speaking, Canadians are pacifists, so terrorist and Canadian do not belong in the same sentence."

Logic evidently confused Evangeline because there was a prolonged moment of silence while she thought of a comeback. "Whatever," she barked. "Your obsession with gay terrorists is not my problem, but I am still your problem."

"And how's that?" Shoshanna asked calmly.

"If you desert your duty, I will destroy your troops. Utterly and completely," she spat triumphantly.

"You do realize there is a dungeon reserved for you in Hell," Shoshanna said.

"Take that back, you nasty old woman," Evangeline seethed with mounting rage.

"I take it back." I could hear the steely edge in Shoshanna's voice. "It's not actually a dungeon, it's just a hole. A hole in Hell, crawling with worms and maggots and other truly nontalented, hideous, stupid people just like you."

"Sticks and stones," the Viper laughed. "Sticks and stones may break my lovely bones, but names will never hurt me. Just remember that, Sue. I own you and all your little friends."

"You don't own Rena. You're paying her."

"Oh, you'd be surprised at the way things turn around, Shosheshe. I don't pay people, people pay me. When you rule the world like I do, everything goes your way. Always."

I heard her stilettos click down the pink marble hall and fade away. I quickly ran back to the couch. Should I let Shoshanna know what I'd heard? No . . . if she wanted to tell me she would.

It took her a few minutes, but my little friend came back into the room as if the hellish hallway conversation had never happened. She was pale, but had a big smile on her face . . . all for my benefit. I was sure I couldn't have loved her any more than I did in this moment. This crazy profane woman was one of the best things that had happened to me in a long time. I was more determined than ever to bring Evangeline's career down in a roaring inferno.

"You made me wet my pants again," Shoshanna laughed. "We need to copyright your warped brain."

"I'm pretty sure you won't make any money off that"—I grinned—"but it could land you a suite in the mental hospital."

"And those products! Were any of those real?"

"Nope," I grinned. "Just in case this pile of poo backfires and lands on us, I don't want to get sued."

"Brilliant," Shoshanna cackled and clapped her hands. "It makes the skanky ho look even stupider than she already is. Goddamn, it would be terrifyingly fucking awesome if we could get her to publicly go on record endorsing Smeerbeer and Bucky's Fried Chicken."

"Yep," I giggled.

"You know, if we could focus your ideas, you might make a fine writer one day."

"And if I turn around three times and click my heels together, little green munchkins will jump out of my ass." I rolled my eyes and hugged her. "I'm a terrible writer and I know that. It's just that I'm not happy being an accountant . . . I think I'm searching for a place to feel good and worthwhile. I love numbers, but as you can imagine, I don't fit in very well in the stuffed-shirt corporate world."

"I can't see someone with your mouth working out too well in an office setting," she smirked.

"Hmm, coming from a woman who touts butt plugs, ass-less leather chaps, and uses the word fuck as a noun, verb, pronoun, and adjective, I'll take that as a compliment," I giggled.

LeHump took a bow. "It was meant as one . . . Rena, I was thinking, you probably won't get paid until we finish. Do you need a loan for a car? I'd be happy to help you out and you can pay me back whenever. No worries."

My stomach clenched and my eyes welled with tears. She was trying to help me escape the Viper without having to reveal anything. I loved her so much it made my teeth hurt.

"Um, no, but thanks. My Aunt Phyllis gave me the money."

"The one with the aliens in the gas tank?" she asked.

"One and the same." I grinned, hoping she didn't notice how glassy my eyes had become.

"She sounds like a lovely lady."

"I'm very lucky." I looked directly at Shoshanna. "I am blessed with some very special women in my life. Women I would be lost without."

"Awww, get over here, you little fucker." She pulled me in for a bear hug. "I know a couple of women who would be lost without you, too."

I smiled and let my tears fall onto her Minnesota Vikings sweatshirt. Life may be complicated, but it's still pretty good.

Chapter 12

Saturday morning rolled around bright, sunny, and fucking cold. Poppy Harriet seemed to enjoy the cooler temperatures. Her house was freezing.

"Would you like a sweater?" she kindly asked. I was sure my blue lips prompted her offer.

"Sure," I smiled, taking the hot pink fuzzy sweater from her. Not really my color, but it was nipple-puckering cold in there.

"I'm trying to save money," she apologized for the frigid conditions. "I'm on a fixed income and it's a bit tight right now."

"I love a nice chilly room," I lied. "It keeps me on my toes." The same ones I feared losing to frostbite.

"The girls should be here any minute." She moved nervously around her cute little home rearranging her chintz pillows and crocheted afghans.

"Why are the ladies coming?" My gut clenched in disappointment. They didn't trust me. Possibly my use of the words *johnson* and *skin flute* might have misled them into believing I had a tiny brain. It still made me feel bad that they felt the need to babysit.

"This is going to be a hard day for me, Rena. I need their support. My life is a little . . . ahhh, messy."

Oh shit, that did not sound good. I'd arrived with a light heart and now it was sinking fast. There was so much more to this story than a few name changes. I had a bad feeling today would lead to more illegal activity on my part. Having a kind-of sort-of date with a cop tonight only made everything worse.

"Do you want to tell me anything before the gals get here?" I asked, hoping to find out what crime I was about to commit.

"No."

"Do you want to give me the paperwork so I can get started?"

"No."

"Do you want to cut a hole in your floor and do some ice fishing?"

"No," Poppy Harriet laughed, tossing me one of the many afghans placed around the room. "Rena, I'm sorry. I'm nervous and a bit gassy from stress."

A little too much information, but she was truly distressed. A change of subject was in order. "So Poppy Harriet, have you ever been married?"

"No, I was never lucky enough to have any gentlemen suitors." She dropped her eyes to the carpet to hide her embarrassment.

God, I felt like an ass. I should probably stick to the weather. With Poppy Harriet looking away, I was really able to study her. She was attractive in a big-boned way, fit, stylish. I loved the little neck scarves she always wore. She must have a ton. Every time I saw her, she was wearing a color-coordinated neck scarf tied in a jaunty little knot at her throat. Her personality was a hoot; she was funny and loving and kind. What in the hell was wrong with men? I wondered if her upper lip had been a source of ridicule when she was younger. I would love for her to let me wax it . . . She did get a tad touchy about things. Bringing up her hairy upper lip might send her into a tailspin.

"What do you write?" I asked, hoping that this subject would cheer her up. I realized I had no idea what her genre was. I knew Nancy was a cookbook queen and Shoshanna loved the whips and chains, but Joanne and Poppy Harriet were still a mystery to me.

She blushed a sweet pink and lowered her eyes. "Last month my amorous tool manual came out."

"Amorous tools?"

"Love tools," she giggled.

"You mean like vibrators and stuff?" I asked out of sheer politeness. I feared her answer the same way I feared Bryant Gumbel.

"Oh, mercy me, no. I'm talking about garden-variety things you can find at your local hardware store to spice up your love life."

"Like what?" Why did my mouth keep moving before my brain could stop it? Although, it was fascinating. Train wreck fascinating.

"Paintbrushes, garden hoses, lawn gnomes."

"Wow," I feigned interest. Thankfully I was able to stop myself from asking how one would use a lawn gnome during sex. Unfortunately I knew I would ponder that one for years to come.

"It's the only thing I can publish that she doesn't want." Her voice broke and she fiddled with her neck scarf.

"You mean Evangeline?"

"Yes," she said flatly. "What I really write is beautiful sweeping sagas about Highlanders. Historicals with breathtakingly brave heroines and handsome, complicated heroes. I adore complex stories where not everything is as it initially seems. My villains are evil, though not at first; eventually they always go down. Violent deaths are a specialty of mine, as well as romantic sex scenes. I'm so in love with Ireland and Scotland. I set most of my novels there because of the mystical beauty and the magnificent landscapes."

"Can I read one?" I asked, blown away by her description. Her books sounded amazing. There was so much more to her than met the eye.

"If you go to O in the romance section of the bookstore, you'll see ten of my novels." Her eyes clouded with tears and her voice was soft.

"I don't understand."

Before she could answer, the front door flew open and the babysitting brigade arrived.

"Holy fucking hell," Shoshanna grunted. "It's colder than a witch's tit in here."

"Poppy dear"—Nancy shivered—"you really must turn the heat up. I'm afraid you'll catch pneumonia."

"Holy Lutheran Jesus," Joanne moaned, bringing up the rear. "I can see my breath. It's warmer outside."

"I'm sorry, girls, but you know I'm on a budget," Poppy Harriet reminded them.

Shoshanna, in a fit of pique, slapped a wad of bills on the table. "My treat, turn up the damn thermostat."

"Fine," Poppy Harriet laughed. "This wasn't such a problem when you ladies were in menopause."

"That was about twenty years ago," Joanne muttered, turning the temperature up to eighty.

"I made a cheese log and I've got some chili going in the Crock-Pot. Does anyone want something to drink?" Poppy Harriet asked.

"Coffee." Nancy was still shivering. "Come on, dear. I'll help you make it."

I wrapped the afghan tighter around me, wishing I'd worn more appropriate clothes, but I hadn't known I'd be visiting Antarctica. LeHump and Joanne grabbed fleece blankets from a stash behind the couch and hunkered down next to me.

"This sucks," LeHump moaned. "How in the hell does she live like this?"

"I have no idea." Joanne was trembling.

"Hey, why are Poppy Harriet's Highlander books in the O section?" I asked, moving closer to Joanne, hoping her larger frame would give off more heat than tiny little Shoshanna's.

"Because they're under O'Hara. Evangeline Slag-ass O'Hara," Joanne fumed. "That horrid woman stole ten books from Poppy Harriet and now she can barely afford to heat her house."

A wave of nausea washed through me and my mood veered sharply to anger. "You're kidding me."

"No, I'm not." She shook her head regretfully. "I wish I was. And now the damn IRS is after her."

"I told her she can come live with me now that Kevin is moving out, but she won't hear of selling her house. It belonged to her mother." Shoshanna shrugged her shoulders and burrowed deeper into her blanket.

IRS. Shit. Maybe I could figure out a way she could get some money back from the government . . . she said she'd paid her taxes, so if she was being truthful, the IRS couldn't touch her. Faking more confidence than I felt, I got up and went to Poppy Harriet's desk. I assumed the large box labeled IRS Bastards would be a good place to start. The ladies turned on the TV and got immersed in Jerry Springer, and I went to work. I was grateful no one was looking over my shoulder. Maybe they did trust me.

The "bastard" box was filled with unopened letters from the Internal Revenue Service and the state of Minnesota Treasury Department. There must have been forty or so sealed envelopes there, dating back almost twenty years. WTF? That was odd, but even more strange, they were addressed to Walter Garski. Who in the hell was Walter Garski? Did Poppy Harriet file with her husband? Wait, she'd said she was never married. Had she lied? Maybe he was an abusive son of a bitch and she pretended he didn't exist . . .

maybe he was a serial fornicator like my Uncle Fucker and she refused to acknowledge their union . . . maybe she'd filed illegally with a friend named Walter. Why in the hell would she do that? Had to be a husband.

"Guys, what's Poppy Harriet's legal name?" I asked, searching her desk for more clues.

"Garski," Shoshanna said, while shushing me with her hands. "Jerry's about to reveal the baby daddy."

"I think it's Carlos," Joanne whispered, eyes glued to the television.

"No," LeHump insisted, "it's Sean. He has a lot of tattoos." The silence, while Jerry took his time opening the paternity test, was killing the ladies. "Open the fucking thing," Shoshanna hissed at the TV. "No goddamn way," she shouted, "I didn't think Billy Bob was even in the running."

"I feel taken advantage of," Joanne huffed.

Oh my God. They're crazy, but at least my suspicions were confirmed. Poppy Harriet had been married. I was a little stymied as to why she didn't want to tell me, but we'd cross that bridge over coffee. Maybe he was dead. I felt uncomfortable opening a strange, possibly deceased man's mail, but if I was going to help, I needed to see what the hell the IRS wanted. Opening someone else's mail was a federal offense. Hopefully my crime spree would be limited to only this.

Envelope after envelope contained checks. Refund checks made out to Walter Garski. And there were letters, inquiring why the checks had not been cashed. I wondered if there was a statute of limitations on the checks. There had to be close to a hundred thousand dollars in undeposited checks there. If Poppy Harriet wanted to live a far more comfortable life, she would have to acknowledge her marriage to Walter Garski. And if he was dead, I'd need a death certificate and a marriage license. This might turn out to be a no-brainer.

"Poppy Harriet could have saved herself a lot of stress if she had opened these." I held the wad of envelopes up to the couch potatoes.

"She never opened anything?" LeHump sounded surprised.

"Nope, she just assumed the IRS was after her." I grinned, happy to have figured this out so quickly. "Can you guys tell me anything about her husband?"

"Her husband?" Joanne choked out, looking as if I'd asked to skin her alive. Clearly this Walter Garski was a very bad man. No wonder Poppy Harriet wanted to pretend she'd never married. "Um . . . well, she ahh . . ." Joanne yanked violently at the newly grown fuzz of her eyebrows.

"Hey, it's okay," I said, letting her know I suspected the worst of Poppy Harriet's ex or current husband. "I'm assuming this Garski guy was or is a class A fucker. Poppy Harriet pretends she's never been married. I get it. I just have to get her to admit to their union so we can cash these checks. There's around a hundred thousand dollars here. Is he alive?"

"Um, yes." Shoshanna's eyes were wide.

God, is he as awful as Evangeline?

"LeHump"—Joanne bounced with excitement—"that sounds like enough for the operation."

"Not now," Shoshanna told her.

"Oh my God," I gasped, "does Poppy Harriet need an operation?"

"Not exactly," Shoshanna muttered vaguely.

Jesus Christ in high heels, what in the hell was going on here? Were they hiding Poppy Harriet's illness from me because they thought I couldn't handle it? My hurt and worry dissolved into anger. The ladies needed to cough up the info, or I was out of here.

"Then who needs an operation?"

"Walter Garski does." LeHump refused to meet my eyes.

"Her husband?" I asked, determined to get an answer.

"He's not her husband," Joanne whispered, trying to find more eyebrow fuzz to pull out.

"Then who in the fuck is Walter Garski?" I shouted.

The crash in the kitchen was loud, but the shrieks were louder. A freaked-out Poppy Harriet trailed by a wild-eyed Nancy came barreling into the room.

"What have you done?" Poppy Harriet sobbed, pacing the room like a caged animal.

"We haven't done anything," Shoshanna snapped. "Now sit your ass down. This IRS crap ends today."

"And so does my life," Poppy Harriet wailed.

"You're fine," Joanne shouted so she could be heard over the ear splitting blubbering. "We trust her. You trust her. She's going to save us from the Viper Bitch Whore from Hell."

I was fairly sure she was referring to me and of course Evangeline. It was nice to know they trusted me. But what secret could be so awful that Poppy Harriet found it necessary to moan and rock as if the world was ending? They all started talking at once. I was this close to having an aneurysm.

"Everyone be quiet," I bellowed. The chatter ceased. Wide eyes peered at me. They looked like naughty toddlers and I bit back inappropriate laughter. "I'll start . . . Poppy Harriet, the IRS is not after you. You are not going to jail, at least not for tax evasion." I did wonder if maybe she had killed or maimed Walter Garski and that's what all the fuss was about. Maybe they all had something to do with it. Fuck, not going to go there. I was going to stick to the facts I'd found in the IRS Bastard box. "Apparently your husband or brother or some kind of relation, Walter Garski, hasn't cashed his refund checks for almost twenty years . . . to the tune of a hundred thousand dollars. I'm not sure if the checks are still good, but I'm sure they can be reissued with proof of backup tax returns. I'm going to take a guess he's not dead because his last refund check is from this year, which means he filed. Am I correct?"

A very pale Poppy replied with a slight nod.

"All right, good," I continued in a businesslike manner. "Are you related to this Walter Garski?"

Even paler, she gave me another almost imperceptible nod. God, this dude must be one awful son of a bitch. Poppy was terrified.

"You're going to have to tell me who this Walter Garski is if you want me to help you," I told her gently.

"No."

"Does anyone else want to jump in here?" I looked around the room at the tight-lipped group.

"It's not our tale to tell," Nancy said, taking Poppy Harriet's hand in hers. "Tell her, Poppy dear, she will understand. She won't judge and she will still love you, just like we do." Nancy gave me a warning look, indicating I would behave exactly as she said. I nodded and Nancy's face relaxed.

Poppy Harriet expelled a giant, tragic sigh and began to untie her smart little neck scarf, revealing a huge Adam's apple. WTF? How could Poppy Harriet have an Adam's apple? Only men have . . . holy fuck.

"Um . . . Walter?" I asked Poppy, tentatively.

"I'm not Walter," she shrieked. "I'm Poppy Harriet. I hate Walter." She clutched her throat, hiding her Adam's apple.

"Poppy Harriet," Nancy admonished gently. "Rena is here to help you."

"Oh, I'm so sorry, Rena," she sniffled. She inhaled deeply and popped all her knuckles. "Yes, I was born Walter Garski, but I always knew God made a mistake. I was in the wrong body."

Her tears fell unchecked. Nancy lovingly rubbed her back. "Go on, dear," Nancy urged.

"Twenty years ago, after my mother died, I decided to live as a woman. I am a female with the wrong plumbing fixtures." She smiled weakly.

"Do you have any other family?" I asked.

"Yes," she hesitated, "I do, but they think I disappeared years ago. I assume they think I'm dead by now."

"But you're living in your mother's house," I shook my head in confusion.

"Walter sold it to me."

"I see," I answered as if that made a modicum of sense. "Did your family know about your, um, other half?"

"Oh, dear heavens, no. And they can't ever know. They're Polish."

I had no idea what that had to do with anything, but knew far better than to ask.

"Poppy Harriet, you have a hundred thousand dollars and . . ."

She cut me off, "No. Walter Garski has a hundred thousand dollars. I am not Walter Garski."

"No," I agreed, "you're not, but without Walter Garski, there would be no Poppy Harriet . . . and the world wouldn't be quite as nice."

She wrapped her sporty scarf back around her neck and placed her hands primly in her lap. "What do you want me to do?"

"Well, I think if you could, um . . . you know, make friends with

Walter and ask him to, um, sign the checks, I could have them cashed for you and we could stop freezing our asses off."

"I'm not sure I can do that. It would be illegal . . . I'd be impersonating a man," she calmly and logically explained.

I was speechless.

"Goddamn it, Poppy," LeHump groused, "sign the checks. It's your money. We're the only ones who know about Walter and . . ."

Joanne cleared her throat loudly. Nancy punched her in the arm and shushed her. "Not now, Joanne." She was using her "don't fuck with me" voice.

She didn't need to say anything; I had already figured it out. Evangeline knew Poppy Harriet was a man and that's why ten of Poppy's books were sitting on the O shelf at the bookstore. I didn't think my hatred could grow, but my contempt for the Viper knew no bounds.

"We won't look," I told Poppy Harriet. "Just go over there and sign the checks. Next week we will legally change Walter Garski's name to Poppy Harriet or whatever the hell you want. You will keep his social security number, so you will be legal, and next year you'll be able to sign your tax returns as Poppy Harriet." I gave her a gentle push.

"It's that easy?" Shoshanna asked.

"I'm pretty sure." I smiled. "Everyone look down or turn away so Poppy Harriet can have some privacy."

She grabbed my arm in a vise-like grip and swung me around like a rag doll to face her. Damn, she was strong. I don't know how in the hell I didn't guess her secret: the big hands, hairy lip, the low voice . . . "I don't think I can do this." She was getting hysterical and her grip tightened.

"Poppy Harriet, if you don't let go of my arm, I'll have to get it amputated." I winced, but tried to keep my voice steady. Riling her up more could be unintentionally life-threatening.

"I'm sorry." She let go, puffed out her silver curls, ran her hands over her hips, and adjusted her breasts. Having to sign checks as Walter was fucking with her femininity.

"Think of it this way," I said, vigorously trying to rub the circulation back into my arm. "Soon Walter will be gone forever. Let him give you this parting gift. It would be a shame to let all this

money go to waste. Maybe you could make an anonymous donation to a transgender support group."

"Or you could have your penis removed," Joanne volunteered.

"Oh, for God's sake, Joanne," Shoshanna groused, "if you put
your foot any further into your mouth, it's going to come out of
your ass."

"That's just mean," Joanne huffed, giving Shoshanna the bird.

I fully expected a slapping bitch fight to start any moment. I ran
my hands through my hair and backed up into the corner. Getting
in the middle of an old lady brawl was not my idea of a good time.

"No. Wait," Poppy Harriet shouted, stopping the smackdown
before it could start. "She's right. With that money I could become
who I really am."

The window of opportunity was open and I climbed through.
"You could think of it as Walter's present to you. Proof of his love
and approval . . ."

"You're right." Her smile broadened and her entire body tensed
with excitement. She paced the room again, but it was different this
time. Her energy and joy bounced off the walls.

"You just need to, um, bring Walter back long enough for him
to sign the checks. Can you do that?" Crossing my fingers behind
my back in hopes that the drama was over, I waited for the other
shoe to drop, for Poppy Harriet's head to start spinning or for a
tantrum about hating Walter to destroy the progress we had made.

"I can do that," she sang with intense pleasure. "Give me those
checks."

I love being wrong. I handed her the checks and she signed
every one of them. "I'll deal with the statute of limitations. There's
a tax specialist at my firm that will be able to get this done quickly.
Do you have copies of your, um, I mean Walter's past returns?"

"Yes, I do." She grabbed a large box from beneath her desk and
shoved it into my arms. "I'd be delighted for you to get this shit out
of my house," she said with a grin.

"I'm on it." I grinned back. "Poppy Harriet, do you mind me
asking how Walter made so much money over the years?"

"Not at all. He owns a chain of hardware stores. You know, the
garden-variety kind." She winked at me and pointed to the gnome
sitting on top of her upright piano.

I rolled my eyes and wondered again how the smiling gnome figured into sex and decided I never wanted the answer to that one. Wait a minute . . . "Poppy Harriet, if Walter has so much in refunds, he must have one hell of a bank account."

"Yes, he does."

"Then why in the hell are you living in the tundra?" I demanded, completely confused.

"It's Walter's money, not mine," she said.

"I think it's time you and Walter had a little talk. Who's been managing all these stores over the years?" I asked.

"People I hired," she said sheepishly. "I work for Walter and receive a small salary to keep all the stores in line. He travels quite a bit and can't actually do the day-to-day." She smiled as if what she said was reasonable and sane.

"Have any of the people who work for Walter ever met him?" I had no idea what would come out of her mouth next, but I knew it would be memorable.

"Oh dear God, no, he's agoraphobic." She shook her head in disgust. All the ladies stared openmouthed. My mouth followed suit.

"Um, Poppy Harriet, would you mind terribly if I had Walter's accounts changed to your name?" I waited for an explosion . . .

She was quiet for several long moments. The girls and I held our breath.

"That would be lovely," she said. "It would make everything so much easier. I'll just let everyone know Walter died and left me everything."

I expelled the breath I'd been holding. "Okay, great."

"Well now you can turn the fucking heat up and leave it that way," Shoshanna grunted.

I smiled and watched all my little ladies hug and cry with each other. A stranger morning I'd never had, but in the end it turned out . . . strange. Good, but definitely strange.

After eating a small amount of cheese log and chili, Shoshanna and Nancy insisted on car shopping with me. Dread ripped through my stomach at the thought of Shoshanna cussing out someone at the dealership, or it could have been the chili. My fears were unfounded. Nancy turned out to be a shark negotiator, and I ended up with an icy blue SUV for well under list price. Nancy could have a lucrative side business as a car negotiator. She's so damn nice the poor car guys didn't realize what they had agreed to until it was too late. There were some tears, but shockingly enough, they weren't LeHump's fault. They were Nancy's. She hugged all the car salesmen she'd bested and told them how wonderful they were and how proud she was of them. By the time we left, everyone had stopped crying. Except for the general manager. He would be crying for a week or so.

I knew I'd chosen the color of my brand spanking new car because of Jack's eyes. That pissed me off some, but what's a girl in lust to do?

After hugging my gals, I drove away in my new wheels, heading home to worry about the evening ahead. Everything had gone so well today that I knew my evening would more than likely blow up in my face. Oh well, two out of three ain't bad.

Chapter 13

Driving my new car to my childhood home felt good. Really good.

Thank God for that, because the evening ahead filled me with angst and was making my eye twitch. I need to relax. I certainly didn't want to show up at my folks' and be questioned about my new tic. I would have enough thrown at me without the addition of a neurological disorder.

"Why in the fuck did I eat Jack's card?" I asked my steering wheel. It didn't answer. The card-eating disaster kept biting me in the butt, hard. I wanted to talk out our history and get our lies straight. I was used to winging it on my own, but winging it in tandem scared the hell out of me. Of course, I couldn't call him because I didn't have his number. I didn't even know his last name, for Christ's sake.

Stepping out of the car, I adjusted my rockin' hot flannel miniskirt and pulled my knee-high boots up. I'd dressed with care, but not because I gave a damn what Jack thought. I didn't want my family to think I wasn't serious about my fake boyfriend because I'd showed up in sweatpants. Who was I kidding? I adjusted my cashmere sweater with more force than necessary and admitted I'd worn a very formfitting top on purpose. I wanted him to suffer. Jack would be punished for making me use Vinnie the Vibrator the other night.

I stared up at my parents' home and wondered what Jack would think. We lived in Hennepin County, one of the ritziest suburbs of Minneapolis, but our home wasn't a nouveau riche McMansion. It was a pretty, classic Hampton design home, bought by my parents long before Edina had become so popular. I sucked in a large amount of oxygen because I knew my sister Jenny would be hogging it inside. I forced my feet to move and walked up the path, prepared to lie my ass off.

"Rena, you look gorgeous." Mom grinned and raised her eyebrows, waggling them suggestively. Shit, this was going to be more painful than I'd thought. "Your boyfriend is lovely. I hope you don't mind me inviting him to dinner." She gave me her pouty face, daring me to answer her truthfully.

"Um, no. That's okay," I muttered, looking for some food to shove in my mouth to avoid having to speak. "He's not here yet, is he?" I grabbed the side of the granite kitchen countertop in alarm. God, the things my family could tell him, without my running interference, made me shudder.

"No, sweetie pie, he's not. I thought you would arrive together." She waited for a response. I decided not to give her one.

"Rena," Aunt Phyllis yelled from the great room, "did you and Jack get back together?"

"Why am I the last to hear about these things?" Mom huffed, giving me that look. The one that implies I've wounded her mortally and she will never recover. It used to work when I was little, but by the time high school rolled around, I had her number. Now it just makes me feel itchy.

"We're fine," I said loudly enough for Aunt Phyllis to hear. I searched the counter for food. Nothing. What in the hell was going on? Mom usually laid out enough to feed and kill an army. Normally I avoid the Crock-Pot dips, but tonight I'd wolf one in its entirety to get out of conversing. "Where's all the food?"

"It's in the dining room, I thought we'd be a little fancier tonight." She chuckled like she'd made a good one. Thank Jesus I didn't get my sense of humor or irony from her.

"Are Jenny and Dirk here?" I asked, hoping my sister was too bloated or her roots were too heinous for her to come this evening.

"Oh yes, sweetie. They've been here for an hour. They don't want to miss a minute of you and your new beau."

"I bet they don't." I grabbed a beer out of the fridge and slammed it shut. I shouldn't have come. I should have waited outside for Jack, told him my family had leprosy, and sent him on his merry way. After I boinked him in my new car.

"Oh, honey bunch, you're not going to drink, are you?" Mom's hands fluttered nervously as she wiped down the spotless countertop with an oven mitt.

"Why?" I narrowed my eyes and waited for her frightening logic.

"Well, um, you're a bit of a lightweight . . ."

"And?" I dared her to continue, knowing what was coming.

"There was that time you drank a little teensy-weensy bit too much and decided streaking would be a good idea."

"Mom," I ground out between clenched teeth, "that was my twenty-first birthday. I found my college roommate in bed with my boyfriend, and I didn't get into my first choice for graduate school. Suffice it to say, that was a really bad day. Not to mention, it was almost ten years ago."

She brought up the streaking incident every time I took a sip of alcohol. I did understand that some of my past choices had been creative, but having to live them down for an eternity was not fair. I smiled, took a huge swig of beer, and left the kitchen. There was only so much a girl could take . . . and it was only six-thirty. Shit.

The kitchen opened into the great room, which opened into the dining room. Basically, the first floor was a wide-open space with a few half walls and a couple of load-bearing ones. It's beautiful, cozy, and warm. Unless my sister is inhabiting some of the space.

Aunt Phyllis and Dad were by the huge flagstone fireplace in the middle of an intense game of dominos. They took their gaming seriously. It's the only time my dad can tolerate Aunt Phyllis. She rarely brings up aliens when she's concentrating on kicking my dad's ass. The dominos would lead to chess and chess would degenerate into what I like to refer to as Profane Poker. It's no wonder I have a mouth like I do . . . For God-fearing Lutherans, my family can swear up a shit storm.

Interrupting their game could result in loss of body parts, so that left my sister to talk to. Crap.

"Hi Rena," Jenny smirked, rubbing her belly while shoving some kind of cheese dip into her piehole. There was a little of it on her chin. Should I tell her? Hmmm.

"Hi Jenny, you look lovely tonight." I smiled, hoping the cheese hardened and stayed there forever.

Her eyes narrowed dangerously. "What's on my face?" she demanded.

Damn it, I shouldn't have complimented her. It was a dead giveaway that something was off. I decided to be nice; maybe she'd cut me some slack when Jack got here. "Cheese on your chin."

She went to wipe it off.

"Your other one." I couldn't help myself, it was just too easy.

"Oh my God, you're such a butthole. I can't wait till you get pregnant. I will give you hell every day," she hissed.

"How will that be different from any other day?" I had a point. Yes, I was a bitch to her, but she usually started it and gave it back ten times worse.

"Oh shut up." Her mouth pulled into a sour grin. "Dirk, will you get me an apple juice? Now."

I hadn't even realized Dirk was in the room. If you weren't careful you could sit on him by accident. He was that quiet and that unobtrusive. I wondered how he stayed married to my sister, but some guys like girls who boss them around. Shoshanna made a living writing about girls dominating guys. Of course those gals use whips and butt plugs, but the basic principle is the same.

Dirk ran from the room like there was a fire. "Wow, that seems like a healthy relationship." I plopped down on the chair, grinning at my evil sister.

"What in the hell would you know about relationships?" she snapped. "You can't keep a boyfriend more than two weeks."

"That's a bit of an exaggeration." I raised my eyebrow in preparation for the kill. "At least I've had boyfriends. You married the first person to ask you out on a date. Oh, wait a minute"—I slapped myself on the forehead—"he didn't ask you out, you asked him. Sorry, I always get that part mixed up."

"No problem," she sneered, "at least he doesn't have a rap sheet."

I couldn't be sure if she was talking about me or one of my former boyfriends. Either way, the shoe fit. Damn, we're a loving family.

"So, your boyfriend Jack, I hear he's a cop." She'd run out of crackers, so she scooped her finger into the cheese dip and stuck it in her mouth. God, that was disgusting. "I didn't think you went for law-abiding citizens."

"I didn't think you went for manners," I shot back, realizing my comeback didn't quite make sense, but I seem to have made my point. Jenny turned a fabulous shade of crimson and placed her cheesy fingers in her lap.

"You said he was in communications. Can't you keep your boyfriends straight?" She smiled and I squirmed. Why couldn't I have a nice sister? Or maybe the question should be, why couldn't she?

"He is," I mumbled. "He's a cop communicator." Shit, that was lame.

"Interesting." She rolled her eyes. I could see her doctor brain working. It was probably a good time for me to lose an arm by interrupting my dad and aunt. "So," she continued, enjoying herself, "his last name isn't Snuffleupagus. What is his last name?"

Why in the hell would she ask me the one question I couldn't make up a lie for? "Why does his last name matter?" I tried to turn the tables.

"I don't know, I just want to hear you say it." She was barely able to keep the laughter out of her voice. What did she know that I didn't? My stomach started to churn. Instead of answering her, I put my entire hand in the cheese dip and shoved it into my mouth. "Oh my God," she shrieked, "that's gross."

"You should know," I said with a mouthful of dip. "Excuse me, I need a cracker."

I ran to the kitchen, washed off my hand, and chugged a glass of water. I hate cheese dip. My heart was bouncing in my chest like a Mexican jumping bean. Jenny knew something that I didn't. She knew Jack's last name. It must be bad. Crap. How bad could it be? I paced the kitchen and stayed close to the front door. I needed to be the one who let Jack in. I needed to tell him about the communications angle and I sure as hell needed to find out his last name.

"Doorbell," Mom shouted.

"I'll get it," I screeched, running like an Olympic sprinter. "Nobody else move."

Skidding to a halt, I smoothed my sweater, shook my hair so it fell wildly around my face, pinched my cheeks for some color, yanked the door open . . . and time stopped. My breath caught in my throat and my tummy tingled. Why couldn't I ever remember how good-looking he was? He made khaki pants look hot. A long-sleeved blue polo hugged his muscular chest perfectly and his eyes appeared bluer, but the part that made me weak was the leather bomber. Knowing he was a cop who looked like a bad boy sent me over the edge.

"Hi, Rena." He smiled his oh-so-sexy smile and tried to step inside.

I gracelessly shoved him out the front door and shut it behind me. I had no time to admire my fake boyfriend. I needed to get him up to speed and I needed to do it fast. An information quickie, if you will. "You're a cop communicator. I'm not exactly sure what that means, but that's what you are. We met at the library a week ago Thursday and you have no problem with the fact I've been arrested." I paused to take a breath before I fainted. "Wait, do you have a problem with me getting arrested?"

"Which time?" He grinned, backing me up against the solid oak door.

God, he smelled good. "Either," I said, putting my hands on his chest to keep him from getting any closer.

"No, Rena, I have no problems." He tried to swoop down for a kiss, but I wasn't done yet.

"Good. Now what in the hell is your last name?"

"Snuffleupagus."

"No, it's not," I giggled. I liked watching his lips move.

"Okay, you got me. It's Sprat."

I had no idea why Jenny thought Sprat was so funny. Jack Sprat. Jack Sprat. What's wrong with . . . "Oh my God. Really?" I gasped. Could his parents have been so cruel as to have named him after a nursery rhyme? Could I date a nursery rhyme?

"No," he chuckled, "not really."

I expelled a huge sigh of relief. "What is it?"

"Careena. My name is Jack Careena." He watched me for a reaction. I didn't have one. I decided the pregnancy had eaten my sister's brain. His name was fine. "Okay, whatever I say in there, just go with it."

"You got it, baby," he laughed, "but the same goes for you."

The use of the word *baby* made my knees weak, I wondered if I had time to drag him to my new car and christen it. No, that could get awkward. My mom had seen me streak, but she'd never seen me do the nasty. Tonight didn't seem like a good time to introduce that one.

"My family is insane," I warned him.

"I wouldn't expect anything less." He grinned, grabbed my hand, and pulled me inside. The look on my sister's face when she laid eyes on Jack would last me a lifetime. She was salivating and her voice stopped working. My mom was acting like a teenage idiot, and I'm fairly sure Aunt Phyllis grabbed his ass. My dad behaved normally, but the real shocker was Dirk. Apparently, Jack had been a legal expert in a trial Dirk had worked on. They both seemed to admire each other quite a bit. Who knew? I didn't even think Dirk could speak. After some small talk, where I quashed any childhood story my mom or Aunt Phyllis tried to tell, we sat down to dinner. I still wasn't sure I trusted Jack completely, but he was a huge hit with the family.

"So Jack," my Dad said, "where are you from originally?"

"Madison, Wisconsin, sir." Jack looked over and winked at me. I didn't know if that meant he was lying or if he wanted to get in my pants.

My dad's face heated up to an unbecoming red. "I'm going to have to ask you something, son. It pains me to have to do this."

The entire dining room went silent, forks clattered to plates, and all eyes were wide. I had no idea where my dad was going with this, but it didn't bode well. Jack's body tensed, and he looked over at me. I shrugged and prayed to God my dad wasn't going to ask Jack what his intentions were or heaven forbid, if we were sleeping together.

"Are you a Packers or Vikings fan?" my dad asked very seriously. Oh, fuck. Jack's answer would determine whether or not he would be welcome in my parents' home again. I held my breath. If he gave the right answer, they'd expect me to marry him. If he gave the wrong one, they'd start forcing me to go to Lutheran Speed Dating. I didn't know if I could marry someone I thought might secretly have plans to arrest me and destroy my life, but I would gouge my eyeballs out if I had to speed-date guys who couldn't pick up girls anywhere other than church.

"My blood bleeds purple, sir. I'm a Vikings fan through and through."

My family let out a collective sigh of relief and my dad got up and bear-hugged Jack. I was mortified, but Jack found the whole thing funny.

"So Rena says you were in Russia for work." Unfortunately Jenny had found her voice. "What did you think of it?"

Jack glanced over at me, his eyes full of amusement. Was he going to back me up or was I going down in flames? "It was cold," he answered. Jenny laughed like he'd just told the funniest joke in the world. It was embarrassing. Even my dad noticed what a dork she was being.

"Oh Jack, you're so witty," she gushed.

My dad cut her off before she could say something truly horrific. I was sorry he stopped her. It was just getting interesting. "What kind of work were you doing over there?" he asked.

"Um, it was . . ." Jack struggled. I could tell he was uncomfortable lying to my dad. I wasn't.

"It's confidential. He's not allowed to talk about it. I don't even know what he was doing over there, but I know it was dangerous and he risked his life at least six times. He may have even taken a bullet." I looked to Jack for approval, but all I got was a raised eyebrow. Maybe I'd gone too far . . .

"I bet it was KGB," Aunt Phyllis blurted out. "They're trying to use the aliens and cyborgs to spy on our government. The zombies running Wall Street are definitely KGB agents."

"Alrighty then," Mom chirped brightly, ignoring Aunt Phyllis's outburst. "Jack, we're having our fortieth wedding anniversary next Friday night at the club. We'd love to have you there."

This was getting to be too much. Did anyone think to ask me if I wanted him there? No. He might arrest me before next Friday. Then what was he going to do? Go alone? Shit, with the way he was being treated, they'd probably love to have him solo. They wouldn't even notice if I wasn't there . . . "He can't come. He'll be in Iceland on a secret mission."

"Oh shoot," Mom said, truly disappointed. "We'll miss you. Won't we, Rena?"

"Tons," I replied, refusing to make eye contact with Jack.

"Actually," Jack informed the table, "the Iceland trip has been postponed."

My head shot up and I stared daggers at my counterfeit boyfriend. "No, it hasn't," I sweetly shot back.

"I got a phone call on the way over," he said staring straight at me. "The trip is pushed back till next Christmas." Crap, he had me. "So Rena and I would be delighted to come."

Had he emphasized the word *come,* or did I have sex on the brain? I decided to ignore him. My inner slut was starting to invade my brain. Looking at him only made the problem worse.

"Wonderful," Mom trilled. "Jack, do you like krum kaka? I made some for dessert."

"Love it, Mrs. Gunderschlict."

I bet he does. He may be hot, but he's messing up my life. I will have so much damage control to do when he's out of here. I'll probably have to move out of state. Damn him, he has no right to make my family fall in love with him.

My mouth felt like sandpaper as I contemplated the reactions I'd get when I told my family the relationship was a sham. Jenny would be over the moon. Why didn't I go with the leprosy plan? That was a really good plan. I grabbed my glass of water and downed it. I wondered whether anyone would notice if I left.

"Oh my God," Aunt Phyllis screamed at me. "You drank my water."

"Jesus Christ, Phyllis," Dad bellowed, "we have more water."

"No, no, no." She paled and began to pull her hair. "It wasn't just water."

Oh fuck no. Had I just drunk some kind of hallucinogenic? Or maybe an antipsychotic?

Visions of me dancing topless on the dining room table while my family cowered in fear blasted through my head. Jack could now add exhibitionist drug addict to my list of illegal activities.

"What was in the water?" Jack asked Phyllis. His voice was calm, but his tone meant business.

Aunt Phyllis was crying now and murmuring to the invisible friends that were sitting on her plate. It sounded like she was praying . . . Was I going to die? I did feel weird, kind of heavy and droopy.

"Phyllis." Jack's authoritative tone snapped her back to reality.

He knelt in front of her and took her hands in his. "What was in the water?"

"I don't know what it's called," she wailed. "It's in my purse."

"Goddamnit, get her purse, Jenny." Both of my dads were pissed. Jenny and her twin sister, who I didn't know, ran over and grabbed Phyllis's purse. They dug through it and pulled out a bottle. Well, Jenny pulled out one bottle and her pregnant clone pulled out another at exactly the same time. How in the fuck did I not know my sister had a twin?

"Rena doesn't look good," I heard Dirk and his doppelgänger say. Wow, he could speak. He had a really nice voice and so did his brother.

I felt Jack's arms wrap around me. It was wonderful. He was so strong and he smelled so good. I nestled my face into his neck and noticed he had two heads. They were nice heads, but I found it odd I'd never noticed it before. You'd think a girl would remember that her boyfriend had two heads. Hmmm.

"It's a tranquilizer," Jenny said, examining the bottle. "Aunt Phyllis, how many did you put in the water?"

"One," Phyllis said, "only one."

"Good," Jenny replied. Or maybe it was her look-alike. "It won't kill her, but she'll be out for a while."

Jenny was a doctor . . . she would know. Or maybe her twin was the doctor. I couldn't remember.

"Why in the hell did you put a tranquilizer in your water?" my dads yelled at Aunt Phyllis and her carbon copy.

"Because I can't swallow pills," she said, wringing her hands and banging her heads on the table.

"Do I need to take her to the emergency room?" Jack asked Jenny.

"No, these aren't very strong, but Rena doesn't do well with meds. She reacts differently than most. Take her home and let her sleep it off."

"She can stay here," Dad said.

"No, wanna go home. Wanna my bed with Jack's heads. Wanna feed cats," I mumbled, trying to sit up.

"I'll take you home, baby," Jack promised, holding me close. "Does she have a cat?"

"Nope," Jenny laughed. "She'll be okay, Jack. Just give her water when she wakes up and make her eat."

Jenny sounded concerned for me. That couldn't be right. It must be her twin. I had to find out her name, she seemed so nice.

The last thing I remembered was being in Jack's strong arms . . . and I kind of remembered my mom screaming something about killing Phyllis with krum kaka.

Chapter 14

I pushed against something delicious, all hard angles and smooth skin. The weight of something masculine was draped across my hip and something very hard and very large was pressing into my stomach. It was a leg across my hip, but it was something else altogether pushing against my tummy.

This was the best, most realistic dream I'd ever had. Images shot through my mind like a movie. An X-rated porno starring me and Jack.

I moaned as big hands caressed my breasts. My nipples hardened painfully and a slow heat started between my legs and moved through the rest of my overheated body. I ran my fingers over his muscular chest. A light sprinkling of crisp hair tickled the tips.

I opened my sleepy eyes and a shot of adrenaline rushed through my aroused body. His gaze was focused and intense. One corner of his mouth lifted and I knew I was a goner. I stared into the most beautiful eyes I'd ever seen. I was nose to nose with every fantasy I'd ever had.

"Hello, sleepyhead," he murmured as his hands continued their exploration of my body.

I loved this dream, but I had to pee. I rolled over and made my way to the bathroom. Thank God it was connected to my room. I didn't have far to go. I peed and brushed my teeth, while reliving the feeling of Jack's hands roaming my body. I wondered if it would feel as good in real life . . . I couldn't imagine it being better than what I'd just dreamed. It was hot.

Why was I still in my sweater? Last night was a bit fuzzy. I yanked my sweater over my head. My ivory bra and matching thong were super cute. I decided to leave them on and go back to bed. Dang, I hoped I could fall asleep again and pick up on my dream where I'd left off.

I wandered back to my pretty peach bedroom and the big, sexy, shirtless man in my bed . . . WTF?

"Oh my God," I screamed. I slapped my hands over my chest, trying to cover my almost nakedness.

Jack leapt off the bed and tackled me to the ground. He scanned the room quickly and reached for his gun.

"What the fuck are you doing?" I grunted, trying to breathe with two hundred pounds of cop on top of me.

"I thought you were in danger," he whispered, not moving an inch.

"Only of being crushed by you," I gasped.

"But you screamed," he said logically, checking his gun for ammo.

"Yes." I tried to shove him off. "Because there was a man in my bed."

He rolled off me and started laughing.

"You're a dick," I said, trying not to stare at his chest. The same one I'd been running my hands over . . . for real. Oh. My. God.

"Be right back." He hopped up and went to my bathroom.

I crawled to my bed, sure that he'd broken several bones in my rib cage. It took all my energy to get myself back up on the mattress. I was so freakin' tired. God, did I have sex with him? If I had, I didn't remember it. Shit. He must think I'm a ho-bag. Why in the hell did that bother me? Maybe because I'm not a ho-bag . . . not even close.

I talked a much bigger game than I could back up with experience. Sure, I'd had sex before, but only within the confines of a shitty relationship. My problem was my taste in men. I'd never met a man quite like Jack before.

I could be a modern girl, sleep with him, and kick him to the curb before he arrested me for stealing jewels that I didn't know I had. My inner slut writhed in delight at the idea, but the rest of me felt dirty. What did it matter? I didn't like him, I just lusted after him. Big difference. What to do . . . what to do . . .

"Scoot over," he said, helping me move my bruised and battered self. He wrapped his big hard body around my soft, curvier one. The heat of his magnificent bod made my decision. I decided to honor my inner slut and become a modern girl. I had the rest of my life to feel guilty about my lack of morals, but right now . . . I wanted what I wanted.

All of a sudden I felt very awake. The pain from my possibly broken bones disappeared. I turned and faced him. Heat crawled up my neck at my state of undress, but at the urging of my lady bits I ignored my embarrassment.

My arms found their way around his neck and I pressed my lips to his. He sucked in a choppy breath and ran his tongue along the seam of my mouth. My lips parted under his persistent ones. He moaned his approval as his tongue very deliberately and forcefully investigated my mouth.

"God, you taste good," he said, as he did nothing short of make love to my mouth.

I pulled back and gave him the evil eye. "Did you use my toothbrush?"

"Yep." He grinned, making my heart skip three beats.

"That's disgusting," I laughed, trying to wriggle away.

"Yep, but I figured since I'd already had my tongue down your throat, it wouldn't matter." His logic was faultless. "You do taste good," he repeated licking his lips and moving in for more.

I turned my head and giggled, causing his mouth to land by my ear. "I bet you say that to all the girls."

"Nope," he whispered, biting the lobe, "only the ones who eat my card."

Shit, I was never going to live that one down.

His lips made a hot trail back to the corner of my mouth. He was making me dizzy. I tried to pull back to regain my bearings, but that was so not happening. I was going nowhere fast. He held me firmly to his body, leaving no wiggle room. With someone else that would infuriate me . . . with him, it lit my panties on fire.

He made his way from my mouth to my neck. *Ohhhh my God. Can't think, can't think, can't think.* "Jack," I gasped.

"Mmm?" he answered, lightly scraping his teeth along my neck and tightening his grip on my ass.

I cried out and jerked against him, pressing all of my soft into all of his hard. Damn these clothes, if I could just . . . .Wait. Small apartment. Kristy was coming home today. She'd give me hell for taking a random guy to bed, regardless of how hot he was . . .

His mouth and teeth were traveling down my body, leaving a fire burning on every spot they touched. In a haze of lust he released my breasts from my bra, unhooking it smoothly. He stopped, mesmerized.

My body stood at attention for him. Every part of me reached for him. My nipples were so hard, they hurt. I tried to pull myself up to him, but he held me down. He held me down and stared at my body. Normally I'd feel shy, but he made me feel so sexy, I thought I'd burst. His eyes were hooded with desire and I had to remind myself to breathe. My back arched wantonly toward him. I wanted him to touch me. I needed him to touch me.

"Oh my God, you're perfect." His mouth descended to one aching breast; he took my nipple into his mouth and drew long and hard. I whimpered my pleasure, raking my nails across his back.

He licked and nipped until I saw stars. He divided his attention between each breast equally. He pressed the lower half of his body into mine, creating a rhythm that was making my head spin. I frantically grabbed his hair and pulled. I wanted his lips on mine. I slanted my mouth across his, drew his tongue into my mouth, and sucked. He gripped my hips with such force, I cried out. I was at the perfect place between pleasure and pain.

Jack laughed delightedly into my mouth. Cupping the back of my head with one hand and my ass with the other, he flipped us over so I was on top. There was no way to get close enough. I wanted him inside me, but I wanted more. The reality of that scared the hell out of me. I chose to ignore it and let my ho-bag take the wheel.

With great purpose, I slid my lips along his jaw. I nipped his ear and felt his body shudder. I slowly dragged my mouth to his neck. With my tongue, I made tight little circles on his skin, loving the taste of him.

My hands traveled down to the waistband of his pants. I knew what I wanted to do. What I needed to do. He went dead still beneath me. His entire body tensed and though it would seem impossible, his erection got bigger and harder.

His breathing became erratic as I scraped his neck with my teeth. He grabbed my ass with both hands, pressing me into his excitement. Fusing my body to his.

"Rena, don't do this if you're not sure," he moaned.

What in the hell was he talking about? I'd never been surer about anything in my life. I laughed lightly and nipped at his skin, running my tongue along the sweet spot where his neck met his shoulder. My inner slut writhed on top of him. I reached down and gripped him through his pants. I ran my hand up and down the length of him. He was gorgeous.

My pulse quickened to the point I thought my heart would burst. He drew my lips back to his neck. His hands shook and I trembled with raging desire. He smelled so good.

Part of my brain tried to warn me that having sex with him could ruin everything. I was fairly sure my inner slut wrestled the reasonable section of my brain to the ground. She wasn't stopping for logic, she was on a mission and I agreed with her. It was so clear to me. I had never wanted anyone so much. Ever. I began to slowly unbutton his khakis.

"Owww!" I shrieked as he pulled me away from him by my hair. "What are you doing?" I tried to go for his pants again. My need was overwhelming. It burned inside me like an inferno.

He flipped me over and pinned me beneath him. His blue eyes flashed. Even through my fury, I could tell he was fighting every instinct he had. Why was he doing this?

"No," he said forcefully. His voice was husky and pained.

"Why?" I whimpered, embarrassed as hell, but more pissed off than mortified.

"Not this way," he ground out. "You were tranquilized by your aunt last night and I unfairly took advantage of you."

"Wait a minute," I shouted. "We had sex and I don't remember it?" My inner slut split in two like Rumpelstiltskin. She was pissed and so was I. Although, I think she was furious because she didn't remember it . . . I was just furious.

"No," he cut me off. "I'm not that much of an asshole. I touched you and aroused you." He paused and ran his hands through his hair in frustration. "I want you to come to me on equal footing. Not when I unfairly seduce you while you're recovering from being drugged. I want more than just a quick roll in the sack."

Last night's drama flashed before my eyes. Shit, shit, shit. "Oh my God." I flopped back on my pillow and stared at the ceiling. He had to think I was a lunatic. "I'm sorry about my family," I muttered, trying to pull the sheet up so there was a bit of a barrier between us. I chose to ignore the part about him wanting more.

"Don't be sorry. I actually liked them." He smiled and gently helped me with the sheet.

All the tension whooshed out of my body like a flat tire, and I turned into a noodle next to him. I tried to suck it up, but I couldn't . . . I cried. I cried from embarrassment, frustration, and exhaustion. And because he was the hottest, nicest, and most gentlemanly guy I'd ever met . . . and I'd probably fucked everything up.

He held me close and whispered sweet things. He played with my hair and kept me warm with his body.

"Sorry," I whispered, pulling myself together. The atmosphere was in need of some major lightening. "You know"—I smiled sheepishly, wiping my tears with the sheet—"my inner slut is really mad at you right now."

"I adore your inner slut," he laughed. "What I just did was the most difficult thing I've done in my life."

"So I take it you don't want me," I teased.

He took my hand, guided it down to the front of his pants and pressed it against some hard evidence to the contrary.

"I want you, Rena—" He grinned. "I want you a lot."

"Well, too bad. That's never gonna happen," I said flippantly, trying to get out of his embrace.

"Really?" His grin widened. He grabbed me and trapped me underneath him.

"Not fair," I screeched, attempting to wrestle him off of me.

"So not fair," he agreed, staring hungrily at me.

The mood got real serious real fast and the merry-go-round began to spin again . . .

"Hey, what the heck is going on in there?" Kristy called out from the hallway.

We froze.

"Did you hear that?" I asked, making sure my imagination wasn't trying to save me from myself.

"Who is it?" he asked quietly, reaching for his shirt.

"My roommate, Kristy," I whispered.

"Rena"—Kristy sounded concerned—"are you okay?"

"Yep, give me a minute, I'll be right out."

"Oookay," she laughed. "Are you in there with Vinnie?" she asked, making me want to kill myself.

"Who's Vinnie?" Jack's eyes narrowed and he crossed his arms over his chest.

"Oh my God," I said, loving his jealousy, "He's no one you need to worry about." I decided it would be fun to make him think he had some competition. I would pretend Vinnie was my other boyfriend. I suppose technically he was.

"I want to know who this Vinnie guy is," he said, getting pissed. His streak of possessiveness scared the hell out of me and turned me on with a vengeance.

"Nope." I smiled sweetly and put my bra back on. I deliberately adjusted my breasts, enjoying how he had to grab his thighs to keep from assisting me.

"Hey, my Vinnie ran out of batteries," Kristy yelled through the door. "Do you have any extra Cs? Or can I borrow your Vinnie's batteries when you're done?"

"I have no idea what you're talking about," I muttered through a tight jaw. The only satisfaction I had was that Kristy would die when she realized a real live man had just heard what she'd said.

Jack's glee at having busted me was intolerable. He was laughing so hard he had to hop around the room.

"What are you laughing at?" Kristy was confused. "You sound like you have a chest cold."

That would be because it wasn't me laughing. A man who would be dead in about two minutes if he didn't shut up was laughing. "I'll be out in a minute," I said. "Meet you in the kitchen."

"Okay. I brought back some cheese curds and I got the new schedule for the Tommy Bartlett Water Show. They have three waterskiing squirrels now. I knew that would blow your mind."

If she kept talking, Jack would self-combust with laughter. He must be about to run from here screaming. He'd met my family, and found out that I have a vibrator and I love waterskiing squirrels. Shit, I'd run if I were him.

"This is one of the best days I've ever had," he said, still laughing.

"You're an ass."

"Occasionally." He smiled, pulling me to him. "So what are we going to do?"

"I have no idea what you're talking about." I eased out of his embrace and yanked on a pair of jeans.

He drew me back to him. "What are we going to do about you and me?"

I watched him silently. I knew he already had an answer to the question he'd posed. I just hoped it didn't involve me going to the pokey.

"We're going to date," he announced grandly.

"Date?" I tried unsuccessfully to bite back my grin of delight.

"Yes, Rena, date. We will date and I will sweep you off your feet so thoroughly, you will very rationally decide to give up Vinnie and spend the rest of your life with me."

"God"—I rolled my eyes—"someone is certainly full of himself."

"Yes, I am." He grinned.

"Are we dating exclusively?" I narrowed my eyes and waited for some backpedaling.

"I don't know." He watched me carefully. "Are you going to keep seeing Vinnie?"

I picked up a pillow and threw it at him. "That depends . . ." I smiled seductively.

"On what?" he asked tracing my lips with his finger.

"On you." I took his finger into my mouth and sucked. Hard.

"Oh shit," he gasped. He pulled his finger out of my mouth and stared at the ceiling, trying to compose himself. "You are so sexy, I can't think straight." He shook his head and backed away. I could see his brain wheels turning. "If you're going to continue to carry on with Vinnie . . . you're not getting into my pants."

"Oh my God." I hurled another pillow at him. "That's going to be so much harder, pun intended, for you than me."

He yanked me flush with his very aroused body and pressed his lips to my ear. "We'll see who it's harder for."

With one final grind that shot through me like a rocket, he lifted me up, tossed me on the bed, and finished dressing himself. He was so wrong if he thought he was getting the last word. So wrong. My mind believed me, but my body was still too busy throbbing from his expert handling to agree.

"Come on, sex kitten. Let's go embarrass your roommate." He held out his hand and smirked evilly. Damn, he was my kind of guy. Kristy turned fifty shades of tomato when Jack and I walked into the kitchen.

"Was he with you this whole time?" she stuttered.

"Yep." I grinned.

"No Vinnie?" she croaked.

"Nope."

"Oh my God." She dropped her head into her hands and started laughing hysterically.

Jack leaned down and kissed the top of my head. "It's nice to see you—" He nodded to a slightly less red Kristy. "I'll call you later." He grinned at me.

"But you don't have my number," I said going for a piece of paper.

"Yes, I do. Plus I know where you live."

That he did. He grabbed his jacket, winked at me and left.

"Boy, you work fast," Kristy said, giving me the thumbs-up.

"What are you talking about?"

"I'm just saying, I've been gone for three days and now you're dating a cop." She shook her head and pulled out the plastic Ziploc bag of cheese curds.

"How did you know he's a cop?"

"Are you serious?" she asked as if I was slow.

"Dead serious," I replied, my stomach filled with lead.

"Rena, that's our new neighbor. The sexy, bad boy cop with the smokin' hot ass. That's why I didn't introduce myself. I already met him."

"You never said the new neighbor was a cop," I accused her.

"I thought I did." She shrugged her shoulders.

"I would have remembered that after all my recent brushes with the law," I hissed at her. Why in the hell was I being mean to Kristy? I wasn't mad at her. I was mad at the cop who apparently lived below me. "I'm sorry, Kristy, I'm being a jerk," I mumbled.

"It's okay." She hugged me tight. "I'm sorry I left the cop thing out."

"Why in the hell didn't he tell me he lives downstairs?" I dropped into a kitchen chair, grabbed the cheese curds and shoved a handful into my mouth.

"I don't know," she mused. "That's weird. But wait, if you didn't meet him in the building, where did you meet?"

"He arrested me last week."

Kristy was shocked to silence . . . almost. "Did it make the evening news?" It was a legitimate question considering my past, but so not what I wanted to hear right now.

"Nope."

"Good,'" she said with a smile. Reading my mood perfectly, she handed me the Tommy Bartlett Water Show schedule and got out the container of black raspberry chip ice cream and two spoons. We spent the rest of the day chilling out and watching bad reality TV. She didn't bring Jack up once. I was tempted to walk downstairs and demand to know why he'd decided to keep his abode a secret from me, but I refrained. He was on crack if he thought we were going to date . . . I couldn't trust someone who omitted large pieces of information like, "I'm your neighbor." My heart felt heavy, but my resolve was strong. I should stick to dating jobless criminals. But none of them had made me feel so happy and empty at the same time.

Chapter 15

After a night of no sleep, I decided that showing up at Evangeline's early to snoop around was a good idea. Let the record show, I also thought streaking was a fine plan.

Pulling up at six-thirty in the morning in total darkness was freaky, not to mention scary. I made my way to her gate and stopped dead in my tracks. The statues that flanked the portico, paying homage to her boobs, were lit up like Christmas trees. Tons of tiny white lights covered the bosom of each, making it the most obscene thing I'd ever seen. I simply couldn't believe she hadn't been cited for this vulgar display. Maybe she'd got something on all her neighbors, too.

I walked through the gate and heard voices. Shit. Who in the hell was here this early? Taking no chance of being busted, I ran and hid behind a rather zaftig naked lady statue in the yard. I picked one close to the house, hoping to slip in undetected. The voices were familiar. Two men and Evangeline. I'd heard the men before . . . I just couldn't put my finger on who they were. Freezing my ass off, I waited to catch a glimpse.

I never would have done something this stupid if it wasn't for that omitting bastard, Jack. His forgetting to mention that he was my neighbor made me think he was still out to arrest me. Oh, I had no doubts that he wanted to get in my pants, but that was probably secondary to wanting to put me away in the slammer for the rest of my life. This brilliant idea had come to me at four-thirty this morning. I was going to prove . . . somehow, that I didn't steal anything. Then when that smug son of a bitch tried to lock me away, I'd shove the proof right up his ass. . . . Damn, that idea had seemed a lot better a couple of hours ago in my warm cozy bed.

"Evangeline, as usual, it's lovely doing business with someone as sophisticated and sexy as you," a man's familiar voice oozed.

Evangeline's giggles made me want to stick bamboo shoots behind my nails. They were on the front steps, close to the house. I tried to peer around the zaftig gal's bottom, but the trio was still hidden from my view. Damn, who was she talking to?

"I just hope you never ever, ever forget where your bread is buttered." She was trying for a sexy voice. It came out constipated.

"Of course not, ma'am," a whiney little voice squeaked.

No fucking way. That can't be who I think it is. I have to be mistaken . . .

"I'm quite serious about stud services being provided," the Viper purred.

"I'd be happy to oblige," a very recognizable deeper voice offered.

Holy hell, was I about to hear a sexual transaction go down between Sergeant Santa, Herbie the Dentist Cop, and Evangeline? Coming here was the absolute worst idea I'd ever had.

"I don't want you," Evangeline hissed. "You're old and probably shriveled."

If that wasn't the pot calling the kettle black . . .

"I want someone young and vibrant with a huge package and big muscles," she spat at Santa. I almost felt sorry for him. Evangeline was one hell of an emasculator.

"I'd be happy to screw you," Herbie the Dentist Cop blurted out, with barely hidden fear and revulsion in his voice. What I wouldn't give to see their faces right now, but if I stepped out, they'd see me. My overriding curiosity could get me killed and buried in a shallow grave. I was grateful for the big fat concrete ass I was hiding behind.

"You?" she laughed disdainfully. "Absolutely not."

I swear I heard Herbie sigh in relief.

"I want the blond one. The hot sexy thing who arrested the twit."

She did not just call me a twit. Yes, she did. Not only that, she wanted to screw my boyfriend. If it wasn't so funny, it would be pathetic.

"Um, I don't think we can make that one work," Santa stammered. "Jack Careena plays by the books. He'd never go for it."

That's my guy. I grinned and then remembered I didn't like him anymore. Who in the hell was I kidding? I was three-fourths of the way in love with him. I wanted him to father my children. I wanted to be Rena Careena. Rena Careena? Oh fuck no . . . now I knew why Jenny thought his name was so funny. If I married him my name would be Rena Careena. It was even worse than Rena Gunderschlict. At least Gunderschlict didn't rhyme. Fuck.

"I'll pay him a huge sum of money," she spat.

"He won't do it," Herbie chimed in.

"Are you two little nothings implying I'm not beautiful and sexy enough for your precious Jack Careena?" she screamed.

Holy shit, someone was going to call the police. Whoops, they were already here. They waited a couple of beats too long before answering her. I heard someone get slapped. WTF? Had she become violent?

"Of course not," Santa insisted desperately. "It's just, as hot and sexy as you are, Jack Careena can't be bought."

"Everyone can be bought," her curt voice lashed out at the idiot duo. "You two little men should certainly know all about that."

My God, she was paying them?

"I just don't know . . ." Santa whined. It sounded like Herbie was crying in the background. He must be the one she'd hit. How could anyone hit Herbie the Dentist?

"Here's what I know," Evangeline spat contemptuously, "You little shits will get Jack Careena to my house on Friday night. He will be my stud until I tire of him. If you don't get him to agree . . . I will destroy you. Am I clear?"

"Yes, ma'am," the jackass team said in unison.

"Here's a little something for your efforts. I expect to see you on Friday, with my willing lover in tow."

If I could see, I'd bet my life she'd just handed them money. They hustled down the steps and into their cruiser, which was parked in the drive. I heard the front door slam and knew I had a long cold wait ahead of me. I was too afraid I'd be spotted if I ran back to my car, so I hunkered down behind the big butt to wait till it was time to go to work.

"Rena, are you okay?"

I opened my eyes to find Cecil squatted down in front of me. I'd apparently fallen asleep on the big butt. Concern showed on his face. I became uneasy under his scrutiny. He didn't seem angry or suspicious, which made it all the more unsettling.

"Oh my goodness," I said, shaking like a leaf. "I got here a little early and felt uncomfortable going in, so I decided to take a quick, um . . . nap." Lame much?

He searched my blue eyes and blue lips, waiting for a more plausible explanation, but none was forthcoming. "Oookay, come inside now." He extended his hand and helped me to my frozen feet. His touch was gentle, and his worry seemed real.

"Thanks," I muttered through chattering teeth. Why did Cecil break my heart? He was supposed to be the bad guy. But the more I discovered about all the new people in my life . . . I realized nothing was as it seemed. Thank you, Poppy Harriet.

I followed him to the kitchen. He made me a cup of hot chocolate and put a warm blanket around my shoulders. I worried Evangeline would catch us, but we weren't doing anything wrong. He stayed silent as he cared for me. I knew he was waiting for me to talk, but I couldn't. I couldn't risk my real friends' and family's lives just to figure out if Cecil had more to him than I'd initially thought.

He stared at me for a long moment. Perhaps giving me another chance to spill my guts. Deciding that wasn't going to happen, he cleaned up. "I'll see you in the office in about an hour," he said quietly.

"Okay. Cecil, thank you for, um, saving me."

"You're welcome, Rena. I'm glad I could help." He nodded politely and left the room. Why did I feel so sad for him? I shook my head in confusion. I would just have to get over it . . . I had a career to ruin.

Pirate Dave hid in his cabin for a week. Occasionally it took that long for body parts to grow back. If he ever got his bare hands on that fucking troll, he'd rip his 'nads off. He knew it had gotten around that he was dick-less. Fourteen rival pirates had tried to steal his ship and treasure. One sneaky son of a bitch had absconded with Shirley, only to bring her back three days later because her voice had ruptured his eardrums.

He slathered some Burt's Butt Cream under his eyes.

He'd heard it was helpful for puffiness. He didn't enjoy the odor, so he doused himself with Scrubby Clean laundry detergent. That turned out to be a bad fucking idea. It burned like a motherfucker when he got it in his eye, but after flushing it out with Aquaman Water, he felt better. So much better, he decided to treat himself to Taco Yo Mama and a Stanley's Junglejuice.

Rumor of Laverne's heroics made him wish he had a schlong again. She had singlehandedly beaten the living hell out of his entire crew and all fourteen pirates who had tried to commandeer what was rightfully his. He suspected she'd handed Shirley over without much fight. Those bitches hated each other.

When his johnson reappeared, he would take Laverne to Smiley Pete's Weenie Shack or possibly Harry's Hotdogs or Jimmy's House of Fried Cheese or maybe even Cyndy's Cylindrical Meat Sausage Shop. She deserved a nice night out on the town.

Pirate Dave doubled over in pain. The area where his love muscle used to reside was burning and itching like a bad case of VD. "What is happening?" he bellowed, knocking over his Mindbendo gaming system in a frantic search for more bottled water, perhaps Aquawoman.

The magic of vampire regeneration overtook him. His body dropped to the floor and he was unable to move. The only relief he had was the use of his thick hairy neck. This gift gave him the power to watch the miraculous miracle that was about to happen.

Right before his not so puffy eyes, his divine rod began to grow back. Boy, he'd love to see the look on that troll's face now. No one fucks with Pirate Dave's pork sword. He watched with pride as his main vein grew back even larger than before! He smiled and winked at his pickle, his long-lost friend . . . But wait, what the hell was going on? Something was very, very wrong. He vaguely remembered reading about this in vampire school, but that was three hundred fucking years ago. This could not be happening. Pirate Dave screamed in anguish, "Noooooooooo."

But no matter how much he cried like a girl, shit still

*happened. Pirate Dave was not blessed with one
tallywhacker . . . oh no, he was blessed with two. Two
raging, erect ding-dongs. What in the hell was he supposed
to do with two skin flutes? He didn't know any women with
two vaginas . . . but wait, maybe he did.*

"Holy God almighty, I never knew there were so many different names for a penis," Joanne said, breaking the shocked silence in the little pink office.

"Yep," Shoshanna said with pride, "our girl has a vast knowledge of anatomy."

I rolled my eyes and tried not to laugh. All the ladies had come for the morning story session. They were jealous of all the fun LeHump and I were having. Thankfully Evangeline hadn't joined us. She was probably in bed, sleeping off her early morning payoff session.

Cecil, seated uncomfortably on the hot pink couch, was pinching the bridge of his nose and avoiding eye contact with all the ladies, especially me. He never commented on the crap I spewed out daily, but I'm almost sure he was holding back laughter as Pirate Dave's two members grew in. Maybe I was wrong. Maybe he was just gassy.

"I brought some homemade cookies and some eggnog." Nancy hopped up excitedly to fetch her treats from the cooler she'd brought.

Poppy Harriet and Shoshanna traded concerned glances. LeHump mimed drinking and then swiped her finger across her neck. Apparently the international sign for, 'Don't drink the eggnog.' What was with the fear of Nancy's food?

Nancy handed everyone several cookies and a cup of eggnog, including Cecil. I watched Cecil through lowered lashes. He examined his cookie and sniffed it cautiously. He took a miniscule bite and rolled it around in his mouth. Nancy was busy packing away the extras, so she was unaware of Cecil's cookie test. The others were not, however, and watched with rapt attention. When Cecil swallowed and gave the gals a curt nod, a collective sigh was released. Shoshanna silently pointed at her cup of eggnog and Cecil shook his head "no."

Nancy turned around and eyed the group. Did she know what

was going on? Before she could tell everyone to drink up, I started talking. Often my conversations made people forget what was on their mind. Occasionally they even forgot their name.

"Cecil," I asked, "how long have you worked for Evangeline?"

"For as long as she's been writing," he said, holding his cup of eggnog, but not drinking from it.

He'd been with that slag for over twenty years? He'd been slaving away for two decades and that horrible woman couldn't even get his name right.

"Cecil's been around as long as we have," Poppy Harriet added with a shudder. I wasn't sure if that was about Cecil or being around Evangeline. Probably the latter.

"Yes, well thank you for the refreshment. I must get back to my other duties." Cecil gave a formal bow and left the room.

"Does he make you as sad as he makes me?" I asked the gals, who sat silently and watched him leave.

"He always has." Joanne shook her head and reached for another Cecil-approved cookie.

After a quick meeting in which I scared the shit out of the ladies with my new Pirate Dave ideas, the gals left. Shoshanna and I buffed the fornicating statues and came up with the worst product placement list imaginable. By the end of the day I was exhausted, but that was my own fault . . . no, actually it was Jack's. One more thing to add to my ever-expanding "I Hate Jack List."

Chapter 16

At quitting time, Shoshanna and I walked out of Evangeline's House of Tacky feeling tired, but good. I glanced across the street to my car and saw something that made my pulse race, my gut clench, and everything south of my belly button dance with joy.

It should piss me off. I should give it the finger, march to my car, and peel out. No, wait . . . first I'll run over its toes and then I'll peel out. Maybe I'll just run it over and kill it . . .

"Holy hot guy almighty." Shoshanna nudged me, almost knocking me to the ground. "Fine piece of man meat dead ahead. And it looks like he's staring right at you."

Jack was across the street leaning on his car. The very same car that had delivered me to the pokey last week. His arms were crossed and his head was cocked to the side. He had that crazy sexy half smirk on his face. His jeans were worn in just the way I like them and his black T-shirt, beneath his leather bomber, hugged his muscles perfectly. Those stupid fucking muscles that I had been up close and personal with only yesterday. *Oh my God, I think I'm in love . . . Whoa. Wait. I don't even like him. At all. He's a lying sack of shit . . . Wait, that's not really fair. He's not technically a liar, as far as I know. That's my department, but he is an omitting sack of shit, and I do not date, screw, or hang out with sacks of shit. Dang it, why does he have to be so hot?*

I stopped on Evangeline's sidewalk, right under the cement boobs, and prepared for a stare-down. Shoshanna, never one to pick up on other people's vibes, left me by the giant mammaries, crossed the street, and walked right up to Jack.

"Hi there, handsome," she said. "I'm Shoshanna LeHump. And you would be?"

"Jack Careena." He took Shoshanna's outstretched little hand into his big one. "It's nice to meet you. I'm Rena's boyfriend."

"No, you're not," I shouted from across the street.

"Yes, I am," he yelled back.

"No. You're. Not." I stamped my foot and stuck out my tongue. Shit, shit, shit. That was so junior high.

"Yes. I. Am."

"Alrighty then, I guess I'll leave you two lovebirds to work out your misunderstanding," Shoshanna laughed and shamelessly slapped Jack on the butt.

She turned and gave me the thumbs-up.

"He's not my boyfriend," I insisted.

"Uh huh," LeHump said with a grin, "good luck with that." With a parting wink at the man meat, she hightailed it to her car, laughing all the way.

Thirty feet separated us. I put my hands on my hips and raised an eyebrow. He chuckled. I wanted to smack him almost as badly as I wanted to jump his bones. Strangely, I thought he would enjoy both. He crooked the pointer finger on his right hand and beckoned me to him.

No way. I will not go to him. He's an omitter. I will stand my ground . . . I will not jump when he says jump. If he wants to talk to me, he can get his ass over here . . . and beg, preferably on his knees.

He made noisy kissy lips and I giggled. He was nuts and he was mine. No, no, no, I had to lose that fantasy. He was not mine. He was just a cop with an awesome butt; they were a dime a dozen. I would walk to my car and I would leave, but I wanted to stay . . . Nope, I was gonna leave. Now.

Apparently while I argued with myself, like a schizophrenic, he crossed the street faster than the speed of light and stood inches from me. I looked up startled, and my traitorous inner slut squealed with delight. Just as the ho-bag trapped inside my body tried to wrap herself around his hot bod, I came to my senses. Taking three steps back, I clasped my hands tightly in front of me. They simply couldn't be trusted.

"Did you have fun today?" Jack inquired warily, probably waiting for my umpteenth personality to emerge.

"Maybe," I answered.

"You, um, seem kind of mad."

"You think?" I shook my head in disbelief.

"Yep." He grinned.

"You think that's funny?" I yelled, itching to slap the smirk off his face.

"No. I think you're sexy when you're mad."

"Oh." What in the hell was I supposed to say to that?

"Rena, tell me why you're mad. I don't like this." He shoved his hands in his pockets. I wondered if he didn't trust his hands either or if he was simply freezing. It was, after all, twenty-two degrees outside.

"You really don't know?" I sputtered. How could he not know?

"I really don't know." He smiled and waited.

"You're my neighbor," I said, teeth chattering. Damn, it was cold out here.

"Yeah, and?"

"What the hell do you mean, 'Yeah, and'? You never told me," I said sharply.

"Are you serious?" He looked at me like I had two heads and laughed.

"As a heart attack," I snapped. How could he think this was not a big deal? Was he a total douche? I was shaking like a leaf now. Part of it was the cold and part of it was my need to kick him in the nuts.

"Come with me." He grabbed my hand and dragged me across the street to his car.

"What are you doing?" I gasped, ducking to avoid knocking my head on the door as he dumped me onto the passenger seat. And if I wasn't mistaken, he copped a major feel of my butt before he went around to his own side.

"I'm ensuring neither of us gets frostbite. I have plans for you. You can't die on me yet." He grinned and ran his fingers across my trembling lips. "Now explain how my being your neighbor disqualifies me from being your boyfriend."

"You didn't tell me," I huffed, playing with the buttons on the dash. Oh my God, he had seat warmers. That was so cool. I flicked it on and waited for my butt to get toasty. I could listen to any bullshit he wanted to spout as long as my rear end was warm.

"Well, I guess I assumed you knew. I was inside the building when I met your mom and Aunt Phyllis and I'd already met Kristy."

"Oh." The heat crawled up my neck. I prayed it wouldn't reach my face.

"So that's why you were ready to dump me?"

"Um, yeah." I hung my head in embarrassment. His explanation made sense and my behavior did not. Shit. I supposed this was where he was going to dump me. Maybe I should explain myself further . . . "I thought you moved into my building to frame me for a crime I didn't commit. And that you were looking for proof to arrest me and lock me away for the rest . . ." I petered off, realizing I sounded deranged. The look on his face indicated that maybe I should have stopped several sentences ago.

He threw his head back and burst out laughing. "Oh my God, I moved into your building because it's a great spot, and I was only subletting my old place. I didn't know you lived there. I signed the lease a month ago and just haven't had the time to move." He was having a difficult time suppressing his laughter, and I was having a difficult time not dying of humiliation.

"Oh well," I muttered, "sorry about all that. I'm just going to go and . . ." I reached for the handle and tried to get out. There was nothing more for me to say. I'd already shoved my foot so far into my mouth it was coming out of my toasty warm ass.

He leaned across me and pushed down the lock. He was so close . . . I wanted to bury my face in his neck and sink my fingers into his hair. I closed my eyes and waited for him to move. He didn't. "You're not going anywhere," he whispered, sending tingles down my spine and calling my lady bits out from their slumber.

"But, I thought . . ." I mumbled.

"Don't think," he chuckled. "Thinking gets you in trouble." His breath tickled my cheek and his scent was making me crazy. "Moving into your building is the most fortuitous coincidence that has ever happened in my life."

"Really?" I asked. I tried unsuccessfully to rip my eyes away from his mouth. It was a work of art and meant to be stared at, so I did.

"Really." He brushed my lips with his. If I wasn't already sitting, I'd be on the ground. "So here's how it's going to go down.

We are dating. We will not sleep together until you trust me. I implore you to trust me soon, because keeping my hands off you is going to kill me." He gave me a lopsided smile that made me dizzy.

"Can we still play kissy face?" I asked, moving in for the kill.

"Only if you beg." His voice was husky and his eyes flashed with amusement.

"Please," I begged, my lips inches from his mouth. "I want you to kiss me . . . please."

"Oh God," he moaned, claiming my lips and crushing me to him. Those were the last words either of us uttered for quite a while.

"Truth or dare?" I giggled, watching him through lowered lashes.

"Truth. I'm not sure I'm equipped for your dares."

"Oh, you're definitely equipped," I purred, watching him squirm.

"If you'd like to find out for sure, just say the word," he shot back. Now I was squirming and my inner slut was break-dancing in my panties. I stared at my hands and made an attempt to pull my mind out of the gutter. We were trying to take it slow. Good luck . . .

We ended up at the coffee shop next door to our building. We agreed our apartments were a bad idea. They both had beds in them . . . The coffee shop, on the other hand, had no beds. It was warm and cozy, filled with overstuffed chairs and mismatched antique tables. After a make-out session that had curled my toes and had me secretly naming all of our unborn children, we decided we needed to get to know each other better. Hence the question-and-answer session over hot drinks in neutral territory.

"Okay, truth," I said, playing with the whipped cream on my hot chocolate. "Why did you become a cop?"

Jack took a deep breath and expelled it slowly, and the light sexy atmosphere we shared disappeared. He ran his hands through his hair and studied his coffee cup. "Both of my parents and my brother were killed by a drunk driver when I was twenty-one. I was in my senior year at college. Back then, I still didn't know what the hell I wanted to do . . . I was kind of a fuckup. The guy who killed my family got off because of shoddy police work. He got to walk away and live his life . . . My mom and dad and brother didn't get to do that. I thought about finding him and killing him myself, but I had an amazing person in my life who convinced me otherwise . . . So"—he looked up and gave me a smile that didn't reach his eyes—"I became a cop. I didn't want anyone else to suffer like I did. Watching that son of a bitch walk out of the courtroom was the worst day of my life."

"I am so sorry," I whispered. Tears blurred my vision, and I felt an overwhelming need to comfort him.

"Me too," he said. "It was a long time ago, but I miss them. So that's why I'm a cop." He smiled again and took my hand in his. This time it reached his eyes. I was falling hard for this beautiful man. "It's your turn. Why did you go into accounting?"

"I like numbers," I said shyly, wiping the tears from my eyes. Talking about accounting made me feel like the nerd I truly am, but if we were going to be honest, he might as well see the real me. "I adore math, and logic and number puzzles . . . Although, I don't fit in well at my office." I grinned. "Number nerds tend to be upset by foul language."

"I've never heard a bad word cross your lips," he deadpanned and I punched him in the arm. "Have you ever thought about going out on your own?"

"I have"—I nodded— "but that takes money and contacts. Neither of which I have."

"How is it that you're able to do this bizarre writing gig with your regular job?"

"I have three weeks of vacation," I muttered, hoping he'd drop it.

"But you're getting paid," he pointed out.

"Um hmm." If he only knew the half of it . . . I wanted to tell him the whole story, but at this point it wasn't my story to tell. I could destroy the lives of four lovely old ladies, my roommate, and my dad if I talked. Not to mention I could end up in jail for grand larceny. Shit.

"I really like this honest stuff," Jack said, rubbing his thumb across my knuckles.

"Me too." In a moment of sickening clarity, I realized I had become the omitter. The sin I'd been willing to break up with him over. I felt a little better by promising myself I'd be able to tell him the whole story soon. Right after I figured out how to save everyone and destroy the Viper Bitch.

"Back to the subject of me being your boyfriend . . ."

"I didn't realize that had been a topic of conversation," I replied dryly.

"Oh, but it is. A very important one."

"Please, do go ahead. I'm all ears." I grinned.

"Well, since I am your boyfriend. Your only boyfriend . . ." He stopped and waited. Rolling my eyes, I nodded in agreement. "I want you to know I'm going out of town for a few days."

"Why?" Maybe he was going to Iceland.

"Remember I said there was an amazing person who stopped me from doing something that would have ruined my life?" I nodded and he continued. "It's my grandpa. He lives in Wisconsin, and he's having gallbladder surgery tomorrow."

"Is he going to be okay?" I asked.

"He's as tough as nails; he'll be fine. He just wants someone there with him. I'll be back on Thursday," he said, reaching into his pocket. "I want you to call me while I'm gone, and I'll call you."

"I don't have your number," I said sheepishly.

He pulled his card out and laid it on the table in front of me. "That's what this is for. Do you think you'll be able to refrain from eating it?"

"Probably, unless you make me really mad."

"I have a better idea. Give me your phone." He put his hand out. I dug through my bottomless Hello Kitty bag and obliged. He put his name and number into my phone and handed it back.

"Can I still have your card?" I asked, wanting something that was his.

"Are you going to eat it?" he teased.

"Only if I get really hungry."

Chapter 17

"No fucking way." Shoshanna let out a long low whistle and dropped heavily onto the desk chair in our poufy pink, pornographic statue-filled office.

"What?" I asked, looking over her shoulder at the computer. It was entirely too early on a Monday morning for LeHump to be dumbfounded.

"She can't do this. It's not possible." Shoshanna's dazed expression made my stomach flippy.

"Can't do what?" I asked more forcefully than I intended, startling Shoshanna out of her stupor. Was the Walking Botox Experiment going after one of the girls? Was she going after me, or my dad, or Kristy? Had she announced her new lover, Jack, on her website? Speaking of . . . I didn't tell Jack about that. Oops. That was a fairly large omission, but I didn't want to worry him when he needed to focus on his grandpa . . . I'd tell him on Thursday when he got back.

"She's going to release the book at the end of next week." Shoshanna looked up at me with eyes as round as saucers.

"What book?" I asked. A small whoosh of panic settled in my stomach and started a slow waltz.

"The pirate book. Your book."

"What?" I yelped. "It's not done. I don't even know what else is going to happen in the damn thing. And how in the hell can you release a book that fast?"

"I guess she's going to self-publish it. If she went through traditional New York publishing, it would take a year to eighteen months," Shoshanna said, staring at the computer as an evil smile slowly spread across her face.

"Why are you smiling?" I asked. The waltz in my tummy increased its pace.

"This might not be a bad thing." She clapped her little hands together in glee. "If she publishes herself, the book will be released with every single word you said, including my favorite, *pork sword.* It will be horrifying," she squealed, bouncing up and down. "Her website says that she has over six thousand pre-orders. It says here," Shoshanna read, "that the national morning shows will be in town to cover her. She will do a reading of a chapter on live television. Hmmm, apparently, her going into independent publishing is big motherfucking news. She says it's her greatest work to date and she dares anyone to deny it. Goddamnit, she's a psycho," she laughed. "This is definitely not a bad thing."

"How in the fuck is this not a bad thing?" I yelled. "I'm going to have to live here at the monster porno house to get this pile of poo finished." I paced the small office. I had to move to counterbalance the tummy waltz that was quickly morphing into a violent tango.

"Oh, oh, oh—" Shoshanna bounced with excitement. "It says here on her site that she's going to unveil her greatest masterpiece at the Midwest Romance-o-Rama Convention next week."

"Oh my God," I gasped. "Wait, what is the Midwest Romance-o-Rama Convention?"

"It's the mac-daddy romance writer and reader convention in the country and this year it's right in our backyard."

"Where?"

"Let me find it." Shoshanna pulled up the convention schedule on the computer and couldn't control her burst of laughter. "This is too good. Every major author, publishing house, and reviewer will be there. She is so going down."

"So it's here in Saint Paul?" I whispered. An icy chill crept up my spine. Getting busted in my hometown so soon after the fucking weather girl disaster was simply too much.

"It's at the WMNS TV station building downtown. God, that's one ugly-ass building."

"Are you sure?" Apprehension coursed through me. Could it get any worse? The thought of having to possibly go to that building and get arrested again made bile rise in my throat.

"Have you seen it? It's uglier than a hat full of assholes."

"Holy hell," I sputtered, forgetting for a moment that my life was blowing up, "did you just make that up?"

"Make up what?" LeHump shook her head, clueless.

"The hat asshole thing,"

"Oh, no. My mom used to say it all the time. You like it?" she asked.

"Um, no. But I may have to use that in the Pirate Dave saga."

"See? I am good for something." She stood up, took a bow.

I pressed my fingers to the bridge of my nose to ward off the panic attack that was hurtling toward Earth and heading straight for me, and I willed myself not to vomit. I had a decision to make and I had to make it fast. It was risky to talk to Shoshanna here at the Viper Bitch's house, but options were getting slim and time was running out. LeHump needed to know . . . I walked to the door, shut it, and locked it. "Shoshanna, I need to tell you something."

And I did. I told her everything. The weather girl debacle, my arrest (both of them), being set up with stolen jewels, being apprehended by Jack, not being paid, Sergeant Santa and Herbie the Dentist Cop's visit, and Evangeline's threats to my dad and Kristy and the writing gals.

LeHump stared at me for a long moment. "I knew you looked familiar," she chuckled, referring to my fifteen minutes of fame as the idiot on the six o'clock news who thought the criteria for the Sunshine Weather Girl job only required showing up and hanging out at the station for a month. "The skank certainly does her homework," she said disgustedly. "You were dead in the water the minute you gave her your name."

"Shoshanna, have you thought this plan out all the way?" I asked, shifting uncomfortably on the couch.

"What do you mean?"

"Well, even if we destroy her career, what stops her from destroying us?"

That wiped the smile right off her face. "Oh, fuck."

I raced down to Cecil's office. If we were going to finish the book, he needed to be there taking notes. I had no clue how Evangeline was going to put my frightening brainchild together, and I didn't care. There were more life-threatening possibilities to worry about. How in the hell had we come up with a plan that still left us as sitting ducks? What if, worst case scenario, people actually liked the book? The movie *The Producers* kept flashing through my mind. Fuckity, fuck, fuck. I was going to have to pull some atrocious stuff out of my warped brain. A hat full of assholes was probably a good place to start . . .

Cecil's office was three doors down from ours. I'd never been inside before. I was curious whether it was as pink as ours. No. It was pinker. How was that even possible?

"Cecil?" I called out from the doorway.

No answer. Where was he? I moved cautiously into his office in case it was booby-trapped. I giggled at my pun. Cecil was nowhere to be found. God, I hoped he wasn't sick today . . .

The office was a mess. Stacks of paper everywhere. The walls were lined with bookshelves and every single inch of space was taken with notebooks and binders. How strange . . . I didn't take Cecil for a slob or a hoarder, but impressions can be deceiving.

I'd leave him a note to come and find us. I waded through the pigsty to his desk and found a stack of magazines that made my eyes pop.

"Hmm," I giggled, leafing through the catalog. I now knew what rocked Cecil's world . . . There must have been at least forty plus-size women's lingerie catalogs piled high on his desk.

He was not getting it on with Evangeline if he liked robust gals. The Viper was a bag of bones. Every other page was dog-eared and many items had been circled. He clearly liked his women in lacy purple undergarments. Crotchless teddies seemed to hold an appeal for him also. Who knew?

After writing a quick note for him to haul ass to our office ASAP, I turned and knocked a pile of notebooks to the ground. "Shit," I groaned, bending down to pick them up. Paragraph after paragraph of Cecil's neat handwriting covered the pages. What the hell was this?

My stomach dropped as I read. No fucking way. I dropped the notebook and picked up another . . . same thing, and another and another. All the notebooks were filled with his neat script. I tripped my way over to the bookshelf. Yanking several down, I opened them and read. The pages were covered with beautiful descriptions of lovers spurned and rejoined. Mind-boggling dialogue and hot, racy sex scenes were described in perfect detail . . . Notebook after notebook was filled with Cecil's handwriting, telling stories I could never even hope to write. The binders were dated and labeled. They went back at least twenty years. First, second, third drafts of all the Viper's novels . . . all in Cecil's neat print.

I pulled down others and read more of the same quality writing. How was this possible? I glanced at the door. No one was there, thank you, Jesus. I would be killed if I got caught. This was bigger than salmonella-gate, much bigger . . . My knees buckled and I slid to the floor. Cecil was not the bad guy. No, my guess was that Cecil was in the same boat we were. Maybe worse . . . I'd bet my car and ten years of my salary that Cecil, the manservant, had been the one originally responsible for making Evangeline a *New York Times* best-selling romance author. Holy fuck.

"Shoshanna," I gasped, fifty shades paler than when I left the room fifteen minutes ago. "I have to tell . . ."

"Hello ladies," Evangeline purred. Her boobs, larger than ever, entered the room before she did.

I stared at her and tried to figure out what could have made her so damned hateful. Studying her at such a close range was alarming and made me realize I'd been wrong about something. Her neck did not resemble a rotted prune, it looked more like an elephant scrotum.

She wobbled her way to the computer and gave us a nasty leer. "I see you've read the exciting news. I believe we're a bit behind schedule. I need the book by the middle of next week for formatting and pre-release to all the major reviewers in the country."

Evangeline the Awful stood at the desk, trying to hold herself upright. She swayed to the left, then she swayed to the right. Was she drunk? It was only nine-thirty in the morning. WTF? Then it hit me . . . She had no balance because her bazooms were too heavy. That was why she walked so strangely and could barely stay on her feet. Holy shit.

"Impossible, you stinky whore," Shoshanna muttered under her breath.

"Shokaka," the odiferous streetwalker hissed, digging her nails into the desk. "When I say it will be done, it will be done." Her voice got thin and shrill. "Do you understand me?"

We nodded mutely. I grabbed LeHump's hand before she called

the smelly ho anything else. I didn't want the Viper to push the due date. What boggled my mind was her confidence in the brilliance of a story that hadn't been written yet. Was she so out of touch that she couldn't see that *Pirate Dave* sucked?

"Aren't you worried about the product?" I asked before I could stop myself. Shoshanna squeezed my hand so hard I heard something crunch.

"Very sneaky, Rudy, very sneaky," she spat, "trying to convince me the book is bad so I'll give it back to you. Never. Going. To. Happen." Her voice got louder and more ear-piercing. "This is my masterpiece. Mine. People will know my name all over the world. I will have free fast food for the rest of my life! Companies will pay me to mention them in my works of art," she was screaming now and I feared a puncture to my eardrum. "James Cameron can shove *Titanic* up his ass because I'm the new King of the World," she shouted and practically fell on her face. LeHump and I didn't move. There was no fucking way we were going to help her. I was kind of hoping she'd have a heart attack or a stroke after her screeching harangue. It would solve so many problems . . .

"You two worthless nothings will get back to work and finish my book or I will finish you." So much venom spewed from her voice I felt dirty. "Oh, and Rita, to answer your question, I'm not at all worried about the product. Cecil tells me it's the book that will change my life and he knows better than anyone," she hissed, throwing her head back, tossing her overprocessed hair, and banging her skull thoroughly on the doorframe. It was all I could do to hold back the Inappropriate Laughing Monster. My lower lip was going to be a bloody mess. Shoshanna didn't even try to hold back. She cackled so hard, I hoped she'd brought another pair of panties.

Evangeline did not look back. She left the room in a daze, hopefully a concussed daze. I'd be very happy if we didn't have to see her again for the rest of the day.

"LeHump, get ahold of yourself. I have to tell you something important," I said, attempting to wipe the grin off my face. She looked at me and dissolved into another bout of hysterics. "I'm serious," I hissed, punching her in the arm.

"Oww," she giggled, trying to compose herself.

"When I was in Cecil's office, I found . . ."

"Shall we get started, ladies?" Cecil asked from the doorway.

"Holy hell," I shrieked, slapping my hand over my mouth so hard I got a headache.

"I understand we have a new deadline. I would suggest we get to work," he said, sitting down and pulling out his notebook and pen.

"Um, sure," I said, "but I'd like to ask a few questions first."

"As long as they are not work related, you may," he answered matter-of-factly.

Crap, they were all work related. What else did I want to know?

"Oh, oh, oh, I've got one." Shoshanna raised her hand. "What's your real name? I've wanted to know that one for twenty years."

"Fred."

"Are you married?" I jumped in.

"No."

"Girlfriend?" I tried again.

"No."

"Boyfriend?" Shoshanna went for it.

"No."

"Are you always this eloquent?" I inquired, racking my brain to find out something useful.

"Only when the occasion dictates," he said with an eye roll.

I was pretty sure he'd just insulted me. "Fine, Fred, tell us something about yourself. Anything. We've been cooped up in this hellhole for a week and I don't know the first thing about you. I'd like to know you better."

He seemed surprised by my request and Shoshanna gave me an odd look. She didn't know where I was going, but in true LeHump fashion, she blindly followed.

"Yeah, Fred, I might even find out I like you," she added. I wasn't sure if that helped or if it scared him to death.

His eyes were glued to his notebook and his shoulders slumped forward. "My name is Fred Smith, and I'm fifty-eight years old. I live with my mother. She's in fragile health, and I take care of her." He sighed heavily and continued, "I don't have many friends. They seem to drift away when you have no time for them. I work and tend to my mother. She loves me. I would rather die than embarrass her." He raised his eyes from his notebook and held mine. "My salary pays for her medicine. Without my job, she would die."

Oh my God. Was that what Evangeline had over him? His

mother's life? But that didn't add up . . . had Fred's mom been sick for twenty years? That was only part of the story. I'd bet Jack's and my unborn children that there was more to this . . .

"But Fred . . ." I wanted the rest of the story.

"Let's get to work," he said firmly, opening his notebook and signaling an end to the cozy get-to-know-you chat. "I'm ready to be revolted by your colorful imagination."

That was the second time he'd dodged me in five minutes, but the twinkle in his eye made his insult seem almost endearing.

"You asked for it." I grinned and started talking.

Chapter 18

Pirate Dave stared at the hat full of assholes and wondered who had sent him such a lovely and unusual gift. He considered trying to fuck them, but since they weren't attached to anything, he decided against it.

Apparently he had a secret admirer.

He'd received daily gifts for a week. Shirley was fit to be tied. She'd tried to tempt him away from thoughts of his admirer by swinging naked from the chandelier in the galley. Bad fucking move on Shirley's part. During her buck-ass naked extravaganza, she'd accidentally blinded six crew members standing nearby when she gouged their eyes out with her toe.

Her lack of remorse was a huge turn-on for Pirate Dave, but she only had one vagina. Pirate Dave ripped open a box of Salty Skeeboodles and shoved them in his mouth. He left the crumbs from his snack embedded in his chest fur. Lice need to eat, too.

He looked down at his expanding stomach and realized he couldn't see his peckers anymore. His inability to find a fuck buddy with two lady holes had led him to eat. A lot. He cared not that his once nicely indented ass had turned as flabby as Poseidon's.

Feeling nauseous and horny, Pirate Dave formed a plan. He would stay awake until he caught his secret admirer. Anyone thoughtful enough to leave him a hat full of assholes deserved a garlic press.

A nasty storm brewed on the horizon. The wind whistled ominously and blinding streaks of lightning ripped through

*the sky, tearing the darkness apart like a go-cart at a
monster truck rally. The ship tossed and turned, causing
Dave's triple bacon cheeseburger, onion rings, and fish
sandwich to threaten a reappearance.*

*"Goddamnit," Pirate Dave railed against the howling
gale, "I hate getting wet."*

*Pirate Dave's head drooped and his shoulders sagged,
for Dave had become too fat to fit through the cabin doors.
He'd been relegated to living on the deck, becoming one
with the motherfucking elements.*

*If only that shit-ass little troll hadn't lopped his wanker
off, none of this would have happened. He'd be happily
porking Shirley. A gag and duct tape had solved the voice
problem. He really did love her as long as she didn't speak,
but . . . Laverne had given him a boner numerous times, too.
Her violent murderous streak made his johnsons stand at
attention. What to do . . .*

"Who's the secret admirer?" Shoshanna asked, shell-shocked
from the words that had just passed my lips.

"I have no idea," I told her truthfully. I figured Cecil-Fred had
realized by now that I was pulling everything out of my butt, so
hiding my ignorance of the upcoming plot didn't faze me.

"Can I take a shot at it?" Shoshanna asked.

I heard Cecil-Fred's sharp intake of breath. Clearly, the thought
of LeHump adding her own brand of crazy to the mix frightened
him. "Be my guest," I said, a little bit afraid myself.

*The storm picked up and Pirate Dave realized the rain
might shrink his ass-less leather chaps. He loved his leather
chaps. They'd become slightly uncomfortable due to his
double cocks, but his vanity overruled his comfort. Of
course his recent hundred-pound weight gain didn't help,
but that wasn't his fault. It was the fault of the formerly
blind stupid fucktard troll.*

*He looked down at his wrists and shook his head in
disgust. Mr. Smee had lost the key to the furry handcuffs
and now he was stuck wearing pink fur and metal until
someone could saw it off without removing his hands.*

*He tightened his braided leather vest. He was so glad it
kind of still fit. He needed the support for his new man-
boobs. He decided to shave his chest and pubic area. Of
course not being able to see his scrotum made this a
dangerous venture, but Dave liked living on the edge.
Unfortunately the only razor he could find was dull and
rusty . . . Oh well, a man's got to do what a man's got to do.*

*He raised the razor to the Heavens for that fat bastard,
Poseidon's blessing. Closing his eyes, he brought the razor
down to his . . .*

"Um, Shoshanna," I stopped her before she could cut Pirate
Dave's double ding-dong off, forcing him to grow back four. I was
surprised I could speak. My mouth had dropped to the floor and
Cecil-Fred was an ungodly shade of red.

"Is there a problem?" she asked.

"Well, yeah. If you castrate him again, four more will grow
back." How was I having this conversation?

"I was only going to cut off one," she explained.

"Yes," Cecil chimed in, turning a deeper shade of red, "but if
you do that, he'll have three."

"How's that?" Shoshanna asked, confused.

"If you cut both of them off, four will grow back. But if you only
cut one off, two will grow back, leaving him with three," I informed her logically.

"Oh my God!" She nodded in understanding. "That didn't occur
to me. Other than that, what did you think?"

I paused for a moment, wondering how much detail I should go
into. I decided none. "I loved it." And I did. It added a hideous fla-
vor I never would have come up with. "Fred, what's your take?"

"First of all, ladies, you must call me Cecil. The Madame is not
aware that you know my real name and I prefer to keep it that way.
As far as the story goes"—he took a deep breath and blushed a little more—"I think it will serve the purpose for which it's intended
very well."

"Cecil"—Shoshanna slapped him on the back—"I never thought
I'd say this to you, but welcome to the club, my friend. Welcome
to the club."

* * *

After one of the most exhausting days of my life, I still had a long and bizarre evening ahead. Thankfully I'd gotten ahold of my only friend at the accounting firm and she'd agreed to take on the Poppy Harriet/Walter Garski case. Her discreet nature and sense of humor were the reasons I knew I could trust her with the delicate matter; plus I'd saved her ass multiple times. Once her hysterical laughter had died down, she promised to have it fixed within the week. I would owe her big-time, but the deadline on Pirate Dave meant I couldn't focus on anything else.

Cecil stayed with us the entire day, giving me no time to share my discovery with Shoshanna. He might have planted himself so I wouldn't say anything, but we did get a lot done and he seemed to be enjoying himself immensely. There was something missing from the blackmail plot against him. I knew asking would lead nowhere. I'd have to discover it myself.

The suckiest part was that Jack and I had played phone tag all day. I couldn't believe how empty I felt at the thought of not seeing him until Thursday. Although knowing his grandpa was doing well made me happy. Thinking about Jack made me happy. Hearing his voice-mail message made me and my lady bits happy. Everything about him made me happy. WTF? Was it possible to fall for someone this fast? Or did the fact that I wanted to see him naked have anything to do with it? I decided to file those thoughts away until I had the time and energy to figure it out. I didn't have the time or energy to even grab anything to eat . . . As promised, in exchange for the car money, I was taking Aunt Phyllis to her first Bigfoot meeting tonight. Fuck.

Chapter 19

The dark, dank back room of the community center smelled like rotten eggs, wet dog, and poopy diapers, or maybe it was the attendees. I couldn't be sure. The ride over to the center consisted of Aunt Phyllis repeatedly apologizing for drugging me with her tranquilizers. No matter how many times I told her not to worry about it, she insisted on apologizing again.

"Aunt Phyllis"—I blew out an exasperated sigh as we tried to find someplace to sit in the crowded room—"I swear to God I will flush all your Martians down the toilet if you don't stop saying you're sorry."

She giggled and pushed me down onto a seat in the front row. "They love the sewer system," she whispered. "If you really want to screw with them, play Céline Dion. They hate that shit."

Oh my God. I knew I didn't fit in here, but I began to wonder if maybe Aunt Phyllis did . . .

A man and a woman entered the room in full camouflage. Their faces were painted green and black, and they carried cameras and camcorders strapped to their backs like weapons. The crowd went nuts as they made their way to the front of the room. I clapped so I wouldn't stand out, but keeping my eyes from rolling was impossible.

"Hi everybody," the woman yelled above the roar of Sasquatch believers. She then bent her knees, lifted her hands like they were claws, and growled at the audience. All around me people lifted their own hand-claws and growled back.

"Is that the secret fucking handshake?" I asked my aunt, laughing until I realized she too had her claws in the air. She elbowed me and gave me "the look." I shook my head, thanking Buddha, Jesus, Allah, Zeus, all the angels and saints, and Brett Favre that I didn't know anyone there. I raised my claws and gave a very halfhearted growl.

"You can do better than that," Aunt Phyllis insisted, growling for all she was worth.

"No. No, I can't." I had entered an alternate universe, and I was going to have to stay for at least two hours. Two hours of my life that I would never get back. Ever.

Turned out the camo-growler was Kim Jensen Johnson and her face-painted cohort was her husband Hugh Jensen Johnson. Kim had to be the size of my SUV and outweighed Hugh by at least two hundred pounds. The vague images of their sex life that kept flitting through my mind were enough to put me into a coma. I decided to put that info into the brain folder labeled "Never Ever Think Those Thoughts Again."

"We are here tonight," Kim shouted, "because we believe." The crowd went ballistic. "Some of us have witnessed the miracle that is Bigfoot and some of us live every day in hopes that, we too will see the Bigfoot."

I heard a strange sound. I glanced around the room to see if anyone was ill . . . Nope. What the hell was that sound?

"People think we're foolish," she yelled like a preacher and the crowd booed and hissed. "That's right, my friends, people think we're foolish to dedicate our lives and our savings accounts to finding Bigfoot. But they are wrong. They have not seen the light!" Kim did the growl thing again and the crowd growled back. Including me, but only because Aunt Phyllis kicked me hard enough to leave a mark.

I heard the sound again, although it had morphed into something more bizarre. It sounded like someone hyperventilating and changed to cats having sex. If you've never heard cats having sex, trust me, it's bad. From the feline intercourse, it slowly changed to a grunting monkey. WTF? I glanced around again and my eyes landed on Hugh . . . I realized it was him. At first I thought he was sick. Then it occurred to me he might be mentally challenged, and I felt horrible for making fun of him inside my head . . . When it dawned on me he was making what he believed were sounds of

Sasquatch, all bets were off. I could ridicule to my heart's content. He was doing sound effects for his wife's sermon on the Yeti.

"We are here tonight for testimonials. If you've seen the beautiful beast, we want you to share. If we have enough sighting stories, we believe we can convince the TV show *Finding Bigfoot* to come and film us." That sent the crowd into a frenzy. So much so, I feared for my and Aunt Phyllis's life.

"I've seen him," called out a man in the back, who possibly had inbreeding in his family tree.

"Tell us, my friend," Kim shouted back as Hugh squealed in a high pitch reserved for dogs and breaking glass.

"It was three years ago. He picked me up and shook me like a can of pop." He sat back down with a satisfied look on his face. Who in the hell shakes cans of pop? Why would he choose that metaphor? Thinking too hard was going to make my brain explode.

"That's nothing," said a mousey little gal two rows back. "Bigfoot came on to me."

The shocked gasp from the hardcore freaks almost made me pee my pants.

"Tell us about it, my sister," Kim bellowed. I wondered if loud was her only volume level. Hugh, if I'm not mistaken, started speaking in tongues.

"I fought him off and he masturbated in the corner of my bedroom." She finished her disturbing tale and sat back down.

"Bigfoot was in your bedroom?" I laughed until realized they were all looking at me with pity. I clearly didn't believe.

"Yes, of course," she replied as if I were an idiot. "He comes at least twice a week."

The double entendre made me bite my lip so hard it bled. I love my Aunt Phyllis, but she would be on her own at the next Sasquatch gathering.

"The last time I saw Bigfoot, he smelled so bad I couldn't eat for a week," a tall bald man said, shaking his head and wincing at the memory.

I felt movement beside me. An icy chill shot up my spine. Aunt Phyllis was ready to add her two cents. This could only lead to her being institutionalized. I tried to stop her, but she would have none of it. "That's nothing," Phyllis jumped up and pointed at the bald guy. "I survived salmonella-gate and couldn't eat for two weeks and three and a half days."

"Oh my God," Kim screeched. "You were there?" Hugh began humming the theme from *Jaws.*

"Yes, I was, and I lived to tell," my aunt said with pride.

The crowd murmured with shock and respect. Several people came up and touched her while a few others knelt at her feet. Was everyone here insane?

The tall bald guy was one who knelt. "I heard it was at Evangeline O'Hara's mansion," he said, extremely impressed. That was news to me.

"I love her books," Bigfoot's mousey girlfriend squealed. "Is she as scary as she looks?"

"Scarier," Aunt Phyllis said, miming big boobs to her rapt audience.

Always the conspiracy theorist, Kim said, "I heard it was a setup. I heard the caterer had nothing to do with it." Hugh was now having his out-of-tune way with the theme song from *Mission Impossible.*

"Where did you hear that?" I asked. Something in the way she spoke made the hair on my arms stand up.

"My cousin's brother's girlfriend's sister works for the Health Department and was the lead investigator on the case. She said something was added to the food. It was not the food itself or the way it was prepared that made people sick. They think Evangeline O'Hara did it, but they could never prove it." Hugh was working up a sweat, beat boxing until Kim punched him in the head. He went flying and everyone smiled their relief that the alarming concert was over.

"What did they find in the food?" I asked.

"Some kind of weird plant extract from Bulgaria, similar to Silly Putty," Kim said, shaking her head in disgust.

Sweet baby Jesus, she'd poisoned people with the same stuff that she pumps into her bosom. I paled and wondered who the poor caterer was that the Viper had ruined. How many fucking people had Evangeline destroyed?

"That doesn't make sense," Aunt Phyllis said. "Evangeline got sick, too."

"That was her alibi," Kim said knowingly. "If she hadn't gotten sick, she wouldn't have gotten away with it." Hugh started in with the theme from *Jeopardy!* but quickly ceased when Kim gave him the evil eye.

"Did they have any idea what her motive was?" Coming to this meeting was more educational than I ever could have dreamed.

"Apparently, she had it in for the caterer, and she hated all the ladies she played bridge with," Kim said.

Every eye in the room went to Aunt Phyllis as she mulled over the new information. "It's a fine hypothesis." She nodded. "That bitch does hate all the bridge girls. We've been kicking her ass for years, but I can't confirm the caterer. I don't know who she used."

"I do," mousey gal volunteered. "It was Nan Thorenson. I have all her cookbooks."

Oh shit. I'd just discovered what the Viper had on Nancy. The food-sniffing made sense now. Oh my God, poor Nancy.

"Did the caterer know Evangeline was suspected?" I asked.

"From what I heard, she took off and hasn't been heard from since," Kim answered, stroking Hugh's head where she had punched him. "She evaded the Health Department. O'Hara testified that the caterer admitted her guilt and took off. Nothing anyone could do if the caterer wouldn't talk."

I'd bet the caterer was still under the impression that she'd poisoned everyone and thought Evangeline was protecting her. I needed to find out if Evangeline had a line of cookbooks . . . My stomach churned and my hands clenched into fists. My only revenge was my story. I smiled and looked around the room at the freaks who were now beautiful to me.

I stood and walked to the front of the room. I hugged Kim and patted Hugh on the head. "Could you guys tell me a little more about Bigfoot? I'm doing research for a book, and I want to make sure I get my facts straight."

The entire room erupted into applause. They made me a believer . . . kind of.

Chapter 20

Pirate Dave had been friends with Hairy Sam forever. Literally. Sam's stench made Dave smell like a flower. Sam was covered in hair from head to toe, hence the name. He'd tried shaving and waxing and electrolysis, but to no avail. He'd even tried burning it off. That had certainly been a bad fucking idea. The hair grew back within minutes, thicker and coarser than before.

The pungent gentlemen enjoyed the game called Fucking with the Future. It was a highlight in both of their immortal lives. Between ravaging large-breasted virgins who pretended they were appalled by sex, stealing treasures, and eating box after box of Shaft Macaroni and Cheese, they enjoyed traveling to the future and messing with undereducated Americans' heads. Especially ones who were married to other family members.

Pirate Dave and Hairy Sam found it amusing to time-travel to the Pacific Northwest or the deep South anywhere between the 1960s and the early 2000s to perpetuate the Bigfoot myth. It wasn't exactly a myth, for Hairy Sam's feet were huge. His shoes were a size twenty-four, matching his doinker to the inch.

Often times Hairy Sam tried to get laid, but usually ended up masturbating in the corner of freaked-out women's bedrooms. Pirate Dave thought this was hilarious. Sam hadn't gotten any in over two hundred years.

Because of Hairy Sam's ridiculously oversized man tool and his vomit-inducing aroma, he had a difficult time with the ladies. But that was about to change . . . for the secret admirer of Pirate Dave was due to arrive and her lady bits were not what they used to be. A hideous bout with childbearing had ended her former career as

*a hooker. She could fit an entire football team in her hoo-ha and
that pissed her off.*

"Jesus Christ in a miniskirt. Where did that come from?" LeHump
choked on her coffee as I ended the scene.

"Aunt Phyllis and I went to a Bigfoot meeting last night." I
grinned as Cecil blanched.

"Um, Rena"—he was having a hard time finding his voice—
"does this have anything to do with the rest of the story?"

"For a Wednesday morning at eight-thirty, I think I'm doing
pretty good," I huffed, grabbing a doughnut and plopping down on
the ugly couch. "Besides, I'm going somewhere with it . . . I think."

"Cecil," Shoshanna challenged, "if you have a bone to pick with
Rena's muse, I suggest you take a shot."

"Yeah, Cecil, you have a go at it," I giggled, imagining what he
could possibly come up with.

"Fine," he said with all the dignity he could muster. "I will."

I pulled my feet up on the couch, grabbed another doughnut, got
comfortable, and waited . . .

He cleared his throat, straightened his suit jacket, and then
cleared his throat again. And again . . . and again.

"Today, Cecil," I laughed, enjoying his embarrassment. It wasn't
as easy as it looked. Coming up with horrific material took some
talent and some serious lack of inhibition. Not to mention some
brain damage.

*The ashes on the deck of the ship were gray mixed with
flecks of turquoise, small pieces of skin, shards of brittle
bone, and dyed blond hair. The gentle breeze off the crystal
blue ocean tossed the gruesome pile about, scaring years off
the lives off the deckhands.*

*"What the fuck is that?" Pirate Dave hissed, angry to be
woken from his sixth morning nap.*

*"We don't know," Captain Crunchy, clutching his blow-
up doll Susan to his sunken chest, stammered uneasily.*

*"It's black magic voodoo shit," Mr. Smee cried out,
brandishing a knife and backing away from the pile that
seemed to be coming to life.*

A whirlwind formed the cinders into a small funnel,
eliciting a gasp of shocked dismay from Pirate Dave and his
below-average crew. Cackling shrieks came from within the
funnel of ash. The men paled and backed away, but not
Pirate Dave.

"What in the hell are you?" he bellowed at the cloud
of ash.

"Your secret admirer," the hideous sight hissed.

"You've got to be fucking kidding me," Pirate Dave
moaned. He'd been hoping for a hot chick with two vaginas.
Clearly he'd fucked a lot of people over through the years to
deserve an admirer like this.

An arm emerged from the ash, covered in age spots and
sporting long hot pink nails. Then a skinny leg revealed
itself, followed by a bony ass, followed by the other skinny
leg and the other liver-freckled arm.

"Get thee from my ship, you ugly Devil," Pirate Dave
screamed. If the rest of her was as awful as what he'd seen
so far, he was afraid he'd lose his lunch from Jack's Ass-
Smack Burgers. It was wonderful going down, but not so
good when it came back up.

The funnel howled with an eerie laughter. The largest
rock-hard bosom Dave had ever laid his eyes on emerged
from the funnel. "Holy shit," he muttered, "I like tits, but
those are disgusting."

The knockers were followed by a shriveled neck and the
most revolting face he'd seen in his very long lifetime.

The crew gasped and hid their faces from the
grotesque sight.

"Hello, Pirate Gabe, did you . . ."

"My name is Dave," he interrupted, hoping against hope
that she had shown up on the wrong ship.

"That's what I said, Steve," she jeered.

"Dave," he corrected.

"What?" she shrieked.

"I said that my name is . . ." he decided to give up.
Clearly she was old and senile.

"So anyway, Javier, did you enjoy the hat full of
assholes?" she leered suggestively.

Pirate Dave threw up in his mouth and tried to run away,
but his girth prohibited him from getting very far.
   The horrifying bag of bones grabbed him by the testicles
and squeezed. Hard. Dave liked it rough, but this was too
much even for him. "You're mine now," she ground out
between clenched false teeth. "Until I get what I want, I
own you."
   "Oh fuck," Pirate Dave groaned. The pain from her
sadistic ball handling was making him dizzy. He
accidentally on purpose projectile-vomited all over her
and collapsed into a heap at her feet.

I never knew what thick silence felt like until now. I was living
a cliché. The cat had my tongue and you could hear a pin drop. Cecil had some real issues with Evangeline and he'd decided to take
them out on her in the book . . . This was fucking great.
   "Holy shit on a stick," Shoshanna shouted. "That's some of the
best stuff yet. You should be a real writer, Cecil." She got up and
slapped him on the back. If she only knew the truth. This was Cecil's chance to come clean. I waited to see what he would do . . .
he did nothing. "I mean it, you sneaky son of a bitch." LeHump
bounced around the room. "You're really good."
   "The framework had already been expertly laid." He winked at
me and grinned sheepishly. "Is it too much?"
   "Do you think she'll actually read it?" I asked, wondering how
much we could get away with.
   "No, she won't. She doesn't like to read," he said, folding his
hands in his lap.
   "Then we're good to go," Shoshanna sang as she skipped joyously around the small office.
   "Is Nancy bringing lunch today?" I asked, pushing Shoshanna
down onto the couch. She was making me dizzy.
   "Nope, she went to Fargo for a few days to visit her daughter."
   Crap, I wanted to talk to her alone. I wasn't sure if all the ladies
knew exactly what the others were being blackmailed for. I didn't
want to risk embarrassing Nancy by talking out of school. "What's
her cell phone number?"
   "She doesn't have one," LeHump said. "No cell, no answering
machine at home, no bank accounts, no e-mail . . . no nothing."

"How odd." I sat back down next to Shoshanna. "It's like she doesn't exist." I glanced over at Cecil. He was avidly brushing non-existent lint from his pants. He knew.

If I was unsure before, I wasn't anymore. Nancy was Nan Thorenson. But never one to leave anything to chance, I kept pushing. "Does Evangeline write cookbooks?" I asked Cecil, who refused to meet my eye.

"Yes, she does," he mumbled.

"Now Cecil, that's not exactly accurate," Shoshanna fumed, hopping up and poking her little finger into his chest. "The skanky hooker doesn't write cookbooks, she steals them . . . from Nancy. For a long time I thought the bitch couldn't write at all; I mean a good handful of her books were written totally by Poppy Harriet, Nancy, and myself. She didn't bother to change a word. Not one fucking word." Shoshanna's voice hardened. "Then I read the Castaway Series, and I realized the hag was a magnificent writer. Ten brilliant books, some of the best I've ever read." She shook her head and her little shoulders fell. "I just don't understand. If she's such a great writer, why did she steal all those books from us? She stole careers and livelihoods and dreams."

I glanced over at Cecil; he was staring down at his notebook. Every part of his body was as still as a statue, except his hands . . . they were trembling. "I must excuse myself." His voice was distant and resigned. He stood up and left. So much for him coming over to our side . . . whatever she had on him was good, and I was going to find out what it was if it killed me.

Chapter 21

Holy hell, it was five-fifteen and Jack was due to get here at six. I twisted my hair up into a messy knot so it would stay dry and hopped into the lemon-scented sudsy tub. I tried to relax, but that was a joke. I've been stretched as tight as a drum all day. Thursday had gone by in a blur. I was so excited for Jack to get back, I couldn't concentrate on anything.

Joanne and Poppy Harriet had spent most of the day with us and each took several stabs at Pirate Dave's adventures. Poppy Harriet's chapters were filled with bizarre and potentially dangerous sexual uses for items you could find at your local hardware store. I was so perplexed by her description of a blow job using a door-knocker, I got a headache. Cecil just looked nauseated.

Joanne, living in a strange and violent place in her mind, chose to do painful and permanent things to Pirate Dave's secret admirer (a barely disguised version of Evangeline). She decimated Evangeline's hair, face, and upper torso. It was so disturbing, I felt myself viscerally reacting.

In the end we kept it all. It gave the book a wonderfully disjointed feeling, a real sense of no direction whatsoever. The reviews were sure to suck. I was curious what Joanne really wrote after that alarming chapter she spewed out. I figured it must be horror or true crime, but we were so busy laughing I had no time to ask.

Leaving the day behind me, I leaned back in the tub and tried to wipe everything from my mind except Jack's butt and the relaxing scent of my lemony bathwater.

"Mmm, smells good in here," Kristy said, sitting on the closed toilet in the bathroom. "What are you wearing for your hot date tonight?"

"My good butt jeans, a pale coffee camisole, that sheer cream sexy top, and my shit-kickin' boots." I grinned, taking off the top layer of my skin with the loofah. I planned to make my whole body as soft as a baby's bottom.

"Well, you better hurry. He'll be here soon and unless you want to greet him in your birthday . . ."

"Hello ladies," Jack said, leaning against the door frame of my bathroom.

"Shit," I screamed; both Kristy and I jumped. I sloshed lemon water all over the floor and all over Kristy. "Oh my God, have you ever heard of knocking?" I yelled. Kristy looked down at the floor, trying not to laugh.

Jack smiled and tilted his head to one side, making me want to hop out of the tub, tackle him, and have my way with him. "The front door was wide open," he said, grinning from ear to ear.

"Oooh, my bad." Kristy winced. "I was carrying groceries in and I forget to shut it."

I rolled my eyes and tried to make sure the bubbles were covering my privates. I'd deal with my ass-hat roommate later.

"Kristy, would you mind giving Rena and me a moment, please?"

"Not at all." She winked at me as she backed out of the bathroom.

"Traitor," I yelled at her. She laughed as she left the apartment, shutting the door behind her.

"I'm naked," I told him, stating the obvious.

"Yes, you are," he acknowledged.

"You have to turn around so I can get out."

"Nope."

"Nope?" I repeated, narrowing my eyes at him.

"Nope." He was grinning. Clearly the eye-narrowing thing didn't affect him. I tried staring him down and he just smirked back. Damn, his eyes were beautiful. "You're breathtaking," he whispered, sending little jolts all through my body.

"I'll be a shriveled prune if you don't leave the bathroom and let me get out," I shot back as I noticed the bubbles disappearing. Shit.

"Let's play a game," he suggested with a glint in his eye. Uh-oh . . . I could see his brain wheels turning.

"What kind of game?" I asked, trying to suppress my inner slut, who was demanding I agree to anything the sexy guy wanted.

"It's called 'Look But Don't Touch.' I promise not to touch, but I get to watch." His voice was husky and low. It was a good thing there wasn't enough water in the tub for me to drown in because he was turning me into jelly.

I examined my pruney fingers and considered his request. I might be able to work this to my advantage if my inner ho-bag didn't get out of line. My plan was to seduce him, make him realize I trusted him, and then ride him like a cowboy until we both passed out.

"Fine," I told him, "you can look, but you can't touch."

I stood up and smiled, letting the suds slowly slide down my body. I had never been so bold in my life, but this man made me feel so sexy, I'd consider streaking again. His hands closed into fists and I enjoyed watching him try to stay put. I leisurely ran my hands over my breasts, my hips, my stomach, and thighs, pushing the rest of the suds down to my ankles. I enjoyed torturing him. Unfortunately I was also torturing myself. I wanted him so badly I physically ached.

I stepped out of the tub and bent over at the hips, my very nice rear end facing him, and picked up a fluffy white bath sheet. My inner ho-bag and slut were high-fiving with joy. I heard him groan and purposely bang his head on the doorframe. Damn, this was fun.

"You are so mean," he laughed.

"Oh baby," I cooed, "I am so just getting started." I began to dry my body, starting at my feet, my calves, my thighs . . . When I got to my bottom, I put the bath towel between my legs, holding it with my right hand in front of me and my left hand behind. All I needed was some cheesy background music and I could be starring in my own porno. I bitch-slapped the inner critic in my head and decided to go for it. I pulled the nubby towel back and forth, watching him the entire time. His lips were parted and his gorgeous eyes were hooded. His hands had unclenched and he was holding on to the doorframe above his head. Evidence of his desire was obvious. Tremendously so.

The towel was creating a friction between my legs that was very close to backfiring on me. Instead of drying myself, I was getting soaked. The look in his eyes and the pressure between my legs made my knees buckle. I didn't even see him move, but move he did.

One hand was on my back, pressing my breasts against his chest. The other was on my ass and sliding lower, reaching with his fingers between my legs. He groaned as he felt how wet I was and reached further, finding the spot that only I was ever able to zone in on. He had no trouble. He began to rub in circular motions with well-aimed pinches in between.

"You're cheating," I gasped, trying unsuccessfully to calm my undulating hips.

"You win, I lose," he ground out as he captured my mouth with his. He wasn't even a little bit gentle. His manhandling was about to make me speak in tongues.

"Jack," I moaned, "you're making me come apart."

"I just want to make you to come," he said as his lips and teeth moved to my neck. His tongue darted to the concave area by my collar bone and I shuddered. His hand was moving so quickly against me I was whimpering. I was spiraling out of control and loving it. His fingers felt better than Vinnie set on high. I bucked against his hand, moaned his name, and raked my nails down his back.

"God, Rena," he whispered against my ear, "you are killing me. So sexy, so beautiful . . . so fucking wet. You're mine. No one else's. Mine." He increased his efforts. My lady bits were literally throbbing under his expert hands. I couldn't speak, I thought I might pass out and fall to the floor from the onslaught of sensation, but lucky for me I stayed conscious. He buried his teeth in my neck at the same time he buried two fingers deeply inside me.

I screamed.

As he made love to my mouth with his own, he worked his fingers in and out of my body. The pleasure from the activity he was engaged in made me see Jesus. I screamed again and swore in at least five languages. My body jerked and tightened like a vise around his hand. I heard him laugh in total masculine pleasure as I kept spasming over and over while his fingers continued to move inside me.

It seemed like hours later when I floated down from the most intense orgasm I'd ever had in my life. I was ready to pass out, but Jack had other plans. He gave me no downtime as his hands went back to work on my most sensitive areas. My body stiffened to reject him, but he wouldn't stop. His mouth found mine as his fingers went to my magic spot and began an erotic massage. I was still tender and swollen from before, but that didn't slow him.

"Jack, I can't," I whimpered.

"Yes, you can," he said. His lips made their way from my mouth to my neck.

"No more," I pleaded, "please . . . no more."

"Yes more, so much more," he said as his mouth closed over my painfully erect nipple and sucked. While my mouth was busy telling him no, my body was telling an entirely different story. My hips pumped against his hand and my back arched to give him better access to my breasts. My inner slut and I had become one and we were having a hell of a good time.

The tightening and tingling started between my legs and traveled upward, sending shock waves pinging through me. I wrapped my arms around his head as he teased my nipples with his tongue and spread my legs to give him better access. He chuckled and bit down on my nipple.

I cried out from the pain and pleasure of what he was doing. My body tried to jerk away, but he held me fast. His fingers continued to plunge into me and he pressed the heel of his hand against my clit. The rhythm of my hips increased to a frantic pace and I let loose a string of swear words I didn't know I knew as my body exploded into another earth-shattering orgasm. I was certain my voice would be gone for six months. Jack held me tight, showering me with kisses as I rode out my second orgasm in fifteen minutes.

"Oh my God," I croaked, "that was . . . I've never. Oh God, you're amazing."

He smiled and brushed my wild hair out of my face, carried me into my bedroom and sat me on his lap. "You amaze me. You are everything I want."

I realized, while I'd had my turn and then some, he had not . . .

"Um Jack." All of a sudden I felt shy. "Do you want to . . . finish what we um . . . started?"

"I would love to," he grinned and my tummy flipped. "But only if you trust me."

"Jack."

"Yes?"

"I trust you. I really, really trust you."

"Thank God," he laughed, tossing me onto my back on the bed. "So, what should we do first?" His eyes raked my body, making me tingle in anticipation.

"I think we already did first. It's time for second. Get naked," I ordered gleefully.

He barked with laughter and obliged. "With pleasure." His voice was hoarse and sexy. Even after what my body had just been through, it wanted more. It took everything I had not to throw myself at him while he slowly disrobed. Obnoxiously slow. With a huge grin on his face, he danced around the bedroom like a male stripper with no sense of rhythm. As I laughed at his show, he removed his shirt . . . then his shoes . . . then his socks . . . then his belt . . . then his pants. Then his boxer briefs.

Oh. My. God. His body was glorious. Strong and muscular and so fucking hot, like satin stretched over steel. His shoulders were broad and his arms were muscular. His chest was perfection with a light sprinkling of crisp blond hair. It tapered down to his abdomen, which was ripped; his cock was long and thick and as hard as a rock. I clenched in anticipation of how he would feel inside me. His eyes narrowed as he watched me like a predator watches his prey. He waited for me to make the first move before he pounced.

Hmm, a new game . . . I hopped off the bed and touched him. He kept his hands still at his sides, letting me do all the work. His muscles rippled under my fingertips and his body shuddered as I lightly ran my nails over his nipples. I liked this game.

I moved lower, taking him into my hands. He felt so good, so perfect, but I wanted more. I kept my eyes on his as I slowly dropped down until my mouth was right where I wanted it. They stayed locked on his as I flicked my tongue out and circled the swollen head of his cock. He groaned and twined his fingers into my hair, pushing my mouth further down on him.

I had never known the taste and feel of a man in my mouth could be so erotic. He was intoxicating. Making him come apart at the seams was as much of a turn-on as riding him like a cowboy. I gripped his hips and relaxed my throat, taking in as much of him as I could.

I felt powerful and sexy as I went down on him. He made the sexiest sounds I'd ever heard and my whole body reacted. His moans spurred me to move faster, taking him deeper and deeper.

"Rena, stop," Jack hissed, pulling me off him. It made a popping sound as my mouth released him. I could still taste him on my tongue and lips as he dragged me up his body. "I want to come inside you," he growled and moved to my breasts. His teeth, lips, and tongue on my nipples were making me lose it. He divided his attention between my breasts, licking, nipping, and sucking me into a blubbering mess.

His beautiful mouth and talented tongue moved slowly down my body, over my ribs, my stomach, and then lower to the center of my universe. He pushed me down on the bed and greedily went after what he wanted. To completely destroy me.

He went to work with an expertise and hunger that was mind blowing. My hips began to buck. I didn't know I had anything left. I gasped and moaned as he licked and nipped.

Tears were streaming from my eyes as he took my sex into his mouth and sucked.

"So fucking hot," he muttered before he pushed his tongue up inside me, while his fingers mercilessly teased my clit.

Right before I had another big O, he stopped. He slid back up my body, placing a heavy thigh between my legs, ensuring I stayed open for him.

He needn't have bothered with the thigh. I could barely move and I would have happily given him anything he wanted. I was wrecked, and we hadn't even done it yet. He stared down at me and I forgot how to breathe. He very gently traced my lips with his finger.

"I'm falling for you," he said.

"Me, too," I whispered.

His smile made my heart skip beats. "I want to hear you scream again, Rena." The finger that had traced my lip moved to my breast. "I'm going to fuck you now until we both come apart."

Holy God Almighty, my body was no longer tired. No one had spoken to me like that. Ever . . . and I loved it. Excitement blasted through me and I could feel the hard evidence of his need pressed against my hip. He got up and grabbed a condom from his jeans. His naked back was as beautiful as his front, but . . .

"Um, Jack, what is that?" I asked, pointing to the large giraffe that covered a good portion of his back.

"What's what?" he asked, tearing the wrapper off the condom.

"On your back. Turn around." I sat up.

Jack froze. I watched as he racked his brain for an acceptable reason he had a humongous giraffe on his back . . . I couldn't think of one and apparently neither could he.

"It was a long time ago. I was drunk," he said, crawling back onto the bed and attempting to kiss me into forgetting he had a giraffe on his back. He clearly didn't know me as well as he thought he did. A large ink giraffe was not something I could let go of.

"Do you like giraffes?" I asked, trying to turn him over to get a better look.

"Goddamnit, Rena, you're killing the mood here."

"I'm not killing it," I giggled. "Your avoidance of the giraffe is."

"Okay—" He blew out a long exasperated sigh. "I lost a bet in college. I had a choice between a giraffe and Jay Leno. I chose the giraffe. End of story."

I bit my lip hard as I imagined a huge Jay Leno tattooed across his back. "I'm glad you picked the giraffe," I mumbled, praying the Inappropriate Laughing Monster would not rear her ugly head and completely ruin the evening.

"Can we just fuck?" he asked, clearly expecting more giraffe questions from me.

I decided to surprise him. "Yep, let's fuck." I grinned. I'd get back to the giraffe another time. Soon.

He heaved a huge sigh of relief and repositioned himself at my very wet and ready entrance. He slowly pushed into me. I closed my eyes at the amazing sensation.

"Open your eyes," Jack commanded. "Look at me."

I did. I didn't think anything could be more intimate than making love with him and his giraffe, but I was wrong. Very wrong. I had never felt so vulnerable in my life as when we watched each other while he entered me. It was empowering and frightening.

He studied me as I adjusted to his body filling mine. I closed my eyes and he stopped. I looked up at him, startled.

"Don't you want more?" he asked, inching a bit more into me.

"Yes," I gasped.

"Then watch me when I fuck you."

"Yes," I whimpered.

With a quick deep thrust he buried himself completely inside me. My body convulsed around his and I cried out. The physical shock of his size was something my body desired, yet fought against. He started slow and steady, but my writhing and bucking wildly beneath him interfered with his rhythm. Before I knew it, he was pounding into me with a force and speed that should have killed me dead. It didn't. I met every thrust with joyful abandon.

He gripped me by my hair and slanted his mouth against mine. His cock and tongue matched each other stroke for stroke. I wrapped my legs around his waist, giving him deeper access. He growled his approval. My orgasm swallowed me like an inferno. I sucked his tongue into my mouth and gripped him inside me with a force that sent shock waves rippling through my body and shudders rocking his.

"You're mine," he whispered. "Say it."

"I'm yours," I gasped, gripping his shoulders.

"Say it again," he demanded.

I did. I'm fairly sure I chanted it as my world kept exploding in gorgeous colors all around me. Jack's body tensed and he shouted as he came, knocking me into the land of impossibility . . . another orgasm.

Chapter 22

Soreness from working out is one thing . . . soreness from having the best sex of my whole fucking life was an entirely different kind of pain. The really good kind. Giraffe or no giraffe, Jack was rockin' in the sack. I glanced over at my future husband and sighed. He had no idea what I had planned for him, but as far as I was concerned he would have no choice. Anyone who can boink me into unconsciousness after giving me multiple big Os was not going anywhere. Ever.

"Hi." He grinned, stretching his yummy body.

"Hi yourself," I giggled, running my hand over his sexy morning stubble.

"Do you want to go to breakfast?" he asked. "Or can I have you for breakfast?"

"Ohh," I flopped back on my pillow, cursing Evangeline for the millionth time. "I can't do either. I have to go to work."

"Call in sick," he whispered, cupping my breast in his big hand and moving my hand down to greet his very excited happy camper.

"I wish I could," I laughed, trying to roll away, "but I can't. I have a deadline."

He wrapped me in his arms and kissed the top of my head. "Okay, but you have to promise we can do it in my car after your parents' anniversary party tonight."

"Oh my God, I almost forgot about that. Do you want to go together?" I asked.

"Yep. I'm feeling a little addicted right now. I'm considering going to work with you today," he chuckled. "Although, apparently I have a meeting about a major donation to the Police Department at the O'Hara estate around six. So I actually will be stalking you at your place of employment." He smiled. "We can leave for the party when I'm done."

Shit, shit, shit. I still hadn't told him about Evangeline wanting him for her concubine. "I have to tell you something." I sat up and got a wonky feeling in my tummy. I wasn't the one who wanted to blackmail him . . . why did I feel so weird? "Jack, there is no major donation."

"Right." He grinned, trying to cop a feel of my ass.

"I'm serious." I swatted his hand away and quickly yanked on a T-shirt and panties. This was not a buck-ass naked conversation we were about to have. "There is no donation," I repeated.

"Okay," he said patronizingly, "if there's no donation, why am I going there?"

I crossed my hands over my braless chest and for a brief moment considered not telling him. Letting him show up totally unprepared to be hit on by an eighty-year-old bag of bones with obscene titties and a face that would scare small children. No . . . I couldn't do that to my worst enemy. "Evangeline is going to try to blackmail you into giving her stud services."

Jack threw his head back and laughed so hard, I thought he might choke. "Oh my God, Rena." He pulled on his jeans and tried to swallow his grin. "That is just so wrong."

"I'm serious," I said.

"Uh huh," he chuckled, pulling on his shoes. "Okay then, after I have sex with my great-great grandmother, we can go to your parents' party."

"This isn't a joke," I insisted. "You're being set up by Sergeant Santa and Herbie the Cop-Dentist."

"Rena, stop." His laughter disappeared. "It was funny for a minute and now, not so much."

"I'm not trying to be funny, Jack. Santa and Herbie are on her payroll and she wants to play hide the salami with you, so they are going to frame you for something and force you to . . . you know." I put on some sweats, thinking he might take me more seriously if I was dressed.

"Enough," he said, running his hands through his hair. "I get that you hate that I'm a cop. With your colorful past that makes sense, but this is ridiculous. I am a cop. I love what I do. If you have a real problem with that . . . we need to have a talk."

"Is that what you think this is about?" I said louder than I intended. I was trying to save him and he was treating me like I was a cop-hating jealous idiot.

"What in the hell am I supposed to think? You just informed me that my boss and a fellow officer are going to blackmail me into sleeping with the most grotesque woman I ever had the displeasure to meet," he yelled.

"It's not my fault you work for ass-monkeys," I yelled back.

He shook his head in disgust. "We are not having this conversation right now. I have to go."

"You're not going anywhere until you believe me." I ran to my bedroom door and stood in front of it.

"Rena, I love the crazy part of you, but you're starting to sound like your Aunt Phyllis."

I was this close to having an aneurysm. "You did not just say that." My anger practically choked me. "Take it back."

"Rena . . ." His voice was full of warning signals that I chose to ignore.

"I am not my Aunt Phyllis and you're not the only one Evangeline is blackmailing," I hissed. "Don't for a minute think I didn't know you were trying to get the scoop on the jewels I stole. I knew you were snooping around, trying to sell me down the river so you could get a big fat hairy promotion."

Jack dropped back down on the bed, flabbergasted. "You stole jewels?"

"No! I didn't steal any fucking jewels," I shouted. "She planted them in that package I was delivering when you arrested me. And now she has me by the balls and I'm not even getting paid for it."

"What are you talking about?" He threw his hands up and looked at me like I was insane. "The box was empty. There was nothing in the box, Rena."

My head spun. The box was empty? Fucking empty? The realization hit with a sickening thud . . . I didn't owe that viper anything. She didn't have a damned thing on me. I didn't have to go back there, ever.

"Rena, I think we have a problem," he said, sounding distant and uncomfortable.

I said nothing. I couldn't speak. The pressure in my chest was building rapidly, and I knew if I opened my mouth I would scream, further proving his case for my insanity.

"If you really think I was trying to have you incarcerated and you insist on libeling my boss . . . I don't know what to say . . ." He dropped his head into his hands and sat silently on my bed.

"I want to say I'm sorry," I whispered. He raised his eyes to mine, hopeful. "I should have trusted you and I do now. I don't have any problem with you being a cop. Just like you don't have any problem with my rap sheet." I gave him a lopsided grin. The beginnings of a smile pulled at the corners of his mouth. "But I'm serious about your boss and Evangeline forcing you to be her boy-toy. I heard the whole thing go down. Herbie even offered to do her, but she was having none of it. She told Santa he was shriveled and . . ."

"Goddamnit, Rena." Jack's smile was gone and his voice turned hard. "I can't do this. You need some help and I need to go." He stood up and moved me from the doorway. "It's probably good it didn't go any further than this," he said coldly, referring to the best night of my life. "I guess I'll just . . . see you around." With a final look of anger and pity, he left.

He walked out of the door and out of my life.

My legs gave way and I crumpled to the floor. I pressed my head to my knees and sat there. For a long time. Never, never again would I give my heart to anyone. I couldn't anyway . . . the one inside my chest had just shattered into a million pieces.

Chapter 23

Going back to hell wasn't an option. For two weeks, that viper whore-bag had had me living in abject terror of spending years in the slammer. She could shove the partially finished Pirate Dave novel up her skinny ass.

I spent two hours packing all my belongings. I was moving out. The thought of running into Mr. Giraffe-back was more terrifying than spending five years in the pokey. I had horrible visions of me begging for another chance and him laughing in my face. Or even worse, running into him with some hot babe attached to his fine ass. To avoid that humiliation, I decided to move to another state. Far away. Accountants are needed everywhere, even in Russia.

I called Shoshanna and explained what had happened and why I wasn't coming back. She was quiet for a long time, and then she told me that she loved me and she was glad I was free from the skank. She even offered to let me stay at her place. That made me feel like a piece of shit, but I held on to my resolve. Her concern for my well-being when I was leaving her to drown was mind blowing. She was a far better person than I was . . . or ever would be.

"What are you doing?" Kristy asked.

"Shit," I screeched, dropping all my high school yearbooks. "Don't sneak up on me like that."

"I didn't. I repeat, what are you doing?" She folded her arms across her chest and eyed the hurricane that used to be my room.

"I'm moving."

"I can see that." She nodded. "Where to?"

"Not sure yet," I admitted. "But it will be far away. Possibly Iceland."

"Interesting," she said. "Any reason for the abrupt departure?"

"Yep," I said, shoving all my underwear into a shopping bag.

"Want to share?" she asked, pushing my box of high school cheerleading trophies over and plopping down on my bed.

"Nope."

"Considering that I am your roommate and best friend and the simple fact that I can't afford this apartment without someone paying the other half of the rent . . . I suggest you spill, or I'm going to call your mom and tell her you're moving to Iceland."

I gave her my best pissed-off look. She laughed.

"Fine," I huffed. "Jack broke up with me because I'm insane and the Viper-slag doesn't really have anything on me because there weren't any fucking jewels in the box. So apparently I'm being blackmailed for nothing. The crooked cops are going to force Jack to screw the Viper-whore and he didn't believe me when I tried to warn him. It turns out Poppy's a man, LeHump was married to a homosexual, and Nancy thinks her cooking was behind salmonella-gate. I don't know what the hell Joanne's problem is and I'm scared to find out. All these women are going down and I can't save them. Aunt Phyllis expects me to attend Bigfoot meetings, and I've discovered I know more terms for the word penis than should be humanly possible. I will never listen to Oprah again because visualizing my future was what got me into this fucked-up mess to start with. But mostly I hate Jack. So I have to move." I crumpled to the floor, for the second time that day, and burst into tears.

"Oh my God." Kristy was on the floor instantly. She wrapped her arms around me and rocked me like a baby. "I didn't follow a lot of that, but I understand the impulse now."

"I ruined everything," I sobbed.

"Not yet," she said.

"What to you mean?" I sniffled.

"I mean, you can still redeem yourself with at least part of that list," she said, stroking my hair.

"I don't want to." I got up and halfheartedly started packing again.

"Well then, you're just a selfish bitch," she said, so matter-of-fact, I thought I had heard her wrong.

"What did you call me?" I stopped packing and stared at her in shock.

"You heard me." She raised her eyebrow in challenge. "You have no heart at all if you leave all those women who love you to be destroyed by that hateful slag."

"You're right about the heart. That got obliterated an hour ago. As far as the rent goes, I'll pay till you can find a new roommate who's not a heartless bitch. And the ladies—" I paused. I felt sick to my stomach and I wanted to tear my hair out in frustration. "I don't know how to help them," I yelled.

"When has that ever stopped you?" Kristy yelled back. "You went after the weather girl job and you threw your hat in to be an author . . ."

"And look where that got me," I snapped, "arrested, black-mailed, and dumped."

"Okay," she caved. "Maybe I didn't pick the best examples."

"Ya think?"

"Fine"—she rolled her eyes—"I picked shitty examples, but you're not a quitter."

"Yes, I am." I zipped my suitcase shut and looked at my best friend. "I'm sorry."

"For what?" she asked, her eyes filling with tears.

"For yelling at you . . . for being a selfish bitch. For just . . . I'm sorry." I picked up my suitcase and the shopping bag of undies and made my way to the front door.

"You're really leaving?"

"I have to. Do you mind if I leave the trophies and yearbooks and stuff here until I know where I'll be?" I asked, trying to hold back my own waterfall.

"That's fine," she said, hugging me tight. "Rena," she paused, "what are some of the other names for penis?"

"The two worst ones are skin flute and pork sword," I said, trying not to giggle. I couldn't believe after our horrid conversation she still cared enough to try to make me smile.

"I've never heard those before," she laughed. "Call me when you know where you'll be. I love you."

"I love you, too."

I dragged my suitcase down to my car and I left.

Driving around for three hours with nowhere to go is expensive and stupid. I got lost six times. The talking lady in my GPS got so confused, it was almost funny. Almost. I pressed about four buttons to turn her off and then I couldn't figure out how to turn her back on.

Conversations with Kristy and LeHump and the rest of the gals played through my head until it pounded. The worst was reliving the pity and disgust on Jack's face . . . the memory left me feeling like I had shards of glass in my throat.

The only reasonable thing to do was to leave. Anyone could see that. My mom and dad would shit. Aunt Phyllis would miss me terribly. And Jenny . . . Jenny would laugh and shake her head, explaining to anyone who would listen what a pathetic loser I was.

Kristy would be okay and the ladies would move on, hopefully without Evangeline. I planned to send Nancy a letter detailing what I'd found out about salmonella-gate. I hoped that would help. Cecil worried me, but I still didn't trust him. I could only pray he'd find a way out. Jack . . . fuck Jack, he wouldn't even notice I was gone. If he did, he'd only feel relief.

With shaky fingers I had called my accounting firm and asked for a transfer. They'd laughed when I requested Iceland and suggested I stick with an English-speaking area, like Iowa. I told them I'd take it. The job would start in two weeks. That gave me some time to get my shit together before I left. It wasn't Russia, but it was far enough that I wouldn't disgrace myself with Jack any further than I already had.

I decided to drive to the travel agent and book my Iowa tickets. I had nothing better to do. I checked my watch; it was three-thirty. I still had a butt load of time to kill before my parents' anniversary party. I drove until I found where I needed to go. I slowed the car to a stop, put it in park, and banged my head on the steering wheel. Five times. What in the hell was I doing? I couldn't go in there. If I went in I would change the course of my life irrevocably. There was no going back. I thought about how great my life was up until this morning, well, most of it, and I stared at the building in front of me. Were the mistakes I'd made too big to overcome? Was Kristy right about me not being a quitter? It didn't really matter. The look on Jack's face when he'd left . . . I'd never forget that one.

I knew I'd made the right decision because the weight in my chest lifted. I was free. I might be impulsive and reckless and foul-mouthed, but I wasn't a quitter. I got out of the car, sucked in a huge breath, and prepared to meet my destiny. I slowly walked up the drive and stopped at the repulsive monstrosity near the entrance. I smacked the huge cement butt of the obscene statue I'd hidden behind the other morning and I went in to kick some ass. Evangeline thought she had me, but she didn't. The tables had turned. She had no idea what she was dealing with now. I had absolutely nothing to lose. I was a dangerous combination of fearless rage and vengeful recently dumped girlfriend. A very bad combo. I still hadn't ruled out Iowa, but I needed to stand up for the people who loved me, despite the fact I was a selfish bitch.

Chapter 24

"You're late," it hissed as I walked through the front door.
"Yep." I smiled and flipped Evangeline the bird as I made my way back to the hideous pink office.

I stood outside the closed door and practiced my deep breathing. I heard several voices and figured they were all in there. My hand shook as I reached for the knob. Would they all be angry at me for deserting them? Did they hate me? Shit. What was I thinking? They didn't need me. I turned to leave and ran smack into my worst nightmare come to life.

"Leaving so soon?" the Viper spat.

Holy hell, what was wrong with her face? Her cheeks looked swollen like a chipmunk's, and what little eyelids she'd had before were gone. "No," I said trying to look away from her. "I was just plotting." Her demise.

"Good," she told me, "because it would be a shame if I had to press charges."

"It would be, wouldn't it?" I laughed.

"You think that's funny?" she demanded, completely confused by my demeanor.

"Yes, in fact, I do. Now, if you'll excuse me, I have work to do. Oh, Evangeline"—I gave her a lovingly concerned look—"you might want to check your boobs. The left one seems a bit smaller than the right one."

She shrieked in horror and wobble-ran down the hallway as fast as her spindly legs would take her. Damn, that felt good.

"Hi honey, I'm home," I said as I walked back into my life.

"Praise Sweet Baby Jesus," Poppy Harriet yelled, smothering

me in a bear hug. "Joanne was trying to have Pirate Dave peel the skin off of his secret admirer while Captain Hook pulled off her toenails with pliers."

"Rusty pliers." Joanne grinned evilly. Holy cow, her eyebrows were growing back. Bushy, just like LeHump had said.

"Welcome back, Rena," Cecil said with relief written all over his face. Who knew Cecil would prefer double doinkers and blind trolls to skin peeling and toenail removal?

I scanned the room looking for LeHump. She sat in the corner with a big shit-eating grin on her face. "I knew you'd be back. Life's just not as much fun without us."

"You are correct, Madame." I grinned back.

"Shall we get started?" Cecil asked, looking exhausted from his morning with the gals.

"Yes"—I smiled at everyone— "we shall."

Pirate Dave was so depressed he'd forgotten he was a warlock. After eating six bags of frozen Schmiggy's Potato Fun Balls, he remembered that he could magic off the one hundred and seventy-five pounds he'd gained over the past two weeks. "Son of a bitch," he yelled, trying to move his lard ass to a wide-open area for the spell.

As pissed off as he was about having two tallywhackers, he missed looking at them. Admiring his man parts had been a large part of his life until he'd gotten too porcine to see his beloved peckers.

He was slightly worried about a heart attack. Warlock spells were vigorous and profane. Would his jiggly girth end up being the cause of his death? Wait the fuck a minute. He was a goddamn vampire, too! Vampires didn't have hearts. What the hell and tarnation had he been thinking?

Pirate Dave danced in a circle and cussed up a storm. Break-dancing was difficult when you weighed almost four hundred pounds. Lightning ripped through the sky as Dave's undulating ripped a great big hole in his breeches. A gust of glittering silver mist engulfed him and swirled across the deck of the ship. He swore twice as hard when a clump of the sparkly crap flew up his nose. Slowly he felt his body

*morph back to the hot, sexy, hairy bastard he'd been before
he had used fast food as therapy.*

*"I'm back," he bellowed, grasping his double man-rod
lovingly. He waltzed with his wieners, turning joyous circle
after circle across the deck. He couldn't wait to show
Laverne and Shirley. The local mermaids heard the ruckus
and came to see what the fuss was about. They pointed and
laughed at poor Pirate Dave's twin wanks, but Dave didn't
care. Those mermaids were whores and they ate their lovers
when they tired of them. Pirate Dave had lost four hundred
and seventy-two friends over the years to those cannibalistic
swimming bitches.*

*He turned his back to the waterlogged hookers and that's
when the screaming began. Horrible screams. Worse than
Shirley on a bad day. He grabbed a mirror to see if possibly
another penis was growing out of his back. No, it was
worse, far, far worse. Pirate Dave's knees buckled and he
dropped to the deck, wailing in agony. That blind
motherfucking troll had given him two gifts. Not only had he
damned Pirate Dave with double skin flutes, he had tattooed
Dave's back with the most heinous, evil, monstrous, enemy
in the entire world . . . Across Pirate Dave's back, covering
it from shoulder to ass, in bright vibrant color was the
feared and hated and dreaded . . . giraffe.*

The silence lasted approximately thirty-seven seconds before the
entire room burst into hysterics.

"Oh shit," Shoshanna said, "I wish Nancy had been here for that
one. Where in the hell did that come from? Do you have something
against giraffes?" she laughed.

"Kind of," I muttered sheepishly.

"A little odd," Cecil agreed, "but strangely entertaining."

"I think you're enjoying yourself, Cecil," I teased. "You'd better watch out; before you know it we'll be showing up at your
house for casseroles and poker."

"It would be an honor, Miss," Cecil said quietly, dipping his
head to hide his blush. Damn it, he was making it very hard to hate
him.

"Well, I don't know about you guys, but I'm beat," Joanne said, pulling out a small comb and gently running it through her eyebrows. "Goodnight all. Rena, I'm so glad you came back."

Poppy Harriet scooped me up into another hug. "Rena, thank you for dealing with the finance issues. The young lady from your firm is outstanding and said it will be fixed next week." She gave me a kiss on the cheek and another big squeeze.

Cecil took his leave with a slight bow and a tiny smile. "I'm happy you came back. We need you."

Then it was just me and LeHump.

"What made you change your mind?" she asked, pulling on her lime-green coat, then straightening our desk.

"It wasn't any one thing," I said trying to figure it out myself. "It was just right."

"I'm glad." She smiled and smooshed my face in her little hands.

"Shoshanna, does the offer to stay with you still stand?" I asked, realizing I had nowhere to go.

"You bet," she said. "Door's always open to friends."

"Great. It'll only be for two weeks, I took a transfer to Iowa," I told her. Why did saying that make me feel nauseated?

"Iowa? What the fuck is in Iowa?" Shoshanna was surprised.

"I don't know, but I'm going to find out. I'm very excited about it; it's a great opportunity." I plastered a huge smile on my face and prayed she wouldn't notice how fake it was.

"Hmmm." She gave me a long stare. "Running away doesn't usually solve anything, little missy, but if you have to go, you have to go. Come on, you can follow me home."

"No, I can't. I'm going to my folks' anniversary party tonight. My stuff's in my car. I'll just change and leave from here," I said, thinking it out as I spoke. "I should be back at your place around eleven. Twelve at the latest. I'll walk out with you. I have to get my outfit for tonight."

"Lead the way, roomie," she laughed.

I rolled my eyes and hoped like hell she didn't snore.

Why had I shoved all my clothes in the suitcase without folding them? I examined the three extremely wrinkled dresses lying on the desk and couldn't decide which one was the lesser of all evils. Jenny would definitely have a snarky comment about sloppy personal hygiene. Although giving her ammunition to insult me would free me up to call her bubble butt or tubby tush or hulking heinie. That made the evening ahead a bit more tolerable.

I yanked on a very expensive and wrinkled wrap dress. At least the teal and navy pattern hid some of the creases. Whatever, the party wasn't about me. It was about my parents celebrating their wedding anniversary. Something I'd never have.

I was unsure whether I would tell everyone Jack had died in a bizarre gardening accident or whether I'd tell them he'd turned out to be gay. I'd have to cry a lot if I went with the dead thing. I'd left my waterproof mascara back at the apartment, so that was out. Gay it shall be. Jenny would love it, but it was better than the truth.

I slipped on the designer pumps that represented most of my last year's salary and said good night to the heinous pink office. Walking through the foyer, I heard voices. Jack and Evangeline's voices. Fuck, shit, fuck, fuck, how did I lose track of the time? I had planned to be out of here by five. Maybe I could make it to the front door.

"Let me show you the foyer, Jake darling," Evangeline purred.

"It's Jack," he politely corrected her.

"That's what I said. Jock." She tried to giggle flirtatiously, but it sounded kind of donkey-like.

I could hear their approach. My stomach lurched and I started to sweat. I wasn't going to make it. Frantically, I ran around the foyer, trying to find a fornicating statue to hide behind. Dang it, none of the fuckers would hide me well enough. This was so not happening to me. Here I stood in a room full of screwing statues, in a wrinkled dress ready to be busted by a walking cadaver with tits who had designs on my ex-boyfriend who thought I was insane. Life didn't get much better.

Just as they entered I made an Olympic dive for the mounds of bejeweled baby pink silk that the Viper called curtains. Safe, but shaking like a leaf, I promised God and Buddha and Peyton Manning that I would be a better Lutheran. I would go to church every Sunday and I'd even try Speed Dating for Lutherans with only a partially bad attitude. I peeked out and realized I was going to be a witness to Jack doing Evangeline, or Evangeline doing Jack, or Jack freaking out on Evangeline, or God knew what . . .

"So Jim," she cooed, looking him over seductively, "have you ever seen anything like this?" She threw her arms out like Maria in *The Sound of Music* and fell flat on her face. Guess the weight of those knockers wasn't compatible with arm movement.

"Oh my God," Jack gasped, helping her to her feet. "Are you all right?"

"I'm fine, Jonsey. I'm fine." She tried to laugh it off as she rubbed her ginormous rack all over him while he helped her up. If it wasn't so pathetic, I'd be pissed.

"It's Jack," he said stiffly, trying to ease her away. "Can I get you an ice bag or something? Your eyes look a little odd."

My teeth clamped down on my bottom lip. Extreme pain would keep me from laughing or gagging. So far, so good.

"My eyes are turquoise and they're feasting on you," she shouted, pointing at him with one clawed hand while death-gripping a statue of a woman performing a blow job with the other.

"I'm sorry, what?" he asked, clearly appalled by what he'd just heard.

"Oh Jeff," she tittered, "don't play coy. It's clear what you want." Her voice lowered and she drew her purple feathered miniskirt farther up her leg. What the hell was she wearing? "I can feel the heat. I've been salivating over the manly bulge in your jeans since you arrived. I feel flattered and a bit frightened of such a large love stick." Had she just really called his penis a love stick?

"There must be some misunderstanding," Jack said, backing away. "I'm from the Minneapolis Police Department. I'm here to discuss a donation, Ms. O'Hara."

"Oooh, you're a kinky one, Jeb. You want to be paid?" she leered, moving to take off her top. "I believe we can arrange a little stipend for services rendered."

"Oh no, no, no, no, no." Jack was either trying not to laugh or not to cry. He moved quickly and shoved her shirt back over her head, pulling her wig way over to the left, revealing a shiny hairless head. Oh. My. God. I had no idea she was bald. Shoshanna would pee her pants. Jack, in a state of panic, attempted to fix her wig before she realized she was sporting a bad, bad look.

"Oh John," she moaned, grabbing her bosom. "I love when you manhandle me like this." She reached out and tried to grab his love stick.

"Jesus Christ." Jack jerked his love stick out of her reach and made an effort to catch her as she slid off the statue she was posing on. The weight of those hooters made her life downright dangerous and Jack wasn't quick enough.

"Enough foreplay," she shrieked as she took a tumble to the ground, knocking her wig clean off her head. "Take me to the boudoir and ravish my bosoms."

Did she realize she looked like Uncle Fester with boobs? Jack blanched and quickly kicked her wig away before she noticed the state of her head. Why he was still being civil was beyond me.

"Ms. O'Hara, I'm not here to have any kind of relations with you or your bosom," Jack ground out, trying to hold on to his temper. "I am here to speak to you about a donation. Just a donation. Nothing more."

"Don't be naive," she hissed. "Your Sergeant Gerald sent you here to be my new paramour. Nothing more." She repeated his phrase and laughed a little maniacally. "You will be my toy until I tire of you. If you don't, there will be hell to pay and I don't think your grandfather or Rena need any more pain in their lives." She repositioned herself on the floor in what she felt was a sexy pose, stuck her claw in the air and beckoned him to her. "Now bring your love stick to me and slap it between my trembling thighs," she said silkily.

Holy hell, she had apparently been reading some crappy romance novels for her dialogue. Holding back my laughter was giving me a headache. If I only had a tape recorder . . . Fuck, if I had a tape recorder I could have blackmailed her into not blackmailing us. I could probably use my phone, but any movement on my part was impossible.

Jack bit back his fury and walked slowly toward her.

"That's right," she purred. "Come to mama."

About a foot and a half away from her, just out of reach, Jack dropped to one knee. Holy shit, was he going to do this? "What do you have on my grandpa and Rena, Ms. O'Hara?" The bridled anger in his voice would have scared the shit out of me, but Evangeline was either too stupid or horny to notice. "Tell me right now," he ground out through clenched teeth.

Evangeline, looking up from her pose, finally had the wherewithal to be alarmed by the furious man she was trying to blackmail for sex. "Call me Evangeline, darling," she said huskily, hoping to distract him.

"What do you have on them?" His barely controlled fury was making her more nervous than I'd ever seen her, but Evangeline never lost and she wasn't about to start now.

"Wouldn't you like to know," she laughed.

"As a matter of fact, I would." He pulled out his phone and held it up in front of him. "Smile, Evangeline," he said.

She did. She even arched her back, so her rack would be more evident. Like that was an issue. "Oh, Jimmy, are these for your private collection?" she tittered seductively, pulling her shirt down off one shoulder to give him a better view of her cavernous cleavage.

He continued to take pictures. She hiked her skirt up and revealed what I already expected. She was going commando. "No," Jack shouted, right before she flashed her goodies. "These are art shots, not sick porn." His relief as she let her skirt fall back into place was hilarious.

"Of course, darling, sexy art shots, so you can masturbate while looking at pictures of me." She smiled as well as she could with her face in a semiparalysis from the Botox.

"These aren't for me," he said and popped his phone back into his pocket. "They're for Facebook, unless you'd like to share what you have on my grandfather and girlfriend." Did he just call me his girlfriend? No way, he'd lost all rights to that term about ten hours ago.

"That will never happen, my love," she hissed. "Now come over here and put your big manly hands on my bosom."

"Put your hands on your head, Evangeline," Jack replied sharply.

"Oooh, we're back to the kinky," she said with rabid excitement. She slowly reached up, her eyes never leaving his, and delicately laid her claws on her head. The look on her face was one I'd never forget as long as I lived, but her scream . . . her scream almost broke my eardrums. "My hair," she shrieked. "What have you done with my hair?"

"Don't worry," he said, smiling, "your hair will not be harmed as long as you cooperate."

"If that's your ace in the hole, you're screwed," she spat. "I have forty wigs upstairs."

"Oh, Evangeline, I believe you may have forgotten I just took three pictures of you. Bald and sprawled. If these pictures get out, it might be a bit damaging to your image." Holy shit, he was brilliant.

She glared at him with burning eyes. "What do you want?"

"Here's the deal. I will ask you three questions. For each satisfactory answer, I will erase a picture. If I don't get what I want, I will go home and upload your shiny head onto Facebook for all the world to see. Do we have a deal?"

"Yes," she shouted, frantically scanning the floor for her hair.

"What do you have on my grandfather?"

"Well, um, there are a lot of things and I can't recall exactly what . . ." she stammered.

"Not satisfactory," Jack barked and Evangeline jumped.

"Fine. We couldn't find anything on your grandfather. He's clean," she said, her lips thinning with anger. Jack erased one picture.

"And Rena?"

"The little slut?" she laughed. "I have plenty on her. She tried to steal from me, to the tune of three hundred and seventy-five thousand dollars. Jewels," she hissed, "she stole my jewels."

"Don't you ever, ever call her a slut again. If there's a slut around here, it's you." I heard the Viper's sharp intake of breath. Jack continued, "Is that all you have on Rena?"

"Isn't that enough? I could send her away for years if I chose to press charges. The jewels were in the box she tried to escape with when you arrested her." She smiled nastily.

Jack erased another picture. "There's a small problem with that. The box was empty," he gave her a nasty smile back.

Evangeline blanched, dragged herself over to her hair, and slapped the wig back on her head. Was he on the last question? Shit, I needed that picture. I could end all the heartache of my friends with that picture. The second half of our not very well-thought-out plan would work if I only had that damn picture, but then I'd be no better than her. I'd be a blackmailing viper just like she was. Maybe she'd fuck up the last answer and he'd post her bald head on Facebook. That could easily break her, and the girls would be free. I held my breath and waited.

"How is my sergeant involved in this?"

"It's not just your sergeant, it's that little midget, too," she laughed, seeing a light at the end of the tunnel. She'd sell anyone down the river to save her own bald head.

"Answer the question," Jack snapped. I knew this was difficult for him. Being a cop was sacred. He would have a very hard time with what he was about to find out.

"I pay them," she said flippantly.

"You what?" Jack was floored.

"I. Pay. Them. They do whatever I want them to do, whenever I tell them to do it," she leered.

"That's against the law and totally unethical." Jack's curt voice lashed out at her.

"Welcome to the real world, pretty boy. Now erase the picture and empty the trash."

My heart sank as the only thing that could save my friends disappeared.

"How long has this been going on?" he demanded.

"That's question number four and you're out of pictures," she spat. "But just because it seems so painful to you, I think I'll answer that. Ten years. Ten years those weak bastards have been on my payroll . . . and it's worth every penny."

Jack's fists clenched by his sides. I could feel him fighting every instinct he had. His breathing was uneven and his cheeks were flushed.

"By the way," she continued, triumphantly, "you'll never be able to prove any of this. It's just your word against mine."

"By the way," Jack replied, as he moved toward the front door, "you are the most repulsive excuse for a woman I've ever seen. Take care. I'll be seeing you soon . . . in court."

"Don't bet on it," she spat, looking uglier than I'd ever seen her look.

He left.

I had to stay hidden for another twenty minutes until her screaming fit ended and I was sure she was gone. If Jack had just believed me this morning, I could have saved him from this, but he hadn't. Although the situation was horrid, it was comforting to see him one more time. No time for pity parties. He thought I was crazy and wanted nothing to do with me. I looked down at myself all tangled up in baby pink rhinestone curtain, my dress more wrinkled than it had been when I had put it on, and realized he was right . . . I was crazy and it never would have worked with us.

Fuck it, I'd go be with people who celebrated crazy and practiced it on a daily basis . . . my family.

Chapter 25

The party was in full swing when I finally got there. Over a hundred people were mingling in one of the nicer rooms at the back of the country club. Thank Jesus it was a buffet. Getting stuck with the same people at a table for an entire evening might have just killed me. Mom and Dad were as happy as they'd ever been, greeting friends and laughing at scary Midwestern humor. I caught them lovingly staring at each other on and off. How in the hell could they still be in love after forty years but I couldn't seem to keep a boyfriend more than three weeks?

"Rena," Aunt Phyllis called out from the other side of the room. I waved and she came barreling over. "Kim and Hugh came to my house last night and we had the best time."

"That's great." I smiled, having no clue who Kim and Hugh were. Were they Martians? Trolls? Gremlins?

"The Bigfoot couple!" she reminded me. "Kim is a hoot and Hugh was able to communicate with the little people inside my TV through his music."

"You mean the scary noise that comes out of him while other people are talking?" I laughed.

"Rena," she said, "that's not nice. He is a bit unusual, but very creative."

Now there's a nice word for certifiably crazy. I filed that one away for future defense.

"Hugh does séances, and we're thinking about calling your Uncle Fucker back so I can give the bastard a piece of my mind." Her eyes lit with excitement at the thought. "Would you like to be there?"

I was mute. No words came to me that would be acceptable in polite company, so I shrugged noncommittally and tried to smile.

"Great, I'll let you know when. Where's Jack?" she asked, looking around for his wonderful butter melting butt.

"He died," I said before I could stop myself.

"Really?" Aunt Phyllis gasped, her eyes filling with tears.

"No, but he's gay."

"Oh my God." She grabbed me and hugged me so hard I felt nauseous. "I'm so sorry. I wouldn't have pegged that in a million years and my gaydar is outstanding."

"Your gay what?"

"My gaydar, dear. It's a radar for gay people," she explained very seriously.

"I see." I nodded, hoping against hope I wouldn't turn out like my beloved aunt. "I'm going to go find Mom and Dad. Do me a favor and keep the gay thing to yourself right now, okay?"

"Should I tell people that he died?" she asked.

"Um, no."

I wandered through the crowd, greeting my parents' friends and escaping quickly when the talk turned to the new boyfriend they'd heard so much about. By the time I got to my parents, I was ready to cry.

"Hi sweetie," Mom said, hugging me close. "You look beautiful as usual." She took a good look at me and pulled me into the corner. "What's wrong?"

"Jack's gay."

"Really?" she said, clearly shocked.

"Um, no. Actually he died."

"Rena, that's awful. Is that true?" She gave me the look.

I paused, racking my brain to come up with a more truthful sounding lie. "No, it's not true. He broke up with me because he thinks I'm nuts."

"That comes from your mother's side of the family," Dad said, having heard the last part of the conversation.

"Dad—" I rolled my eyes— "Aunt Phyllis is your sister."

"Is she really? I suppose I blocked that one out," he chuckled, giving me a hug. "That guy is an ass if he doesn't appreciate you for who you are. You are perfect and don't let anyone tell you otherwise."

"I love you, Daddy."

"What am I, chopped liver?" My mom horned in on the hug I

was giving my dad. I might be in a yucky place right now, but it could be worse . . . although I wasn't really sure how. But I did have good friends, amazing parents, a kooky aunt whom I adored, and a . . .

"Hi Rena," my sister interrupted. "I heard Jack is gay and that he died." Oh, right. I also had a bitchy ass-wad of a sister.

"Girls," Mom warned, "you will be pleasant to each other this evening."

"I didn't even say anything to her. She just walked her hulking ass over here and started in on me," I whined.

"You take that back," Jenny spat. "Dirk says my ass is like J.Lo's."

"Dirk's on crack," I muttered.

"Enough." Dad cut off Jenny's comeback before it passed her lips. "If you can't be civil, then separate. Tonight is for your mom and me. I expect you to remember that."

"I'm sorry, Dad. Sorry, Mom . . . sorry, Jenny." The last sorry was a little like chewing glass, but Dad was right. We were behaving like children.

"Sorry, too," Jenny said. I noted that she didn't actually apologize to me, but her mea culpa seemed to satisfy the folks.

"All right." Mom smiled, hugging us both. "We need to mingle with our guests. You two behave."

They wandered back into the crowd, leaving me and Jenny in the corner. I fidgeted uncomfortably and wondered what in the hell had happened to us. When we were little, we adored each other. I guess we weren't so little anymore. Well, she wasn't.

"Are you going to behave?" I asked her.

"No. Are you?"

"Nope." I grinned. "Maybe we should take this elsewhere so we don't upset Mom and Dad."

"Sounds like a plan," she agreed. "After you." She stepped back and let me lead the way. That alone made me a little nervous. Clearly she had something hateful planned to do or to say. I quickly thought through all the big butt references I'd come up with earlier and tried to remember every mortifying thing she'd done in high school. I didn't know if it would be enough. Shit.

It was fucking freezing outside. The cold didn't seem to faze

Jenny. She did have a lot of extra padding from the pregnancy. And then there was her butt . . .

"What do you want?" I asked warily.

"I don't know." She smiled innocently. "I just thought it might be fun to talk about the demise of your latest relationship."

"That seems like a lovely topic, but I'd rather measure your ass. I'm sure they have a tape measure or two inside." I moved away from her to go back in.

"What happened? Did he realize pretty packages on the outside are often not so pretty on the inside?" she asked nastily.

"Yep." I nodded. "I showed him my spleen and he ran for the hills."

"No, really Rena, did he figure out how crazy you are? Did he decide to cut ties and run before you ruined his life? I mean, come on, spill."

I was speechless. I had no comeback.

"Maybe he heard how quickly you go through men and didn't want to be another notch in your belt. Was that it?" she inquired blandly.

My entire body was shaking and it wasn't from the cold. What had we done to each other to end up like this? I was still unable to speak. I didn't trust myself not to cry. I was not going to let her see me cry.

"I'll bet it was the crazy thing. Did he find out about the Sunshine Weather Girl mishap? I would think a cop might have a hard time dating someone with a rap sheet," she laughed. "You never told me how you met. How did you meet?"

"Stop, Jenny," I said quietly.

"Is that your best comeback?" She shook her head in pity. "I'm sure you can do better than that."

Everything from the past two weeks hurled through my mind, making me dizzy. She was small potatoes compared to the other problems I had. Did she need to win that badly? Maybe she did . . .

"Rena, Rena, Rena, you finally find a good one and you screw that up just like you screwed up all the others," she goaded.

"Fine, Jenny," I yelled. "You win. I lose. Again. You want to know why he dumped me? He kicked me to the curb because he thinks I'm crazy. That should help you sleep better at night." My voice broke miserably, but I didn't care anymore. "And you'll love how we met. It's absolutely darling. We met when he arrested me for breaking my restraining order." Jenny looked really weird. Everything looked weird. Then I realized the tears I was not going to cry were making my surroundings blurry. Shit. "Do you want to know what the best part is?" I shouted as hot tears rolled down my cheeks, "I'm in love with him and he doesn't want me." I sank to the cold ground and deep sobs wracked my body. "He doesn't want me," I whispered to no one in particular.

"Oh my God," Jenny said, squatting on the ground next to me and trying to put her arms around me. "Oh God, Rena, I'm so sorry."

"Go away. Leave me alone," I said, rigidly holding my tears in check. "You should be able to enjoy the party now."

"Fuck, Rena, I feel sick to my stomach. I'm just so . . . so sorry." She tried to hold me again and I moved away.

"Jenny, I'm tired. I'm tired of you and me and life. You got what you wanted, so just please, leave me alone." I pressed my head against my knees and closed my eyes.

She sat quietly next to me. The silence was nice. I couldn't take any more. My breaking point had finally come.

"I've always been jealous of you," she said softly.

I snorted in disbelief. "Jealous? What do you have to be jealous of? You're a doctor with a husband and a baby and a house." I stared at her as if she had two heads.

She pulled her knees to her chest, well, as much as she could being pregnant and all, and stared off at the stars. "You were always so funny. You had tons of friends and boyfriends . . . When people would find out I was your little sister, they couldn't believe it." She sighed and shook her head. "I wasn't pretty and silly and creative like you. I didn't have your charm or your balls."

I stared in shock. Maybe Aunt Phyllis had slipped me a hallucinogenic. This was not my sister.

"Jenny, stop. It's okay. You don't have to say all that stuff to make me feel better. I'll be fine. Eventually."

"I mean it. Even your screwups are funny and wild. I'm not brave or strong like you. Don't get me wrong, I'm happy with my life. I'm a good doctor and I love Dirk and I'm going to have a baby, but there's still a part of me that wishes I was you." She put her hand out. I hesitated, and then tentatively took it. "I guess I was just jealous again. There you were with this gorgeous guy . . . you looked like a supermodel couple, for God's sake," she laughed. "I didn't want him, but I'm ashamed to say, I didn't want you to have him either."

"Well, he's gone." I smiled weakly. "And just for the record, I always wanted to be more like you. Smart and organized and sane," I giggled.

"You don't want my butt," she teased.

"Actually, Dirk is right. You do have a J.Lo butt. It pops, it's sexy." I grinned and squeezed her hand.

"Will you put that in writing?" she asked.

"Only if you put all the shit you said tonight in writing." I narrowed my eyes at her.

"No fucking way," she laughed.

"Ditto," I giggled. "You know, Jenny, I've missed you for a long time."

"Me, too." She smiled and put her head on my shoulder. It felt good. "Rena?"

"Yeah?"

"Jack really fucked up. That ass-monkey just lost the best thing that could ever happen to him," she whispered. "If you ever decide to take his sorry ass back, I'll be happy for you, but . . ."

"But what?" I asked.

"But I think I'll always have to call him ass-monkey for the rest of his life."

I started laughing and I couldn't stop. Jenny joined me. If anyone saw us they'd think we were wasted. I rolled around on the ground with my pregnant sister in the freezing cold and laughed like a hyena. I hadn't felt so happy in a long time. Who knew it would take my life blowing up to get my sister back?

Chapter 26

Saturday rolled around and I found myself trapped in a shrine to the Minnesota Vikings. Believe me, I love football, but this was three and a half yards too far.

Shoshanna's home was done entirely in purple, gold, and white. Very comfortable, but extremely scary. A life-size cutout of Brett Favre with a cardboard caption reading "Green Bay Sucks" was the focal point of the room. I had a difficult time believing her gay husband had lived here for any amount of time. All of my gay friends have superb taste . . .

Beggars can't be choosers and I was grateful to my little friend for putting me up. I felt safe and loved. Nobody cared about my crazy here; in fact, it was embraced. Speaking of which, it was time for more Pirate Dave.

We were minus Cecil. He had to take his mother for routine testing at the hospital, so the girls and I decided to work from Shoshanna's.

"We have to finish this piece of art by tomorrow night," Shoshanna said.

"Why?" I asked, moving her collection of bobble heads from the purple couch to the gold coffee table so I could sit. "I thought we had until Wednesday."

"Nope." She shook her head. "Cecil needs to format and upload it by Tuesday afternoon. It will be available Wednesday at five o'-clock. The she-devil goes on live at the convention with Anderson Cooper, Wednesday at six."

"Back the fuck up," I laughed. "Anderson Cooper? I thought it was the morning shows."

"You missed the memo." Poppy Harriet clasped her hands together in glee. "The massive pre-sales for this book are unprecedented. National news has picked up the story!"

"She's going to read a chapter live on TV," Joanne said, popping her compact shut. Ever since the brows started coming back, she couldn't stop looking at herself.

"Oh my God, no." My fingers went to my mouth and I started chowing down on the cuticles. Hiding my terror was impossible.

"Yep." Shoshanna grinned, pulling my hands away from my teeth. "The skank informed us yesterday while you were out driving around finding yourself."

"Holy shit, isn't the network going to insist on seeing what she's going to read?" I asked. Surely they wouldn't let her loose like that.

"We convinced her to refuse to show them an advance copy," Joanne giggled. "We said it would be more financially beneficial for her to hold on to it till the last second."

That made very little sense to me, but sense and Evangeline didn't go together. Time was running out and I still had no way to free the girls from her. The Viper had nothing on me. Poppy Harriet and Shoshanna were fairly safe, but I knew Poppy Harriet didn't want her Polish family to find out about her alter ego. Nancy wasn't responsible for salmonella-gate, but I had no evidence to implicate Evangeline. And I still didn't know about Joanne or Cecil . . .

"When does Nancy come back?" I asked, hoping it was soon. I needed to tell her what I'd learned.

"Wednesday morning," Shoshanna answered. "She is going to love this turn of events."

"Guys, the Viper can still bring us down. We can ruin her career, but she can still destroy us," I said. Even though I was in the clear, the thought of her hurting my friends made me furious. I realized in that moment, I was prepared to go down with the ship.

"No time to worry about that," Joanne said firmly, putting an end to my hopes of finding out what her deal was. "We need to finish the book and worry about the rest later."

"She's right," Poppy Harriet agreed. "Our good Lutheran God will make sure nothing bad happens."

I wanted to ask her where her good Lutheran God had been for the last twenty years, but even I wouldn't go that far. I decided to believe her; plus I did recall recently making several deals with Him . . .

"Okay fine," I muttered, trying to find my Pirate Dave place. With so many thoughts and worries dancing in my head, I wasn't sure if I could focus. What the hell was I thinking? I didn't need to focus to come up with horrific plots. I just needed to open my mouth and talk.

Crooked Jim wandered the deck of the ship, moaning in agony. Scurvy sucked and his recent hobby, knife juggling, had resulted in the loss of four fingers on his left hand and two on his right. He feared his days as the ship's seamstress were numbered.

"Woe is me," Crooked Jim wailed, banging his head on the railing and knocking out his front tooth. Sometimes it doesn't pay to get up in the morning, he thought. He put the tooth in his pocket, hoping maybe the Tooth Fairy would pay him a visit and leave a gold coin or a fifth of gin.

He sat down on the deck and put his head in his basically fingerless hands and said every cussword he knew. Twice. What he didn't know was that he was being watched . . .

An ominous wind blew and out of the shadows came the biggest, most uneven and lumpiest set of knockers Crooked Jim had ever seen. "Argghhhshitfuckpiss," he screamed in terror, trying to cover his eyes. Damnit to hell, having no fingers made it difficult to cover his eyes, for Crooked Jim had teeny-tiny palms.

"Oh shut up," the head on top of the boobs sneered.

The rest of the body belonging to the grotesque badoinkies was somewhat normal. It was almost impossible to get past the flesh melons protruding from her chest, but Crooked Jim was a decent sort. He tried to look at her face.

"What do you want?" he stammered, hoping it wasn't anything that involved getting within five feet of her.

"I want to help you keep your job," she purred, revealing sharp little teeth.

"Who are you?" he asked, slowly scooting away. He

*wanted to keep his seamstress job, but she looked kind
of hungry . . .*

"I'm Pirate Dave's secret admirer," she hissed.

*Crooked Jim had heard about her. Apparently she had
left a hat full of assholes for his beloved captain. While
Jim found that impressive and creative, she was fucking
frightening. No wonder Pirate Dave preferred Laverne
and Shirley.*

*Crooked Jim felt bad. Judging people by their looks
was shallow. For God's sake, Jim knew he was uglier
than hell. Who was he to be appalled by someone with
disgusting boobsters?*

*"How can you help me?" he asked, deciding he would
befriend the unsightly woman. Even someone with revolting
rib balloons needs a friend.*

"Can you still sew without any fingers?" she inquired.

*"Yes," he said proudly. "My seams aren't as straight as
they used to be, but I'm working on it."*

*"The messier, the better," she spat, arching her back and
pushing her bazoombas further out of the shadows and into
the light.*

Crooked Jim gulped and tried not to puke.

"Oh, oh, oh," Joanne yelled. "Can I jump in here?"

"Sure," I said, wondering what heinous malady was about to be-
fall the secret admirer.

"Great," she said.

"What's your name?" Crooked Jim asked.

*"My name is Eviline." She smiled demonically. Her
head spun around three times and Crooked Jim passed out
from fear.*

*"Goddamnit," she shrieked. She got so pissed off she
began to peel her skin from her body . . ."*

"Um, Joanne," I cut in on her diatribe before she had Eviline in
chunks on the ground.

"What?" she asked, coming out of the violent part of her brain.

"That's really interesting and quite unsettling, but we should probably wait till the end of the book to kill her."

"Do we have to?" Her shoulders sagged and she looked so disappointed, I almost gave in.

"Yep, we have to," I told her gently.

"Maybe she has nine lives," she mused, "and we could kill her nine times."

"Joanne, it's a fucking romance novel, not *Silence of the Lambs.*" Shoshanna rolled her eyes.

"You're right," she blushed. "I'm sorry. I just can't seem to help myself. Poppy Harriet, you take a turn."

"May I?" Poppy Harriet asked.

"Are you going to kill her?" I queried warily. She did have a flair for the dangerous, especially where garden tools were concerned.

"No," she giggled. "I'm going to make her have sex with a scurvy, fingerless pirate and a lawn gnome."

And she did.

Thank Jesus, the girls were gone. At five-thirty all three of them left in a rush to make Happy Hour at Shenanigans. Finally, I was alone. I pressed my ragged, bitten down fingers to the bridge of my nose. My headache pounded through my skull. I was done. I didn't think I'd be able to sleep or eat for a week. Plus, my cell had been ringing all day. Jack had left several messages. I had no idea what he'd said because I'd erased them. All of them.

When it rang yet again, I was tempted to throw it at the wall, but I was too afraid of damaging Brett Favre. Caller I.D. let me know it was Kristy.

"He's been up here like six times today," she said. "He looks pathetic."

I moved the phone to my other ear and put my feet up on Shoshanna's coffee table. She had put her feet on mine; I figured I'd return the favor. "You didn't tell him anything," I said to Kristy, feeling wonky and excited.

"No, of course not, but he seems really sorry."

"He should be sorry. He compared me to Aunt Phyllis."

"Oh my God," she gasped, "he didn't."

"He did. He also said I need help."

"Ewww." I knew she was wrinkling her nose. "What are you going to do?"

I paused and tried to reorganize my feelings. "Kristy, if I see him, I'll go back to him and fall even deeper than I already have."

"What's wrong with that?"

"What's wrong," I explained, "is that it will happen again. My crazy gene is embedded fairly deep in my head. I'll do something he thinks is nuts and unacceptable and he'll dump me again. I can't take that." As I spoke, my eyes welled up with tears. I was glad Kristy couldn't see me.

"Okay," she sighed, "I get it. Rena . . ."

"Yeah?"

"You're not crazy in a bad way. You're crazy in a good way. The kind that everybody wants to be around and wishes they had," she said.

"It's too bad that you're the only one who thinks so," I laughed without much humor.

"Oh, I'm not the only one. In fact, I know I'm not the only one," she hinted.

"Kristy, stop. I have to not think about him. I have to finish Pirate Dave and figure out how to save the girls. I can't lose focus."

"Any leads on how to make that happen?" she asked.

"No, but I have about eighty-four hours left." My tone was optimistic, but my stomach was knotted. "I'll get it done."

"I know you will. When he comes back up, should I tell him anything?" she asked.

"Tell him I'm moving to Iowa and he should find a nice girl without a rap sheet."

"He's not going to like that," she laughed.

"I know," I sighed, wondering if I was being stupid. "Neither do I."

Chapter 27

"Do it. Do it. Do it," they chanted. Shoshanna, Joanne, Poppy Harriet, and Cecil sat crammed together like sardines on the hot pink couch in our ugly pink office, bouncing up and down, encouraging me to finish our masterpiece.

We'd spent the entire Sunday spewing out gross situation after gross situation. I'd never laughed so hard in my life.

Cecil was on a roll. Joanne was as violent as ever, and Poppy Harriet introduced us to the many and varied sexual uses for wood putty, weed whips, soaker hoses, and a pack of sunflower seeds. Gardening was now ruined for me. Forever. Shoshanna had to excuse herself to the bathroom, muttering something about needing adult diapers.

We were now at the end, and they expected me to finish it.

"Rena, you started it. It is only fitting that you should end it," Cecil said.

"He's right," Shoshanna agreed. "This is your baby, you need to put it to bed."

"Or cover it with dirt and put a headstone on it," I giggled.

"That, too," she said with a grin.

"Okay, here I . . ." I stopped short when the scent of evil, greed, and over-Botoxed old lady drenched in ass-loads of perfume reached my nose.

"Hello, little people. Are we done with my novel yet?" Evangeline stood in the doorway, sucking every bit of joy and life from the room.

"Almost, Madame," Cecil said in a clipped tone. He removed himself from the couch and from us. He had turned back into the mistreated butler I didn't trust.

"Ruby," she purred, "you missed my exciting news. I will be the featured star on the Anderson Cooper show on Wednesday."

"I heard, Evelyn." I smiled and gave her a thumbs-up.

She looked confused for a moment. I suppose the thumbs-up negated the use of a random name because she went on. "Do you old ladies realize the irony of my pairing with Cooper?"

We all stood silently trying to figure out what the hell she was talking about. The vision of her sprawled and bald while reaching for Jack's love stick was impossible to erase. I itched to yank her wig off, but I tamped down my impulsive desire.

"Um, no, can't say we do," Shoshanna said.

"I wouldn't expect you out-of-touch old biddies to get it," she laughed derisively. "I look like his mother. I am the spitting image of Gloria Vanderbilt," she shouted, striking a pose and thrusting her tatas out.

"In your dreams," Shoshanna muttered under her breath. "You know . . . I think you should tell Anderson that." She grinned. "On the show."

"I believe I will." She narrowed her eyes at Shoshanna and altered her pose before she got stuck. "Of course, he'll see the resemblance immediately." She clenched her claws in excitement and went off into her own disturbing dreamworld.

She looked nothing like Gloria Vanderbilt. Gloria Vanderbilt was a beautiful woman, a fashion icon, and a philanthropist. Evangeline O'Hara was an unattractive, horrifically overaltered, no-talent, Botox-infested, blackmailing liar. She was not Gloria Vanderbilt.

"You should definitely tell him on the show." I nodded, imagining Anderson Cooper's face when she threw that juicy tidbit out. Her confidence in herself and her looks was almost as appalling as the Pirate Dave story.

"I will," she snapped. "So here's how it will go down. You will finish my book. Cecil will put it on the computer thingy so I can get richer and more famous. Then I will be immortalized and worshiped on the Anderson Cooper Show. I will read out loud to my adoring fans, and I will procure a date with Anderson. I expect all of you to be there to witness my triumph." She laughed manically and struck another pose, vaguely resembling a frog with boobs on the dissecting table. "Where's Nancy?"

"She's with her daughter," I said. Was the Viper on crack? Procure a date with Anderson? Was she going to demand he put his love stick between her trembling thighs? I considered sending Anderson an anonymous tip, but with my luck, I'd somehow end up getting booked for sexual harassment and arrested . . . by Jack. "Nancy will be back on Wednesday. She wouldn't miss your explosion into the homes of America for anything."

"Good. I have a procedure to get to," she informed us. "I'll check back with you idiots later this evening."

"Oh, Evangeline—" I stopped her and gave her an earnest wide-eyed stare. "You should ask Anderson Cooper out on a date on live TV. He'll have to say yes."

She stood in the doorway, weighing the pros and cons of my suggestion. When a lascivious smile spread across her frightening face, I knew I'd scored. "That's the first good idea you've ever had, Ruth."

"Thank you, Your Greatness." I bowed my head demurely and bit my lip to quell the laughter that wanted freedom.

"Get to work," she commanded as she left us.

"You heard the hooker," Shoshanna laughed. "Get to work."

Eviline danced around the deck of the ship in the moonlight, striking pose after pose. A cool ocean breeze ruffled her wig. These fucking wigs made her head sweat profusely, but a beauty without hair was not a beauty. Her child-birthing year had been unkind to her. She'd lost all her thick, curly, fiery red tresses and her nether regions could swallow a watermelon. Whatever, she'd have her revenge soon enough . . .

Convincing Crooked Jim to sew the twins back together was easier than she'd thought. She'd told him Pirate Dave would honor him with a night at a strip club for midgets if he secretly did such a wonderful thing.

She cackled and ran around the deck, bumping into everything. The weight of her coconuts made her balance precarious at best. She cared not, for her cannonballs were her proudest asset. After the sixth fall, when she gave herself a mild concussion, she slithered back into the shadows.

Pirate Dave would be devastated when he found his paramour Shirley sewn back to her sister Laverne. Eviline had procured some magical string from a blind shape-shifting fairy-like troll years ago. The string was magically permanent, so the twins would be forever conjoined. She grinned at the thought of Pirate Dave killing himself in agony over losing his fornicating privacy with Shirley.

This was a win, win, win for Eviline. Not only would she destroy Pirate Dave by decimating his sex life, she'd get back at the two people who had stretched her hoo-ha to the point of no return . . . her daughters. Laverne and Shirley.

"No way," Poppy Harriet squealed, "no wonder you didn't want us to kill her earlier."

"I understand now," Joanne said, "but promise me you'll kill her. Violently."

"I promise," I said, needing a short break before the grand finale.

I grabbed an apple and plopped down next to Cecil, who had clearly rejoined our team once Evangeline left. What in the hell did she have on him? It had to be good . . .

"So Rena," he said, proofreading my latest addition to our novel and blushing uncomfortably in the process, "do you go back to work next week?"

"Um, no." I bit a huge chunk out of my apple, hoping he'd forget the question by the time I'd finished chewing.

"Oh my God," Poppy Harriet gasped, "did you get fired over my financial issues?"

I shook my head no. I had a massive mouthful of apple, making speech impossible.

"She took a transfer to Iowa." Shoshanna let the cat out of the bag. "She leaves in two weeks."

I gave her the evil eye and tried to chew faster. I wanted to rip her a new one for telling everyone. My plan had been to slip away quietly in the night.

"Oh no." Joanne grabbed me and shook me, causing me to swallow a rather large piece of un-chewed apple. "You can't leave us. We need you." Big fat crocodile tears rolled down her cheeks. "We love you."

I punched my chest to dislodge the chunk of apple wedged there and answered hoarsely, "I love you guys, too, but I need to get away from here."

"Why?" Cecil asked.

"It's a great opportunity for me professionally, and I think Iowa is a vibrant and interesting place. I'll be able to, um, eat a lot of corn and make new friends. Hopefully get laid by a big strapping farm boy. Well, not a boy, I mean a man. A big strapping farm man and . . ." I petered off. They were staring at me as if I'd grown another head. Shit.

"She got dumped because her ass-whacker boyfriend thought she was crazy," Shoshanna told everyone.

"How do you know that?" I gasped.

"I pried it out of Kristy," she said guiltily.

Kristy was so dead. I would freeze every undergarment she owned when I got ahold of her.

"You're not crazy," Joanne huffed. "You're creative."

"Thanks." I smiled weakly. Me and Hugh the Bigfoot guy . . . creative. Fucking great.

"Do you want me to kick his ass?" Poppy Harriet inquired. "I'm not sure if you remember, but I used to be a man. I may look lovely and feminine now, but I'm pretty sure I can still bust some backside."

"That's very sweet, but no," I said. It was the first time she'd referred to her former self without a freak-out attached. I was so proud of her. She'd be okay.

"Do you love him?" Cecil asked.

I practically choked on the small amount of apple remaining in my mouth. Why on earth would he ask me that? That was personal and rude and mean and unnecessary and . . . "Yes, I do . . . I mean, did . . . I mean, I don't know. Shit, how can I love someone who doesn't like who I am?"

"How old is this relationship?" Cecil inquired, taking notes. Seriously? Notes?

"Um, a couple of weeks," I muttered.

"What exactly do you mean by a couple?" he asked. He was a pushy bastard.

"Two. Two weeks," I snapped. "Go ahead and laugh. How in the world can I be in love with someone after two weeks? Right? Well, I am . . . was . . . shit, am. I'm still in love with him and I knew immediately. The minute I laid eyes on him I knew he was mine. Fuck, I sound like a character in a cheesy romance novel," I groaned.

"No," Cecil smiled, "a character in a beautiful romance novel."

"I do?"

"Yes, the best kind," he said.

"What am I supposed to do now?" I asked, hoping he had the magic answer.

"I would suggest we finish the novel first, watch the horrid plastic surgery victim implode on Wednesday, and on Thursday sit down and make a solid plan to get your man back," Cecil stated matter-of-factly.

We all stared openmouthed at Cecil. He'd never directly uttered a derogatory word about Evangeline . . . till now. I knew positively I would find out what she had on Cecil and clear him, too. I had no fucking idea how I would do it . . . but I would.

"Shall we get back to Pirate Dave and his randy adventures?" Cecil inquired, loving the fact that he'd rendered us speechless.

"That's it," Shoshanna shouted.

"That's what?" Poppy Harriet screeched, hitting a karate pose to defend us from whatever Shoshanna had spotted.

"The title," LeHump yelled, bouncing around the room like a Mexican jumping bean. "Pirate Dave and His Randy Adventures."

"Brilliant," Joanne said reverently.

"Yep," I said, "I like it.

We all turned to Cecil. In the short time we'd been together, he had become our voice of reason. Although anyone with a modicum of sense would have qualified for the job. That pretty much knocked me and the gals out of the running so by default the honor went to Cecil.

"It's perfect," he agreed. "Let's get back to work."

"Make it disgusting," Shoshanna grinned.

"I believe I can do that."

I felt better than I had in a while. I didn't know if it would work with Jack, but the thought of trying calmed all my jangled nerves. I was ready to put Pirate Dave out of his misery . . .

"*Pirate Dave,*" *Hairy Sam squealed in terror, making his way to his captain.* "*It's awful. The blood, it's everywhere. Crooked Jim has lost his fucking mind. He keeps talking about naked midgets . . . He's killing them!*"

"*He's killing midgets?*" *Dave asked. Why would anyone kill a midget? All the midgets he knew were lovely. Well, there was that bastard troll who branded his back with the dreaded giraffe and gave him two peepees, but was a troll considered a midget? Pirate Dave was so confused, he sat back down on the deck.*

"*Get up, you two-pronged jackass,*" *Hairy Sam yelped.* "*You have to save your women.*"

"*My women?*" *Pirate Dave stood up, braving the elements.* "*Crooked Jim is killing my women?*"

"*That's what I've been trying to tell you,*" *Hairy Sam bellowed.*

"*No,*" *Dave yelled back.* "*You said Crooked Jim was killing midgets. I don't have any girlfriends who are midgets. Not that I'm opposed to that. In fact, it's a fine idea. Do you know any attractive midgets with two vaginas?*"

"*Oh for fuck's sake,*" *Hairy Sam rolled his eyes. He grabbed Dave by the chest hair and dragged him to the upper deck of the ship.*

What Pirate Dave saw would stay with him for the rest of his immortal life . . . it was awful.

Laverne and Shirley were hog-tied together and strapped to the ground. Crooked Jim stood above them, doing some kind of bizarre bloody ritual. Blood ran dark and red all over the deck.

The girls howled and cried out in pain and terror.

"*What the fuck are you doing?*" *Pirate Dave bellowed.*

Crooked Jim turned to Pirate Dave with an ecstatic expression, "*It's a surprise!*" *he screamed joyously, jumping up and down.* "*Do you love it?*" *he gushed.*

"*Love that you're killing the two women I'm screwing? Are you a fucking imbecile?*"

Crooked Jim had always been an odd one, but Dave liked to gather misfits. Not anymore . . .

Pirate Dave began to swear and bump and grind his way around the deck. He slipped twice in the blood while doing complicated moves. His crew backed away in fear. Pirate Dave's spells didn't always work out right. No one wanted to be in the line of fire when he got going.

"Shitmotherfuckerpisscocksuckerturdpoopdamnfart," he cried out, contorting his body and sweating like a pig.

The storm stilled and a wall of golden glitter whooshed across the deck. The pirates began to sneeze and cough. This was the biggest most deadly wall of shimmering crap they'd ever seen Pirate Dave conjure up. The sparkling mass morphed into a giant flesh-eating snake and slithered through the air toward Crooked Jim.

"Noooo," Crooked Jim squawked. "She said you would be happy. The hat full of assholes, boob lady said you would love it," he wailed, but it was too late. The glitter snake wrapped itself around Crooked Jim's neck. He tried to pull it off, but he had very few fingers and teeny-tiny palms. He didn't stand a chance against Pirate Dave's rage magic. The angry snake choked the life out of poor Crooked Jim. The crew stood by and watched, thanking Poseidon that Dave hadn't fucked up and killed everyone within 5.3 miles.

Pirate Dave slipped and tripped through the blood to get to his loves. They lay bound together, barely breathing. "Why?" Dave shouted at the heavens. "Why have you taken my concubines?"

Lightning flashed and thunder rumbled, tearing a hole in the sky. From the hole fell the formerly blind troll fairy bastard. He tumbled from the blue yonder and landed right on top of the practically dead twins.

"You," Pirate Dave hissed. "You are responsible for this." He threw the troll across the deck and dove after him.

"I didn't do this," the troll shrieked. "I came back to apologize for the giraffe."

"You didn't set Crooked Jim up to kill the women I fornicate with?" Dave asked.

"Um, no."

"Were you also going to apologize for giving me two ding-dongs?" Dave demanded.

"Um, no."

"Fine," Dave said, grabbing the troll by the hair and dragging him over to the bloody mess of his gal pals, "if you want to make it right, fix them."

The troll examined Laverne and Shirley closely. He gasped when he saw the string. He recognized the string, for it was his. "They've been sewn back together." He shook his head in sorrow.

"Then separate them," Dave said.

"I can't," the troll whispered sadly. "No one can."

"Of course they can," Pirate Dave insisted. "They did it before, they can do it again."

"No. They've been sewn back together with magical string. They can never be separated again."

"Nooooo," Dave howled in anguish. "Why would someone do this to me?"

"Because you're a hairy asshole," came a voice from the shadows.

"Show yourself," Pirate Dave bellowed.

Out from the darkened corner of the ship came the most foul and disgusting tits followed by an okay body. The pirates looked away, for those jugs were repulsive. "You could have had me," Eviline spat. "I have a hoo-ha that could have accommodated your deformity, but no . . . you laughed in my face and carried on with the sluts that ruined my hoochie in the first place," she screamed, her face contorting into a hideous mask.

"Mother?" Laverne and Shirley whispered weakly.

"Don't call me that." Her face reddened unattractively with fury. "You're freaks and you ruined my vagina. You don't deserve to have a normal life," she screamed. "I'm glad you despise each other; now you are connected for eternity." She laughed maniacally and fell on her face due to the weight of her hooters. No one helped her up.

"Actually," Laverne said, giving Shirley a shy smile, "I don't like you much and your voice makes me want to tear my own head off, but I've missed you."

"I've missed you, too," Shirley whispered, trying not to offend anyone with her power of speech.

"Girls," Pirate Dave squealed like a pig. "Do you know what this means?"

Everyone stared at Dave in confusion.

"You are now my perfect woman! You have two vaginas!"

The crew broke into raucous applause, whistling and high-fiving with joy. The happiness of their fearless leader meant the world to them.

"Shut up," the foul and repulsive giver of hats full of assholes screamed. "I will kill all of you! You will not be happy!" She pulled an AK-47 machine gun from between her knockers and prepared to blow everyone away.

"Not so fast," the troll stepped out from his hiding place behind Mr. Smee and Captain Crunchy. He lifted his hand and froze her where she stood. It was a highly disturbing pose, with her sharp little teeth bared and her ginormous cantaloupes thrust forward. "Um, guys, if you want a photograph of this, you should take one now. She's not going to be around much longer."

The pirates pulled out their cell phones and snapped away. The troll went to Pirate Dave and knelt before him. "I'd like to make amends for defiling you with the giraffe," the troll said.

"What about my multiple dicks?" Dave asked.

"That turned out pretty well," the troll countered.

"You're right," Dave agreed, fondling himself. "What do you propose?"

"Getting rid of that," he said pointing to Eviline.

"Can we watch?" Dave asked.

"Of course." The troll nodded.

Pirate Dave magicked up some chairs and popcorn and Candy's Liquid Party in a Can and Kurt's Fried Cheese Curds. Everyone got comfortable and waited for the festivities to begin.

The troll didn't disappoint, dismembering Eviline in ways his bloodthirsty audience could fully appreciate, right down to feeding several of her body parts to the mermaids. Finally, he waved his hand and she disappeared.

The crowd went wild.

The troll took eight bows and blew kisses all around.

"Holy shit," Pirate Dave laughed, holding his women close. "That was the most fucked-up thing I've ever seen in my life."

"Thank you," the troll said modestly. "Are we even?"

"Absolutely," Dave grinned. "Come on, girls. Are you ready to fuck?"

Laverne and Shirley squealed their delight and followed Dave to his mouse-infested cabin below. No one saw them for six days and everyone lived happily ever after.

The End

Chapter 28

Who in the hell had turned out every light in the house? I'd already run into three fornicating statues in the foyer while trying to find my way back to the icky pink office. Forgetting my cell phone had been stupid and inconvenient. I considered leaving it at the mansion overnight, but my parents might call. If I didn't answer, they'd drive to my apartment and find out I had moved. I had no energy to deal with that fallout.

Cecil and the gals had made Shirley Temples to celebrate the completion of *Pirate Dave and His Randy Adventures*. Turned out Poppy Harriet was a recovering alcoholic. Well, she wasn't . . . Walter Garski was. We got pretty rowdy and Cecil actually told three jokes. They weren't funny, but we laughed anyway. He'd come so far out of his shell, we'd do anything to keep him there.

"Motherfucker," I whispered, nailing my shin on someone's cement butt. It was creepy in there at night. I wondered where Evangeline was and prayed I wouldn't run into her.

I quickly grabbed my phone from the office and made my way back to the fuck-foyer. Getting out of there was very necessary. The house had a sinister feel that late at night. I was almost home free when I heard soft moaning. Oh Sweet Jesus, was Evangeline getting it . . . wait, it was a man . . . and he was moaning in pain, not pleasure. Shit, had the Viper beaten the crap out of Herbie the Dentist Cop again?

Every instinct I had told me to leave. To run like hell without looking back, but I couldn't. Whoever was moaning was in a bad way. I couldn't leave someone there like that . . . even if it was Herbie the asshole Dentist.

I felt my way over to the wall. My worry about being caught by

Evangeline evaporated, overtaken by my concern for whoever was moaning. I flicked on the light and my knees buckled. This had to be a nightmare.

"Oh my God, no," I gasped. My insides clenched and I had to suppress the impulse to scream. "No, no, no," I cried out, running to the foot of the staircase where Cecil lay crumpled and bleeding. "Cecil," I whispered, "oh my God, Cecil, what happened?"

"Rena?" Cecil looked up and tried to focus on me. His eyes were dilated, a sure sign of a concussion. His lip was swollen and bleeding and there was a deep gash over his left eyebrow. Those were the injuries I could see; I worried about the ones I couldn't.

"What happened to you? Did you fall?"

"Rena," he choked out, "you have to leave. Now."

"Clearly you've been smoking crack because I'm not going anywhere," I told him, pulling some Kleenex out of my bag and pressing it against the gash. "This will hurt, but we have to stop the bleeding. You're going to need some stitches."

"Listen to me"—his voice was horse—"go home now. She'll be back."

WTF? "What do you mean?" I shook my head, trying to wrap my brain around the thought of Evangeline harming Cecil this way. "Answer me, Cecil."

"I can't." His eyes pleaded with me, "Please leave, I'll be okay."

"You are not okay," I said trying not to cry. "I'm going to call an ambulance." I pulled out my recently recovered cell and started to dial.

"No," he hissed grabbing my arm in a vise-like grip. "Don't. Please God, don't." He winced and his face went slack with pain. He tried to hold his ribs, but his body fought him and he collapsed back to the floor.

"Shit, fuck, shit, shit," I muttered, feeling panic swell inside me. He needed medical attention. Now. "Listen to me, Cecil, I promise I won't call an ambulance, but I'm going to call my sister. She's a doctor. You're a mess and I don't know what to do," I said as my eyes welled up.

"Can you help me to the office?" he asked.

"I have no idea, but my answer is yes."

Twenty minutes later, Cecil was in the office and Jenny was

about ten minutes away. It took a hell of a lot of convincing to get her to come here instead of meeting her at the hospital, but when I promised her she could pick the return favor, no questions asked, she caved. I snuck back out to the foyer and waited for my sister. Cecil wasn't talking. I'd threatened, begged, and whined, but he wouldn't tell me what had happened. I thought I couldn't possibly hate Evangeline any more than I already did. I was wrong.

A soft knock at the door yanked me back to my horrific reality.

"Holy hell," Jenny whispered, looking around the foyer in shock. "What is this place?"

"My office." I grinned weakly. "Come with me."

I had filled Jenny in as much as I could when I'd called her. She'd asked pointed questions about Cecil's injuries and had brought the instruments and meds she thought she would need.

"I shouldn't be doing this," she said. "We should be at a hospital."

"I know, but this means more to me than you'll ever know."

"How old is your friend?" she asked as we quietly made our way back to the office.

"Late fifties."

"Okay, and how do you think this happened?"

"I think Evangeline hit him and he fell down the stairs," I said.

"Those stairs?" She pointed to the grand marble staircase and cringed.

"Yeah, I found him crumpled at the bottom." The panic began to surface again.

"Rena, if he fell down those stairs, you never should have moved him," she said, shaking her head. "Actually, if he fell down those stairs, he's lucky to be alive."

"He wouldn't let me call you unless I helped him to the office." My tears spilled down my cheeks. "What if he dies because I moved him?"

"Was he able to walk?" she asked, wiping my tears away.

"Kind of," I said, taking a deep breath and trying not to flop to the floor and become a useless blubbering mess.

"If he was able to move on his own, it might not be as bad as I think," she said reassuringly. "Take me to him."

After Jenny grilled Cecil with questions, took his blood pressure and all sorts of other doctor things, she stitched his eye and lip. When she went to lift his shirt, he adamantly refused to let her examine his ribs.

"She's a surgeon, Cecil." I rolled my eyes. "She's seen people's insides, for God's sake. Your naked chest isn't going to offend her."

"I'm fine," he said, standing to prove it. The second he was upright his eyes rolled into the back of his head and he passed out. Thankfully the heinous pink couch was there to catch him.

"Oh my God, is he dead?" I gasped.

Jenny ran over and checked his vitals, "Nope, just passed out from the pain."

"Alrighty then." I glanced at my sister and started to laugh. The Inappropriate Laughing Monster decided to pay me a poorly timed visit. Thankfully he knocked on Jenny's door, too.

"Help me with his clothes. I'll check him while he's out," she said when she got control of herself.

We gently peeled off his suit jacket. Jenny hung it over a chair and I carefully unbuttoned his shirt. I froze. Oh my God, another missing puzzle piece smacked me in the head. Cecil didn't like plus-size women. Well, he might like them, but he certainly wasn't buying lingerie for them . . . he was buying it for himself.

Underneath Cecil's crisp white dress shirt was a purple teddy, and if I remembered correctly, my guess would be that it was crotchless. Probably made going to the bathroom easier for the average guy who likes wearing women's undergarments. This was what Evangeline had on him, but how would she even know? I couldn't imagine why this would be such a big deal, but Cecil was from another generation and I'd bet a million bucks his mother had no clue.

"Um, Jenny, just because a man wears women's underthingies doesn't mean he's gay. Right?"

"Why in the hell would you ask me . . . Oh my," she giggled, taking in Cecil in all his purple lacy glory. "Just because a man likes lacy panties doesn't mean he bats for the other team. Do you remember Uncle Carlton?"

"You mean Uncle Fucker?" I corrected her.

"Yes, exactly," she said, smiling. "He wore Aunt Phyllis's undies all the time."

The Uncle Fucker stories were never-ending. Maybe I would go to the séance. It might be enlightening . . .

"Are Cecil's ribs busted?" I asked.

"Let me feel around," she said. She examined his rib cage and shook her head in bewilderment. "Call me crazy, but I think the boning and padding in his teddy may have saved his ribs. He's bruised, but it doesn't feel broken. We're still going to get an X-ray. He may have cracked a rib and I'm worried about internal bleeding or a punctured lung, although his vitals are strong," she said. "I just need to rule internal issues out."

"So I see you've discovered Cecil is nothing but a useless fag," Evangeline spat derisively from the doorway.

"Jesus Christ," Jenny shouted in abject horror as she flattened herself against the wall. "What is that?"

I couldn't stop the laugh that flew out of my mouth and had no desire to. Thank God, my sister had been born without the thought filter gene. The look on the Viper's face was priceless.

"Were you in an accident?" Jenny stammered, digging an even bigger hole. "I mean, my God, your face. It's just . . . just—" She shook her head and slapped her hand over her mouth before anything else came out. That made me sad; it was just getting good.

"I have no idea what you're talking about," the Viper hissed, "but I do believe you're trespassing. Breaking and entering is a crime." She smiled nastily. "I think I'll alert the police."

"Not so fast," my sister said. "I'm a doctor and you have a very injured man here. From what I understand, this man is your employee. Why haven't you called for medical assistance?"

"I was busy," she snapped, "and he'll be fine. He's probably faking it. He's not my problem"—she waved her hand dismissively—"but I am yours, Doctor. I didn't call you, which means you are in my home illegally. That should make a lovely headline in tomorrow's paper, don't you think?"

"What I think, Ma'am, is that you have slightly larger problems on your hands." Jenny spoke slowly and her enunciation was perfect. She was scaring the hell out of me. "My husband is a lawyer, and he'll be representing Cecil when he sues you for attempted murder."

The Viper's bulbous lips thinned and her nostrils flared. "Oh, he won't be suing me," she guaranteed and pointed her claw at me, "he'll be suing the slut who pushed him down the stairs."

"There is so much wrong with that statement, I don't know where to begin." Jenny chuckled as if she were talking to an old, amusing, and slightly senile friend.

"Do go on, little trespasser," Evangeline purred and absently began massaging her breasts.

Jenny was stunned to repulsed silence for a brief moment, but she loved a good fight. "My sister may be a lot of things, impulsive, reckless, profane, out of control, rude . . ."

"Um, Jenny," I cut her off.

"Right," she said, "but she is definitely not a slut. Furthermore, Cecil is lying here passed out in this pink . . . I suppose you'd call it an office. There is no possible way you'd know he was pushed down the stairs unless you did it yourself." Jenny tucked her hair behind her ear and perched casually on the edge of the desk, "You see, as many bad qualities as Rena possesses, and there are many"—she winked at me—"she would never, ever harm anyone. And lastly, whoever your plastic surgeon is . . . the man should be shot and his license should be revoked. You're a hot mess."

Evangeline turned the most unattractive shade of purple I'd ever seen on a human. Of course her humanity is debatable . . . "My plastic surgeon is a woman," she shrieked.

"I find that hard to swallow," my sister shot back. "A woman's touch is far less heavy-handed than the business you've got going on there. I'd be curious to take a look at the scarring under your wig. May I?"

My sister was forevermore going to be my hero. If Evangeline could have split in two like Rumpelstiltskin, she would have. "My hair is real," she screamed, shaking with fury. She clutched her bosom as if it were a life line to sanity; too bad it was just Bulgarian silly putty. I worried a little bit about her coming at us. After we'd seen her handiwork on Cecil, who knew what she was capable of. I half expected her to pull an AK-47 out from between her knockers like Eviline had.

"I'm going to my boudoir," she ground out. "I expect you to be gone in five minutes. And take that pathetic fag with you."

"Just because he's a cross-dresser doesn't mean he's gay," I said, sticking up for poor passed-out Cecil.

"Oh, please," she laughed, "any boy who's worn girls' panties since grade school is not a boy." She turned on her stiletto bedroom mules and wobbled out.

"That's the famous writer?" Jenny asked in disbelief.

"Famous? Yes. Writer? Debatable," I said.

"Rena?" Cecil called weakly from the couch. "What happened?"

"Nothing," I told him softly. If he hadn't heard that exchange, he never needed to know about it. "Cecil, you have to go to the hospital. You could have internal bleeding and my sister's risked her career and her medical liability insurance to come here."

Cecil lay silently on the couch while we watched. He raised his hands to his head and tried to sit up. His tortured gasp when he saw his shirt open tore at my insides. I hadn't seen a grown man cry in anguish since my grandma's funeral. My dad's heartbreak had been an awful thing to watch. Somehow, even though death wasn't involved, Cecil's breakdown was equally as painful.

"Cecil, it's okay," I said putting my hand on his arm.

He turned away to hide the tears. "I'm so ashamed," he whispered brokenly through his sobs. "I'm so sorry."

"Cecil, my Uncle Fuc . . . Carlton wore my aunt's underwear for years. It's not a sin," I said, gently closing his shirt to give him back his dignity.

"Cecil, we have to get you to the hospital," Jenny said. "If you won't let us take you, I'll be forced to call an ambulance. The choice is yours."

"I'll go," he said, "but Rena, would you . . . ."

"Yes, I will." I walked to the desk, got a pair of scissors, and cut him out of the teddy. His head slumped in embarrassment. It was devastating to think that he felt he'd committed a heinous and unforgivable crime by wearing some ladies' underthings. What had happened to him in the past?

"Thank you," he said. "Please don't . . ."

"Don't worry, Cecil, this goes nowhere. Ever. I promise."

"Nowhere," my sister agreed. "All right, let's go."

Cecil checked out at the hospital okay. Miraculously, no broken ribs or internal bleeding. A concussion and severe bruising were the major issues. He was a very lucky man, although lucky is a relative term. When Jenny filled out the report, Cecil firmly insisted he'd tripped and fallen.

"That's bullshit," I said. "Cecil, you can't let her get away with this. She could have killed you."

Cecil stared at his hands and repeated his lie. After twenty more unsuccessful minutes of trying to pull the truth out of him, I gave up and drove him home. He lived in a cute little house in an older section of Minneapolis. The tree-lined streets were well maintained and the homes were charming.

"We're here," I said, waking him up. He was exhausted from his injuries. It was also two in the morning.

"If you could help me in, I'd greatly appreciate it," he said, looking away. Clearly he didn't like asking for help and no doubt he could feel my anger about the stupid lies he'd told at the hospital.

"Of course," I said.

After a very slow walk through the house, I got him tucked in. I set six alarms to go off hourly. I was worried about the concussion. I made him promise to text me each time he woke up. I threatened him with coming back over and raiding his underwear drawer if he didn't. He blanched and promised he'd text.

As I turned to leave I noticed something odd. A picture of a young Cecil, about twenty, with two women. One was clearly his mother and the other bore a striking resemblance to a pre-surgery Evangeline. "Cecil, how long have you been working for Evangeline?"

"Twenty years," he answered sleepily. "Why?"

"No reason. Get some sleep," I said. When he turned over, I slipped the photo into my bag and left. Of all the freaking puzzles I had to piece together, Cecil's was the most difficult. Logic puzzles were one of my favorite things, but time was running out and this one defied reason. Shit.

Chapter 29

Monday was a clusterfuck. Cecil, of course, didn't show up. Evangeline was nowhere to be found, and no one had any idea how to format and upload the book.

"Shoshanna, you're a world-renowned professor, for God's sake. How can you not know how to work the computer?" I groused.

"That's what graduate assistants are for," she said.

"I can do it," Joanne said, with more volume than confidence. She smeared some kind of gel into her ever-blooming eyebrows and sat down in front of the computer. She resembled a deer caught in the headlights with shiny eyebrows.

Poppy Harriet, in a knuckle-popping frenzy, paced the room like a caged tiger. "We're fucked. If we don't get this right, we're fucked. We are totally fucked. Fucked."

"I'm sorry," Shoshanna laughed, "I'm not sure I understand. What are we?"

"We're fu . . ." Poppy Harriet stopped, realizing how many times she'd just dropped the F-bomb. "Well, we are," she giggled.

"No, we're not. If we can't figure it out, we'll go to Cecil's and get him to help us," I said. Give me a bunch of numbers and a spreadsheet and I was brilliant. This stuff, not so much.

"Nancy could do it," Joanne informed our group.

"Do you see Nancy?" LeHump asked irritably.

"No," Joanne answered, looking around the room. "Do you?"

"Joanne, I was being sarcastic." Shoshanna shook her head and laughed.

"You know I don't pick up very well on irony." Joanne wagged her finger at LeHump, who, in turn, flipped her the bird. "Now *that* I understand," she chuckled, returning the gesture.

By three-thirty, after a lot of middle finger salutes and an absurd amount of swearing, we agreed we were fried. In a majority rules vote, it was decided I would go to Cecil's and figure out how in the hell to upload. I thought it was unfair, considering I had been up half the night, but nobody wanted to hear my bitchin', so I went. I didn't tell them I had been planning on going anyway to check on Cecil. It was way more fun to bitch and complain.

"Holy crap, why in the hell couldn't we figure this out?" I flopped back on Cecil's couch and closed my tired eyes.

"Because you all spend too much time coming up with rude names for male genitalia and making obscene gestures at each other."

I laughed. He was right.

Cecil looked like hell. His eye had practically swollen shut and the gash over his eyebrow appeared red and angry. He moved like an old man and his speech was labored. On the flip side, his home was lovely—warm and comfortable, with cushy armchairs and lovely art, mixed with beautiful Oriental rugs and cut-glass vases overflowing with fresh flowers. I was so at ease, I wanted to curl up and sleep for a week.

"Hello dear, you must be Rena," an exquisite old woman said. Her eyes were riveting, a beautiful blue, almost turquoise. "I'm Delona, Fred's mother." She smiled and held out her frail hand. "Fred said you were lovely, but he didn't do you justice."

I was so caught up in her magic, I didn't even notice how delicate her health seemed. "Um, thanks," I said, feeling self-conscious heat crawl up my neck. "I'm Fred's friend from work."

"I want to thank you for taking care of him last night," she said, seating herself next to me. "He is so clumsy," she chuckled and smiled lovingly at him.

"Does he fall often?" I asked.

"Oh yes." She shook her head. "Last summer he fell at work and broke his arm in two places, and he's forever getting black eyes from running into file cabinets."

"Really?" I glanced sharply at Cecil/Fred, who was looking everywhere except at me. My face felt hot and flushed. It was no longer from embarrassment; it was rage.

"Yes, I never knew being a stockbroker was such dangerous work," she said.

It took everything I had not to scream. She didn't even know what her son did. Why in the hell all the secrets? And what in the hell was that photo about?

"This is the first time I've met anyone from Fred's work. What is it that you do, dear?" she asked kindly.

"I'm a numbers girl," I said, thankful I didn't have to lie. "I do internal audits, financial planning, corporate taxes . . . boring stuff," I laughed.

"Oh, that doesn't sound boring at all," she said, squeezing my hand. "I love a smart independent young woman. It's so different now than when I was young, of course. My si . . ."

"Mother, it's time for you to lie down." Cecil cut her off and gently aided her up from the couch. "I'll help you."

"No sweetheart, you're a mess. I can make it to my room all by myself," she said with a twinkle in her eye. "I'm a big girl. You spend time with your friend."

She slowly made her way out of the room. I inhaled deep breaths to calm myself. My desire to rip Cecil a new one was intense. I tried to quiet my inner fury so I wouldn't scare his mother when she was safely in her room. I kept reminding myself not to yell. That was going to be fucking difficult.

When I was sure she was gone, I felt free to start ripping. "Would you like to explain yourself, Cecil?" I hissed.

"Please call me Fred here," he said, not meeting my eye.

"How about Lying Sack of Shit?"

"That would work, too," he muttered, straightening papers and nervously rearranging his desk.

"Spill it," I ground out.

"There's nothing to spill," he said. "Can I get you something to drink or eat?" he asked. "You probably didn't get a chance to eat lunch and I don't want to be a bad host. So if you . . ."

"Fred, shut up." My heart was hammering in my chest. "I'm not hungry or thirsty, I'm pissed. At you. You have let that skank beat on you for probably years, you've lied to your mother about what you do . . . what are you waiting for? For Evangeline to kill you? Because it will happen; it could have happened last night." I glared at him. "What will happen to your mother if you're dead? And how in the hell could Evangeline tell your mother your secret? She doesn't even know your name is Fred, for fuck's sake."

Fred's body sagged. "Rena, I can't." His voice was low and tormented. "This disgusting and shameful compulsion I have . . ." He paused, white knuckling the chair as his body shook. "My mother can't know." He sighed heavily, his voice full of anguish. "It would kill her."

"Fred, I find that hard to believe. She adores you."

"She adores her son, not the freak who can't function unless he's wearing women's undergarments. I can't leave the house without . . ." He stopped; his face was bleak. "I'm not gay," he whispered.

"I didn't think you were. In fact, when I first met you, I thought you might be boning Evangeline."

The shock on his face made me laugh. Hard. So hard, it was contagious. Fred tried not to join me, but it was impossible. He held his bruised ribs as he belly-laughed and moaned in pain at the same time.

"That is the most repulsive thing I've ever heard pass your lips," he groaned, clutching his ribs, "and I sat through two weeks of Pirate Dave."

"When you're good, you're good," I giggled. "Fred, will you please talk to me?"

He sat quietly on the couch. I could feel him weakening. I waited, praying he would help. I knew he had the key to getting the goods on the viper whore. The question was, would he give it to me?

"I'm sorry, Rena. I can't."

"Fine." I stood up and shoved my arms into my coat with far more force than necessary. "Just think about this: your silence is ruining the lives of four wonderful women. And"—I held up my hand when he tried to interrupt—"you're underestimating your mother's love for you. You're a fucking idiot to think your taste in underwear would make any difference to her at all."

"You don't have the whole story," he said quietly.

"No duh, and I suppose you're going to enlighten me."

"No."

"Well, Cecil or Fred or whomever, it was nice knowing you. I hope your life turns out peachy. With or without your help, I will bring the Viper down and I will clear all my friends . . . including you."

I turned and left the broken man on the couch. I was so tempted to go back and comfort him, but I had work to do. Fuck, fuck, fuck, why was it all so hard?

Chapter 30

Tuesday morning rolled in with a vengeance. Six inches of snow blanketed the ground. The utter depressing grayness of the day matched my mood perfectly. Nancy had called Shoshanna's and I went ahead and filled her in on what I had found out about salmonella-gate. At first she tried to deny she was Nan Sorenson, but as my story unfolded, she admitted everything. The sucky thing was, I still didn't have any evidence to clear her. She didn't care. She was so overwhelmed by the news that she hadn't caused salmonella-gate, she let loose with a string of swearwords that almost burned my ears off. We hung up after I promised her I'd do everything in my power to get proof.

"What are you going to do?" Shoshanna asked, eating cling peaches from the can with her fingers.

"I have no idea. Is that your breakfast?" I inquired as I watched her drip peach juice all over her Minnesota Vikings flannel pj's.

"Yep, want some?" She offered me the can.

"Um, no. I have a better idea."

We met Kristy at a diner not far from my old apartment. Apprehension danced through my tummy at the possibility of running into Jack, but Kristy assured me that after he'd banged on our door this morning for the umpteenth time, he went to work.

"You really need to talk to him," Kristy said, smearing cream cheese on a bagel. "He keeps coming up at all hours looking for you."

"He's got it bad," LeHump said as she stole the bacon off my plate. Her manners never ceased to amaze me.

"No, he doesn't," I said, slapping her little hand as she went for my toast. "Why in the hell didn't you order anything?"

"I'm not hungry," Shoshanna said. I rolled my eyes and handed her my toast.

"Why didn't you butter this?" she asked. "Now it's too cold for the butter to melt."

I held up my three middle fingers and smiled. "Read between the lines, LeHump."

"Very high school, Rena," she laughed. "Kristy, are you going to finish your bagel?" Kristy considered her bagel for a moment, then handed it over to the human vacuum.

"So what else has Mr. Sexy Buns done?" LeHump asked with a mouthful of Kristy's former breakfast.

"He knocked so long yesterday, our reclusive little neighbor came out and threatened to call the police," Kristy laughed.

"Oh my God," I giggled. "What did he do?"

"Flashed his badge and apologized."

I pondered my scrambled eggs, which I had put way too much salt on, and wondered if I was making the hugest mistake of my life by not seeing him again. I pushed my eggs over to Shoshanna, who took a bite and pushed them right back.

"I can't see him. I know Cecil wants to help me make a plan, but he's going to be laid up for a while and I don't like him right now anyway." I ran my hands through my hair and sighed. "I'm moving to Iowa and I've grown up a lot in the past two weeks. Mostly against my will, but getting blackmailed by a soulless set of boobs can do that to you. The old me would have run back and begged Jack for another chance, and I would have tried to change for him. I would have tried to be what he wants instead of being me. It would work for about a month or so and then he'd realize I was a fraud. I'd be so in love with him by that time that when he dumped me again, I'd have to stay in bed for three months to recover. He doesn't like who I am. He thinks I'm nuts." Any appetite I had was gone. Going out for breakfast was a bad idea.

"A man who bangs on the door eight to ten times a day likes who you are," Shoshanna said. "You should at least hear him out."

"If it's meant to be, it's meant to be," I said.

"What are you? A fucking fortune cookie?" Shoshanna chuckled. "Sometimes what's meant to be doesn't happen unless you help it along."

"She's right," Kristy agreed.

I stared at my old best friend and bizarrely enough, my new one. "I agree with you, too."

"You do?" they said in unison.

"Yep," I said, "but not about Jack. I'm going to apply that little nugget of wisdom to something else. I'll see you guys later." I dropped some money on the table to pay for the breakfast I'd ordered and Shoshanna had eaten, and I left.

"Listen to me, Fred, if you don't help me, everybody goes down. Including you. If you think for one moment she's not going to sing like a fucking bird after we destroy her career, you're an idiot," I said, sitting across from him at his house.

"Please keep your voice down. My mother is resting."

"Sorry," I muttered, trying to figure out how to convince him. I actually considered blackmailing him, but my mind didn't work that way. I giggled at the irony. I'd been arrested twice, yet I made a shitty criminal.

"You find this funny?" he asked, surprised. He still looked like hell. His eye was purple with a hint of greenish-yellow. The gash above his eyebrow wasn't quite as angry, but his movement was stiff and his skin was pale.

"Hilarious," I snapped. "I can't wait until the world finds out that Poppy Harriet is a man and that the respected Professor Sue Lumpschlicterschmidt's alias is Shoshanna LeHump. You know, the porno-writing granny who was married to a gay man. Nancy will be thrilled to be outed as Nan Thorenson, the perpetrator of salmonella-gate, and Joanne . . . I don't know what the Viper has on Joanne. Whatever." I threw my hands in the air in frustration. "Oh, and don't let me forget, I stole jewels. Of course, there were no fucking jewels in the box, but the Viper is paying off the police, so I'm sure something will stick." I stopped and stood in front of the sad old man I'd come to care about. "And you . . . you have the chance to tell your mother yourself, or you can let that bitch do it for you."

"Rena, it's not that simple."

"It is that simple." I got down on my knees, forcing him to look at me. "It is that simple. I know somewhere in that disaster you call an office, you have proof of what she's done. Am I right?"

He closed his eyes and didn't move a muscle.

"Answer me," I pleaded.

"You can't be sure she'll talk," he insisted. "You don't know that for certain." He sounded desperate. Was he that scared of his mother knowing? It didn't add up.

"Fred, think about it. The Viper will not go down alone. She will take everyone she can with her. I don't know what happened in Evangeline O'Hara's childhood to fuck her up so badly, but she is pure evil."

Fred's spine straightened and his face reddened. "She had a wonderful childhood," he sputtered indignantly. "Her parents were lovely people."

"How in the hell would you know that?" I demanded. I'd had enough of other people's cryptic bullshit to last me a lifetime.

"I'm surmising," he stammered.

"Surmising, my ass. You tell me what you know or I'll . . . I'll, hell, I don't know what I'll do, but it will be bad."

Fred stayed stone-faced and silent.

"How about I start with what I know," I said sarcastically, folding my hands and putting them primly in my lap. "I know your name is not Cecil or Jeeves or Belvedere. Your name is Fred. You're not a stockbroker, you're a *New York Times* best-selling romance author who's had his books stolen by a plastic surgery addict who is probably more synthetic than human."

"Rena, stop."

"Nope, it's my turn and I'm taking it," I said, cutting him off. "You're working for a woman who physically and mentally abuses you, and one of these days, she will kill you. You have the chance to bring her down and at the same time save some wonderful women who are being blackmailed just like you are and you won't do it. You are so afraid your mother will disown you for having a ladies' underpants fetish, you can't see past your own selfish fear. I would suggest you pull up your big girl panties and loosen your bra straps because they're obviously cutting off the blood flow to your brain."

"Fred?" Delona stood in the doorway with tears running down her cheeks. "Is all that true?" she whispered.

"Mother," Fred gasped, jumping up and going to her. He dropped to his knees and buried his face in her dressing gown. He looked so much like a child, I turned away. It was too private. I would have left if I could have, but they were blocking the doorway.

"You're working for Evangeline?" she asked with despair in her voice.

What in the hell was going on? How did she know the Viper? Her knees started to buckle. Fred was so immersed in his own shock and anguish, he had no clue. I literally flew across the room and caught Delona before she fell on top of her son.

"Come sit down," I said, helping her to the couch. Fred stayed on the floor, unable to look at anyone.

"Thank you, Rena," she said, pulling herself together, "for more than you know. Fred, come here." It wasn't a request.

"How much of that did you hear?" I asked, feeling sick to my stomach. My intention was for Fred to tell his secrets . . . not me.

"All of it," she replied, taking Fred's hands in her own. "Fred, when your father died I thought it would be a good thing to move back to Minnesota and be near family. You were so young and I was so sad." She gently reached under his chin and lifted his face. His eyes were desolate and I felt my own fill with tears.

"Maybe I should go," I said, standing up to leave.

"No, Rena," Delona said. "Please stay." I sat back down. "I thought being around my parents and sister would be a good thing for us . . . I was wrong. I knew she was sick, but I had no idea you were still in contact with her."

The lightbulb in my brain began to light up, dimly, but it was on. The photograph now made sense . . .

"Fred, I want you to know that I've always known." She smiled, trying to lighten the morbid pall in the room. "I've known since you were ten and my underwear starting disappearing."

Fred sobbed and dropped his head into his hands. "I'm so sorry. So sorry."

"Why are you sorry?" she asked gently.

"Because I'm a freak of nature." His voice ripped from his throat. I looked down at my hands. It was simply too painful to watch. "I don't deserve to live. I'm worthless and stupid and an embarrassment to you," he said. "You were never supposed to know." His head drooped and his shoulders slumped. "I'm so sorry."

"On my God, Fred. Why would you think that?" She put her arms around him and rocked him like a child.

"She told me. She said it would kill you . . . you would hate me. Oh God, I'm so sorry."

"Fred, you're a grown man. Why would you believe such a thing?" she asked, touching his bruised face and frantically searching his eyes.

Fred's cries tore at my insides. Evangeline had damaged him far more than I'd thought possible. "Eleven," he sobbed. "I was eleven and she caught me. Every day . . . every day."

"She's told you every day since you were eleven?" The words flew from my horrified mouth before I could stop them.

Fred, unable to speak, nodded his head and refused to make eye contact with me or his mother.

"Rena," Delona said. Her words had an edge of steel that reminded me of Evangeline. Although the Viper was out for herself, her sister, Delona, was out for her son. "I heard there may be a way to help, to . . . end this. What did you mean by that?"

I put my hand on Fred's shoulder, asking permission. Without raising his eyes, he clasped my hand and squeezed. "I think Fred has proof of what Evangeline has done over the years to him and many others. I want him to give it to me."

Delona's turquoise blue eyes, so similar to her sister's, studied me. "What will you do with this information?"

"Take her ass down, set it on fire, and watch it explode," I told her, meaning every word. Metaphorically, that is.

"Fred, I want to be very clear with you. Look at me," she said. "I love you. I have always loved you and nothing you say or do can change that. I have no problem that you like ladies' underthings. When your father was alive I enjoyed his boxers from time to time, so you probably come by it naturally." She grabbed his chin when he tried to turn away. "What was done to you was horrific child abuse and I know you probably don't believe me when I say I love you. We have a journey to take now. We will do therapy together and you will do it alone, too. You are a beautiful man and the best son a woman could ask for, goddamnit. I ask you for one thing."

"What?" Fred whispered, obviously wanting so much to believe everything his mother was saying.

"I want you to give Rena the proof."

"I want that, too," he said. "I wanted that all along, I was just too weak to . . ."

"Stop," I interrupted. "It's not too late. Just tell me where it is and I'll do the rest."

Fred handed me a key to a drawer in his office and made me promise to go after eight this evening. Evangeline was having a procedure on her nonexistent eyelids at six and everyone should be gone by eight. She would be so drugged up by then, it should be simple to get in and out.

As I was leaving, I heard Delona ask Fred about his writing. As he spoke with pride and she laughed with delight, my heart felt lighter than it had in a while. Fred was going to be okay.

I went back to Shoshanna's and had a two-hour conversation with cardboard Brett Favre. He was very nice about my dumping all my issues on him and didn't seem to be the least bit offended by my colorful language. I thought I might ask Shoshanna if I could take him to Iowa.

Waiting to go to the Viper's to get the proof was killing me. I was loving life so much, I almost called Jack . . . almost.

At eight o'clock, I picked up the folder. It was thick. I drove right back to Shoshanna's and started reading. And oh boy, it was some heavy reading. At three in the morning, I closed the folder . . . Tomorrow was going to be a very busy day.

Chapter 31

I hadn't been back to my apartment building since I'd moved out. My trembling hands and somersaulting insides were proof enough that I should stay away from Jack, but I wanted to give him something. Kristy was fairly sure he had gone to work, but he hadn't knocked at our door this morning. My busted heart broke a little more at that news.

I pressed my ear against his door and listened. No noise. Thank you, Jesus. I got down on my hands and knees and tried to shove an envelope underneath. A tiny part of me was disappointed he wasn't home . . . all right, a huge part of me, but it was better this way.

"Dang it," I said, trying to push it under the sealed door. Peeling up the rubber to make room for the envelope wasn't working. The only success I had was breaking two of my already short finger-nails. Failure was not acceptable. I considered taping it to the door, but this envelope could not fall into the wrong hands. I dug through my purse looking for something that could cut the rubber enough to make room for my delivery . . . gum, hand cream, lip gloss, phone, wallet, tampons. Ah ha, the butter knife I'd borrowed from the diner last week because Shoshanna didn't have any. I knew what she was getting from me next Christmas.

I wedged the knife under the door and tried to peel the rubber back. The knife bent in half. Shit, what in the hell did they make this crap with? Tinfoil? I sat back on my butt and tried to figure out what to do. I had about two hours before I needed to implement the next part of my plan. There had to be a way to make this work. I rammed the misshapen knife into the rubber and started sawing. I put all my weight behind it and went to town. This might actually . . .

"Rena?" Jack asked, opening the door.

I tumbled into Jack's apartment, landing at his running-shoe-clad feet. Fuckity, fuck, fuck. "I have something I need to give you," I said with faint hysteria in my voice. I was still on my hands and knees at his feet. This was so not happening.

"Okay," he said, squatting down to my level. "And you figured carving out a hole in my door would be a good way to deliver it?"

"Um, yes. Yes, I did." So much for the I'm-not-crazy campaign.

"I've been trying to find you," he said, grabbing my hand and pulling me to my feet.

Son of a bitch, he was gorgeous. It wasn't fair. His legs were covered in tight winter running pants and his black long-sleeved running shirt hugged every muscular inch of his upper body. I was tongue-tied and stared at him openmouthed. At least I'd dressed with care, on the outside, outside chance I would run into him. He took in my Captain Crunch T-shirt, and a sexy grin split his face. My knees went weak and my heart ping-ponged around my chest.

"Here." I handed him the envelope, shocked that any words came out.

"What's this? A restraining order?" He smiled, slipping around me to close, lock, chain, and double bolt his front door. My insides clenched in excitement at the thought of him forcing me against my will to do all kinds of things with him. Of course force would have nothing to do with it . . . me and my inner slut would do anything he wanted. Anything. Happily. As many times as he wanted. In fact, I could probably come up with a few interesting new positions to try . . .

I backed away before I slammed him against the wall and played tonsil hockey with him. "No, it's something I think you need."

He carelessly tossed the envelope onto the table next to his door. "The only thing I need is you," he said in a husky voice that made me tingle all over.

"Jack, I . . ."

"No, Rena, listen to me. I am so sorry. I was wrong not to believe you. I was an asshole and a jerk and I said some awful things." He moved toward me and put his big strong hands on my upper arms, sending jolts of electricity through me and straight to my panties. "My life just sucks without you."

His hands were warm and I knew he meant what he said, but . . .
"Jack, it will happen again."

"God, I hope not." He winced, clearly reliving his evening with
the eighty-year-old silicone knockers. "Wait," he stammered, having no idea I knew what he was referring to. "I don't mean you. I
mean, um . . ."

"I know what you mean," I said.

"No, you don't." He grimaced.

"Unfortunately, I do. I was hiding in the curtains," I admitted
guiltily.

"Oh my God," he laughed, then shuddered with disgust. "I'm almost glad someone can verify that actually happened. Why were
you in the curtains?"

"I was about to leave and I heard your voices and I didn't want
to see you or for you to see me. I tried to hide behind a naked fornicator statue, but it wasn't big enough, so I dove behind the curtains and then I . . ." I petered off, realizing how insane I sounded.
This was exactly why it wouldn't work. I straightened my spine
and slipped out of his arms. "Jack," I said in my best accountant's
voice, "I think you'll be extremely interested in the contents of the
envelope. I hope your life goes very well and I'm sure someday we
can be friends. I have other errands to run and I'm moving to Iowa
with Cardboard Brett Favre in two weeks, so, um . . ."

"Rena, what can I do to make you give me another chance?"

I was caught off guard by the urgency in his voice. "I don't . . ."

"I'll let you look at my giraffe and even make fun of it," he offered, taking off his shirt.

"You will?" I giggled. An express shuttle of excitement tore
through my body straight to my lady bits at the sight of his naked
chest. "You're not playing fair," I said in a voice that belonged in
a porno.

"Nope," he agreed. "I'm not." He pushed his hands into the
waistband of his running pants and slowly eased them down his
legs.

Oh. My. God. My mouth went dry and my inner slut fought me
for control.

"I will resort to anything to get you back," he said sexily.

"I will not have sex with you," I said, pulling my own shirt over
my head.

"Okay," he said, unbuttoning my jeans and sliding them down my legs. "No sex. I got it. Anything else?"

"Um, yes." I felt like a breathless teenager. "I won't date you. I'm going to find a strapping farm man in Iowa and Cardboard Brett Favre is pretty damn hot," I said, quickly removing my bra.

His eyes raked my body hungrily. "I thought Brett Favre was married."

"Cardboard Brett Favre is single," I gasped as he removed my panties. His slightly callused hands ran slowly up my legs, firmly planting themselves on my bare ass. Thank Sweet Baby Jesus, I'd shaved my legs this morning.

I felt a little dizzy. My nipples were so hard they hurt, my heart was lodged in my throat, and the moisture pooling between my legs needed attention immediately.

"So my getting into your pants doesn't mean you forgive me?" he asked, leaving my ass behind and running his thumbs over my nipples.

"I'm not wearing any pants." I arched my back to give him more of my aching breasts. "And there's nothing to forgive. You were right, I'm crazy," I gasped as his lips closed over my nipple and drew hard. I plunged my fingers into his hair and held him close. His scent and his body were the most perfect things I'd ever had the good fortune to touch. I wished . . .

"Rena, I want to make love to you. I need to make love to you," he moaned.

"I want that, too," I whispered. Thankfully he didn't notice the tears in my eyes. This was so bittersweet for me. Making love with the person I loved, whom I couldn't be with because, as much as he thought my crazy was okay, eventually it would destroy us.

"Come with me." He practically dragged me to his bedroom. His bed dominated the room. It was huge. Dark blue sheets and a squishy down comforter covered the mattress and tons of pillows littered the bed. I could get lost in that bed. "Don't move," he said, pushing me against the wall and giving me a kiss that curled my toes. So much for doing it on his bed . . . I watched as he frantically searched for a condom. The muscles in his back were so hot. They flexed as he tore through his bedside drawer. His giraffe seemed to come to life with his movement. I tried unsuccessfully to stifle my laughter.

"I know what you're laughing at." He grinned as he tore the condom open with his teeth. "And I give you full permission to laugh at it for the rest of your life."

Oh God, if only. I pushed those thoughts out of my head and concentrated on watching him slide the condom over his massive and gorgeous erection. Everything in my body tightened in anticipation of the feeling of him inside me.

His frenzied pace had slowed and he walked toward me like an animal stalking prey. "You are so fucking beautiful," he said in a low voice. Shit, all he had to do to make me come was keep talking. He looked like he wanted to devour me and that was A-OK with me.

He grasped me by the waist and lifted me in the air. "Wrap your legs around me," he said gruffly, running his open mouth across my collar bone and nipping at my shoulder.

The wall felt cool against my back in contrast to the heat of his hard body. My breasts were smashed on his chest, and I could feel the swollen head of his cock pressed against my pelvis. One of his hands reached around my body and between my legs to test my readiness. "Oh God," he muttered, burying his fingers in my moisture. "You are so fucking wet. I need to fuck you. Now. I need to be inside you now."

My pulse quickened to heart attack levels. I reached back and guided him to me. He held me up by my ass and lowered my body onto his. The exquisite burn of something so large entering me made my head spin. He was going too slow . . . I wanted, oh God, I wanted . . .

I screamed as he read my mind and buried himself to the hilt. I started to rock back and forth on him. This felt so much deeper than the last time and tiny explosions were going off inside me.

"Rena," he ground out, "look at me." I opened my eyes as he forcibly slowed the movement of our bodies. "If you won't believe my words, let me show you how I feel with my body. Please."

I nodded my head. I didn't trust my voice. My heart thumped wildly in my chest and I was so close to telling him that I loved him, I had to bite down on my tongue. He smiled and lifted my body like it was a feather, slowly up and down his own.

As his body invaded mine I moaned and ran trembling fingers through his hair. His slow pace ended quickly as I writhed against him. Wrapping one arm around my waist and the other under my ass, he plunged into me with hard powerful strokes. He whispered in my ear, but I had no idea what he was saying. I could barely think . . . barely function. The sound of our flesh coming together was so hot, I forgot how to breathe.

His lips moved to my neck as his lower body increased the speed, making my control snap. I screamed as little frissons of white-hot pleasure shot through me. His avid attention to my neck made me lose brain cells.

A slow heat started low in my abdomen, traveling upward at a blindingly fast pace. My body jerked as shock wave after shock wave ricocheted through me. My body tightened like a vise around his cock and his eyes went wide with pleasure. I think I was speaking Russian because I couldn't even understand what I was saying.

Jack threw his head back and shouted as he came. He crushed my mouth to his and we rode out the aftershocks connected to each other in every way.

My bones had turned to water. That was not just sex. I'd had sex before, not a lot, and never with a law-abiding citizen, but this was more than just sex. It felt like my atoms had shifted, like he had fundamentally changed me. The more he gave, the more I wanted to give back, and I knew losing him would be losing part of myself. I didn't want that to happen. Maybe it could work . . .

He walked me to his bed and gently laid me on top of his comforter. He wrapped his big strong body around mine and stroked my hair. Cardboard Brett Favre just wouldn't do. "Jack, I want . . ." I froze and looked at his ceiling. WTF? "You have a mirrored ceiling?" I gasped, wondering if I had gotten all the signals wrong and he was a big old player.

He started laughing, "It was here when I moved in. I haven't had time to take it down. Why?" he teased. "Do you like it?"

"Um, I don't know," I muttered, feeling the heat crawl up my neck. I looked up at our reflections and noticed something odd. No fucking way. "Did you give me a hickey?" I shouted. I had so much to do today. I didn't have time to explain to everyone that I'd gotten my brains screwed out by a cop with a vampire fetish. Shit.

"Ohhh," he said without an ounce of remorse, "I guess I did."

There was no hiding the huge red hickey he'd put on my neck.

It would even peek out from a turtleneck, unless I wore it up over my mouth. "What are you, Bigfoot?" I yelled.

"Bigfoot gives hickeys?" he asked, totally confused.

"How should I know? I've only been to one meeting." I slapped my hands over my mouth and burst into tears. Why did I always sound crazy around him? I hopped up and ran to the other room. I yanked on my clothes and grabbed my purse. I wanted to burst out of my skin. He sprinted out of the bedroom completely naked, almost making me forget my name. "Don't say a word," I warned as he opened his mouth to speak. "It won't work between us. I can try to be what you want, but I will always go to Bigfoot meetings. I will babysit my aunt's Martians because I love her and it makes her happy. I will say and do stupid and embarrassing things till the day I die. You need a normal girl and I need to move to Iowa and get married to a cardboard cutout who doesn't give a damn what comes out of my mouth."

I tossed the envelope from the side table to him. "That contains canceled checks from Evangeline to your Sergeant and Herbie the Dentist. They date back over ten years. It's your proof to bring down some crooked cops if you want to." He was speechless. I wasn't sure if it was all the things I'd just said or if it was the information I'd brought to him. It didn't matter, I was out of there.

"Rena, please," he said in a broken voice.

My back was to him as I gripped the doorknob. "Jack—" I heaved a heavy sigh. "I am in love with you . . . and that's why I'm leaving. I already know what will happen if I stay."

I opened the door and left without looking back. Any remnants of my heart lay scattered all over his floor. I took a deep breath and moved forward, one step at a time. Tomorrow I would crawl into bed for my three-month mourning period. Today I needed to suck it up and save my friends.

Chapter 32

I walked into the packed lobby of the WMNS building with the folder tucked securely under my arm. My fear of being arrested for breaking my restraining order, yet again, made me tremble. Shoshanna assured me the black wig and horn-rimmed glasses made me unrecognizable, but I wasn't so sure. Of course the scarf around my neck just made me look fashion impaired, but I wasn't going to take any shit about my hickey. I meandered by the coffee shop. If the boys didn't recognize me, I knew I was good to go.

"Rena," Vito whispered in my ear.

"Fuck," I shouted. "How did you know it was me?"

"Your ass," he whispered loudly.

"And your rack," Angelo added quietly. "You have the most stupendous rack I've ever seen."

Vito nodded solemnly in agreement with Angelo.

"Um, thank you," I muttered, wondering if that was the appropriate response to two little Italian men in their sixties who ogled your boobs. "Do you think anyone else will know it's me?" I was freaking out. Not to mention creeped out by their photographic memories of my privates.

"Absolutely not," Vito said. "No one has studied your ass and rack like we have. Right, Angelo?"

"Correct." Angelo nodded. "Are you in trouble? Because all we have to do is make a call and we can have whoever is bothering you six feet under by eight o'clock tonight," he offered.

Shit, I could have had them take care of Evangeline three weeks ago. Not. "No guys, thanks for the offer, but I'm bringing this one down alone."

They looked disappointed that I didn't want them to kill anyone, but seemed proud I was taking the matter into my own hands.

"If you change your mind, you know where to find us," Vito said, waggling his substantial brows. They eased their way into the coffee shop back to back. I loved them, but they were weird.

The lobby was full of women hoping to catch a glimpse of their favorite author, Evangeline O'Hara. Gals of all shapes and colors and sizes chatted animatedly about the Viper's books and characters as if they were real. The excitement was palpable. If they only knew.

I spotted a stage at the far end of the lobby. TV cameras and lights surrounded the podium and a large logo sign with Anderson Cooper's name floated above the stage. How in the hell did they do that? I couldn't see any wires. I glanced around with dismay. How was I supposed to find Shoshanna and the girls in this mess? There had to be five hundred women milling around.

"Rena," Nancy whispered.

"Motherfucker," I gasped, grabbing my chest. She was the third person who'd recognized me in less than two minutes. "Am I that recognizable?"

"No," she laughed. "You look awful. Shoshanna described your disguise to a tee."

"Okay," I mumbled, kind of hurt that she thought I looked icky. My heart rate slowed and I realized ugly was better than incarcerated.

"The show starts in fifteen minutes. The girls are here. They'll meet us in five, they're scoping out the stage," she said. "Rena, I have to tell you something. No matter how this all turns out, the day you came into our lives was one of the best things that ever happened to any of us." She hugged me tight. "I can only hope we've added something other than trouble to yours."

"Oh my God, Nancy"—my eyes welled up—"I love you guys. It might have been less stressful under different circumstances, but I wouldn't change any of it."

"Good." She smiled lovingly at me. "You stay here. Poppy Harriet went to the ladies' room ten minutes ago; I'm getting worried that she fell into the commode. I'll be back."

I wasn't sure if she was serious or joking, but my stomach was in such a knot I decided to let that one go. I had emailed the proof of Evangeline's guilt in salmonella-gate to Bigfoot Kim earlier in the day. Fred had kept the receipts for the Silly Putty substance from Bulgaria and he had the invoices for the people paid to poison the food, all signed by the Botox bitch herself. They correlated with the dates of the party exactly. Kim promised to have her cousin's brother's girlfriend's sister, the health inspector, show up. I'd instructed her to tell her brother's cousin's whatever to stand close to the stage. After hanging up with Kim, I realized the health inspector's relationship to Kim was strange, but then again, so was dedicating your life to finding Bigfoot.

I watched all the fans and kept my eyes open for security. Paranoia was beginning to consume me. I could have sworn on the drive over I was being followed. Maybe I'd been watching too much TV. At one point I even thought it was Jack, but he was naked when I'd left him. There was no way.

The countdown had started. The Viper's book had been released an hour ago. I spotted women avidly reading their Kindles and Nooks with looks of appalled disgust on their face. I had to physically stop myself from bouncing up and down with glee. *Pirate Dave and His Randy Adventures* had hit the Net and by the looks of it, he was doing his job beautifully.

"Oh my God," a typical Midwestern housewife gasped. "This is filth. Gladys, did you read any of this crap yet?"

Gladys was the color of chalk. "This is awful," she cried out, trying to recover. I wondered which section she'd read. "I can't believe I paid ten dollars for this. I want my money back."

The consensus through the crowd was the same. Maybe they would rush the stage and kill the Viper. That would solve all my problems. The headlines would be great. Angry Mob Kills Author Over Disgusting Pornographic Shit. I grinned at the thought.

Where were the girls? I wanted to explain the contents of the folder. I had done a front sheet with all the bullet points. I'd organized all the data inside and written a page per person that Evangeline was blackmailing. The returned checks I'd given Jack were the originals, but I had made copies for the folder. Just in case Jack decided against pressing charges, I wanted Santa and Herbie the Dentist to go down.

I still wasn't sure what the gals were going to do with the folder.

That was Joanne's job to figure out. Fuck. Joanne . . . There wasn't anything in the folder about Joanne. How had I not noticed that? An icy chill raced up my spine. I whipped through the folder again, hoping I'd missed something. Nothing. What was I going to do? It would be my fault if Joanne went down and everyone else was saved.

Where in the hell were they? Anderson Cooper walked out on the stage for a pre-show warm-up and the crowd went wild. God, if they didn't get here soon, none of this would work out. My mouth felt dry and the pounding in my head alerted me to the migraine that would be paying a visit soon. Ohgodohgodohgod, where are they? If I could find out what in the hell Evangeline had on Joanne, I might be able to figure out a logical excuse that could clear her.

I could barely hear my own thoughts over the screams of the crowd. My four partners in crime pushed their way through the masses and surrounded me.

"Do you have it?" Shoshanna shouted at the top of her lungs. With the noise I could barely make out what she was saying, although I had a good idea.

I held up the folder. Joanne grabbed it, gave me a thumbs-up, and slipped back into the crowd. "No," I screamed, trying to stop her.

"What's wrong?" Poppy Harriet yelled.

"What does Evangeline have on Joanne?" I yelled. She put her hand to her ear, indicating she couldn't hear me. I repeated myself. Louder.

"Ruffing," Poppy Harriet shouted, smiling like she was drunk.

WTF? What was ruffing? And why was she so happy about it? Maybe she *had* fallen in the toilet. There was little I could do. We'd have to deal with clearing Joanne after the fact. I prayed ruffing wasn't something really awful or illegal. It sounded slightly gang related. Nausea consumed me. We'd come so far. Too far for a fuckup like this.

"Cover the exits," Shoshanna yelled. "Be prepared to tackle the skank's ass if she tries to escape. Beat the hell out of her and then turn her over to the police. Move out," she shrieked. I realized two things. Shoshanna was dressed from head to toe in fatigues and I wasn't going to be able to get their help with Joanne. They disappeared as quickly as they'd shown up. Fuck.

I moved to my assigned exit and waited for all hell to break loose. I stood up on a bench for a better view and realized there were huge monitor screens all over the room. Very considerate of Anderson Cooper. There wasn't a bad seat in the house. I was terrified of having to look at Evangeline on something that rivaled a movie screen, but I figured I could close my eyes if it got too alarming.

"Rena?"

"Holy shit," I squealed, falling off my bench. Fred caught me and winced in pain. "Oh my God," I gasped. "How did you know it was me?"

"Shoshanna texted me a picture," he chuckled. He was wearing his requisite suit with his mother, Delona, on his arm.

"Are you well enough to be here?" I asked, glad that the crowd had quieted some and I didn't have to shout.

"We wouldn't miss this for the world." Delona smiled deviously. "May we join you?"

"Of course," I said, grinning. Fred and I helped her up on the bench and we stood on either side of her.

A hush went through the crowd as the screens flashed the word "Quiet." Women held hands and some were crying. This was insane. I could still hear people grousing about Pirate Dave, but fewer than before. Shit, what if the book wasn't enough to ruin her? Could her fans forgive her? I had tried so hard to present a pile of confusing, offensive, unreadable shit . . . What if I'd failed?

"Good evening, ladies and gentlemen," a very excited and overly medicated announcer's voice boomed over the sound system. "Welcome to the live edition of the *Anderson Cooper Show*."

The crowd went wild and two women fainted. "Quiet" flashed on the screen again and the crowd got hold of itself as paramedics dragged the passed-out, overexcited fans away.

"Anderson will be back out in a moment," the faceless voice continued. "Make sure you watch the screen. It will instruct you when to clap, laugh, sigh, cry, boo, and shut up . . . I mean quiet down," the voice chuckled nervously. I was thinking this guy might need to look for a new job tomorrow. A lot of the fans seemed to take offense at the "shut up" comment. "Anderson will be interviewing Evangeline O'Hara tonight, and she will read from her new book. The reviews are coming in as we speak, and we will read several on the air."

The murmuring in the crowd was music to my ears. I heard "piece of shit," and "did she have an aneurysm?" and "I might sue to get my money back." Fred gave me a high five and pulled his shirt open just a touch to show me his lavender teddy. I giggled and hugged him. Everyone was going to be okay. I just prayed that Joanne would be all right, too.

"Fred, what does Evangeline have on Joanne?" I asked, hoping he could help me solve my dilemma.

Fred looked stymied and shook his head. "I've never seen anything on Joanne."

"Oh my God," I moaned, "this is bad. Poppy Harriet said something about ruffing."

"What does that mean?" Delona asked.

"I have no idea, but it sounds gang related to me." My panic level was rising.

"We will deal with it," Fred said firmly. "Whatever it is, we will make sure she's all right."

Fred's confidence calmed my jangled nerves and I focused back on the stage. It was set up like a talk show. There was a desk for Anderson Cooper and a pale green couch next to it. Down stage and to the left stood a podium. I assumed that's where the Viper would read to her adoring fans. From my high vantage point, I could make out Joanne standing next to the stage near a set of what appeared to be stairs. What in the hell was she planning to do? I got a sick feeling. Next to her stood an official-looking woman carrying a briefcase. She chatted easily with Joanne. I assumed she was the health inspector. The circus in my tummy got more violent with each passing second.

"And now, ladies and gentlemen," the announcer squealed, "here's Anderson Cooper!" The screens flashed the words "go nuts" and the crowd obliged with gusto.

"Here we go—" Fred grinned, grabbing my ice-cold hand and squeezing.

The jugglers in my stomach started tossing daggers. I gave Fred a weak smile and squeezed his hand. "Yep," I choked out, "here we go."

Chapter 33

"Hello, ladies and gentlemen. How is everyone feeling to-night?" Anderson Cooper yelled as he came out onto the stage. The crowd went ballistic and completely ignored the flashing sign to be quiet. He stood there smiling at the nutty audience. Dang, he's cute. "Tonight we are very lucky to have *New York Times* best-selling author Evangeline O'Hara. She has thrown her hat into the self-publishing world with a preorder that defies reason. I haven't had the honor of meeting her yet, but I look forward to sitting with such an incredibly accomplished icon."

Oh my God, he's in for a treat. A producer walked out onto the stage and handed him some papers. Anderson nodded his thanks and continued. "Right here in my hand I'm holding the early reviews for *Pirate Dave and His Randy Adventures.* Am I in the room with Evangeline O'Hara fans?" he asked the audience. They screamed rabidly. Anderson Cooper looked slightly alarmed by the response, but he was a pro. "Would you like to hear what the papers are saying?" he yelled, holding the reviews above his head. Again, they screamed like they were on fire.

He glanced at the paper he was holding and blanched. The dagger throwers in my tummy started juggling pillows. He quickly flipped through the sheaf of papers in his hands, getting paler with each discovery. "Well, um," Anderson Cooper stuttered, "maybe we'll, ah . . . hold off on these until later in the show."

The crowd, clearly in love with Mr. Cooper, cheered like maniacs. Anderson glanced over to the producer, held up the reviews, and gave him a WTF look. "All right, my friends"—he popped right back into his TV self—"after the break we'll be back with Evangeline O'Hara."

"He didn't read the reviews because the book sucks," one woman hissed.

"I agree," another said. "It's an obscene pile of disconnected crap. It's not readable."

My fists clenched with excitement and my eyes sparkled behind my horn rims. Fred and Delona grinned and nodded. So far, so good. Anderson Cooper left the stage. I was sure he had some choice words for his producer.

A hush went through the room as the Viper stepped onto the stage. Evangeline made her entrance with two young producers from the show. The crowd murmured in shock. She looked like a dead hooker who had been reanimated by zombies. Her skirt length was obscenely short. It was turquoise feathers with gold sequins. Her top was a gold lamé halter and her stilettos were covered in gold glitter. Her considerable boobage was spilling out of her halter in a very bad way. I glanced at Delona, whose jaw had practically hit the floor.

Evangeline wobbled her way to the couch, relying heavily on her escorts. As she seated herself, she grabbed on to the dark-haired escort's love stick. The crowd gasped and the escort shrieked in terror, turned, and hightailed it off the stage. The other escort backed away in fear and quickly followed his buddy. She made the international "call me" sign to their backs as they escaped.

"She did not just grab that poor guy's privates," I laughed.

"Yes, she did." Delona raised her eyebrow in disgust. "I hope he sues her. God knows there are enough witnesses."

Evangeline looked out at her fans and did the Queen's wave. The camera guy, who had a sense of humor or was just as mean as a snake, went in for a close-up, and stayed. A sixteen-foot picture of Evangeline's face was projected on the big screen all over the lobby. People turned away in horror and some started to cry. I realized what little eyelids she might have had left were completely gone. Her eyes were bulging out of her head. Her makeup was on the garish side and her neck looked like an elephant scrotum at its finest. Fucking awesome.

The canned music came back on. Anderson Cooper ran back onstage and seated himself at his desk. He turned to smile at Evangeline and startled so badly, he threw himself backward. He and his chair toppled over. Producers, PA's, and security ran out onto the stage to help their star. Within seconds he was righted, his TV face was back on, and he was ready to go.

"Sorry about that," he told the viewing audience at home, "there seems to be a malfunction with my chair. All fixed now!"

"Malfunction, my ass," I giggled.

"This is making my year," Delona gushed, hugging both me and Fred.

"Ladies and gentlemen, I'd like to introduce you to Evangeline O'Hara." Anderson Cooper smiled out to the crowd, trying to avoid looking directly at the Viper. The smattering of applause was in direct violation of the screen, which was urging us with desperate flashing to "go nuts."

"Thank you, Andy," she purred, running her claw up his arm. He gave her a lovely smile and discreetly moved out of her range.

"It's actually Anderson," he corrected her politely.

"Oh Andy," she tittered seductively while everyone in the lobby cringed, "you don't have to be so formal with me. I'm the spitting image of your mother. Everyone tells me so."

Anderson Cooper was speechless. He turned a rather mottled shade of purple and straightened all the papers on his desk. "Yes, well," he said, gathering himself, "let's talk about your book."

"Of course I'm only sixty," she cooed and touched her bosom lightly, "but the resemblance is uncanny. Don't you think so, Andy?" Several women in the crowd rolled their eyes at her age lie, others downright laughed.

"Um, no, I don't. So let's get back to the book." He smiled, but I could tell it cost him. "You have over forty best-sellers on the *New York Times* list, so why self-publish?"

"They're all crap." She flicked her hand dismissively. "All those books were awful. I'm embarrassed to have my name on them."

The crowd gasped and several people booed.

Evangeline's head snapped around and she glared at the audience. "You all are idiots if you liked those books," she laughed. The poor audience couldn't tell if she was kidding or serious. Neither could Anderson Cooper. Everyone laughed weakly along with her, wondering if they'd entered the Twilight Zone.

"You must be joking," Anderson said, uncomfortably.

Evangeline's tiny brain wheels started working, and she realized the crowd was not with her. "Of course I'm joking," she crooned. "I love all those books and all the little people who buy them."

"Oo-kay." Anderson's eyes were large and he shifted in his seat. "Why don't you tell us about *Pirate Dave and His Randy Adventures*? The pre-sales are phenomenal, absolutely record breaking."

"Yes, well, when you're as prolific as I am, this kind of thing is not a large surprise." She smile-grimaced and Queen-waved back at all the little people in the audience. *"Pirate Dave,* as I like to call my tome, is my greatest work to date. It's based on a true story about the time-traveling vampire warlock who discovered America."

"I'm sorry, what?" Anderson Cooper snorted.

"Gesundheit," she replied. "Yes, not many people know the truth behind the discovery of America and I felt it was my duty as a citizen, a celebrity, and a style icon to make all the little people aware. It's also a sweeping love story about conjoined twins. There are some wonderful midget fairies and lots of my trademark graphic sex." She leered at Anderson.

"The midgets are gay?" he choked out.

"Oh no, darling," she tried to giggle, but it sounded like a belch. "They're fairy shape-shifters and there are also flying magical trolls."

"And this is all true?" he asked.

"Absolutely, Andy."

Anderson looked pale. "We are going to go to a station identification break and we'll be right back with Evangeline O'Hara."

The canned music came back on and Anderson Cooper ran off the stage. No one spoke to or offered Evangeline anything. The audience was so confused that some members started to leave. I noticed Joanne speaking animatedly with the same producer who had given Anderson Cooper the sheets of bad reviews. She was showing him the contents of the folder; he was nodding and smiling. Oh. My. God. Was Anderson Cooper going to confront her with her crimes on the air?

The show started again and my body forgot how to breathe. Anderson Cooper took his seat and completely ignored a pouting Evangeline until the cameras rolled.

"Evangeline, before you read an excerpt, I understand there is someone here who can enlighten the world on your career."

"That's lovely," Evangeline said, not listening to a word, "but there's something I'd like to ask you, Andy."

Oh my God, no. Was she really going to . . .

"I'd like to ask you out on a date. I find you extremely attractive, and I think we could make beautiful music together." She eyed him suggestively and put one of her claws into her mouth. Women around me gagged.

Anderson was speechless for the second time in ten minutes. My guess was that this was a first for him. "I'm seeing someone," he muttered with murder in his eyes. "I'd like to bring on your good friend Joanne Krakowski. Welcome, Joanne."

Joanne ran up on the stage and shook Anderson Cooper's hand excitedly. The crowd waited in anticipation and Evangeline just looked confused. I, on the other hand, was about to puke. Joanne must have no idea that there was nothing in the folder to clear her of ruffing, whatever the hell that is.

"Fred—" I grabbed his hand. "Evangeline will eat her alive. I have to go up there and . . ."

Fred held tight to my hand, not letting me move. "Rena, Joanne is smarter and tougher than you think. She wouldn't go up there without knowing what she's doing."

"God, I hope so," I muttered.

A crew person ran on and clipped a wireless mike to Joanne's sweatshirt as she seated herself next to Evangeline. The camera went in for a close-up. Her eyebrows looked fantastic—she'd be so pleased. It looked a little like she'd penciled in where they were still sparse, but she'd done a great job. While her brows were stellar, her body trembled with fear.

"Joanne," Anderson Cooper said warmly and with massive relief, "we're so glad to have you on the show and we're waiting with baited breath for your inside scoop."

"Well, Anderson Cooper," she giggled, "I'm very nervous. I've never been on TV before."

"You're doing a great job so far." He smiled. "Isn't she doing great?" he asked the bewildered audience. They started slowly, but the audience roared its approval for someone normal and sweet. Joanne was a hit.

"Oh my goodness," she gushed. "Thank you, everyone. Anderson Cooper, I think I'm starting to sweat a little bit, so I'd like to get started before my eyebrows melt off."

The audience laughed, relating to her beautifully. I hadn't realized till this moment how attractive Joanne was. The dimples in her cheeks were adorable and her eyes were a clear blue under the lights. Her nervousness caused a pretty flush across her cheeks and her purple sweatshirt made her sparkling eyes pop.

"What's going on here?" Evangeline hissed. "This is my interview. I don't even know who this woman is. Make her go away, Andy darling. This is our time, my love."

"No can do," he replied, focusing all his energy on Joanne. "What exactly is it you'd like to share with us, Joanne?"

"Well, Anderson Cooper, I'm here to inform the world that Evangeline O'Hara has never written a book in her life. She's been blackmailing four people for over twenty years."

Oh shit, not four. Five. Oh my God, was she forgetting about Fred?

"Get the police," the Viper shrieked. "This unkempt piece of white trash is slandering me. I mean, for God's sake, look at what she's wearing." That was her fatal mistake. Over half the women here were dressed almost identically to Joanne. Purple sweatshirts were a fucking staple in the wardrobe of any self-respecting Minnesotan. Period. Evangeline glanced out at the little people for support and all she got was hostile glares. She howled like an animal and lunged at Joanne with her claws. For a round little gal, Joanne moved quickly. She hopped up on the couch and Evangeline tumbled to the floor, knocking her wig off in the process. Women in the audience screamed in horror and delight as she crawled around the floor swearing and trying to find her hair. Thankfully she disconnected her mic when she flew off the couch, or else the viewers would be getting a blistering string of profanities thrown at them. This had turned into the *Jerry Springer Show*.

"What are you saying?" Anderson asked, getting excited at the turn of events. "Did other people write her novels?"

"Yes, they did, Anderson Cooper." Joanne moved closer to the host and farther away from the screaming mimi writhing all over the floor.

"Do you have proof?" he asked hopefully.

"Of course I do, Anderson Cooper," she replied. "Do you think I'd risk my life like this if I didn't have proof?"

The crowd cheered and began chanting, "Proof, proof, proof . . ." The lead ball in my stomach wasn't getting along with the dagger throwing jugglers or the chocolate I'd shoved down my throat on my drive over. My eyes welled up and I dropped my head into my hands. I couldn't watch Joanne go down.

Fred gently lifted my chin. "It's going to be okay," he said. "I promise."

"Where in the fuck is my hair?" Evangeline screeched. "I will destroy you all," she wailed, still crawling around. The crowd booed her, which in turn made her start swearing at the crowd. Thank God her mic was gone.

"The proof is in the folder." Joanne smiled, and pinched Anderson's cheek affectionately. Instead of recoiling, Mr. Cooper grinned and leaned in for more. "The writers are here tonight. They've been deprived of tens of thousands of dollars and they've lived in fear and slavery for twenty years." Joanne's pretty eyes filled with tears. "It's been a living hell," she whispered.

Anderson Cooper took Joanne's hand in his own. "Would you like to bring them up?"

"Yes," she sniffed, "and I would like to clear them of this awful weight they've been carrying for twenty years."

"Audience," Anderson yelled, "would you like that?"

The roar was deafening. I watched as Shoshanna, Poppy Harriet, and Nancy made their way to the stage.

"Fred—" I pulled on him— "you have to go up."

"I can't," he said, shaking like a leaf. "I can't."

"Delona," I pleaded, "make him go."

"He's a grown man, Rena. If he wants to go, he will."

"Son of a bitch," Evangeline shouted. She'd found her hair, but the weight of her knockers made getting back up an impossibility.

"This is Shoshanna LeHump," Joanne said proudly as Shoshanna took the stage in her full-on camo. "She wrote the entire Pirate series. All fourteen books."

"I love you! Those sex scenes saved my marriage," a woman in the back screamed at Shoshanna.

"I love you, too!" She grinned, giving the crowd the peace sign. The fans went nuts. No direction screen necessary.

Joanne continued, "This is Poppy Harriet. She wrote the best-selling historical series. All ten of them," Joanne said, giving her friend a huge hug.

Several women shrieked and started sobbing. They ran to the edge of the stage and tried to touch Poppy Harriet as if she was a freakin' rock star.

"Thank you," Poppy Harriet murmured, completely overwhelmed by the attention.

"Anderson Cooper, I'd like to bring the Minnesota State Health Inspector to the stage, if I may." Joanne smiled shyly at her new best friend, Anderson.

"By all means," he told her gallantly.

Joanne gestured to the gal with the briefcase. She walked to the podium with an official air, cleared her throat six times, and began to speak. "I am holding proof in my hands that Evangeline O'Hara was the perpetrator and mastermind behind salmonella-gate." The happy audience turned on a dime. Angry shouts erupted from all corners. A few threw their convention programs at Evangeline, causing her to drop her hair again. Salmonella-gate was no joke here. It was serious fucking business. "We have signed receipts for the illegal substances that were used and copies of checks made out to the people hired to place the poison in the food. Charges will be filed tomorrow. Thank you." She closed her folder and left the stage.

"Liars, big, fat, ugly, casserole-eating liars," Evangeline yowled from the floor. She was ignored.

"That brings me to Nancy," Joanne went on, "also known as Nan Thorenson." The crowd gasped. "She's lived in hiding for many years, believing she accidentally poisoned two hundred and fifty innocent bridge players." Nancy meekly walked onto the stage and took her place next to her friends. Joanne took her hand and announced, "Nancy is the author of all twenty-one of Evangeline O'Hara's cookbooks."

The crowd cheered as if Nancy was the new quarterback for the Minnesota Vikings. Anderson Cooper was in hog heaven. The grin that split his face was something to behold.

Once the roar died down, a quiet murmur began. The audience spoke in excited whispers and then a voice broke from the crowd.

"Who wrote her best work?" one lady demanded. "Who wrote the Castaway Series?"

Joanne smiled. "That is one of the finest series ever written," she agreed. "The Castaway series was written by Fred Smith."

"Nooooooo," Evangeline howled like an injured animal. She dragged herself to the podium and pulled herself and her knockers into a standing position. "Fred Smith is a cross-dressing faggot," she spat into the microphone. "He's an abomination."

Fred's face paled and he sank down to the floor.

"Just wait one second, you over-Botoxed skank," Joanne yelled. "Fred Smith is not a homosexual. I should know, because we've been doing the nasty for over six years, and he's an animal in the sack!"

A woman in the back added, "My husband wears my underpants. I think it's hot."

"That's nothing," an older gal from the other side of the lobby shouted. "My man and I go lingerie shopping together. He picks out my stuff and I pick out his!"

"So there." Joanne stuck her tongue out at Evangeline, who dropped back to the floor . . . boobs first.

I squatted down next to Fred, who was the color of a tomato. "Well, well, well—" I grinned. "Somebody has been busy." He wouldn't meet my eyes, but he couldn't hide his delighted smile.

Anderson Cooper made his way to Joanne. "Joanne, I am clear on how the other people were wronged, but what does that awful woman have on you?"

I froze. My body turned to ice.

"Oh Anderson," she said, "you're so sweet to think about me." He preened under her praise. "Evangeline O'Hara has nothing on me. Nothing. I'm not a writer either. I just couldn't stand to see my friends persecuted this way."

Nothing. Ruffing. Nothing. Ruffing. I collapsed on the floor next to Fred and laughed till my sides hurt.

"So you stood by your friends for twenty years? Suffering along with them?" Anderson Cooper sounded amazed.

"That's what friends do, sweetie," she said. "Oh, I have made one error. Evangeline did write *Pirate Dave and His Randy Adventures* . . . all by herself." She grinned evilly.

"Goddamn right I did," the Viper squealed from the floor.

"And the reviews are dreadful," Anderson said, retrieving them from his desk. "Most offensive dreck ever written . . . Career-ending book . . . Profane and stupid . . . Politically incorrect drivel . . . An abomination." He grinned.

Still down on the ground next to Fred, I punched him lightly in the arm. "You knew. You knew she had nothing on Joanne."

"Yes, I knew," he said.

"Excuse me," a familiar voice yelled from the crowd. "I'm with the Minneapolis Police Department."

No fucking way. My heart was pounding so loudly in my chest I was sure it was going to bounce out of my mouth. What was Jack doing here? I stood up slowly and searched the crowd. He was striding across the stage much to the delight of all the ladies in the audience . . . and he was half naked . . .

Dressed in his tight running pants, one shoe, no shirt, and his leather bomber jacket, he still looked like sex on a stick. I felt an insane desire to smack all the women drooling over my man, only he wasn't my man . . .

"You're an officer of the law?" Anderson Cooper asked doubtfully of the woefully underdressed hottie striding toward the podium.

"Yep." Jack flashed his badge and handcuffed a foulmouthed Evangeline. "Mr. Cooper, I was wondering if I could say a few words?"

"Why not?" Anderson threw his hands in the air and grinned. "Everyone else has."

Jack nodded his head curtly in thanks and approached the podium. My insides got wiggly and I used Fred, Delona, and the wall to hold me upright.

"I would like to say, on, um . . . national TV that I am a jerk. I am also an idiot and an ass-monkey." He smiled sheepishly, cleared his throat, and scanned the crowd. He didn't see me. I giggled. I couldn't believe he'd just said ass-monkey on TV. "Rena, I hope you're here and if you're not I pray to God you're watching this on TV. I want you to know, I love your crazy. My life is empty without you and your crazy . . . Anything I have to do to prove it to you, I will. These last couple of days have been the loneliest and worst of my life." He ran his hands through his hair and examined the crowd again. I ducked down as his eyes passed my group. Shit, too late. He'd seen me—his delighted half smirk proved it. How in the fuck was everyone recognizing me?

"Holy God almighty," a lady near me said. "If this Rena gal doesn't want him, I'll divorce my husband for some of that." All the surrounding women agreed.

"I will go to Bigfoot meetings and I will babysit Martians and I'll, um . . . even remove the giraffe from my back. I will do anything if you'll give me another chance," he said, staring right at me. "People don't believe in love at first sight . . . but the moment I laid eyes on you, my world stopped."

A huge sigh erupted through the lobby. All the women were a-twitter. This was a romance novel come to life.

"I am head over heels in love with you and I can promise you I will treat you a lot better than an Iowa farm boy . . ."

"Man," Shoshanna corrected him. "An Iowa farm man."

"Excuse me," he chuckled. "An Iowa farm man. And I'm definitely a lot warmer than Cardboard Brett Favre."

My insides began to tingle and my inner slut was urging me to rush the stage and jump him.

"Rena, my life sucks without you in it. Will you please come back to me?"

I held my breath and wondered if we could really make a go of it . . . I looked at the man of my dreams and my fantasies and my reality and I knew . . .

"Is she here?" someone yelled from the crowd. "Because if she's not, you can come home with me."

"Me, too," another yelled. "And you can keep your giraffe, whatever that means."

"She's here," Jack laughed. "She's definitely here."

"Answer him already," a lady toward the front shouted.

"Yeah," Shoshanna threw in her two cents. "Don't be a fortune cookie. Answer the poor man. He's dying up here."

I couldn't believe she didn't say "fucking." My hands were trembling as I reached up and removed my wig and glasses. I handed them to Delona, who winked at me and gave me a little push. My eyes locked on his and I started the long walk from the back of the room to the stage. The crowd parted magically before me and I couldn't believe my legs didn't give out.

My insides were jumbled and I could hear my heart beating wildly in my chest. All the ladies I passed were oohing and ahhing as I made my way to Jack. Tissues were a-plenty. One gal stuffed a wad into my hand. Thank Lutheran Jesus, because my tears were rolling freely down my face.

"This is so romantic," a woman said as I passed.

"I'm crying. This is making me cry," another said.

I got to the edge of the stage and raised my arms up to Jack. He lifted me effortlessly and held me in front of him. We stood silently looking at each other. He was the most beautiful man I'd ever met, inside and out. Anderson Cooper hustled over and shoved a handheld mic into Jack's hands, effectively ruining the moment. I realized this was all being caught on film and broadcast to the world . . . and I didn't care.

"Will you give me another chance?" he whispered. Anderson Cooper's hand wedged between us and pushed the mic closer to Jack's lips.

I giggled at the craziness of the situation and realized it was fitting. If Jack could deal with something as insane as this and still want me, we would definitely work. I mean, for God's sake, he called himself an ass-monkey on national television. "Yes, I will give you all the chances in the world . . . as long as you do the same for me."

"Deal." He grinned, crushing me against him and planting the hottest, most mind-shattering kiss I'd ever had in my life.

The crowd of romance lovers went berserk.

"I love you," I said, grinning from ear to ear.

"I love you, too," he answered. "You do realize I have to arrest you for breaking your restraining order, don't you?"

"I figured as much." I shrugged and laughed. "Can we at least screw in your car on the way to the station?"

"Oh my God, yes." He grabbed me by the arm and practically dragged me from the building. As I was leaving I shouted my goodbyes to Shoshanna, Poppy Harriet, Nancy, Delona, and a very lip locked Joanne and Fred. Who woulda thunk?

I love my life. It's fucking awesome.

Epilogue

The back room at the country club had been expensive, but worth it. I'd used every last penny from my stash of Aunt Phyllis's mattress money to host a party for all the people I loved.

I glanced around the room and giggled. Vito and Angelo stood in the corner drinking wine and rating racks and asses. They promised, with great sincerity, that no one's privates would outscore mine. That's some fucked-up loyalty right there.

Shoshanna brought the newly married Kevin and Steve. They complimented me profusely on *Pirate Dave and His Randy Adventures,* telling me it was the funniest and most frightening thing they'd ever read. All of their friends had replaced the word *penis* in their vocabulary with *pork sword.* As far as compliments go, that was one of the most alarming I'd ever received. Apparently Pirate Dave had become quite the underground hit among the gay community. Thankfully, due to Evangeline's impending time in the pokey, all the proceeds from the book were going to charity.

The Viper's charges were numerous and ugly; she was looking at anywhere from five to ten years. Somewhere inside myself I felt a little bit sorry for her, but she was bad. What makes a person do the things she did? Even Delona couldn't shed any light on that one. I had taken her to see her sister at the county jail. I was worried she might kill Evangeline, but she stood quietly and stared at her, pity written all over her face. Evangeline begged Delona to bail her out, but Delona just gave her a Mona Lisa smile and continued to stare. When the Viper realized her sister had no intention of helping her, she swore a blue streak that made even me uncomfortable. Not an easy thing to accomplish.

"Rena." Vito grabbed me and hugged me in a slightly inappropriate manner.

"Yes?" I kindly disengaged myself from his embrace.

"This is a wonderful party," he announced.

"Thanks."

Angelo nodded his agreement. "Most of the asses and racks here rate about a thirty-seven."

I choked on my own tongue. "What?"

"Don't worry." Angelo patted my lower back, dangerously close to my bottom. "You're a sixty-nine."

Speechless, I nodded my thanks and decided I would block this conversation out of my head. Permanently.

"Oh," Vito added, "even though it's not Italian, the food is tremendous."

Nancy had outdone herself. She'd insisted on catering the party, free of charge, and there wasn't any cream of mushroom soup in sight. She had done French cuisine with an Asian twist. It was delicious. Nancy's catering business was back in demand and she'd received a six-figure advance from one of the big publishing houses for a line of romantic cookbooks.

Speaking of, all the ghost writers had received huge advances and publishing contracts. After twenty years, Fred, Shoshanna, Nancy, and Poppy Harriet were going to be recognized and compensated for their talent.

"I got a job," Joanne giggled, giving me a squeeze. Fred stood next to her beaming like a besotted high school boy.

"You did?" I asked, grinning at them like an idiot. Their happiness was contagious.

"I'm going to be a traveling correspondent for the *Anderson Cooper Show*! Anderson Cooper had the highest ratings of his career at the convention and he told me I was the main reason!"

"Oh my God," I squealed. "That's fantastic, but what about . . ."

Fred read my mind and cut me off. "I'll be traveling with her." He smiled sheepishly, putting his arm around Joanne. "I can write from anywhere."

"Rena—" Joanne and her beautiful bushy eyebrows got right up in my face— "none of this would have happened without you. I love you."

"I love you, too," I whispered as my eyes filled. I bit down on my lip when they informed me they were going to the coatroom to make out. Joanne ran off with Fred following like a puppy.

I laughed when I spotted my sister. Jenny looked terrified standing in the middle of the room flanked by Bigfoot Kim and Soundtrack Hugh. Dirk, who was now legally representing all my friends, was in a deep and animated conversation with Kim about Sasquatch sightings. I prayed to Lutheran Jesus and Brett Favre that he would soon take my place and accompany Aunt Phyllis to her meetings.

"Oh. My. God," Kristy gasped, pulling me behind some drapes. "Why didn't you tell me Jack's new sergeant was so hot?"

"I didn't know he was. I haven't met him yet."

Jack had a new sergeant. Before he'd showed up half naked at the convention, he'd delivered the canceled checks and a hasty explanation to the Minneapolis Prosecuting Attorney's office. Sergeant Santa and Herbie the Dentist Cop were going down in a bad and very public way. Their disgrace had the added benefit of increased time on Evangeline's slammer vacation.

"He's been staring at me all night," Kristy hissed. "When he asked me my name, I said Carol."

"Oh my God," I laughed. "Why?"

"Because," she moaned in agony, "I forgot mine."

"Do you want me to fix it?"

"Hell, he's going to think I'm crazy," she said, pulling on her wild curls.

"From what I hear, cops like crazy girls." I grinned.

She froze, her eyes got wide and a goofy smile pulled at her lips. "They do, don't they? I'll be back," she said, hightailing it to find her future husband.

Mom and Delona hit it off beautifully. They were deep in conversation about Fred's books. Dad, showing admirable restraint, listened grudgingly to Aunt Phyllis's new theory on the telepathic capabilities of houseflies. I grabbed a glass of champagne when my mother wasn't looking and realized I was surrounded by my ladies.

"So, are you still moving to Iowa?" Shoshanna teased as she shoved fork food into her mouth with her fingers.

"No, I'm not," I laughed, completely grossed out by her manners, yet again.

"Will you go back to your old firm?" Nancy asked, handing LeHump a wad of napkins.

"Um, no." Shit, I so didn't want to explain my current employment status, but I knew they would harass me until they were satisfied. "Actually, I, um . . . called Iowa first to decline the job and, ah, when I called my office here, they'd already filled my spot." I felt the heat crawl up my neck. At least it would hide the remnants of the hickey I was still sporting.

"Hold the fuck up," Shoshanna laughed. "Are you telling me that you spent your every last dime on this shindig and you don't have a job?"

"I don't really find it all that funny," I said.

"Sweet Moses in a Basket," Nancy gasped. "You're broke and jobless?"

"That's fantastic," Poppy Harriet shrieked, giving Joanne a high five.

The gals bounced up and down with excitement. WTF?

"Tell her," Joanne insisted, punching Poppy Harriet's shoulder. "Tell her or I will."

"Tell me what?"

"Well," Poppy Harriet said, way too slowly for my nerves. "The girls and Fred and I are in the market for an accountant/business manager. You know, someone to run our finances and guide investments and teach us new terms for the word *penis*," she giggled. "And it just so happens, right before Walter Garski died, he bought an office complex right here in downtown Minneapolis . . . and it's still empty!"

I felt a little dizzy. I was fairly sure I knew where they were going with this, but use of the English language had deserted me.

"So," Joanne cut in, "here's how we see it. Jack said one of your dreams was to go out on your own and now you will. We've already outfitted your new office and Fred has set up an incredible computer system."

"Walter forbade me to take rent on the place. He needs a tax loss." Poppy Harriet grinned. "We thought Kristy might like a little space there, too. She could do her paperwork and have a fundraising staff for the shelter."

Still, nothing came out of my mouth.

"It's a big-ass building," Shoshanna said. "So we'll all have offices there, too."

They stood silently and waited. I felt shaky and excited and overwhelmed and scared out of my mind. Could I do this? Could I really have my own firm? Was I good enough to make it work? The penis references were no problem, but handling every aspect of my friends' financial lives? The prospect made me a nervous wreck, but I was good at this. I loved numbers like they loved words. A feeling of happiness started at my toes and raced through my body, giving me my answer.

"So, what do you say, oh wondrous inventor of the term pork sword?" LeHump asked, knocking me back into my body.

"I say yes," I whispered as tears spilled down my cheeks.

Shoshanna handed me the wad of napkins and all the gals smothered me in hugs.

"You're the reason we're all standing here today," LeHump said in a rare sentence without a swearword in it. "You saved us and we will never let you go." If they had told me that the first day I met them, I would have run for the hills. Today it meant the world.

Two strong arms circled me from behind and two lips kissed my neck. I turned and buried my weepy face in Jack's chest. "Jack"— I looked up at him— "they want me to be . . ."

"I already know, baby." He smiled and pulled me closer.

I felt tingly all over in his arms. I was in love for real. For the first time in my life, I was head over heels in love. The irony that I had Evangeline to thank for my happiness was bizarre, but I figured the hell she'd put me through made us even.

"Are you having fun?" I asked him, running my fingertips along his lips.

"Yeah"—he smiled his sexy half smirk—"but I have a really good idea."

"You do?" Excitement took the express shuttle through my body.

"Yep. You see, I have a set of handcuffs burning a hole in my back pocket and a room rented at the hotel down the street." He discreetly moved my hand down to greet his very happy camper.

"Jack," I giggled, "we're at a party."

"Have you said hello to everybody?" he asked.

"Um, yes."

"Then I'm afraid I'm going to have to place you under arrest. You will have to come with me now or else I'll have to restrain you and carry you out of here with force," he whispered in my ear.

"Will you strip-search me?" I asked, using my hand to make his happy camper even happier.

"I believe that could be arranged." His quick intake of breath made my knees weak.

"All right, officer, I'll go with you, but it better be good."

"Oh baby," he groaned. "It will be 'I can't walk tomorrow' good." He grabbed my hand and whisked me out of my own party so quickly, it made my head spin.

I love my life. It's fucking awesome.

ROBYN PETERMAN writes because the people inside her head won't leave her alone until she gives them life on paper. Her addictions include laughing really hard with friends, shoes (the expensive kind), Target, Coke with extra ice in a Styrofoam cup, bejeweled reading glasses, her kids, her superhot hubby, and collecting stray animals.

A former professional actress, with Broadway, film, and TV credits, she now lives in the South with her family and too many animals to count. Writing gives her peace and makes her whole, plus having a job where she can work in her PJs works really well for her.

You can follow Robyn at robynpeterman.com or on her Facebook author page. She loves to hear from her fans.

Don't miss these other exciting eKensington titles,
available now.

LINDSEY
BROOKES

JIMMIE JOE JOHNSON:
Manwhore

"The most hilarious
book I've read in years—
maybe ever!
—*New York Times*
bestselling author
C.L. Wilson

a Possum Hollow novel

Be careful
what you reap.
You might fall in love
with her…

GRAVE
INTENTIONS

Lori Sjoberg

MORE THAN THIS

Is love between friends worth the risk?

SHANNYN SCHROEDER

CPSIA information can be obtained at www.ICGtesting.com
Printed in the USA
LVOW08s1442280616

494433LV00001B/134/P